MÉNAGE

Ewan Morrison is the author of the novels *Swung*
and *Distance* and a collection of stories, *The Last
Book You Read*.

D0635540

ALSO BY EWAN MORRISON

The Last Book You Read
Swung
Distance

EWAN MORRISON

Ménage

VINTAGE BOOKS
London

Published by Vintage 2010

2 4 6 8 10 9 7 5 3 1

Copyright © Ewan Morrison 2009

Ewan Morrison has asserted his right under the Copyright, Designs
and Patents Act 1988 to be identified as the author of this work

First published in Great Britain in 2009
by Jonathan Cape

Vintage
Random House, 20 Vauxhall Bridge Road,
London SW1V 2SA

www.vintage-books.co.uk

Addresses for companies within The Random House Group Limited
can be found at: www.randomhouse.co.uk/offices.htm

The Random House Group Limited Reg. No. 954009

A CIP catalogue record for this book
is available from the British Library

ISBN 9780099520726

The Random House Group Limited supports The Forest
Stewardship Council (FSC), the leading international forest
certification organisation. All our titles that are printed on
Greenpeace approved FSC certified paper carry the FSC logo.
Our paper procurement policy can be found at
www.rbooks.co.uk/environment

Mixed Sources
Product group from well-managed
forests and other controlled sources
www.fsc.org   Cert no. TT-COC-2139
© 1996 Forest Stewardship Council
FSC

Typeset by Palimpsest Book Production Limited,
Grangemouth, Stirlingshire

Printed and bound in Great Britain by
CPI Bookmarque, Croydon, CR0 4TD

Ménage

Pronunciation: Ma'nazh
Function: Noun
Etymology: French, from Old French –
mesnage, dwelling; from Vulgar Latin –
mansionaticum
A domestic establishment; Household;
also Housekeeping
See *Ménage à trois*

I just point my camera at people then they do things they wouldn't normally do, I suppose. Even when I film myself, it stops being me. I don't really think of myself as an artist anyway. I'm probably at least three people in one body. I mean, sometimes I'm a guy and other times two guys or three girls or ... I don't know, I just don't buy into this big artistic genius thing. It's sick. Who wants to be stuck on that pedestal? I'd die of loneliness.

Dorothy Shears, 1999

Dorothy Shears

nine works

Video installations, 1992–2009

nine works

introduction

Trust. 1993. Video installation. 32 mins. Variable dimensions. Private collection.

THE NINE WORKS here form an intrinsic part of the iconography of what came to be known as the Young British Artist (YBA) scene, a period that started in 1992 and endured for almost fifteen years. Many of the artists from this 'movement' are now represented in major international art collections, with their works commanding impressive sums. As the movement has received institutional acceptance, however, it has inevitably fallen into decline.[1] Dorothy Shears is one of the few key artists to have survived the collapse of the YBA brand and to have consolidated her status.

The typical image of the YBA was that of grungy cockney post-punks living in squats, making thrown-together streetwise art in rebellion against Thatcherism and Consumerism.[2] Shears does not fit that prescriptive schema, being from a different class background, but her work shares many common features with her peers. Being made with 'cheap throwaway materials', in her case domestic home video, it crosses over into the realms of installation and performance art, and was originally made for exhibition in backstreet Dockland and East End warehouses.[3] Graduating from Goldsmiths College within a few years of Hirst at the time of what was to become Britpop,[4] the hype machine was quick to pull her into its orbit.

Some claim that Shears's initial success was a product of 'Van Gogh syndrome',[5] with much tabloid hype being made out of the speculated history of her mental health. But unlike several of her peers, Shears has carefully protected her past from the public eye.[6] Against the ironic zeitgeist of her time, Shears created intimate, personal works that were in many ways a record of her own artistic 'becoming' in a secret coded visual language. As such, her work survives beyond explanation and plagiarist reproduction in the many forms that have attempted to exploit it across the years.[7]

The following discussion of the nine works sets out not to analyse or explain, but to pay respect to the enigma of the works and the woman herself. As she has, throughout the years, invited viewers to lay aside judgement and trust her, so I too beg you to close your eyes, and enter the darkness with her.

Owen Morgan, 2009

1. While still in their artistic infancy, recent art graduates were plucked from obscurity by Charles Saatchi, making this the first artistic movement in history created by an advertising magnate. His rapid buying of an entire show and all the artists within it, then his swift reselling of certain works, rewrote the rules of art galleries which had formerly been concerned with building an artist's career over a lifetime. Many former YBA 'successes' now make a modest living as teachers.
2. Saatchi & Saatchi was responsible for the successful election campaigns of the Conservative Party through the Thatcher years ('Labour Isn't Working') then through the 'lame duck' administration of John Major, in which the YBAs emerged. Saatchi, reinvesting the money he made through advertising into art, made a mockery of the hype that promoted these artists as 'rebels'.
3. Group exhibitions were temporary in nature and held in non-art spaces with names like City Racing (an old betting shop) and Die Yuppie Scum. The warehouse shows in Camden, Hoxton and Docklands would not have passed health and safety standards, but were exhilarating.
4. Britpop bands like the Stone Roses, Blur and Pulp were selling millions internationally. New Brit became a brand for both music and art. Jarvis Cocker (musician and former art student)'s showing his arse while Michael Jackson sang at the Brit Awards became a symbol for this typically irreverent British attitude.
5. Van Gogh syndrome – the belief that certain artists are only

appreciated and elevated to a high status because of their tragic personal histories. See R. Clements, *The Life and Death of Jean-Michel Basquiat*, Random House, 1999.

6. WRT – Tracey Emin, the claim that Emin's documentation of her working-class victimhood became unsustainable as she climbed the commercial ladder. See J. Cambridge, *Variance*, IFP, 2003, 'The Oppressed Minority of One'.

7. Note the many pop promos, advertisements and political campaigns that have exploited Shears's 'vérité' grunge images.

THE LANDLINE IS ringing. It should not be, not outside working hours, not ever without warning. He has taken great care over the years to keep his number from everyone, apart from the editor and the picture desk, going ex-directory so that the artists whose work it is his work to destroy cannot trace him.

It is still ringing.

Friends are few and all know that acts of spontaneity will be ignored. It could only be his mother or ex-wife. But his mother seemed well enough when he called for his quarterly check-in and the ex no longer calls. It could be a fuck-buddy, but they always ring his mobile as is his rule.

Still it rings. It must be to do with the image. It is everywhere: on the tube, fly-posted twenty feet across, in the pages of the *Guardian*, the *Telegraph*. No escaping it. This advert for this exhibition with this photo of a man's face in obscene sensual agony. They have been ringing and emailing – the gallery and the agent – asking him to return their calls and emails, to consider writing the text for the catalogue for the international touring show by Dorothy Shears. What they don't know is how that image has almost forced him into hiding this past month. Of how that obscene sensual face in that artwork from 1993 is his own.

It keeps on ringing so something must be wrong.

He has his rules; if he picks it up he knows the night will be ruined. Tonight was going to be the one, which so rarely occurs, when, having found time away from the work he's paid to write at a certain number of pence per word, he would commune with self and attempt to write his diary

6

or a poem or a critique of this or that advert or image or any other damn thing that's invaded his privacy and reminded him that there's no escape from images.

The usual ritual had been gone through. The second gin and tonic and the bottle in the freezer ready for the top-ups if inspiration hit. Radiohead on repeat. The secondary plan, if words failed, was to check in on CANDYGIRL. She might be in her bath, or bed, or at her PC and he would instant message her. She is the only person he allows to chat to him at night. She knows him as Nocturc9 and he pays eighty-nine US dollars per month for the privilege of watching her 24/7 on her four webcams. He would put on the used pink frilly girlie panties he bought from her which she mailed FedEx and touch himself as he watched her touch her tight firm eighteen-year-old body in her student flat in Los Angeles. These were the limits of his deviances now. There are mental techniques for their control.

But it will not stop ringing. He does not have an answer-phone because it only encourages them. He could turn the ringer off but still the little red light would keep flashing on and off, and in the reaching, he might, after the G&Ts, upset the handset from its cradle and then the caller would hear him pick up and know he'd deliberately hung up and so it would start again. Pull it from the wall then. But he is unsteady on his feet as he reaches for the plug socket and already enraged over so many things. And the fucking world will not go away no matter how strict you make the rules, so he picks it up and shouts: 'Who the hell is this?'

A male voice saying 'Owen. Owen Morgan. Hey, it's me.'

'I'm going to hang up. I have no idea how you got my –'

'Chill, man, it's me . . .' (cough) '. . . Saul.'

(Silence.)

'Freaking you out, eh? Sorry, been a while. So how you doing?'

'Sorry . . . Saul . . . how did you . . . ?'

7

'Hey, buddy, yeah, they're doing Dot's show on telly later, just wanted to let you know. You going to review her show?'

'I don't think so.'

'You ever see her around . . . galleries and that?'

'No . . . Saul, so what are you . . . ?'

'*Late Review* tonight. Just thought I'd let you know.'

'Well . . . thanks.'

'Piece in the *Independent*, couldn't believe it, one of the old videos, how did that happen eh? Picture of you. Saw it on the tube.'

'Look . . . could you give me your number? I'm kind of in the middle of something right now.'

'Sure, yeah.' (Laughter.) 'The fucking Lieder, eh! Who'd have thought, huh? Hey, you going to review her show?

'No, I try to avoid –'

'I was there, snuck in, her opening . . . man, you should see her now, beautiful. Didn't say hello. Still mad as a brush, her, not . . . she's got a kid too, you know.'

'Yes, I read that.'

'Looks like her mum. Dot – a mum – Jesus! You know with the medication and all that. Wassit called – birth defects – those pills she used to –'

'Saul, it's great . . . you sound well, but it's late and I'm sorry but I've got work tomorrow.'

'Course, course, career man, yup, OK, sorry for calling . . . just wanted to . . . well, to say sorry if I put you down, I was always putting you down. You proved me wrong though, eh? What did I know? Good on you, partner. The *Guardian*, eh?'

'Well, freelance actually.'

'Who'd have thought . . . and Dot, she's quite the artist, eh?'

'Look, if you could give me your number I can call back when I have –'

'You still in Hoxton?'

'Well . . . no, a bit . . . further out.'

'Big place, is it? Amazing the changes, eh? Hope you didn't over-mortgage on a big yuppie place. Amazing what's happening out there, eh? It's all going to hell, man. The end of capitalism again, eh? We're all going down.' (Laughter.)

'Where are you exactly, Saul?'

'Me, getting by . . . living in Dalston, been here a few years now.'

'Really?'

(Silence.)

'Hey, Owen, fuck, eh? Member that time we watched Bergman what was it? No, no, the one with the . . . no, maybe Tarkovsky, anyway . . . I kissed her, her hand, I mean and . . . it was . . .' (Laughter.)

'OK, Saul.'

'. . . thought it was hers! It was your fucking hand!' (Laughter.)

(Silence.)

'OK, fine, look . . . what can I do for you, Saul?'

'No need to –'

'How did you get this number anyway?'

'You know, I know my place, man, happier than ever, no need to get all –'

'Saul.'

'Never been happier – Jesus Christ, I'm talking to Owen fucking Morgan – you grow that beard yet?'

'Saul!'

'Hey, 'member when she pinched that chicken?!'

'What do you *want*, Saul?'

(Silence.)

'I love you, man.'

'OK.'

'No, I mean it. Just had to say it.'

(Silence.)

9

'Always have done.'

'OK, thanks for calling. We'll speak soon. Got to go.'

'Love you, partner.'

'OK. Bye.'

He hung up. Seconds then, just staring at the phone. The past coming back to haunt you was an old bullshit lie from movies and therapy. The voice from the past with its apocalyptic overtones. 'We're all going down.'

He resisted the sudden desire to call the ex-wife in Paris. Fuck it all. He needed to fuck. He scrolled through the fuck-buddies on his mobile: Alexis, Angie, Annabel, Beth, Carolyn, Camilla – but then an old Saulism came to him: 'Endless consumer choice masks the fact that there's no choice at all.'

He felt guilt now over his tone with Saul, for having got rid of him so abruptly, for not even having had the politeness to ask how he was, if he made a living, or was in a relationship, had kids even, or ever finished that artwork or written that book. Guilt, for having withheld his address, for having harboured the fear that Saul was lurking, waiting. Looking for a place to crash. Stalker.

He turned on the TV and there was *Late Review*. Dot wasn't there, just the usual three critics in round-table discussion about whether this show was the epitaph for YBA. The post-feminist was saying the early works marked the end of Marxist feminism and the birth of gender fucking. The tabloid nu-lad was saying: 'It's a rip-off, you can find better video stuff on YouTube.' The black Oxbridge academic said he found her work typical of work from the Aids-panic era. The usual round of tediously well-balanced argument but all he could focus on was that image on the back wall behind the critics from that night when Dot and Saul had tied him up and took turns kissing and slapping him. This image now called art. Now called *Trust.*

Images flooded him. He was searching for loose change

and shoplifting to eat – waking to find Dot running her cunt-wet fingers over his lips as he slept beside Saul – dancing to Saul's suicidal music – the needle and the blood – the green tube of her intravenous drip – kissing her torn knuckles as she drifted in and out of consciousness – praying for her to wake and, in time, come to forgive, if she lived.

Stop it. End it again. The images wouldn't go till it was done. OK, he told himself. He would go and see Dot's retrospective, get it done in ten minutes, have it over with, put the past back where it belonged – on the cold dead white of a commercial gallery wall.

*

Abandon Hope All Ye Who Enter Here – that should have been the sign above our door. It was the Thursday, the week after Black Wednesday 1992, the year of Dot. The stock market had crashed; Communism was dead; Whitney Houston was just about to start a three-month run at number one; and Saul and I were under threat of eviction for our failure to find a co-tenant and our five months' worth of rent arrears. For two years I had endured Saul's self-imposed poverty while he sat and quoted his aphorisms at me ('To confront death every day is the only way to really live!'). I could no longer endure the squalor, but made one last attempt to save myself from the street by putting adverts up in all the local shops. The wording had been his.

FLATMATE SOUGHT

To share basement flat, Whitmore Road, Hoxton, w/two aesthetes (male). Rent – cheap, conditions – rudimentary. No limits on sex, race or age. Strictly no hoodlums. Only lovers of Wagner need apply. Call 071 338 9865. Ask for Owen.

My brain was so starved of nutrients that I no longer even knew how I'd got trapped there. It was supposed to be a stopover, the lowest rent in London and probably illegal for occupancy. One of the council houses Thatcher couldn't sell off. The two floors above were totally derelict and our 'basement' seemed dug from the foundations. My window had iron bars on it and a view of the four lanes of Shoreditch overpass. The whole place was dank, dark, fungus-ridden and could have come down at any time, the security door was busted and some moron, or maybe many, used the communal hallway as a toilet.

I returned from sticking up the adverts late in the afternoon and still he had not risen. I stared despairingly into the spare room, knowing we would never rent it in such a state. It was stacked high with three months' worth of blue-bottle infested bin bags and had the sickly sweet malodour of a mortuary. I was damned if it was going to be my turn to clean them out, as I had done the task over fifteen times previously, without him lifting a finger.

Damn him, that very day he would have to take respon-sibility for our situation or I would leave, I told myself, knowing full well there was no way to beat him in the stand-offs. He could have eaten from a maggot-infested plate before admitting it was his turn to do the dishes. Hygiene! He often ejaculated with disgust – what has a more filthy history than cleansing? Think of the Nazis and the Serbs!

As I waited for him to wake I prepared my ultimatum speech. Saul rarely woke before 2 p.m. as he generally kept me up till dawn with his drunken plans for 'the most trans-gressive artwork of our time'. Every day it was the same: he cursed me for waking him, with his smoker's sotto voce, then for letting him sleep so late again, shouting, 'Another day wasted. It's pointless! I'm going back to bed, we'll start again tomorrow.' But tomorrow, I knew, it would be the same. It struck me then that this was what old people did, curling up in bed waiting for death, and saw clearly how it could happen to us both. When Kerouac was our age he'd been driving Route 66. Why were we wasting our halcyon days like this? For what? For art? What the hell was halcyon anyway? There were galleries starting up around us, but Saul was convinced they were all beneath him. That he'd never even made a start on his great artwork he blamed on the fact that there were no functioning light bulbs in the flat and so we were in almost perpetual darkness.

The kitchen had no windows and the light bulb in there had been the first to blow months back and had never been replaced. As I stood in the doorway, I could sense a squirming in the sink beyond. I had to eat something before confronting him, to get my strength up, but all I could make out among the stacks of encrusted plates was a halved orange skin, scooped out and refilled entirely with cigarette butts, like some sick surrealist artwork.

Vomit rose and I swallowed it, took another Rennie and considered how malnutrition was affecting our judgement. Starvation produces ecstatic visions, he often said, and I knew for a fact that the majority of what passed his lips most days was regurgitated phlegm. For three months we had eaten nothing but pasta with no sauce, not even butter, as he had grown weary of stealing it from Spud-u-Like. The occasional can of beans (stolen) or banana (same). Everything else was spent on his necessary Don Quixote (sherry). He considered my concern over nutrition 'reactionary' and advised I reread the Marquis de Sade, although what sexual mutilation had to do with nutrition I had yet to work out. My gut was aching from, perhaps, liver failure. I sneezed constantly from the spores and had to take Rennie and paracetamol to kill the side effects of the antihistamines. After paying for all the drugs, buying food was out of the question.

When finally I plucked up the indignation to knock on

his door, he opened it and struck a dandyish pose, as if he had been waiting all along.

— Yes? What can I do for you?

His appearance never failed to throw me: eyeliner, stubble poking through layers of foundation stretched into cracks around his mouth, high-street girl's T-shirt, far too tight, which read 'BABE', army boots, bare legs and his kimono. That damned kimono. The way his dick would peek out from it occasionally, as if checking whether the coast was clear. The whole issue about sex was very confusing and I had lived those two years without it because every time I tried to pick up a girl he showed great disdain, muttering things like 'Don't forget – all they want is to steal your talent, and you have precious little of it to spare'. Naked bodies disgusted him, and as for sex, he said, 'All that grunting and sweating, it's like doing push-ups till you're sick.' No, I was convinced he was as asexual as he was amoral and our relationship was platonic (although I did once dream I let him sodomise me in exchange for him taking out the bin bags).

He waited in his doorway for me to challenge him, his stereo blaring – *Thus Spoke Zarathustra* – as if claiming Nietzsche was on his side in the pending argument. His breath was already heavy with sickly sweet breakfast sherry.

I was afraid of confronting the eviction issue too directly, so said, — We need to have a big talk, and I can't if you insist on hitting the bottle before breakfast.

He silently drew on the last strand of fag end, staring at the ground before venting his riposte.

— Hitting? The bottle! As you may have noticed our penury has reduced us to drinking from boxes. And if anything is being hit it is me, by the poverty of your imagination!

I knew what was coming.

— Ungrateful peasant. My God, may He rest in peace, it was me that dragged you up . . .

14

— I know, I know – from the proletarian slime . . . but if we're going to be able to get a flatmate we need to clean the place and if we're going to clean the place we need to buy light bulbs so we can at least see the extent of the horror.

— Buy? *Buy*? Did you not know they invented a light bulb that lasted for a lifetime but the capitalist bastards decided it would put them out of business? I will not subsidise planned obsolescence! Go forth and procure some by the usual methods!

I protested that I'd almost got caught red-handed last time. There were only so many times I could go to the pub's pisser and replace their live bulb with our dead one. I proposed candles.

— Candles are for hippies!

— Well, if we went to sleep at a regular hour we could wake before it starts getting dark and clean up using daylight; it's free by the way.

— I have my best ideas at night. The dark suits me.

I laid out the cost of light bulbs for him, seventy-five pence from Sadhi's, sixty-five from Woolies.

— Do you have sixty-five pence?

I did not and told him so.

— My God, may He rest in peace, but what happened to your dole cheque?

And so I went though our weekly costs. Don Quixote and Golden Virginia, photocopying and pasta shells. I suggested we roll back the carpet and look for spare change, if not our own then from the previous occupants.

— We did that last month. All is futile. I'm going back to bed.

He did just that and pulled the covers over his head. It must have been 4 p.m.

— For Christ's sake, I protested, are you seriously telling me we're going to be evicted just because you refuse to save up enough to buy a light bulb!

15

— Money money money, you're like a fucking song by Abba. Why don't you sell your soul and get some real work, like you really want to, then we could afford all your horrible bourgeois necessities.

Stupidly, I ventured that he might also try to find work.

— Jobs, my dear, are for those such as you, who are scared of a moment alone with one's thoughts. Sustaining idleness is the most difficult vocation of all.

Oh, how he loved to tease me about my little scraps of freelance writing for the *Hoxton Advertiser* – a hack from the Borough of Hackney, he called me. I was not proud of what I had to do to earn a crust and did not know how it came to pass that I paid for everything and was poorer than before. To this day I still have no idea how Saul had managed to stay on the dole for seven years, only hints. Something to do with faking a psychology test and his 'affliction'. He was on invalidity benefit although he was able-bodied, or at least would have been if he for once tried to eat and didn't smoke so much. He said Thatcher invented all these new benefits to bring down the unemployment figures, and even though he decried the welfare state and railed against scroungers and hypocrites, he nonetheless every second week cashed his giro as an invalid. He was, as he said, 'gainfully unemployed'.

I digress. I should be telling you about how I met Dot, but it is important for you to picture the mire she was just about to wade into.

To resolve the crisis over flatmate and electric light, I, as a last attempt, proposed that we go to one of the gallery openings that night – there were many at that time. It was at Dazed and Confused and there would be wine to steal. Perhaps, I thought, if Saul got wasted enough he might help me clean up. Saul, shook his head – I could pinch sherry from Sadhi's much more easily, he exclaimed, so I added the prospect of real toilet paper. While he had often insisted that my complaint over using newspapers for the purposes of anal cleansing was reactionary, I knew that he harboured a secret nostalgia for quality loo roll ('Tabloids are smoother on the anus,' he'd declared, 'being cheaply made on thin, inferior paper, while *The Times* and *Guardian* do lead to chafing and occasional bleeding. Such is the burden of intelligence.') That was it then: the promise of some pinched Kleenex and white wine had him motivated. As he got dressed I secretly searched my mind for a plan to leave him. I did not for a second really hope or believe that anyone would or could enter our lives and save us from ourselves, certainly not one such as Dot.

Arseholes was the name of the exhibition, and it was, quite unexpectedly, a series of eighteen high-gloss cibachromes, about a metre square, of human anuses in extreme, almost medical, close-up. (There was no way the *Hoxton Advertiser* would publish a review, which would leave me twenty quid short the next month.)

I set about locating and stealing the wine bottles while Saul got to work distracting the masses.

— Such a succinct sphincter, he pronounced as he gesticulated before a tight pink arsehole, — but my favourite is the one with hairy haemorrhoids, very Jackson Pollock!

He soon had quite a circle round him. I located a hidden place beside the drinks table, with bottles well within reach. And so Saul stared ranting about Damien Hirst; how he'd first met him three years ago and told him: — Darling, you're flogging a dead horse with this art of yours. Why don't you just in fact exhibit one?

The sheep and the cows in formaldehyde that then followed Saul claimed as his own, to rapturous laughter from the circle.

— He has still to do a horse, though. I think he's afraid I might sue.

I grabbed two bottles while Saul went on. Pearls before swine, he muttered. Pearls before swine. As he threw back a glass of wine I heard him start his old favourite.

— Did I ever tell you about the Duchess, he ranted, — the mistress of Duchamp? She once walked down Fifth Avenue with a corset built from a birdcage, with a live bird inside it!

Bottles stuffed in bag, I snuck to the back and, before heading to the toilet, paused and stuck up an advert for the spare room. On looking up I noticed this girl was staring at me. Quite beautiful in a way, skinny-looking with long mousy hair, not dyed or cropped. Young, privileged, but not hip. Twenty-one was my guess. Flat sensible shoes, not retro heels or Doc Martens like the rest, and an Aran sweater. Something freakish but endearingly geekish about her, profoundly uncool, but still an elegance, the high cheek-bones and large sky-blue eyes, a sign of good breading, a trophy mother maybe. It was not my fault that Saul taught me to read class background from faces. He liked to joke that Dr Mengele was right. Eugenics would be on the pages of *Vogue* soon enough. I imagined her in time lapse, a hundred people buzzing around her in a soft blur of excitement about what's hot and what's not, and her standing so still, staring out at the arseholes.

From across the gallery, Saul nodded to me to proceed with phase two. So I ducked away and headed to the toilet. The process was tricky as I'd made the mistake of swapping light bulbs before attempting to steal the toilet roll and so had to work in the dark with my penknife to open the big white metal thing. (Did they do that to stop toilet rolls being stolen? Were there others like me?) It was a real treasure, though, a whole new roll, about a foot in diameter. It was hard to stuff it into the shoulder sack with the two bottles and the bulb in there already, but the thought of actually cleaning my arse on something other than Saul's stolen tabloids got me through the humiliating process. Then there were knocks at the door and posh voices laughing and I was crouching by the door, listening like a cat, trying to will the bodies away, feeling rather like Raskolnikov in *Crime and Punishment*.

I was out and mumbling apologetically about the damned light bulb that had just blown, as a couple laughed past me and entered together. Coked up, obviously, going for a kinky shag. I searched through the bodies for Saul and the door.

The girl was still there at the noticeboard, in front of my advert, and I realised what a stupid mistake I'd made. How easy it would be for anyone to work out that the guy loitering by the noticeboard had been the toilet thief. My name and address there for all to read. I feared she was maybe the daughter of the gallery owner and was about to have me arrested. She smiled as if with a look of pity, or embarrassment. Anxiety gripped me.

I pushed through the thickening trendies to the exit. Outside and round the corner, I waited for Saul. As my breath calmed and I counted the minutes, I was suddenly crushed by the pettiness of what I had found so all-consuming just minutes before – the theft of a light bulb, toilet roll and two bottles of wine. As I had to pay for both our tickets on the late-night bus and as Saul would consume all the wine himself, I calculated that, even after such entrepreneurial exertions, I was left at a loss of something like forty-seven pence.

As I rested my head against the cold wall and closed my eyes, her smile came to me. And a phrase – 'Alone among the arseholes'. I thought that, as with most things of beauty, I would never see her again.

Five flatmate interviews were scheduled for the day after next, but still the stand-off on the bin bags had not been resolved. To make matters worse Saul had dressed in his most offensive attire to greet the potentials: that wedding dress he'd torn in half to make into a T-shirt – grey with grime – his red rhinestone cowboy boots and a huge beauty spot over his stubble. — Try to have some common sense for once, I begged, to which he replied, — Sense is far too common for me! I decided it was best he stayed out of the proceedings and had dragged only the first of the stinking bags out of the door when they started arriving.

First there was a lovely, elderly Francis Bacon type, who found it 'all so bohemian' and was dying to meet my 'chum'. Who seemed oblivious to the stench and was just 'so thrilled' about sharing with 'two young aesthetes'.

Saul played the Osmonds and would not open his door.

Then a young German student guy with bicycle clips on his chinos, who arrived just as a bag burst in my arms and I was covered in fungal noodles, and insisted I lower the rent for reasons of basic hygiene and common decency. And Saul played that terrifying album by Einstürzende Neubauten, with the chainsaws as musical instruments. In desperation I did all that I could. I climbed up to the fusebox, and flicked off the power. The sound of his stereo dying. That was it for him, that roused him. I threatened to move out if he did not help me with the flatmate situation.

— Go then, he said, — you'll find nothing much out there, believe me, it's a void.

The doorbell rang again and he turned, flicked the electricity back on and ran back to his room, his kimono flying behind him.

I took a deep breath and opened the door. It was her. She offered her hand and her name and laughed nervously

— Dorothy, but people call me Dotty. I guess I am rather, sometimes.

She was a final-year student at Goldsmiths, a painter. Her voice was very pukka-pukka, like royalty. She seemed ashamed of it, putting her hand over her mouth. Perfect

American TV presenter teeth, a slight stutter, she did not finish her sentences.

I invited her in and no sooner did I indicate Saul's room, than 'Happiness in Slavery' started up from behind his door – that track with the S&M noises. I led her swiftly away, then to the kitchen, apologised for the lack of light, then showed her my room – the only one not toxic – apologising that we hadn't had time to clean the spare one, but really, she could trust me, it would be fine and was about the same size as mine and really cheap.

She left with a smile and said we seemed very interesting, but I could tell she was glad to get away. As if in celebration of her departure Saul turned up the volume: the sounds of electric guitars and a man being whipped filled every room.

Why had I sacrificed my life to be his apologist and slave, I asked myself in the days that followed as I made plans to move out. It took me back to that very first time I met Saul and the question of why I moved in. I'd been in my third year, studying for a BA in political theory and journalism at the London School of Economics. I was twenty-one, and much angered by the decline of the Left. It was just after the Wapping dispute, Rupert Murdoch and the great cull of permanent staff at the newspapers. I swore I would never walk past a picket line even though I needed work to pay back my student loan. I was a member of the Socialist Workers Party and stood every weekend, outside Camden tube station, beside the alkies and bums, trying to sell papers with headlines like TORY SCUM; DESTROY THE CAPITALIST MACHINE. But the more I studied Trotskyism the more my thesis on working-class solidarity bore no relation to the world around me.

I'd been going through a messy break-up with my then girlfriend, Debs, who was angered both by my sexual inadequacies and my revolutionary beliefs – the latter she saw

21

as a pathetic excuse for the former. It had been on a day when I had been struggling with my thesis and had failed to sell a single paper after six hours shouting, 'This week's *Socialist Worker*,' a day when Debs had given me an ultimatum to move out. Facing homelessness, I came across an ad in a shop window. The rent was cheap and I was pushing well into my overdraft.

I heard his music before I saw him at the door. Some kind of terrifying art-student experiment. But it was his face that really scared me: he was wearing foundation and looked like the Joker in *Batman*. He nodded at me, reluctantly, then let me enter. I found his rudeness perplexing, as all previous potential flatmates had given me the tour like they were estate agents. I walked to the back room and 'squalid' would have been a compliment. I entered his dark cavern of a room with questions about rent. He gave me a figure, ridiculous, then, as I was about to leave, he cut it in half. Two hundred . . . and then he added thirty more. He asked me to sit, and as I set down my stack of unsold papers, he laughed. I asked what he found so funny. He read the front page aloud: — 'Support the Wapping workers.'

— Waking the masses from their slumbers, are we?

I took offence and explained that Marxism was an analysis of –

— Yes, yes, yes . . . he interrupted, – cultural hegemony, historical necessity and all that jazz.

I was shocked that he knew the lingo.

— I'm sure equality seems lovely to you, but let me tell you, people will always find a way to fuck each other over. You see, there's no such thing as Left and Right, there are simply those who shaft and those who get shafted!

I picked up my papers and headed for the door.

He called after me: — In time you may come to see the simple beauty of this.

With no money for the tube I headed to the intersection

at Shoreditch in a fury. A minicab screamed to a halt before me; I passed a sex shop, beneath the shadow of the high-rises where drug dealers loitered – the shafters and the shafted, and how dare anyone say this was anything but ugliness and hell. The sky was bearing down on me, burning yellow. On the overpass thousands of headlights screamed red beneath my feet. I looked up and an ancient tramp was there, ten feet from me, alone at the railing. What little change I had I decided to offer him, and walked to his side.

— Lovely, ain't it? he said, almost to himself. The head-lights lit his drunken teary-eyed face that seemed moved as if by poetry. He did not take my money but smiled, turned and walked slowly away, carrying his one plastic bag. I stood where he'd stood and stared out.

It was then as I felt the cars push wind on my face, as I surrendered to their power, that I realised I would never escape from that voice that dared to show me the world in negative, to turn all I had known inside out, and speak to me through other people and things. In that moment all judgement fell away and I glimpsed the fatal beauty of it all. The cars were unstoppable in their force, capitalism could not be overthrown, these things were not external to me, to be critiqued, but inside me, as alive as the toxic car fumes in my lungs. I was of it, and it of me, and the head-lights became stars that wept for me. I roared with laughter then and fell headlong into that scepticism that had long been brewing. I fell and all I once believed in fell away. At the end of the overpass I threw my papers to the ground and walked away. Within the week, I had said my goodbyes to Debs and my degree and I became the student of the terri-fying laughing man who saw beauty in the crap of the world.

It seemed a miracle. I had been scanning the For Rent pages when Dot rang to say she would move in. I said yes, uncon-ditionally, then recanted: I'd have to clear it with Saul first.

23

He agreed on two conditions: that we lie about the price, and that she paid us, not the council, so we could skim a couple of hundred off the top. Six-fifty a month was ridiculous (as we both paid two hundred) and it was humiliating to have to call her back but he hung over my shoulder the whole time whispering the price. Money was not a problem, she said. She liked us and would move in the next day.

Why the hell she would want to live with us? It was an hour or so's commute to Goldsmiths. She had mentioned that her father had bought her a flat in Golders Green but she felt lonely there and she needed the company of 'real artists'. Were we? Con artists more like. I felt guilty about bleeding those extra hundreds out of her, and Saul was despicable, yet his deceit had saved us from eviction. I couldn't help but marvel at what the promise of a few hundred quid had done to him as he dived into the spare room and started carrying out the remaining rancid bin bags and stacked them out the front. Slime was dripping stinking trails across the floor, as he declared: — I suppose wealth is preferable to poverty, if only for financial reasons!

Of course he had disclaimers – we weren't to speak to her – she was a capitalist cash crop – women were a distraction, nothing more. He made me swear I would not succumb to the temptations of the flesh, that if I slept with her he would leave without discussion. I made my vow of abstinence as we stood there with twenty reeking bin bags between us.

We made a shoplifting trip to Pricecutter for Neutradol – the world's number-one room spray odour destroyer – and some cheese because he was peckish. All we bought was a copy of the *Sun*, because it was the cheapest thing in the shop. As soon as we were outside he threw the paper to the ground. He had no ethical issues over stealing from Pakistanis or subsidising Rupert Murdoch to the value of twenty pence, now that we had real toilet paper.

As I tidied her room for her arrival, I wondered what Dot would make of Saul on actually meeting him: an obnoxious character, no doubt. Beneath his hundred ironic veils, the clashes of cultures he played with daily, was there an essence to the man, an essential Saul? There were some basic facts. Saul was by no means tall. Five foot seven was my guess, although he was rarely barefoot and his Cuban heels added three inches and his cowboy boots perhaps two. (They looked vaguely orthopaedic and may have had a few hidden inches inside.) His feet were extraordinarily large, a size twelve, and the rumour about feet and their correlation with male endowment, I gathered, from glimpses through his ever-shifting kimono, was in fact the case. On the few occasions I saw him almost naked I determined that there seemed not an inch of him that was not covered in thick black hair. In two days he could grow a moustache that would have taken me three weeks, and when he wore foundation his five o'clock shadow spiked its way through at around 3 p.m. He had a Kirk Douglas chin, and his nose was large and long and slightly crooked, which gave him the appearance, on his days in a trench coat, of being some modern-day Fagin (although he denied Judaic origins). His eyebrows added to the effect, being heavy and almost meeting in the middle, although I recalled that time – he was going through his Dolly Parton stage – when he shaved them off entirely and wore eyeliner instead. He was prematurely greying, although that would be a premature judgement as he carefully concealed his age. I'd guessed somewhere between twenty-eight and thirty-two. The hair came and went in length too, some days a 'yuppie ponytail', others shoulder-length, once he wore it in two pigtails – one on either side of his head – like a schoolgirl (an effect he called pornographic), most days it was matted, but never dread-locked, as he despaired at the Rastafarians. His chest, beneath the hairs, was as sunken as his arm muscles were shrunken,

25

lending validation to the impression that he'd never done a day's exercise in his life.

This – the man naked, pieced together from fragments I was maybe not supposed to have seen – still did not answer the question.

Any time I got close to some truth about where he had come from I got the same riposte. 'I am who I am today, nothing more.' I gathered that he had spent his twenties studying the arts and political sciences but whether at university or in his bed, I did not know. He liked the word 'autodidact'.

His accent should have given me clues, but it was a hybrid of many things – some Americanisms from the adverts he quoted, but largely the nineteenth-century affectations he'd pinched from Nietzsche. It was only when he quoted in French that I detected the tiniest trace of something that may have been from the north of England. (Had he a Brummy French teacher in school?) He despised rave culture – the Happy Mondays and Stone Roses and even before that the Smiths. The sensitive socialist Morrissey was maybe his public enemy number one, which may have been more evidence to prove that he was born within a mile of the man's home. As he would not discuss his parents or childhood, disclaiming it all as 'just so much Freudian nonsense', I was left none the wiser. Perhaps his quest to be a new person was the product of some deeply embarrassing truth about himself, a childhood of squalor in Manchester perhaps, a single mother, a working-class background (which may have explained his hatred of the proletariat; maybe his father had been one of the miners that Thatcher crushed?). He did after all frequently say, 'Art saves us from the prison of history.' But as soon as I started examining I would hear him incanting: 'The truth of oneself is not hidden inside, it has yet to be invented!'

As I waited for her arrival Saul declared that he had

changed his mind and did not want to meet the 'incumbent'. I was to handle all the practicalities of her move as he would be gathering his thoughts and was not to be disturbed. He went to his room and put on a record. As the cheesy synths jangled through the flat I knew it was the dreaded one. 'Disparu' by the Duchamps. They were some long-disbanded failed eighties band a bit like Spandau Ballet meets Stockhausen meets a karaoke singer doing Pavarotti. It had audio samples of animals played backwards and the keyboards sounded like a kiddie's home computer. As I tried to shield my ears from it, the vocals came on. The notes were flat and the voice was of a sick androgyne singing falsetto and mispronouncing French lyrics with a trace of a Yorkshire accent.

'J'ai disparu, nous avons disparooo, vooo disparooo.'

It was possibly the worst and definitely the most pretentious album of all time. An album so up its own bottom that no one perhaps other than Saul could have ever found it; that symbolised Saul's ethos of rebellion against the forces of mass culture, the elevation of obscurity to a virtue and his belief in worshipping failure in a world based on the cult of success.

He had played it to me that first time I met him, as a test, and somehow maybe in a kind of fucked-up way I had gone from fearing, to loathing, to kind of loving it. I had to laugh at what the girl called Dot's first reaction would be upon hearing the sounds of 'Disparu'.

It was surreal, this company she'd hired, three men in matching overalls, carrying in her possessions in identical boxes: a music stand for, maybe, a violin; eight or so boxes of books or CDs; a large television. She apologised profusely for her many things: a cappuccino machine; easel; surround-sound stereo; teak bookshelf; one of those new Apple Macintoshes and a printer.

Saul's door was locked throughout, 'The Ride of the Valkyries' blaring from within. The council clone came again to the door and the scene was impossible but beautiful. Him demanding the back rent and Dot extending her hand to shake.

— Hello, my name is Dorothy. Who are you?

Her posh voice must have freaked him — and the Wagner and the wad in her wallet. He called her 'ma'am' then, said thank you again and again as she gave him the dosh, then backed away, his lowered shoulders and posture that of a subservient dog. She had paid our arrears. I chatted to her after, helping her plug in things and apologising for the lingering smells and Saul's absence and his Valkyries.

— He'll maybe say hello in a few days.

As if hearing me he strode past us both as if on a catwalk, wearing his bare-bottomed leather cowboy chaps, a Winnie-the-Pooh pyjama top and ballet pumps, without even casting a glance at Dot.

— Hello . . . she tried to say: — Saul?

But he slammed the toilet door and within seconds we heard him retching. His stomach was sensitive to any changes in routine and he'd asked me for two quid earlier which I was sure had gone on a box of Don Quixote.

— Is he OK? she asked anxiously.

— Oh, yes, this is perfectly normal. He just takes a while to get used to.

I committed to spending the evening with her, chatting. To not come across as mercenary as Saul. To find the real person, not the chequebook. In her room I saw her paintings stacked against the bed – abstract and brightly coloured – and I worried then, because Saul despised paintings and colour in all its manifestations. Furthermore, she was a trust-fund kid and somewhat hippy-ish and on a daily basis he screamed for the genocide of both. She put on her favourite record for me: Joni Mitchell – and if there was one thing

Saul despised more than anything it was the 'heart-felt mewings of that menstrual monster'. I tried to smile as the acoustic guitar started up.

All week it had been coming, this scene of the most crushing despair. From her locked door I heard her sobbing and it took me back to two years before, when, having just moved in and filled with enthusiasm, I attempted to show Saul my latest writings.

She'd talked to me for hours that morning about how much her art studies meant to her, when Saul wandered through in his kimono, curious, no doubt, to find out what he was being excluded from. He said very little, but was judging, I could tell. He returned to his room and in excitement she followed, carrying two small canvases. I could not stop her, so sat, peering round the door, as she set the canvases by his wall and asked what he thought.

They were too far away for me to hear clearly, I only heard bits when Saul raised his voice . . . Bourgeois . . . reactionary . . . obsolete! You may as well destroy them! The eraser says more about you than any mark you wilfully make. If you must paint, then paint your face, or your room, tattoo your tits, or graffiti a flyover. Do it like Warhol if you must − car crashes in lilac, electric chairs in pastel peach − a hundred a day. There is more art in my ashtray than in a hundred thousand paintings. Why not exhibit my soiled bed sheets, a more damning indictment of our time you will not find! Fuck art and turn yourself into an artwork. Steal a video camera and record yourself eating, sleeping, taking a shit!

As she wept in her room, he played Bach's cello solos in his, the ones in the minor keys, as if the necessary destruction of egos caused him some subtle pain. The same record he played after my ego-death.

I worried for her then, with her fragile ways. The quiet

29

way she carried herself, the look on her face, of fear at the simplest of things. Her inability to finish her sentences, the waiting when you had to guess and then she said, 'Yes,' as if it was easier for her to let you speak for her. She was in her last year at art school and had to have something to show for her graduation. Perhaps he had already destroyed her education. I had to go through and see if she was OK, apologise on his behalf. Confess that I too had been thwarted by him, how her fear of the empty canvas was the same as mine of the empty page.

But yet, as I paused at her door, I told myself that, perhaps, she would come in time to see that he had done her a great favour as he did for me. His critique of Western civilisation was correct. What was the point of adding more art, more reproduction of the same to the stinking stockpile of crap that was our culture? Why give the wealthy the opportunity to buy status objects that told them how sophisticated they are when their wealth was made on the suffering of millions? Stop being creative and embrace the beauty of destruction. And in that moment of suicidal despair, reach for your first breath as a truly free soul. That was what Saul believed, or did the last time I'd asked.

In the days that followed she hid herself away and went for long walks alone. I took the liberty of peeking into her room. The things she'd moved in: packs of bedlinen, towels from Marks & Spencer, unopened, three Sainsbury's ready meals; a stack of notepads, books on psychotherapy, self-help, *The Prophet* by Kahlil Gibran and one by the Dalai Lama. Her canvases lay by her bed, torn from their frames.

I imagined her then walking aimlessly through streets in tears, remeasuring the world. Disillusionment with all is the first stage in the conversions of Saul. The Road to Damascus is long and very few survive the revelation that the figure at the end is a man on the dole. I told myself not to worry, she would come back, as I did.

After she had returned and tiptoed past my room, I decided to confront Saul. To ask him please, try to be nice, give her some appreciation for the rent situation. What did he actually want to achieve by this war of attrition? For her to give us money and then leave?

— That would be ideal! he said, as he put on a track by Rapeman. — Women, he said, — pah, they leave smells and cosmetics in the bathroom. Have you ever witnessed a bloody tampon in a toilet bowl?

Could he at least stop scaring her, sit down and talk with her? I asked.

— Talk, talk, talk, Freud was an imbecile, talking cures nothing.

I knew there was no possibility of an apology as he closed his door on me. I waited, fearing the worst and it came. Japanese avant-garde industrial noise music. Recordings of buildings exploding and women wailing. Hiroshima on a twelve-inch. Nagasaki on the B-side. That was it, I couldn't stand it, I had to at least apologise to her for his conduct.

I heard not a 'come in' or a 'hi', just a noise, affirmative, telling me it was OK to enter. She was sitting by the window on that office chair Saul and I found in the street, hands upturned on her lap, as if meditating. There was no view from that window, just the wall and ten years of accumulated crap that could be a garden if anyone cared. I sensed I was intruding on something horribly private and I was embarrassed, no longer sure why I'd come in. But she gestured towards the bed for me to sit.

— Sorry, I've just taken a Valium.

— Really? I asked her. She nodded slowly. The silence between us was violated by his music. I apologised.

— He can play it rather loud at times, he's just probably

31

a little freaked out about having another person here. He's eccentric, but he means well. The fact that he's ignoring you and so rude means he's scared, that's all. He considers fear the basis of devotion, if that's any help.

— There's a little tree out there. I have to find positives, my shrink says. She's a cognitive behaviourist.

She pointed and I was grateful then for the excuse to get closer, to touch her shoulder as I leaned to see. And yes, there was a tree, growing from the rubble. She allowed my hand to linger on her shoulder. Saul couldn't stand my touchy-feelyness. I sat back and tried to recall what it had been like in that time before Saul's voice had sat in judgement of my every action. She stared at her upturned hands.

— Lithium for breakfast, Prozac for lunch, Valium before bed.

It was like a little song to herself. I told her it was quite a cocktail, that Saul and I believed medication was a form of oppression, even though we did hash and speed when we could blag it.

— My mum's on antidepressants and Valium too. I'm not supposed to do hash because it can set me off – I'm manic-depressive, she said as if she'd just introduced herself. I got the impression that this was a rite for her, something she told everyone or was told to tell everyone. She was staring at her hands again. The strangest thing, this kind of honesty would have usually had me running for the door, but something told me that my presence was not a problem. Time was different for her. Valium time.

— Well, that was the last diagnosis. I dunno. My dad thinks I might have an obsessive personality disorder too.

All of this made me feel quite awkward, but morbidly curious.

I searched for something to talk about and saw a little folder on the floor.

— Are those more of your paintings?

— Just old photos, I was just looking through, you know, trying to remember why I started in the first place.

I thought if I expressed an interest it might repair some of the damage Saul had done.

— Can I see?

She motioned for me to sit next to her as she picked it up. I calmed to her pace and listened as she flicked through the pictures. We weren't flirting: there was just this incredible candidness. The photos were of her many paintings from maybe since pre-puberty. At first figurative and amateurish; people's faces, then many self-portraits, the face gaunt, teenage, skull-like, the details growing as the skill developed as the face aged.

— I did these ones in art therapy – after my episode.

— Your episode?

— Yeah, my mum had one too after Josh died – he was my brother. They say it's hereditary but I don't believe it – the episodes, I mean.

A dead brother. I didn't want to pry. I asked to see more. In every self-portrait that followed the style changed: one was like Munch, then Rembrandt, then Picasso, the lines thinner, then bolder, harsher, black and white, then cubist, then torn and collaged, as if exhausting every art movement, looking for the one true face.

— These are really good, I said. — So who started you on art therapy?

— My dad. He prescribes my medication too. He's a –

— Your dad's a shrink?

— Yes, Harley Street, stinking rich.

That was weird. Very controlling. I was developing a theory about her art being an attempt to escape a sick mother and tyrannical drug-administering father.

— It was kind of handy when I went nuts, she said.

— I'm sure you weren't crazy at all. Maybe you were

33

just rebelling against some people who were trying to control you.

— How very sweet you are, she said and gave my hand a little squeeze.

— Can I see the rest?

— They're really crap, she said. But I insisted. As the paintings became more abstract and the faces vanished from the surfaces, I could feel Dot relax beside me. Swathes of colour, imaginary fields and planes, bright and luminous. I sensed how much her art meant to her, how painful a voyage it had been from those first tentative scratched pencil portraits to the bright bold washes of pure primary colour.

— These are really lovely, I said, but then my eyes came to rest on the torn paintings by the door and I remembered Saul's venom. How could he have dismissed all her effort and struggle as if it were all a joke? My chest grew tight as the anger rose.

Her hand was on my shoulder.

— Hello? You OK?

She told me I was hyperventilating and took my hand and squeezed it, explaining that it was acupressure and might help.

— You want a pill?

She held these things in front of me. Plastic and silver wrapping. Beta blockers. Or if I wanted she could give me half a Valium. And she was sorry, people often responded like this when she showed them her past. I said yes, to all, to both tablets. She asked if I was sure. I said please. She placed two pills in my hand, got me a glass of water.

A knock on the door.

In all the time we had been in there Saul had paid us no heed and had played Ministry and Foetus and Millions of Dead Cops and even *William Shatner Sings the Blues*, but now, his ugliest records exhausted, he was at her door.

Mister-and-something-else-is-happening-and-I'm-excluded –
so I want to be part of it.

— Hi, he said, all cutesy in a whole new get-up: torn
flares and his Prince T-shirt and purple eyeliner, doing that
oh-so-awkward-I'm-so-sensitive-lost-for-words-staring-at-
the-floor thing that he did when he wanted something.

She gestured for him to sit and he seemed so excited
or was faking it.

— So what's going on?

I tried to explain, but she was before us with the contents
of her medication cabinet. I played it smart.

— We're doing drugs.

— Drugs, huh. I did three acid before breakfast once
and it had no effect whatsoever.

The liar.

— Mind-contracting drugs, now that's what we need.
My mind's over-expanded enough as it is!

I wanted the Valium, just because he'd have to take it
too, and I knew for a fact he'd not taken half the drugs he
claimed. He'd never hugged strangers on E, or been lucid
on speed like Lou Reed. He found all these things signs of
weakness in me. And I knew he would only heap scorn on
the confessional Dot and I had just shared. It being something about depth and truth.

She gave us three pills each and we sat with them in
our hands like kids in school taking their vitamins, as she
explained what each did and how the lithium wouldn't
really have any effect because it had to be taken every day
and build up in your metabolism. She was laughing but I
was worried, the forever practical me, that in taking them
we were depriving her of what she needed.

It was strange to see the new rapport between them.
Her forgiveness of his former obnoxiousness, and the transformation in him, like a goofy kid.

Valium. It's nothing. Things happen and you feel nothing.

Things that were boundaries or taboos collapse. All of my anxieties vanished, but there was no sense of the liberation, of the break or the joy of overcoming. Just nothing.

— Bit of a disappointment, Saul declared. — If we're going to explore the void, we may as well listen to some Abba while we're at it.

In Saul's room, Dot was looking through his records on the floor and he was putting on track after track, no memory of what, none of my usual analysis of what mood he was in by reading his music, no sense of excitement or dread over his next choice. Iggy Pop or Parliament or Mahler. And in that Valium nothing I did not care; he could have overdosed or slashed his wrists and I would have just stared at the turntable going round and round. Horrific, that her father had fed her these pills for years. In the name of love, these pills that make love or hate impossible.

We ran out of tobacco and were all quite spacious so I suggested we play the Rizla game. Dot had never done it before, so we taught her.

Saul wrote HITLER and stuck it on her head. I wrote THATCHER and stuck it on his. She wrote MADONNA and stuck it on mine. Dot didn't quite get the rules, but found the whole thing hilarious.

— Wait, am I John Wayne? Or no, no . . . what's his name?

— You're the one who's supposed to guess!

— Superman?

Saul, as always, was the first to work out who he was and I was sure he always cheated and had a little mirror stashed somewhere among his mess. When it was over, Saul turned suddenly pale, excused himself like the perfect gent and ran, hand to mouth, to puke in the kitchen sink. I thought perhaps the mixture of sherry and Valium. When he came back through Dot told us both, — No more drugs, not for you, not for any of us.

We watched as she flushed all of her pills down the toilet. I asked her if it was a good idea, wouldn't there be withdrawal symptoms or . . .

— You've convinced me . . . I don't need them any more, she said, but would not explain what I had said or done to convince her. She smiled with a gentle wisdom that told me she'd survived depths I had only glimpsed and Saul had only read about. In that moment she seemed the most beautiful creature I had ever witnessed.

It was the last week of September 1992.

one

PlayBoy. 1992. Video loop. 25 mins. Installation view. Private collection.

THE WORK COMPRISES two video projections on free-standing screens, twenty feet by fourteen feet, placed facing each other at a distance of twenty feet. The audio is in sync with the pictures. The footage is hand-held and 'home movie' in style. The subject is a woman in her early twenties (the artist).

The location of the footage is a domestic toilet. Both pieces of footage are almost identical. In each, the artist faces the (bathroom) mirror with a video camera, filming her reflection, striking poses and talking to herself. In the first, the artist is in a loose-fitting top, her areolae visible; in the second, she is wearing a 'fake' moustache. In the first, the content of her dialogue (with herself) is entirely negative and derisory: 'Ugly bitch', 'droopy tits', 'useless cunt'. In the second, she compliments herself on her 'male' image. 'Hunky bastard', 'cute spunky man', etc.

The placement of the two screens facing each other gives the impression that the artist is recording the other self on the facing screen. This uncanny illusion is reinforced by the fact that at one point in the screening, which may or may not be a happy accident,[1] the 'male' artist on screen two seems to speak to the 'female' artist on screen one – 'What you fucking looking at?' – at which point the female artist lowers her eyes as if in shame and says, 'Nothing. Sorry.'[2]

Many viewers have commented that this artwork is 'spookily alive' and feel they're intruding on a very private experience. Others feel that they can relate to this daily self-criticism before a mirror and have felt trapped between the two screens, becoming 'the third person' to whom both of the screens address their comments – the stated 'What you fucking looking at?' refers to the art viewer him/herself and is as such a critique of the ways in which gender identity is constructed within consumerism.[3]

Less favourable responses have come from the tabloid press. The 1994 headline in the *Sun* was: '£50,000 FOR A GIRL IN THE BOG'. The story claimed that the footage was 'just a typical stoned posh student mucking about with a new video camera'.

It's worth bearing in mind that in the year this work was made, gender and sexual identity were issues of greater importance than they are now: Madonna's *Sex* book had just been banned by the Vatican; Sinead O'Connor had torn up an image of the Pope on US television over the issues of homosexuality and contraception; in the UK the Operation Spanner trial raised a political outcry within lesbian and gay communities; the artist Cindy Sherman had, at this time, created the seminal works in which she enacted gender stereotypes for her camera, while artists such as Jenny Holzer and Barbara Kruger were deconstructing 'male language'; the Aids activists ACT-UP toured their artwork and theatre worldwide; in fashion culture, sadomasochistic-style PVC clothing made it into high street stores such as Dorothy Perkins and H&M; sex shops made it onto the main streets and the first 'drag kings' were reaching the public eye through the popularisation of the queer scene.

Whatever conclusions we may draw from *PlayBoy*, no matter how 'trivial' or 'dated' it may now seem, Shears has, undoubtedly, held a mirror up to her time. In that mirror we see a generation who came to sexual maturity beneath the shadow of the Aids epidemic, under the 'back to basics' reactionary 'family' politics of John Major's Conservative Party. A generation who had grown up witnessing the fall of the Berlin Wall, the collapse of Socialism, the defeat of union power, of resistance politics, and the co-option of dissent into mainstream culture.

42

If nothing else, this is a simple, non-judgemental document of what it meant to be a young woman growing to maturity within the many contradictory messages of modern consumerist culture. For all its simplicity, this, ultimately, is of greater historic significance than the work of so-called politically engaged artists.[4]

1. See Duchamp on accidents in *3 Standard Stoppages*, quoted by T. Schwartz in 'No Accidents in Art', *New European Critique*, June 1973.
2. See *Taxi Driver*. Also used as 'found footage' by Turner Prize-winner Douglas Gordon.
3. This 'schizophrenic critique' is reminiscent of *How to Explain America to a Dead Hare* by Joseph Beuys (1965) and *USA* by Vito Acconci (1964) in which Acconci filmed himself arguing (with himself) over the evils of American imperialism versus his love of and immediate need for a can of Coca-Cola.
4. Ironically, the political artists who fought for the self-expression of sexual minorities – gays, lesbians, sadomasochists, etc. – did not foresee how their 'liberation' goals would lead to the sexualisation of the culture as a whole and to the increasing commodification of the body. Shopping malls worldwide selling sadomasochist-inspired lingerie and sexual aids, the reduction of radical oppositional identity to passing fashion and individual consumer choice, was surely not on the original liberation agenda. See Z. Bauman on *Individualisation and Consumer Society*, RKP, 1996.

'I'LL HOLD,' Owen said. The call-waiting jingle started up, just like a call centre but it sounded religious. Probably Arvo Pärt, he thought, typical for a high-end gallery.

A car alarm was wailing outside. Owen took a peep out the window: some hooligan had thrown the next-door neighbours' FOR SALE sign onto the bonnet of a trendy retro Beetle. He checked to see how many of the other FOR SALE signs were still there. Nope, no change.

The call-waiting choir was singing in Latin in a cathedral.

He escaped the alarm noise, took the cordless phone through to the empty back room and sat on the window ledge, picking at the lining paper, fingering the dust. Funny, he thought, that he'd hardly ever been in here, that he'd not actually got round to redecorating the place, never got beyond that first burst of energy that was stripping out and white-washing every trace of the ex, filling it up with odds and sods of second-hand furniture – when was it? Year of the war? Was it Iraq? That far back?

The choir sang in his call-waiting ear. Jaysooo Chreestay.

The morning post thudded on the floor and he tiptoed along the half-varnished floor, phone still to ear. Bills, bills, bank statement – not to be opened – then another one of those bloody estate agent brochures. In the recent hysteria some moron had got the addresses mixed up. One of the adverts was of the place just across the road, identical to his own.

FIXED PRICE £295,000. It had been FIXED PRICE £320K last month.

As the choir sang Dominum, dominum, he scanned the

44

printed hype: . . . *pleased to offer this spacious 2-bedroom 2-floor Edwardian maisonette in Balls Pond Road, blah blah blah . . . two double bedrooms, en suite water closet, a third room ideal for a small child, the property benefits from blah de blah* – Jesooo Chreestay – *Location is ideal – to the east is Dalston, tipped to thrive from the Olympic boom and a new tube station, to the west you have central Islington and trendy Upper Street . . .*

Wonderful, he told himself, how they missed out any mention of the concrete towers of the housing estate, the shadows from which even now were growing menacingly along the street. Still, he'd been bloody lucky that the bank had let him remortgage to buy out the ex's share. Bloody lucky not to be out on his ear. To be going absolutely nowhere. The choir were cut off mid crescendo.

'Sorry,' the girl on the phone said, 'Miss Shears is in Hamburg till the 22nd at the Freiberg Institute.

Thank fuck, thought Owen. They belonged in different worlds and there was absolutely no way he was going to sneak into Dot's exhibition if there was any chance of her actually being there.

As he caught sight of the video surveillance footage of himself getting onto the tube escalator at Angel, he thought of the many ridiculous lengths he'd gone to over the years to avoid her. Of the many openings, group shows, biennales, in Paris, Frankfurt and Berlin, he'd attended while secretly mapping her schedule of appointments. Thankfully, now, she was just like many other artists, spending almost half the year touring with her art, so the chances of bumping into her locally had much diminished. He was notorious for turning up at private views just before they started, whisking round in ten minutes, and then leaving before the drinks were opened and the hundreds arrived. He gave the excuse that meeting artists socially would cloud his judgement – he refused point-blank to do face to face interviews. Of course, while this had brought him even more respect, skirting around her and not being at the epicentre of the scene had damaged his career. He was sure this was why at the age of thirty-nine he was still without pension plan, or salary, precariously scraping a living from bits and pieces for so many different magazines and papers.

'There is no drearier and more repulsive creature than the man who has evaded his own genius,' Saul had once said. Nonetheless, this failure to face up to his greater potential was a lesser humiliation compared with what hell could be unleashed if he ever did come face to face with Dot.

The real challenge came when he had to review a group show that had her work in it. If he had refused the job it would have aroused suspicion. So he developed a technique: he never praised or was overcritical; he gave her the column inches that befitted an artist of her standing with words carefully cribbed from other critics' reviews, but with absolutely no value judgements of his own. They had never agreed on this course of action, there had been no secret negotiations through third parties. Although all the world knew of, and almost celebrated, her suicide attempt, she, or her PR people, had taken great care to hide the truth about the love triangle that had led to it. He wanted it kept that way.

Owen turned the corner onto the King's Road and saw the sign on the austere modernist facade. The Lieder Gallery.

On entering, it was the usual: the vast reception of white that was supposed to instil reverence and symbolise purity and timelessness but which he knew was no more than the antechamber to a spectacle as empty and fleeting as fashion, desire and fashionable investment.

At the front desk, two girls in black suits with headsets

46

on were busy with visitors. There were brochures in full colour with a portrait of Dot. A new one, possibly Leibovitz. He slipped by and went to look on his own. The layout was very much like that that she'd had at the Venice Biennale. That night when his avoidance techniques had been almost slapstick.

It had been 2003; he'd known she was in town with *Walking Blind 2* in the International Salon, so he'd snuck away early from the opening and headed to the Italian Pavilion to see the seventies Viennese performance art retrospective, only to look up and see her ten feet away sipping champagne with the Wilson Twins. He'd ducked swiftly into the darkness of a walled installation – early video works on monitors on the floor of naked artists smearing themselves in the blood of suspended dogs' carcasses – only to realise that the space had two doorways and that Dot had entered from the other with the twins. He'd turned away swiftly, knocking a glass of champagne from some woman's hands, it smashing on the floor, him trying to say sorry but not wanting Dot to hear his voice. Him hunching his shoulders, trying to change his appearance as he hobbled away from her, then almost running through the throngs to the door, not looking back. He harboured a suspicion that she'd secretly sensed the identity of the man always running away from galleries.

He was just about to enter one of the enclosures when the PR woman ran to catch him.

'Excuse me, are you Owen Morgan?'

She'd got him. He nodded and had to smile. He couldn't help but wonder if they had CCTV at the door and a member of staff employed to search for critics.

'Are you here in connection with a review in the *Guardian*, or concerning the essay for the catalogue? Mr Schwarz isn't here right now, but we could book a time for you –'

'Sorry,' he said, 'before I write anything, I'm going to just see if it's any good, that OK?' Fucking PR people, he thought. The last thing they want is for anyone to see the fucking product they're selling. 'I just need ten minutes by myself, that OK?'

She backed away whispering into her headpiece, eyeing him up and down.

He paused at the white-walled maze-like entrance to the artwork known as *Name Game 3*. He calmed himself and told himself to withhold judgement: this is Dot's work but Dot is a fashionable media fabrication too – like Hirst in the pages of *Vogue* and Sam Taylor-Wood posing naked in *Harpers & Queen*. He must resist the temptation to write a review in his head. That is not the purpose of this exercise. No copy will be filed. He is here to erase.

He entered and the projections were epic in scale: three faces on free-standing screens, two men and one woman; each face had a name on a piece of paper on their heads, each taking turns to guess what their head-names were. The bits of paper read: STALIN, JESUS, COBAIN. The faces asked questions of themselves – Am I still alive? Am I a woman? Am I a film star?

It cannot but disappoint – this expensive remake of that stoner game they'd played many times, only Dot had filmed it and so it entered the canon of art history. The people in this remake are professional actors, their lines scripted. The lighting and production values, superb, almost Hollywood. Their faces, all different in ethnic mix, reflecting the pressure to be politically correct that Dot's work in the last few years has succumbed to.

It does not touch him as the original did. He walks out. There are many other walled enclosures to choose from. He wants to go to that room, the one that has his face. He returns to the front desk and asks the PR woman where it is, laughing to himself that she has probably seen that face a hundred times but does not know that it is his.

She shows him the floor plan and offers the information pack. As she talks and smiles Saul's voice returns again, scorning him, Jiminy Cricket-like.

'Art critics are people who can't write, interviewing people who can't talk, for people who can't read.'

When Saul said it, it had been funny, but living it was no joke. Yet Dot must have been haunted by Saul too. Every artwork she'd ever made came from something Saul had said, even the titles. Some of them had been jokes he'd made that she'd taken seriously. Most of her speech on accepting the Lieder Prize in 2002 had been Saul's words.

Owen thanks the PR woman for her help and walks the long white corridors. He passes four other rooms with the newer works, all of it is, as he knows, as they said on *Late Review*, recreations/reinventions/re-explorations of the works from that one incredible year when Dot made the works that her career has since rested upon. As he turned the corner before entering *Trust*, Owen closed his eyes and laughed at himself over that little beat, that pause of reverence that was required, before stepping in and looking up at the screen.

The face – the hair was long, grunge-like; he'd been told often that he looked like Cobain, like Jesus. Anorexic, anaemic. A blur round his chin, that first growth of a goatee. His face covered in lipstick kisses. The light was bright in his eyes while all in the background was black. Every fifteen, twenty or thirty seconds Saul or Dot entered to kiss or slap him. The face twitching in anticipation.

What the other critics failed to notice was the smile. A smile you may have had to live through to understand. To be kissed and slapped by your secret lover and the man she said she loved, your best and only friend whom you had betrayed with her. To be at the heart of that love triangle, sitting in the dark, not knowing if it was she or he that would strike you, fearing violence. An hour the whole video had taken to make, the clip was thirty minutes long. The critics said the light-blinded man was a critique of consumerism, the stimulus-response model of taught tele-visual consumption. Pavlov's Dog.

But the face, twenty feet wide, contorting in expecta-tion. This almost static portrait of the act of waiting. Some audiences wept, it was said. Others jumped when the kiss or slap hit.

And your own face, Owen, if you could only see it now.

The camera had been turned on, she said, they were recording. He had to keep a straight face, no giggling. He couldn't, was laughing at how the whole thing was absurd and sorry for spoiling it all. A shot broke the silence. A sharp noise to his left. He turned to see but his eyes were branded by the glow of the bulb. Dot's command to face the light. Then a hand, so gentle, stroking his cheek, and the brush of a kiss. Then nothing, only the waiting for another kiss, but it was a vicious slap.

The noises echoed round the empty gallery. Owen guessed the tape had another five minutes to go. He'd stay for its repeat. He was trying to anticipate the next blow, but it did not come when expected and when the face was struck it was by a kiss. So out of sync. He edged closer towards the screen to see more clearly but got too close and the image broke into thousands of multicoloured pixels. He turned back and was blinded by the projector light, and then startled by a shadow on the projection screen. He apolo-gised to the unseen person only to discover that the place was empty and the shadow was his own.

As he hit the street it was not the video but what happened just after the camera had been turned off that lingered: flashes of flesh, the sharing of her body in the dark.

Back on the Piccadilly Line at South Ken, he found

himself staring at the reflection of his face upside down in the bevelled glass, between the shoulders of a man and a woman, above the empty seat between them. The skin was neon green, the features stretched, aged, ghostlike. He closed his eyes and waited, it would be another ten minutes till his stop. The Northern Line, the way it was really two lines that joined then split then joined then split. If you missed the change at Euston, you had to go to Camden then double back south to Angel before the long walk home.

He shouldn't be here, he knows this. The choice of exits: Old Street, City Road North, City Road South – he picks the old one, passes a beggar dressed in red like a Hare Krishna with a chalk drawing of spirals beneath his bare feet. 'True beauty only survives in the gutter, where the guardians of high culture have overlooked it,' Saul once said. The old familiar street signs: Ring Road A11, A13 and A2. Finn's Court, Hackney Housing, sixties mosaics and graffiti, just as before. The old high-rises to his left. To his right – a trendy skater shop. City Best Kebab where it was, then all the new FOR LET signs. Old Street Moroccan and Mediterranean Cuisine. He laughs to himself thinking of Edna and Dot and the plaster-cast penises and smoking Moroccan black. Edna was dead now, four years back, maybe more. He passes the new blue recycling bins. There was an authentic Banksy somewhere near here. The locals had protested that his anarchic graffiti had pushed up property prices, forcing them out. The irony of it would have made Saul laugh, or puke over the original Banksy on the wall. Now they'd be welcoming as many Banksys as they could get.

The warehouses have been mostly converted into studio flats. He passes the sex shop now called Sh! – devoted to women's pleasure – gentlemen only welcome when accompanied by a woman. In this very same alleyway, he had gone down on his knees and begged Dot to let him eat her cunt. There had been a Chinese here, and a bin. She'd joked about the smell of sweet and sour.

Hoxton Square. White Cube gallery. Blue Bar and Kitchen. Yelo. Ziegfried and Underbelly. Another gallery he has never been to. An exhibition called *Through a Glass Darkly*. He puts his face to the glass and sees that one of the artworks is a hole in the gallery floor and that had been another joke Saul had said, a dare to an artist – 'Why not just dig yourself a fucking hole. Let's form an escape committee and get the fuck out of here!' He walks to the top of the square and hears the screams of children from St Monica's. The faces as before, black, the laughter is as it always is with all children. He walks the hundred yards then to the dole office that is called a jobcenture now. As soon as he turns the corner onto Hoxton Street it will be two blocks to 102 Whitmore Road. Saul had always said that the thing the place was lacking was more wit.

The old pie-and-mash place, then Bacchus – the franchised S&M chain. Hoxton Kicks – another new sex shop. The new Hoxton community garden, a pile of weeds and stones and broken bottles when he first saw it, before it became a community anything. The green metal signs for Hoxton Market arching over the street. The FOR LEASE signs diminish as the council houses grow around him. Miles of state-subsidised housing, inescapable poverty, incorruptible and pure in its way. Untouchable by the wealth in the square behind, which is now receding again.

The Queen's Head is boarded up and a sign says under new management and he is thankful for that because he hopes now not to find what he was looking for as he is about to turn that corner and is searching for any excuse not to go there.

She passes him in a miniskirt and he turns to look. She

has a tattoo of a Manga character on her ankle. She's eighteen, maybe twenty, Japanese-looking but Williamsburgesque, her arm in that of her androgynous beau. Just look at them. Their matching dyed green hair and deliberately slashed clothes. One earpiece in each of their ears sharing the iPod, the cable stretched taut pulling their faces closer to each other. And he feels for how they feel. Your angriest music in your ears and the world is only what you allow in and what you steal to give you enough hatred to laugh as you march through it. You see how much your games offend the order, and the eyes that stare with judgement only fuel you and tell you you are breaking nothing less than all the rules. They are all nothing and you are really something, you are really happening.

They stop and take a photo of themselves, just before the sign for Hoxton Market and now they seem fake. Everything now is copies of copies of copies, just as Saul's Baudrillard predicted. He watches them walk away, and now the disappointment turns to himself. Youth is wasted on the young, Saul said, but that line too had been copied.

He has to stop for a cigarette. But he is on week three again on his eighth attempt at quitting. A pack of Marlboro Lights from the pub. But it is boarded up and smoking in pubs is now illegal. So it has to be the street and no smokes, just the smouldering need.

Owen, look at you. By the time you are home and turn off the burglar alarm then all this will be lost again. Do something now, fight the need to run home, do something radical, stupid.

The Asian shop is the answer. It takes so long to decide what it will be, this product he must slip into his pocket and walk out without paying for. It's like he's drunk. This responsible man of thirty-nine years who wrote what many see as the most probing reviews of the works of two former Turner Prize-winners.

First it was the chocolate aisle, then bacon and poultry. Then anxiety over security cameras and being seen on some screen somewhere, going to the canned produce, touching a few, looking round then setting them back. The products before his eyes are surreal and enigmatic and their names are: Spaghetti Hoops in Tomato Sauce and Heinz Mushy Peas and Burga-mix. And Saul loved Warhol and he is thinking of cans and hands and pockets and he is for the first time in so long so alive and he has to do it now or he is nothing.

The Asian man is staring at him. He made that mistake Saul taught him not to, which was to make eye contact, that other – to smile back. The can of Heinz Mushy Peas is staring back at him, telling him he is a coward and hypocrite. Shut up, shut up, he is telling them. And they reply that they contain only 22g of fat per 100g and that they are very tasty.

Shut up! Silence them in pocket.

Checkout counter. Running over Saul's rules.

Don't walk out without buying something else – so chewing gum. He is telling the Asian guy that he just needs some gum because he's giving up smoking. Keep your cool, wittering is a dead giveaway. Shut up. Make the guy feel he owes you something. Rule 5 had been Dot's. Be rude to the shop assistant before you leave. If you placate it is abnormal. They are Asian. It's normal to be rude. England is racist.

He tries not to say thank you but can't help himself.

The adrenalin still coursing through him even after the tube ride home. He sets the mushy peas on the counter. He will never eat them and they seem to know it, staring blankly back at him, telling him there would be no escape from impulsive incidents until he had done the one thing he feared.

The phone is in his hand and he is dialling. The gallery girl picks up and he gives his name. She is only a receptionist or intern, he has no time to be asked who he is again or to wait to be put through to some other nobody who can assist him after the same questions. He asks her to get a pen, to leave a message; he has to get her to repeat it to him when it is done.

'OK, so, your name is Owen Morgan and you'd like to do an interview with Dorothy Shears, about her show, for her catalogue, is that right?'

*

It must have been around Halloween '92. Saul despised conventional festivities but took Dot under his wing as the new student of his ways and taught her how to dress, and shoplift clothes for herself, giving her lessons on the arts of working in twos and threes in supermarkets to distract the checkout girl and in concealing foodstuffs under trench coats. In turn she started loaning him money, as much as he wanted and more. As for me, my first real bits of work were coming in from the *Hoxton Advertiser* and as the autumn leaves fell we all three marched hand in hand in hand through the crap-strewn streets.

Dot had barely been to art school since she'd moved in with us, then one day she'd travelled to Goldsmiths to inform her tutor that she was giving up painting. Her announcement had created an uproar with her tutors who insisted she was throwing her life away on a whim as she had only six months to put together her graduation show – there had been much 'painting is dead' hysteria in the air at that time. On the way home Dot stopped off in Leicester Square and bought a super-cool video camera, a Panasonic. Striding in, she showed it to us.

— I'm going to turn my life into an artwork!

I worried then that it was unwise for her to have taken what Saul had said weeks before so literally. Did Saul even recall that he'd advised she record her life? My anxieties, however, were soon drowned by her enthusiasm, and I told myself that unfamiliar as I was to happiness, it was not to be feared.

I plugged her new camera into the back of Saul's TV and she set it on top facing the room and we spent most of the day reading the manual, taking turns pushing buttons, watching ourselves on the screen, moving in and out of shot. After an hour of her filming the pizza-coloured seventies vinyl carpet, Saul's scattered records and the woodchip wallpaper, walking round eye to Panasonic, bumping into things then playing it back, her energy started flagging.

— Filming life 'as it is' is banal old school socialist miserablism,' Saul declared. — You must remain true to your beliefs [which were his] and record your own radical transformation, he said, invoking Nietzsche, although Nietzsche never had a video camera.

We had a break for some pasta and Dot filmed that too. Saul declared it was like *Eat* by Warhol – a forty-five-minute single shot of one of the Factoryites eating a mushroom, so we put on the Velvet Underground in homage. Saul said we should nick lots of tinfoil to wallpaper the room with – à la the Factory circa '64, and that Dot could, with a bit of a makeover, be the next Edie Sedgwick. A few books scattered and images of Edie later, Dot stood before Saul's Victorian wardrobe as he, in the depths of the thing, threw out things for her to try on.

— Could you film for me? she asked, a little nervously, handing me the camera.

His camouflage military trousers; his SLUT T-shirt; his stolen Armani jacket with the holes in the elbows; his spray-on black PVC trousers; his Palestinian headscarf – all the time he ran back and forward to change the records – to create the optimum environment for the birth of a new self, he declared, explaining his philosophy of attire, — 'Jeans are banned, they stink of James Dean and napalm' — 'One's attire should be offensive' — 'We cannot transform the masses but we can at least have a revolution in our own wardrobes' — 'Every item should clash with every other as it was for the punks and surrealists' — 'A contemptuous semiotic montage' — 'One should endeavour to be a new person every day: three incompatible people every hour. To face a face one does not know in the mirror and destroy the bourgeois colonialist myth of the self'. And other such Saulisms. I sat on his bed laughing to myself, recalling the first time I had stripped for him to dress me.

Saul's enthusiasm soon overwhelmed Dot's shyness and in no time she was standing in bra and panties, then trying on his shoes, then motorcycle boots, army boots, his filthy 'Kerouac' plimsoll trainers. Then his T-shirts – his Elvis one, then the one that read 'JESUS IS YOUR FRIEND', his seventies stripy lady's vinyl blouse, his goth winklepickers, his Black Watch tartan military trousers, his pinstriped Hugo Boss business shirt. — If two things go together then I know I've got it wrong. It's the same with people! I despise monogamous clothing, he proclaimed.

I filmed her laughing at herself in the mirror and Saul's hands hovering around her, not touching, proffering ever more absurd changes as if he were Picasso conceiving a cubist masterpiece. Then army boots, bare legs and his long T-shirt, the one with the picture of Carlos the Jackal from Saul's ultra-left terrorist period.

— But it's too short, she protested. — It's like I'm wearing a nightie!

— Ah yes, but you are putting the ass back into class! Besides, the pornographic effect is offset by the military boots and the terrorist chic: little Red-Army Faction slapper. You see, not a cliché in sight.

She twirled around, almost falling in the outsized boots

as Saul smoked, contemplating her image, dissatisfied with his *Demoiselles d'Avignon.*

— I don't know. Is it really . . . me? she asked.

— My dreary dear, the essence is to have no essence, think of yourself as a work of surrealism. The Duchess once wore a birdcage as a corset, with a real bird inside!

— The Duchess? she asked. Thankfully, he spared her the entire history of his favourite transgressor.

Her giggles infected us all. The flashes of her skin between changes, soft flesh pulled tight by elastic, by leather belt. I chastened myself and tried to see beyond her feminine forms. Was that not Saul's mantra — to eliminate all preconditioned desires? She turned to the camera, asked me what I thought, had we made art yet? We watched the playback, all huddled up together on his bed before the tiny screen. It looked like a home video, nothing more.

— I'm crap.

— No, no, not at all, it's just . . . Saul left us waiting for his aesthetic judgement.

— The hair is the *big* problem, Saul finally pronounced. He looked at me for affirmation. What did I know?

— Yes, those curls are far too preppy, the whole damned lot will have to come off.

I thought he'd gone too far when she got up so suddenly and ran to the bathroom. I reproached him and told him to go a little easy on her.

— It was beastly, bourgeois beastly.

We heard sound of the bathroom door, slammed, locked.

— Seriously, she might be in there slashing her wrists for all we know.

— Change is the only thing in history that never changes!

Minutes passed as I sat and smoked. I was freaked, I must admit, at how fast she'd jumped at his suggestion. He could be fickle and sometimes say things to dare people to acts of great stupidity, like the time we gatecrashed that rave in that mansion house in Islington and there were all these rich kids out of their tits on E. We were spliffing up on the third-floor balcony and he dared that stoner kid to jump. Everyone watched as the kid lowered himself over the edge then fell beyond sight, and everyone started screaming. But then the rich kid came limping back wanting to do it again, at which point Saul declared he was bored and wanted to leave.

She called us from the bathroom and I ran through, Saul following slowly. I glimpsed scissors in the sink, a trace of blood on the ceramic bowl. I pushed in to find her shorn skull confronting me, but radiating with a smile.

— Can you do the back for me? I can't reach.

— Ah, *mon amour*, Saul declared as she stood before us, fists full of hair.

— Can you film us? she asked me. And so I did as Saul trimmed the back of her head to, practically, a skinhead.

So we were back in Saul's room and the volume was turned up and Nico was singing 'Chelsea Girls' as Dot paraded in front of the camera giggling to herself, her fingers feeling their way through her ravaged tufts, watching her new face on the live feed from the TV.

And I had known this. That your face could be a stranger to you as you learn the contours of the world according to Saul. The sense of rebirth in the brutality of the scissors. With me it had been the opposite. I was too 'socialist realist' and had to grow my hair long, he insisted, to embrace the fop within.

For hours we watched her striking TV poses. All of us singing along to 'Heroin' and 'Sunday Morning' and 'Venus in Furs' while Dot judged her face, pulling her skin tight, then pouting, checking herself against the Edie photos. Sticking her tongue out at her own TV-face. Laughing like a little girl, then falling silent as we watched the playback.

— *Mais, je suis pas Edie Sedgwick,* Dot said glumly.

— *Non? Mais tu es fantastique! Superbe! Beaucoup* better than Edie, *mon petite cabbage. Tu es un très bon garçon* he pronounced.

— *Moi, un garçon?* She loved the idea. I had not said a word in French all night and had to say something.

Her hand reached to bring me closer, then she brought Saul closer too, we got ourselves into position for the camera, all three of our heads on the TV screen, while she kissed us both.

— *Nous sommes les trois, toi et toi et moi.* She giggled.

Finally – something I could say. I got in there fast before Saul could.

— *Et nous sommes Jules et Jim!*

Laughter, but then she asked,

— *Et moi?*

I didn't know the name of the character that Jeanne Moreau played, Saul seemed similarly perplexed, and I felt like a fool because the film was inappropriate – it ended in suicide, but none of us seemed particularly worried by this detail.

We watched the playback but Saul was not convinced it was art. — It needs something more, he proclaimed, — a leap of faith, a jump into the dark!

— Oh, but we didn't film the cutting. I am so bloody . . . Dot was lost for words and threw the video camera onto the bed. Saul said, not to worry, he would film the hair in the sink. So we stood there in the bathroom as he did. But Dot was still dissatisfied.

— We can't miss any opportunities again, she said, — we must take a leap immediately and record it! She asked us for ideas, but I could think of nothing and Saul's eyes were drooping from the drink. We slumped before the TV and Dot sat there between us, filming the screen: a surreal news report about President Bush throwing up in the lap of the Japanese prime minister. Dot recorded it and we played it back. Although he tried to hide it there was a dangling bit of noodle visible on his lip. We wept with laughter as we replayed it again and again. The world suddenly seemed impossibly beautiful.

Dramatic changes occurred within Saul – I recall waking one day to find Dot filming him waltzing in a Miami shirt with the vacuum cleaner while Abba played at full blast. — Look, look, he declared with a flourish— it's like Eno's *Music for Airports,* or *Fanfare for the Common Man.* I envisage a whole series – music for chain smoking – music to sleep to – to take a shit to – *Now That's What I Call Hoovering Volume Twelve!* I marvelled at how the presence of her camera had made him do a thing he'd maybe never attempted in his life.

The very next day it was shoplifting that was the subject of Dot's video life lesson. I went into Saul's room and she was already sitting on his bed, dressed in his pinstripe flared trousers and authentic antique Nazi trench coat with real Luftwaffe swastika insignia and the pockets that, torn, went all the way to the bottom of the lining – ideal for the theft of shirts and spaghetti, nothing too large as that would ruin the line of the coat – and she was recording his infamous oft-delivered lecture on the ethical necessity of theft.

— If everyone was to do it, he declared, invoking Kant's categorical imperative, — we could finally destroy the rotting corpse of English capitalism . . . or at least the Hackney branch of Woolworths!

He really was atrocious. I doubted he'd told her how he'd shoplifted almost his entire wardrobe from charity shops, his favourite being Save the Children in Islington because all the yuppies dropped their designer labels there, there was no electronic tagging and the old woman at the counter was half blind.

Saul was testing her on strategy.

— So, you walk in, then what do you do?

— I take five or six things to the changing room . . .

— Aha. And then?

— Put on three layers of their stuff and then the trench-coat on top, and return the three others to the rails.

— And then?

— Leave?

— No, no! You must buy a little shitty something, a 99p Depeche Mode CD or some socks, and have a little chat with the old dears. About anything really, the starving in Ethiopia or Bosnia or God or whatever, they're so ecstatic to be talking to a nice young person who believes in their good work that they'll never suspect you're wearing five layers of their stuff.

— But why don't we just buy the stuff? Isn't this a bit . . . unnecessary?

— My dear, the only thing that saves us from the total-itarian tyranny of common sense is random acts of pure folly.

How could she, I or anyone argue with such reasoning?

As was agreed, we went to Save the Children and I was to record it. I considered this a dead giveaway but Dot, in miraculous ways, played it to advantage. She went straight up to the old dear and asked: — Is it OK, to film ourselves? We're doing an art project for college.

The old fossil seemed thrilled to bits. I was both dumb-founded and perplexed but followed Dot's direction. To the hilarity of the old dear, Dot play-acted looking at clothes, then put them on one layer on top of the other. From beyond the eyepiece I could see Saul twitching by the doorway.

— Keep filming, Dot winked at me.

She pulled on a nice Armani-looking number and then a raincoat, all the time pulling funny faces for the old dear.

Then with a nod at the camera, she paraded herself to the doorway as if on the catwalk. I kept on filming and could hear the old dear's giggles. As soon as Dot was outside, she paused, then without warning broke into a run. Saul and I shot each other a terrified glance. We looked at the old dear and saw the truth dawn on her face. We ran like fucking hell, as the screaming started.

After three breathless staggering blocks we finally found her in the alleyway by Lucky's Chinese. A siren screamed towards us, and we froze. It turned out to be an ambulance.

— That wasn't what I taught you! Saul shouted at her. Then smiled. — But it was bloody good nonetheless! Much to learn, you have, my apprentice, Saul grinned, — much to learn, as he shook his head, invoking Confucius or perhaps Yoda.

So she was his apprentice. Who was I then? Perhaps she would take my place and I would become the femme de ménage for them both. As if she sensed my insecurity, she turned and kissed me, then made a show of kissing him too as she wrapped her arms round our shoulders and jumped into a puddle, splashing us both.

Because we were not competing for her affections, not each trying to seduce her, due to our vow of amorous abstinence, because neither Saul nor I was trying to win her over to one side, the simplest, most banal of daily domestic tasks crackled with the electric static of sublimated desire. We found an old pot of paint in the street and danced around as we painted the kitchen bright orange. She made up names for us both. I was called 'O' as in 'Oh', which often came out 'Oh-Oh'. And she called him Zarathustra after the Nietzsche he was trying to teach her.

— There's nuthin' Neetcha can't teach ya!

Typically of an evening they would be in his room

watching TV cuddled up together under the duvet, laughing at the so-called intellectuals on *Newsnight* debating for the nth time Fukuyama's predicted victory of Western capitalism. The End of History and this is as good as it gets and the biggest shopping mall in the world has just opened. And I would pine to be in there with them as I sensed if I missed out on a single moment then she would be drawn more to him, but I fought the impulse to possess.

The desire to kiss her was at times unbearable. I saw it on Saul's face too but our gentleman's agreement kept us from crossing that line. She was neither mine nor his. Every time she hugged one of us she would hug the other. We were as chaste as children, living without ownership or envy.

Was this what life was like a hundred years ago? When lovers had chaperones and could not kiss in public? My God, I thought then, if I never have sex again, if I could just live like this in this constant repression of the urge, in which it grows and finds its way out, blossoming, not in acts of selfish possessiveness but in generosity, to two not one. If I could live like this, forever seeing the struggle in Saul's face, to resist possessing her, to not betray me.

The way she became then, in those weeks, some subtle liberation growing within her. She walked around in various states of un- and re-dressing, completely without embarrassment. She would pee with the door open, and read his books legs tucked to her knees on his sofa, with no panties on, giving us ample display of her peach-like buttocks and pouting pussy. She said coming off the antidepressants made her feel herself again. Saul thought it at times hilarious – a habit of the decadent aristocracy, the aristocracy always parade around half naked, he said. — My God, the Duchess is alive and living in my living room!

You may not believe what follows but it is as factually true as that old cliché that declares joy harder to depict than conflict. All of our great narratives are of conflict and so joy goes undocumented and it is said that by documenting joy, we diminish and destroy it, but we found the opposite to be true. Our happiness was absolutely a product of her omnipresent camera. She would point it at me in the midst of – what? – sorting out my socks, and say: Action! And suddenly this banal chore turned into a performance. I would pull them on slowly as if I were Marlene Dietrich with silk stockings.

We said 'cut' a lot. It became our way of saying: this is boring, let's do something else. Saul no longer moaned or bitched at me, because he did not want to be caught in such a mood on camera. He woke and dressed before I even rose, as if ready for his close-up, Mr de Mille. Dot bought a hundred pounds' worth of blank videotapes, and we got through half of them in a week. It even changed the world around us – one day we walked down Old Street arm in arm, all three, and because she held her camera at arm's length filming us no one who passed said a thing. Some scary proles even jumped in our way, all smiles and waved to the lens, asking: — This for da telly, darlin?

Our shadows reached long into the streets on those October evenings as we searched for things to film. We always ended up kicking about in the warehouse, off Old Street, the door long since booted in, brainstorming. Dot suggested we run around naked. — Cut! Saul shouted. — Too performance art. The whole nudity-as-truth thing is a modernist fallacy.

I proposed that we could dance around to music. — Cut! he called out. — It's been done before by that annoying socialist artist girl who danced in a shopping mall in Peckham, and besides, all the first MTV pop videos had pop bands dancing about in abandoned warehouses.

No matter what ideas Dot and I came up with he found reasons to abandon them. — Cut! It's no use. Stop trying to be interesting, he insisted. — You cannot compete with advertising. The only way to strike profundity is to aim one's sights at the utterly banal and to miss completely.

When he said things like that Dot shouted, — Stop, I have to record this. But by the time she got her camera ready he'd lost momentum and couldn't pick up the thread again. Everything had been done before, he said, even the saying of it had been said before.

I started to sense we'd get nothing done and that we were damaging her chance of an art degree. She had yet to learn that Saul's encyclopaedic knowledge could be crippling. If it were not so then he would not still be have been with two wannabes, at age – what? – twenty-nine, thirty, hanging out in disused warehouses. The only way to be a true nihilist without being a hypocrite was to do absolutely nothing, he had often said. But when the camera was turned off we felt rather empty, melancholy.

As per a typical night I shoplifted Pot Noodles on the way home and we added ketchup and chilli pepper to make up for the lack of sustenance by way of stimulation, then degreasing it all with boxes of sherry.

— Oh 'O', she said to me, — I'll never make art at this rate, I'm rubbish.

Saul, suitably loosened, declared the answer was not to think of something arty to film, but to live more dangerously. He started on one of his rants about the Duchess.

— She could not be contained, restrained. Her blood itself was in rebellion against the constriction of her veins. Likewise her gut, bladder and cunt. Every orifice puking, pissing in the face of convention.

Dot was perplexed.

— Who? Where? So I explained that Saul's great muse was from New York, in the twenties the mistress of Duchamp, of most of the surrealists, in fact.

— Nonsense! Saul shouted. — She *was* surrealism itself!

Walking down Fifth Avenue wearing nothing but a trash can! A Chinese fan hanging from her anus. Did you know, he whispered drunkenly, — her talents at disguise were so accomplished she could go undetected even among her closest friends?! She dressed as a man, sporting a fulsome moustache, and wore a cucumber in her pants. She seduced rich men with homosexual tendencies, then blackmailed them, just for the hell of it.

— No way! Dot said, but was transfixed.

— That's nothing. She was richer than Chrysler, some said, but lived in a hovel in Greenwich Village. She married an Austrian count and had him butchered, two days after the wedding.

— That's horrible!

— Absolutely. She stole fur coats from Macy's and handed them out to passing tramps. She was filling the streets with mink. She grew vegetables in human excrement and lived on nothing but champagne and opium! I have the book somewhere and if I ever find it you can read for yourself.

Dot was enraptured. I left them alone so Saul could recount more of the gory decadence. In that moment, truth be told, I felt a little jealous for the sense of wonder she'd just discovered. From now on she would wake each day, her head bursting with surrealism and song.

Back in my room, as I lay back, as if in déjà vu, I knew what would happen next and sure enough it did. I heard the stereo start up, then those ridiculous keyboards, that sounded like a kiddie's toy version of Duran Duran meets a church organ – 'Disparu' by the Duchamps.

'J'ai disparoo, tu as disparoo . . .'

Our secret album and he was sharing it with her. I fought a small surge of jealousy, then conquered it, telling myself that yes – through her I was already, in many ways, reliving my conversion to the wondrous ways of Saul. I

smiled to myself as the synthesisers wangled and the backwards audio samples of cats miaowing got louder and the
she-man's voice rose to an epic operatic flat note.

'Nous avons deees – par – oooo!'

There are markers, signs, points of no return in every relationship, tests to be endured and questions to be answered,
a yes or no as to the future. In ancient times men went to
a seer or oracle. And so Saul insisted we take a trip to
Hackney to visit Edna – the exemplary living artwork. Funny,
how he never said, — Let's go buy some hash from Edna:
His many paranoias and claims included that our phone
had been tapped by MI5, due to his previous undisclosed
subversive activities.

As he readied himself in suitably contradictory attire,
it fell on me to explain the deal to Dot. The more I told her
the more absurd every word seemed.

Edna lived in a high-rise on Hobbs Estate, which was
mostly abandoned. She dealt mostly in hash, downers,
hallucinogens and handed out spliffs like cups of tea. She
held Saul in great esteem as they had some secret history.
In her clouds of hashish smoke with her mystical wind-
chime vinyls, she was surrounded, daily, by a harem of
stoners who worshipped her every word. Saul believed
Edna existed beyond the limits of the known world – on
a good day.

For some reason I tried to shy clear of the most important fact.

— Oh, and she's a man, I mean she has a penis, she's
saving up to get it cut off.

Dot, giggling, said it would be cool if she dressed in
her new men's clothes again. I voiced some concerns, as
that part of Hackney was pretty rough.

Saul emerged, to the sounds of the Revolting Cocks,
head to toe in leather biker's gear with a Chanel scarf round

his waist, bandit-like, and two beauty spots on his left cheek. Dot was inspired and ran off to get her camera so as to film him. He struck pouting poses for her in his doorway while I got changed. I really had nothing that could compete. Even the things I borrowed from him sometimes just didn't sit well on me, being too tall and gangly. As I tried on thing after thing, I could hear them laughing beyond my door and I got to worrying about this whole Edna thing.

The first time I met her/him was like an exam, as if Saul was testing my endurance. I got scared and hogged the spliff and got so high I whited out and ended up walking through the depths of black Hackney till 4. a.m. trying not to throw up. Amazing that I wasn't mugged.

We headed out together, and I had only managed some eyeliner by way of transgression. Yes, something was up, some great mystical evaluation of Dot's future. She was bouncing along, arms interlocked in ours, all questions, in her shoplifted jacket with eighties yuppie shoulder pads. We took the 58 bus and Saul sat quiet and cool just telling her, wait and see, which only fuelled her excitement.

The incredible thing about Edna is that she is a white man with breasts that have grown from years of hormone therapy, but she seems, quite simply, to be from another planet. Her dreadlocks, mousy brown and three feet long with extensions and sometimes ribbons; the kaftans and Japanese kimono trousers; the Jesus sandals. Miraculously no one ever shouts 'Poof' or 'Queer' at her in the street. They must assume she's some kind of hybrid Hindu swami meets Rastafarian bong queen meets, I don't know, Hare Krishna. The question of her true sex never arose, neither did her skin colour and she was so clearly white, whiter still since she never left the hash smoke to see the light of day and lived like her home-grown weed in curtain-drawn darkness with only UV lamps to light the way. Her sex/race seemed inconsequential to the total alienness that emanated from her. Which was why it was both baffling and astounding to behold her boyfriend, Dan – a deeply homo-phobic 'real' East End bloke, who could have been a bricklayer or football hooligan shouting, 'Here we go, here we go, here we go.'

I tried to confess my anxieties on the bus but Dot was trying to film Saul as he had her in hysterics over Edna's plaster-cast penis collection.

I feared Dan though. Maybe he'd just done too many drugs and didn't actually notice that Edna had a dick, a very large one too, she often said. When she got enough money to get it cut off, she said, she was going to have it embalmed and exhibited with the plaster casts on her shelves. Dan never missed an opportunity to scream at fucking poofs and nonces. Maybe he was just in denial, maybe it was the return of the repressed, or the fact that, as Edna said, he's manic-depressive and paranoid schizo-phrenic. He always seemed to have wet lips, a sure sign of medication, and he could become terrifyingly animated at times, waving his hands about and shouting, and was over six three. Edna always calmed him with a spliff. I was not sure that was wise given the other medication he must have been on.

We were at the entrance and I was twitching, nervous about the locals.

— For God's sake, put that camera away, muttered Saul.

Before us, the shellsuits and shaved heads, the black urban poor, that Saul called buppies. No one was over four-teen and all of them deadly looking, and a girl, no more than twelve with a pram. And there was Saul with Max Factor and Dot dressed as a man.

To get in, you needed to ring her outer buzzer. Saul always did this; he had a password he wouldn't reveal to me. Sounded like Balzac or ball-sack. Dot clung to my arm as he led the way inside. The place gave me the shits. Most of the windows on the twenty-eight floors were boarded up with metal. I reassured her that while it looked quite terrifying there were only twenty or so people left inside, all on different floors, all on drugs, all minding their own lucrative business. A weird kind of inverted Thatcherite Neighbourhood Watch scheme, watching out for the cops.

Up the needle-crunching shit-smelling steps. The sign above the buzzer said: *Dr Edna Archimedes: Philanthropist, Homoeopathist, Herbologist, Unnaturalist, Poetess.* The sticker below that read: *No fucking shoes.* Sure enough, shoes were lined outside her door. Four pairs, mostly hippy moccasins and varieties of Jesus sandals, one pair of Doc Martens with painted flowers on, sitting below the holly-hocks and petunias that surrounded her doorway, a miraculous growth of nature in a place of concrete as terri-fying as the graffitied promises of death that we met in the stairwell: DEEDEE POSSE; GANG BANGED SHONA HERE; £5 A SUCK.

Dan answered the door, like Frankenstein's monster, not acknowledging faces. His own was already slack with meds. Saul led the way in, Dot reached back for my hand, her eyes darting round. I tried to whisper explanations as we were led deeper into the boudoir, the Bedouin tent, towards the sound of Tibetan chimes from the living room. The corridor, strung up with scarves and silks as if corners and right angles offended Edna's circular yin and yang feng-shui sensibility. There were plants everywhere and the heavy sexual musk of patchouli, bergamot, Moroccan black, sinsemilla, inhaled and exhaled, sweated through plant lungs. It wasn't like entering a flat, but an organism, the walls themselves seemed to breathe, the red silks billowing every time there was a draught or someone moved.

There were silent nods as we entered. Edna was in the

midst of it, rolling her infamous eight-skinner. A nod from her to Saul. And there was that woman there too, the one who'd been trying for years to ape Edna, the post-colonial PhD scholar from the London School of Economics.

Dot gripped my hand tighter, scared, as I was, at the sight of Edna, lighting up with the Hindu gods behind her, and things which might have been shrunken heads from Borneo sitting on her stereo. The eight-skinner was passed on and Saul went to her, smooching. She whispered, — Who are these people? Even though I'd been here three times before. Saul whispered back then took the spliff. After that she was all arms round Dot, complimenting her on her suit jacket.

— What a handsome young man!

Edna leaned to whisper to her and Dot blushed. Edna pulled down her kaftan to show her breasts, asking Dot to touch. Dot anxiously did as told. Giggling as she touched Edna's nipples.

— God, they're bigger than mine!

Edna play-acted an orgasm, declared that we were cool and could stay. Saul nodded as he passed back the spliff. Dot was her best friend then with many whisperings and tokes passed between them. The Tibetan chants were put on and it was time for the initiation.

There were seventy-five of them, made over a period of fifteen years. Each one cast by hand by Edna applying the plaster to the member. Each sat erect above eye level on the shelf that she had put up where the dado rail once was. Like Greek statues around the Parthenon. Like saints round St Peter's. And she had sucked or fucked them all, and had many stories, of their different lengths and girths and textures and personalities. — And this is Mathieu and this is Kahil and you have to see Jose. So many, almost impossible to give them all the common name of penis. I could never stop myself wondering if there was this much variation in other human organs: eyeballs, kidneys, tonsils. I always got a visceral reaction to them. A kind of sickening in my stomach. The one up there at the back, how was it possible, how could it be real? As long as my forearm and as thick as my wrist. My God, how could Edna ever have ... ? I always had to take a Rennie.

Dot found the whole thing hilarious as Edna brought them down for her to feel and assess, as if antiques from some golden age now lost to humanity.

— And this is Dave, God, he was a god.

— Wow, Dot laughed, somewhat embarrassed, as I was for her. As I am every time I witness Dave's superhuman, Übermenschian girth. I'd passed on the spliff.

— Where is Dave when we need him? Dot giggled.

— We don't ask about Dave, Edna muttered then went back to her meditative pose, cross-legged. The Tibetan wind chimes, the breathing.

And I knew from reading between the lines that Edna had lost many lovers. That this was why she dealt drugs. That she wanted to talk about the cocks but the truth was she had survived when so many of them were sick or dying now. When she talked it was not of now or five years ago but of 1978, before the plague.

Saul was oblivious to my anxieties. He took a deep draw and passed one of the acolytes the money for the quarter.

Dot was kissing Edna's cheek and telling her she was the most amazing person ever – all she wanted to do was film Edna for an hour, a day, could they hang out together and make an artwork? Which was the worst thing to do because then there would be the photos and the records and the photo album, which was Edna's history.

— Oh, yer a smasher! Edna declared — Here, I've got just the thing for you. We watched then as Edna went into her art box and got out some glue and some scissors. She cut a bit of Dot's hair, then all was hidden from us. Minutes later Dot turned to us, sporting a moustache. All were laughing as Dot and Edna struck poses. Dot asked me to film and took my hand.

Then the most disturbing thing happened. Dan, as if woken from a coma, suddenly started shouting at me and Dot, waving his fists.

— Ya fackin' nonces! Poofy bastards!

Terror. All the acolytes left hastily with their pills as Edna tried to calm the monster. We thinly scraped out without any actual violence, with many apologies.

Heading home on the bus, I was spliff-sick and Dot was ranting about how radical Edna was. Saul fell asleep on her arm as she stroked his head and I fought the jealousy impulse.

Edna saddened me, though I didn't tell Dot this. The names changed, the locations, but it was always the same story with her – about how she'd been in every band from the Sex Pistols to Suicide (and even the bloody Duchamps) and knew Vivienne Westwood and Dee Dee Ramone and Warhol and Debbie Harry and Iggy Pop and Ginsberg and Valerie Solanas and Andreas Baader and Che Guevara and had fucked them all and they told her she would be the greatest artist ever. And how she was going to be fabulous again as soon as she got the operation and she'd almost saved enough, another five years. I'd known her for two and it was five back then.

In another five she would be dead.

Her hash was cheap, too cheap.

The trip to Edna's had greatly inspired Dot. It was strange but the more she dressed as a man, the more enthusiastic she was and the more attractive to my eye. Saul too seemed to be struggling with new emotions, as he was grumpy with her at times, a sure sign of attraction.

We were walking through Hackney, days later, her with Edna's moustache reglued to her face.

— How do I look? she squealed as she bounced along.
— Am I a man yet?

— It takes more than a few props, you must learn how to walk like one, Saul snapped at her, — Stop looking around with amazement.

So his lecture began.

— Look at your feet, stop bopping about. You've got to resent everything and everyone. To own the very ground you walk on. If anyone comes near you, growl and defend your space. This is what men do.

Dot tried it, playing the man on the street, clumping along; it was impossible not to laugh as she filmed her own feet.

— You see, Saul expounded, — masculinity is as fake as Barbie, it's all learned responses. Tell her about school, he said to me.

And as she pointed her camera and we passed real person after real person, I started, quietly, so the real people wouldn't hear – of how I was bullied at school, after my dad left and we moved to a new town, a poor town, for not knowing how to walk right and talk right. 'Ballet dancer,' they called me, 'Poof.' Each word reinforced with a punch to the nose, the face in the dirt. How I'd learned to survive by practising the moves in a mirror.

Dot kissed my cheek.

— So, show me, she said then. And so I taught her the prole walk. Two legs wide apart, the upper torso stiff, shoulders rigid, the hand in fists, as she filmed and Saul expounded.

— Yes, you see, like the pavement is yours and everyone else can fucking die. Someone wants your space, some refugee mother with a child, you take wider strides to say fuck off. Spread your legs, like you have a humungous cock.

— But I –

— We'll fashion one later with a sock.

Later we shoplifted a can of beans and headed home and I felt like he was Henry Higgins and she Eliza Doolittle. The rain in Spain stays mainly on the plain – By Jove, I think she's go it! A woman passed us by. Dot lowered her eyes.

— What in hell's teeth do you think you're doing? Saul muttered.

— Sorry, what – what?

— Women! My God, don't you know this? You're supposed to stare the poor bitches down, once they've passed, turn and ogle their arses. It's despicable and bestial, I know, and I've never done it myself, but I'm told they like it, women that is, even expect it of you. We have yet to evolve.

Dot tried to man-walk but she was too curvaceous.

— No wiggling and giggling!

— It must be so dull being a man, she laughed.

— Indeed, I try to avoid it as much as possible, Saul muttered in utter seriousness.

Back on Old Street, Dot asked me to take the camera and film her, as she ran to a certain point then turned and walked slowly back towards us both, trying to eradicate that swing of the hips that had so aroused me. She stumbled and we both reached to help her up, our hands meeting round her waist. We marched then, *à trois*, struggling to keep straight faces as we passed the many that stopped and stared at the three apparent men, two with moustaches. But Dot was disappointed, people had thought it a joke and she wanted to *pass* as a real man – in Safeway's or the Queen's Head. It could be her first artwork. We were all drunk and it was crazy. To 'go for a pint' as men. A joke gone far enough.

It was almost 4 a.m. but Dot insisted on binding her breasts with a bandage to make them lie flat, and asked me to help. As I assisted my fingers brushed her areola and I had to leave swiftly to address my growing affliction.

I must have been dozing off when I heard her voice in low tones.

— C'mere, you sexy man – yeah you, you're so cool, so hard.

I opened my eyes but she was nowhere to be seen. I crept to my door and discovered her in the bathroom, the door half closed. Again I heard her say, — C'mere, sexy guy, big strong man. I peered through the gap in the door and there she was in the mirror, flexing her muscles in the mirror, talking to her own moustachioed face, filming herself. I must have made a noise because she opened the door and caught me there. After a humiliating silence she burst into a fit of the giggles. She laughed so hard her moustache flew off into the toilet. I fished it out and we stared at it as if it were dead. I returned to bed telling myself I was not to fall in love. It was a weakness, Saul said, and I thought him right.

We'd been hit by a plague of moustaches. In the days that followed she scrawled them on every available newspaper and magazine visage. I vividly recall a very large Nietzschean one on the lip of the newly elected Clinton. She'd taken her moustache video to Goldsmiths and it had not, however, gone down at all well. Nonetheless, she was unperturbed in her quest to pass as a new man. Saul insisted she desist.
— We are being emasculated, he claimed in utter seriousness and went clean-shaven in protest.

The Queen's Head was a terrifyingly proletarian establishment full of old piss-head cockneys and young concrete-covered builders and a barmaid who looked like Dolly Parton's mother and always had red lipstick on her teeth. Even when it was just Saul and me in the pub we were invariably threatened with death, so for us to turn up with a moustachioed Dot was beyond insanity. However, her promise of free drinks had Saul reaching for his coat.

Dot had her video camera primed but I insisted it would only draw attention and proposed we at least hide it. As we hesitated before the pub entrance, and she checked to see if her moustache was still in place, I had a sudden urge to hold her hand and tried one last time to talk some sense into them both – it would lead to A&E tonight. But Saul was already marching in with Dot's twenty in his hand, proposing Scotch malts. It was not that I did not want to appear a coward, but rather that I thought they would be safer with me there, and so I followed.

Old leather seats, neon lights and Formica tables. No one batted an eye as we stood at the bar. Dot kept re-adjusting her moustache and I worried that with all the fiddling it would fall off in her hand. The stench from the Gents was exactly the same as the beer, as if they were actually drinking piss. An old fuck was slumped in a corner, alone, a pool of fluid beneath his feet, with a catheter tube visible. Two builder types were boasting of some fight with acted-out punches.

— Facka went for me and I ducked and got him a left hook on the fackin' vera. An' the uver caant comes at me, knowhatahmean.

— The inherent violence of the proletariat is a result of their failure to embrace their revolutionary potential, Saul muttered discreetly. — One always turns one's failure against oneself.

He seemed oblivious to the very real threat as he ordered the first round, pints and whisky shots for us all. Dot was shaking and I had to control the need to hug her. Saul whispered to us both, — Stop looking around. The savages are distracted. Just stare at your pint and consider it a phenomenological event à la Sartre.

A scar-cheek asked us where we woz from. Dot was too scared to speak. Saul, having downed his shot and half his pint, had the Dutch to reply on our behalf.

— Idaho, he said in a voice that had no trace of American about it.

— Well, fuck me, the old stinker spat, — they's Yanks, he called out to the blood-teethed bar bimbo and the assembled pissers. — Wot the fuck you doing here then?

Saul muttered something about a Mardi Gras, which left the old pisser perplexed, and took Dot to one side then, for a whisper. I got the gist – she was doing fine, just to nod and grunt, that he would handle this. I was stuck next to the old pisser, hoping the interrogation would stop soon.

The two bricklayers, just feet away, were doing slo-mo punch moves. The story of violence never-ending.

— ... wiv a fackin' bottuw, so I's duckin' daan, an' turned on the caant an' smacked him a Tyson rite in is fackin' kissa! BAAAYYYM!

I needed to pee although I'd only drunk a mouthful. Pissing myself with fear, perhaps. I prepared our escape plan but the old stench was shouting: — A round, for the 'merican boys.

But then he turned to Dot, nudged her elbow.

— Oi, wassat – wassat all abaat then? Fackin' 'merican football? Daan't geddit, paddin', an' helmets anat, bunch of fackin' sissies, pardon me French.

She looked at me, terrified. Saul whispered in her ear.

— That's it, no need to reply, just swear under your breath, a few fucks and cunt or two or some muttering.

The old fuck was passing the drinks. He raised a glass to clink with Dot.

— Wassat den, that 'merican football, eh, eh?

I could see her twitching, preparing to speak.

— CUNTZ! Dot shrieked, suddenly, extremely high in pitch.

My eyes shot to the doorway, as the place fell silent and the old fucker's face was deep in the depths questioning, joining the dots. Saul's face turned white.

The old stench's hand was on Dot's shoulder then, the size of a builder's breeze block, his eyes on me and Saul. I was ready to run.

— You fackers callin' me a cant?

Dot shook her head nervously, covered her moustache.

The old cunt burst out laughing, patted her on the back.

— CANTZ! he shouted. — FACKIN' CANTZ, his glass in the air. — WE'RE ALL FACKIN' CANTZ HERE!

Cheers from the back. — CANTZ, CANTZ! A veritable canto of cunts.

Weird, what the old urinal did then, leaning over to kiss Dot on the cheek. — Had you there, didn't I? Good one, eh. No offence, mate. Maybe he sensed that there was something alluring about her he couldn't quite place. Maybe this was something very drunk old men did, kiss other men.

Maybe London was too drunk to notice or care if you were two men and a woman with a fake moustache.

Saul, anxious, wanted us to leave immediately but Dot whispered that she wanted to stay. He headed for the door and I was caught in the middle. I spent the next ten minutes running back and forth from him outside to her inside, trying to get us to stick together.

Saul marched off towards Hoxton Square. I dragged Dot along, as she laughed about the adventure, oblivious to Saul's mood. We finally caught up with him,

— Fucking stupid! he muttered.

— Oh Sozzle, they were lovely, it was perfectly safe.

— Do I look scared? he snapped. — And take off that fucking ridiculous moustache!

It had been our first outright fight and they were both silent all the way home, me between them, trying my best to get them to talk. She tried to take his hand but he pushed hers away. She held mine for a minute but must have felt it was wrong, and unequal, so let it go.

I could understand her confusion – had Saul not filled her head with all this talk of the Duchess and craziness, only to walk away when it all got too real?

He locked his door to her that night, but she did not come to talk to me. For the first time in two months we were each very alone.

It had been a wake-up call. The very next day Dot had been a good student and put in a whole day at art school. She returned with a bunch of flowers and a box of sherry for Saul and a video to watch, by way of making it up to us. It was called *Withnail and I* and was basically a shaggy dog story about two losers who live in squalor, both failed actors. The scene in the pub had been very much like our one of the day before, and she'd wanted to show us it, so we could laugh about it all. Saul sat stone-faced throughout.

— See, you're so Withnail, she joked, trying to tickle him, but he did not respond. Her plan had backfired horribly as the film's message was only too clear: Withnail was a drunk and waster and 'I' would go on to greater things – it was, after all, his story. The story of I. I was not such a bad role. I was in fact rather flattered to be I. By the end Saul asked us to leave the room as he wanted to be alone. As soon as we were in the hall he locked the door behind us.

Dot was outside his room for nearly an hour after, apologising. He would not let her in, or speak. It had been foolish of her, but understandable. She wanted to show Saul how much she understood him but made the mistake of reducing him to an existing image. He had to be the total innovation of himself, he was not Richard E. Grant, no matter how closely the film mapped our lives. It was perhaps some subconscious revenge on her part. Saul had made her slash her canvases and now she had exposed his vulnerabilities.

I couldn't help but laugh though as I stared at the kitchen sink. There's something moving in there. It may be a mouse. Then the bastard will rue the day!

Did not Saul have this same fixation on vermin months back? Did he not swear that a rat came out to watch the telly every time he put an art-house tape on? Did he not say at the time, — The vermin is obsessed with Bergman!

— Please open up and stop being so grumpy, I heard her say to his closed door. — It's just a silly film. But the damage had been done. The power of human weakness is greater than strength. She would be banished from his affections.

That night I finally gave in to the impulse to competitiveness. The event had revealed his weaknesses at last and she would be repulsed. I have to confess that I masturbated with her panties thinking of how she now favoured me more than him.

But, my God, how wrong I was.

— Nothing happened, OK, she said as I found her in only a T-shirt, staggering out of his room. But the fact that she ventured the excuse before I had even asked the question was proof enough. And the guilt on her face, eyes not meeting mine. They had slept together that night. As if overcome with guilt, she ran to the bathroom and threw up.

As if all the world was conspiring against me, I had to sign on that day and declare my earnings from the *Hoxton Advertiser*, which was then deducted, so it all came to nothing. A whole hour and a half in which I had to leave Saul and Dot alone, as I sat there in the dole office.

On my return she was still wearing his T-shirt and little else and they were in the bathroom together, giggling. Dot rushed out. They'd just made her a new moustache from

Saul's hair. It was so much more wiry and convincing, didn't I think?

In a fit of jealousy I tried to put her down.

— So how's the art coming along? Any plans for your graduation show?

I became the secret double agent, trying to find the split between them. In a moment alone with Saul I told him we shouldn't be wasting so much time with Dot, he had his book or play or film or art concept or whatever to create, and surely it was time now to really get down to some serious work.

But he was oblivious and so I concocted a plan. I suggested we really should teach Dot how to shoplift food. I had visions of her being caught red-handed, and wanted to see if he would stand up for her when the police came. Saul was all smiles and post-coital stupidity and unaware of my subterfuge. I had time with Dot alone as I ran through the rules. An avocado, some parsley, or a can of beans. Her moustache could be a problem, but I didn't say it. I wanted her to be arrested. I ran through the moves with her, there in his room, before his eyes, and revelled in making him watch.

In those minutes while I instructed her, I had her full attention and Saul was silent, and I knew then that they had fucked and this whole thing of humouring Owen had been planned to make it seem like nothing had happened. Saul was a hypocrite and a whore. Never let a woman come between us, indeed. She would be caught and he too and then they would do their penance. Or if I was caught and they ran it was a sure sign that they had conspired together.

Poundstretcher on Old Street. Saul had his reservations but Dot was enthused and I had the petty pleasure of forcing him to do as I pleased.

All three of us entered separately, minutes apart. Dot was to be at the magazines, Saul at the vegetables, me at the canned beans and fruit. The plan was to swap positions and for Dot to steal a can of Heinz Baked Beans and some Ambrosia Creamed Rice, with Saul distracting at the cash register.

But Dot was scared, shooting anxious glances at me and Saul, staring up at the CCTV. As I passed the canned aisle I saw that there were no Heinz beans left, and so the plan was shot. I felt guilty, as it was only a matter of seconds till she would be caught. I had to warn her, but communication was a dead giveaway, the fuckers watching you on the monitor as you started whispering. I checked out the ancient Asian shop woman and wanted to call it all off. Dot was in the poultry aisle, the wrong place entirely. Saul was obviously onto the problem because he was up at the counter, talking, I think about a lottery ticket, getting the woman to bring out one then the next.

I caught a flash of Dot stuffing something immense under her jumper. Her belly, the size of a basketball, what the fuck was it even? She walked past me, looking pregnant, then broke into a run as she exited. I headed for the door. The woman started shouting.

Outside, round the corner, me first, then Saul, perplexed. Dot was nowhere to be seen, was maybe running round while the cops scoured the streets for a pregnant woman with a moustache. We waited in silence, Saul sneaking glances round the corner.

— Boo! She appeared behind us, doubled over in laughter as she pulled the thing out – a self-basting extra-large chicken.

— Happy Christmas!

— *Mon Dieu!* Saul exclaimed. — *Mais c'est Novembre, quelle obscenité!*

It was hard to hate them, even though, once we were back, I heard her slip back into his room. Self-basting. How the fuck could a dead thing prepare itself for the oven? Over the weeks that followed I found it a metaphor for my cowardice and my slow-burning rage. Even after it had rotted no one would touch it and it sat there weeping its stinking blood onto the Formica and floor while I had to endure the sounds of their laughter and her many cries and moans.

two

Negative Leap. 1993. Video installation. 12 minutes, video loop.
Variable dimensions. P. Buchler Collection.

THE INSTALLATION COMPRISES two large screens of projected video footage played in extreme slow motion in black and white. On the first screen a woman falls backwards through darkness. On the second many hands reach into the air. This latter footage is in 'negative'. Both pieces of footage come from a 'hardcore' concert in 1992 and represent what is known as 'stage diving' or 'crowd surfing'. This is one of the most powerful examples of the *détournement* of found footage in recent art history.[1]

Negative Leap is generally seen as Shears's first major work. It quite literally became the 'leap' into her career as an artist. In it, the 'amateur' nature of the video footage is transcended by her intelligent recontextualistion. The beauty of the work is that the images on the two screens, separated by a distance of over thirty feet, never come together in 'sync'. While in the real-life filmed action, a woman would have leapt from the stage to be caught by the audience, here the hands are in a perpetual state of waiting. The body too seems trapped mid-leap, in just a few seconds, repeated on loop, as if locked in a space and time of endless falling. The hands wait and reach for a point of contact that never arrives. The fact that the footage is played in total silence adds to this sense of a void between the two screens, between action and repercussion. The act of union, in which the body is caught by the hands, exists only, on the third (non-existent) screen – the one that exists in the viewer's imagination.[2]

The crowd and the falling woman in 'cruciform' pose have often been compared to images of religious ritual and ecstasy. Crowd hysteria and individuals taking 'the leap of faith'[3] being common to the vast majority of religions and cults.[4] However, interpretations that pose Shears as in any way commenting on 'pop culture as the religion of the masses'[5] seem wide of the mark, as Shears has never expressed any concern with politics.

This is the first work by Shears in which her triumvirate of thematic concerns come together into a coherent combination greater than the sum of the parts. They are: play, swapping roles and trust. It was, at that time, uncommon for women to 'stage-dive', and so in her leap, she has taken a masculine position; nonetheless, she is conceding control and placing herself at risk – the crowd may not catch her, may let her fall. This throwing oneself into the dark many find deeply unsettling.

The work is not 'about' a subject in both senses (the content and the 'human subject') and Shears defies our need to think of her as 'an artist' with a 'singular message'. Some see in this a failure to take responsibility for her own authorship and criticise the communal processes involved in the making of her work (she did not hold the camera, the footage is merely a document, her role in it is just 'showing off', etc.). But the message of Shears's work is a non-negative or anti-message.[6] It invokes a desire for escape from the isolated identity, from the responsibility for and self-management of the ego.[7] Through playing games with identity, swapping roles and taking a leap into non-identity, she is asking us, as she asks herself, to become 'nobody' and to join with and trust others. If we believe that the role of the artist is to be an exemplary individual with a singular message then we would indeed find Shears's actions empty, meaningless and 'negative'. If, however, we find the culture of the constructed self oppressive, then Shears's selfless leap is one towards freedom.

1. Found footage: see Nam June Paik, Douglas Gordon, Baldassarri, Warhol, Duchamp, Debord. Ironically, the use of found footage has become so popular that certain artists have been exposed as lying about the origins of their material – having actually shot it themselves while trying to hide this fact. See controversy around J. Albert's *Trovato*, S. Burgin, *New Left Review*, June 2001.
2. Discussion of the return of dialectical thinking, post-demise of deconstruction. E. Voltimer, *The Invisible Third*, CUP, 2003.
3. S. Kierkegaard, *Either/Or*, Penguin, 1992.
4. G. Bataille on the origins of pre-historic religious ceremonies/ human sacrifice, *Eroticism: Death and Sensuality*, City Lights, 2001.
5. A. Kaplan, from 'The New Opium', in *Screen*, vol. 45, 2003.
6. Shears has often claimed that her work 'means nothing' – 'I didn't even make it myself', *Harper's*, September 2004. See strategic use of feigned naiveté in Warhol.
7. Theory that the project of individualist self-emancipation in the sixties has led to an even more oppressive culture in which the mechanisms of state and power have become micro-internalised, in which each person polices themselves, in health, psychology, sexuality, behaviour and consumption. The only way to escape 'the prison of the self' being through the ordeal of the negative, to explore nihilism's end and confront death. 'One must put into play, show up, transform and reverse the systems which quietly order us about.' Foucault, 1968, quoted in J. Miller, *The Passion of Michel Foucault*, Flamingo, 1994. See also F. Nietzsche, *Human, All-Too-Human*, Dover, 2006.

SAUL STAGGERED BAREFOOT by the side of the motorway. The sun pounded down on his red leathered head as he searched for roadkill, a fox, a rat, to cook later in his billycan. The cars screamed past and teenagers jeered at him, but he had long ceased noticing the scorn of passing faces and it had been many years since he'd even glimpsed his own. He shaved now with a piece of broken bottle and tied what was left of his grey hair in an old piece of twine from a packing crate. Beneath his concrete flyover, as he drank from the stagnant stolen milk cartons, he cursed the passing cars and swore again his vow to never again succumb to the need of that road with its service station and its promise of ice-cold water and the charity of passing drivers. How could he live in the modern world, every day being confronted with the images, the adverts, newspaper and magazine covers, with their many smiling photo faces all of which reminded him? How could he not scream at the sight of those images of a success that was rightfully his, stolen by a woman, a mere child, a thief and plagiarist. Had he not taught her every-thing she knew: the meaning of irony, of punk, Dada, of rebellion itself? In the darkness of his dripping underpass home, when all the world slept, he would take out the box of newspaper clippings, and carefully lift them by candle-light, taking care not to spill the wax, then place them in such a way, shrine-like, to stare until the tears came, fighting with himself, against the urge to tear her face to pieces. In his piss-stinking sleeping bag, from his most secret hideaway space behind the stolen supermarket trolley, beneath the scavenged food cartons and empty boxes of sherry, he would, nightly, retrieve the wet and warped, much annotated mass-market paperback of *Thus Spoke Zarathustra* and whisper the memorised words:

Each virtue is jealous of the others, and jealousy is a terrible thing. Virtues too can perish of jealousy. Surrounded by the flame of jealousy, one will in the end, like the scorpion, turn one's poisonous sting against oneself.

After the usual time he would place the clippings back inside the box and pronounce again, silently, that he had grown wiser than the sage and would never again descend with his message for the masses to face the humiliation of their ignorant laughter, he would leave all images and roads forever and go deeper into more forgotten spaces of the desert they called the real.

This image of Saul was the one that came to Owen whenever he felt a twinge of jealousy over Dot's career, in those days, which caught him unawares when Dot's face, without warning, appeared at the turn of a magazine page. There but for the grace of God go I. Saul in the desert was the only thing that saved him from those moments when he couldn't face the fact that, yes, he might just envy her success. A dubious sidestep, no doubt, to transfer his sense of failure onto a now fictional persona, but how could Saul have survived Dot's success without having dropped out, moved to another country, gone in search of God? For years now Saul had aimlessly wandered the desert so that Owen could stride with purpose through the world.

But today, Owen was doing his penance. The PR woman from the Lieder had called back to let him know that Dorothy Shears had agreed to meet for an interview. They were excited to 'potentially' have him on board and he was on their list of potential candidates for the 'big job' – an essay on the nine works in the show for the catalogue for the international tour, starting in Zurich, in two months' time. None of this could be leaked to any newspapers and he could not reuse any of the material in other formats or countries; if he did it would be a case for litigation, as per item 5 in the contract which they would email, that should be signed by his lawyer and returned as per soonest possible date.

He had only wanted to see her again, but already it was getting convoluted and legal and too late to back out of and anxiety crept over him – that Dot had agreed so easily; that these fifteen years fearing her had been his own invention; that their reunion could have taken place long before and saved him the angst that had become a way of life.

And what the hell would he even write about her art? He'd noticed recently that the adjectives around her work had changed from 'radical' and 'challenging' to 'compelling'. 'Compelling' was a variation on 'interesting' and betrayed a lack of confidence in the artist's brand name and a downturn in investment. The video-art bubble was bursting because of YouTube – some teenager in Pakistan had recently committed suicide online after getting viewers to vote on whether she should see it through. A guy in Germany had cut off his dick in front of half a million global viewers. Hundreds of thousands of barely legal-age girls the world over had twenty-four-hour webcams recording their every living moment for cash. It was rumoured that Saatchi was looking to buy online Islamic web porn as art. The truth was Dot's work was an interesting footnote in the onward destructive march of the moving image.

If he had the integrity of Saul he would have called it all off, but the PR woman made it very clear that, even after the interview and their analysis of his essay, they reserved the right to give the job to another writer. And that galled him, to still be the whore, fighting for a cheque counted at pence per word.

The time, date and location of the interview had been picked – her studio between London Bridge and Southwark.

He was actually going to meet Dot again. Today. In two hours, forty-six minutes. He would first of all apologise for not keeping in touch, then, ice broken, apologise for all that had happened. Those would be the words – 'Sorry for all that happened.' Two beta blockers were all he'd managed by way of breakfast.

But then his clothes had caused him grief. The linen suit or jeans and one of his remaining ironic-sloganed T-shirts? 'Today I'm wearing mostly black' or 'Your band sucks'. He caught himself, after a third change, standing in front of the mirror in grey socks and paisley-patterned boxers, staring at his paunchy, hairy belly button, wondering who the hell he was trying to be. Had Dot mapped a story of his fifteen years in her head? Thought him a coward yellow-belly for hiding from her? Or worse, had she barely thought of him at all? Only on opening a newspaper, and seeing his face, maybe once a year. His twenty Xmas-present tips for *Time Out* five years back that he should never have agreed to put his name to. They must not talk about the past when they met. If they did, she would learn very quickly that he knew too much, that he did in fact have a press-clipping box, two in fact, filled with her many faces.

The clothes he finally picked were designer grunge.

Images wouldn't leave him alone on the walk to Angel. A whole street of FOR SALE signs, newspapers with Wall Street traders, heads in hands; 27% fall on the FTSE index. Meltdown Monday they'd called it, just a month back, but still the economy was smouldering into nothing. It struck him that he'd first met Dot just after Black Wednesday, that his career had been a tenuous thread stretched between two troughs of depression. There was something reassuring about being in a recession again, the comfort of being just another failure among millions, of not having to try to be someone any more.

He fought his way through the morning crowds, swiped

his Oyster card and headed to the Northern Line. There were video adverts on the down escalator, all showing images of sexy young things, eyeing each other on a virtual escalator, all the video monitors in sync. Match.com. 'Has your future partner just passed you by?' Would he actually recognise her when he saw her? The latest promo photo showed her thin-boned with short white hair. Warholesque. A little Paula Yates circa late eighties, but without make-up. White not to shock but maybe to hide grey.

He waited on the platform and caught himself looking at the waiting women: a tall Swedish-looker in designer leathers, a shaved-headed dyke with denims. Strange, to be checking the faces as if looking for her.

No, he had not followed her slavishly; there were at least three years of almost total denial. Freelance work, travelling, building a reputation, jobbing it for anyone that would take him, lifestyle columns on fashion, pop, hairstyles, cover bands, photographers, community workshops, children with disabilities making murals in Bradford, music rehab projects for junkies in Birmingham. The time of attempted domesticity. Telling himself that Dot's world was fake. That a quiet life, with a wife, planning a child would be the antidote to the hype.

What the hell would he say to her after the words of hello?

The anxiety grew as the train arrived and he climbed on board and found a seat. Across from him a young emo couple shared an iPod between them, just as the Hoxton couple had done, one earpiece apiece. He looked up and there above them was an advert for iPod showing a silhouette of a young couple doing exactly the same thing. 'Consumers are manufactured now, not products,' Saul had said.

He would not tell her of the years of exhaustion and of his wife's creeping disappointment in him. Her desire for a child and his constant attempts to reassure her that they should wait till things were more 'secure'. But being free-lance, every job was a struggle to tie down, and he came to dread the confining limits of the marriage he'd bought into. After another year of it she screamed that he was always postponing, running up and down the country and for what? Just another couple of hundred quid. 'There's never a right time to have a kid,' she'd said. 'We have to believe in ourselves, take a risk.'

Moorgate. A peroxide blonde was suddenly beside him and he jumped. He watched the way she held the metal pole as if she was a lap dancer. Her breasts in a low-cut top were on display. A short man in a business suit kept staring, trying to edge closer. As the train jumped Owen was sure he saw the man rub his crotch against her and she did not flinch. Her face – steel.

He recalled the time Dot had been nominated for the Turner Prize, 2001. The embarrassment he'd felt as he sat beside Becky and watched the award ceremony. She'd pointed at the TV saying: 'Didn't you know her?' And he'd lied. The time of lies. For the next few months, Becky had bullied him into trying to make babies, and each time he'd faked ejaculation. After that it was the secret drinking, the secret porn habit, and, most bizarre of all, his secret search for that old album of Saul's – *The Duchamps* – for weeks on end, in all the retro shops and online, everywhere, an obsession. When she found out, it was the last straw. She left him to chase her image of a partner more fit to be father, a man with a future, with money.

The first stop was Old Street. A group of trendy twenty-somethings got on, with retro hippy hair, talking excitedly. He was feeling light-headed and took a Rennie to calm his churning gut. At the end of the carriage there was a mother and child, poor-looking, olive-skinned, possibly immigrant. He wondered how old this child Dot had was, this Molly.

A hot flush rose up his neck and he tasted salt. He took a second beta blocker and contemplated another antacid.

One more stop till London Bridge. If he'd just had a drink to calm his nerves. But it was only 11 a.m. and he had rules about hours and times and quantities. As the human surge left at Bank – it was as if the world was giving him secret coded messages – he glimpsed that image of his face smeared in lipstick and the words writ large: *Nine Works* – before it vanished into the multitudes of other advert faces accelerating into tunnel darkness. Then it was a woman, with huge fake gold earrings reading *Dazed & Confused* and on her page was the image of the sculpture of Kate Moss cast in gold. 'Gold and art are the only two safe investments in a global recession,' Saul had once said, 'because neither can be mass-produced.' As the tube sped by and the stench of sweating tourists filled his nostrils and anonymous bodies dug their elbows into his ribs, he closed his eyes and surrendered to the images.

Dazed, nine years back. She was long-haired, dyed blonde and wearing sunglasses on the arm of a hunky punk guy on the centre pages; then she was in a Ghost dress at a gallery opening in the society pages of *Tatler* in 2002; in *Vogue* in a bikini on a beach with her lover and the father of her child, gallery owner Hans Gershoon. Every time it had been the fury that these men were beneath her, that she could let herself stoop so low. No, he'd not been jealous – all of it was contemptible and if she had fallen for it then she was a hypocrite and whore. The relationship with the gallery owner Gershoon had been despicably calculating, made even more so by the fact that other artists had done similar things. If he had just acted differently, on that one day in May 1993 – stayed with her till she woke, then he could have saved her from this. They could have been together, maybe with a child of their own. It would have been almost sixteen now, old enough to leave home. He opened his eyes and the iPod couple were whispering together, as if about him.

Out and up the tube steps. London Bridge and factories and warehouses converted into apartments and artists' studios. Three streets of towering sand-blasted brick and fifty TO LET signs and more adverts and the number was hard to find: 752. There was graffiti on the walls but it didn't look real, more like some artist's project, some pseudo Banksy. He was at 684, his gut tightening. As he walked the numbers, up the cobblestoned streets that once ran with industrial and human waste, he passed a sign for an estate agent that, beside it, had an advert for Hirst's diamond-encrusted skull. The words of Saul: 'I fear irony is dead. We shall be laughing ourselves into mass graves.'

Finally, it was 752. He took a deep breath as he entered and found the old cast-iron lift as the gallery email told him he would and pushed the button for the fifth floor.

The vast metal doors opened and, of course, the place was immense and she was nowhere to be seen. But even given the great deal he knew of the workings of contemporary artists, he was surprised to find that her studio was basically no more than a storeroom for artworks. Several hundred packing crates covered in Post-it notes. Polystyrene packing, plastic wrapping, FedEx boxes. Not an artwork in sight and no sight of her.

On rounding a stack of crates he found only a woman, middle-aged, scrawny-looking in jogging pants and T-shirt on a phone, Dot's assistant, no doubt. He walked past her into the space when her voice called out.

'Hi, there.' He turned and found himself once again in those big open eyes. She motioned to her phone, waved her hands around in a frenzy that he took to mean have a look around I'll be a minute. He had been wrong, not scrawny, just slender, and the jogging clothes were more hip or hip hop. He did not want to be caught looking. If he could just find an excuse to delay, to leave.

He heard her hang up but no sooner had she done so and he turned back nervously to speak, than her mobile rang. She threw her hand in the air in some mime of sorry and picked it up. As he watched her she seemed like a Wall Street broker or PR girl for some transient product that was basically herself. Minutes more he fidgeted by her packing cases, increasingly embarrassed as her every moment was taken up with admin. A woman entered and started asking her questions. To Owen's horror she turned out to be that deadly serious Israeli artist who made quaint watercolour landscapes with her own urine, whom he'd panned in *Time Out* a few years back.

He was hiding himself behind a crate that read 'Barcelona' when the hand touched his shoulder. She smiled at him, was trying to talk on her mobile and kiss his cheek all at once, her mobile about to fall from her hand. Her eyes had tiny crow's feet but glowed still in that way he knew.

'See how crazy it is?' And before she had time to explain she was talking to the other voice in her ear.

'No, the screens have to be Panavision Presentation, twelve by eight. Wait, I have the number for the hire company here somewhere.' Then she was flicking through laptop screens. 'Fucking formats!'

No animosity or vengeance, no sit down and let's face the past. He was making hand signs that he should just go, another time maybe, but she indicated to stay, sit, but there was nowhere to sit. As he stood there awkward, she undid a blouse button, fanned the air as if it was too hot. From where he was standing he could see the lacy outline of her bra. So casually then, as she phone-talked, rubbing her neck, her collarbone, as if inviting him to stare at her increasingly visible cleavage, as if he was an executive toy she was idly playing with.

'I could resend it on PAL? DVD. And the projector is six thousand LM, luminance? . . . It has to be because it's quite a dark image, can you confirm that for me? No, that's great, yes, send my regards to Ed, tell him I love him to bits and I'll be there for the opening.'

He was looking round to see if excretions-woman was anywhere to be seen, if he could find a way to leave, discreetly.

'*Bitte*,' she said to the phone. '*Vielen Dank*.'

As she hung up she suddenly stopped touching herself. He was stuck, struck speechless.

'God, but you know the thing is . . .'

'What?' And 'hello' and 'sorry' he wanted to say. But this was so Dot, so old Dot – the way she'd start midsentence, even after an argument, after an absence of hours, even days, and say: 'And another thing . . .' He waited for the next fragment.

'. . . what the fuck am I even doing here?' He was about to reply that yes, he felt somewhat the same and if she wanted they could call the whole thing off.

'Sorry, I should have . . .' she said. And there was no moment when they stood apart and took time to assess what time had taken from them or hopefully healed, or even said hello as two total strangers might, only this weird familiarity in fragments. She had not even said his name.

'. . . I mean, my sugar level. I'm about to go hypoglycaemic, we have to eat NOW!'

'Oh, I see, OK. Yeah, sure.'

Over the chichi sushi lunch, in the fusion place a block away, which she wolfed down – some indication perhaps of the damage she'd done to her system in the year of near anorexia with him and Saul – he tried to keep it business. They had been talking art, not past, just art.

'So . . . how do you find time to make any new work?'

She stuffed raw tuna into her mouth with her second Diet Coke.

'Truth is I haven't really made anything, not since . . .'

He thought she meant like the neo-conceptualists, Douglas Gordon et al. He'd witnessed Gordon at work before. At his laptop, he didn't even have a studio; his work had almost become pure concept. Like, say a wall in the Schwartz Gallery covered in the names of everyone he could remember in a day. Around two thousand. One version was in the Gallery of Modern Art in Edinburgh. He wrote down the names on the plane and in arrivals emailed it off to the gallery with a list of dimensions, font size and number of hours it would take a team of a certain number to stencil the names on the wall, then turned up for the opening.

'No, no, God, I wish I was that smart,' she mumbled as she stuffed down his hardly touched Thai noodles. 'I mean, nothing at all, for years, I'm serious, nothing new . . . I'm like a photocopy machine or a –'

'But surely, you must want to . . . again.'

'No, I'm just glad it's a day job, you know, making sure they've got the DVD players in Barcelona, and the layout maps and the PR's up to date. I haven't had a creative thought in years.'

'You're joking?'

'Seriously, I'm done with art, I mean, what's the point, I've made all this money and now I'm probably gonna lose it all with the banks going down anyway.'

'But I thought the government was protecting savings over, well, a certain amount.' His voice sounded banal in his ears.

She looked at him as if to say, Silly man, I've lost millions, already.

He wanted to say, Isn't it funny, we met after Black Wednesday and now we're on Meltdown Monday. He wanted to say he'd rather write off the fifteen years between and go back to total poverty as there was at least some comfort in it.

'I dunno . . . I just want to grow vegetables or knit socks

or . . .' she said. 'Cos since Molly, she's my . . . she's four, you'd love her, all this travel, God! New York, Frankfurt, Tokyo, this was just in the last . . . I mean the flights, Tracey says the same thing.'

'Sorry, this is Tracey Emin?'

'Yeah, yeah, and this subversive thing, they always say she's so subversive, I'm so subversive, blah de blah. But we're so totally square. I mean, what's left to subvert anyway? What do they want us to do, kill ourselves?'

He could have said that indeed it was not a joke. Her premature death would probably quadruple her market value as it had done for Basquiat, that there had been conspiracy theories about possible murder, but he considered it in poor taste.

'Where was I anyway?'

'Uh, you were talking about your daughter, flights . . .'

'Yeah, yeah, no, I mean, they keep asking me to make new work, and I try and try . . . Did you see it, that one at the Lieder, with Molly in it? It's shit, I mean . . .'

He had not seen it and apologised.

'I pulled it from the show, last week, so there's only eight now. Fucking thing's called Nine and everyone's embarrassed cos I've got to take the Nine to Zurich. I was kind of hoping you could maybe . . .'

'Hoping I could?'

'Well, give me some ideas. I know, sorry, it's a dumb idea, I should never have asked, sorry you're . . .'

'No, not at all.' He was flattered, but still reeling from her onslaught.

'Anyway, I'm just worried that when broadband gets good enough they'll just stream all my stuff and I won't have any FedExing to do any more and I'll be out of a job anyway . . .'

Dot! he wanted to say. Hello Dot, can we just slow down, say hello and start again? She seemed drained by all the talking and reached for his hand.

'Can't we just go snooze?'

'Ah . . . really? Sorry?'

Still there had been no addressing of the question of the years. No 'I forgive you', or 'I hate you'.

'I'm whacked . . . I'm so . . .'

'Sure . . . but where?'

'Home.'

She laughed as she touched his hand, burped, then giggled, covering her mouth in that way she used to.

'Sorry, I mean . . . my place.'

On the taxi ride to Notting Hill he picked up more fragments. It was an affluent des-res town house, a full three floors in a trendy tree-lined street, but as soon as he stepped inside he cracked his knee on a packing case and with every step there was even more mess. Dot was fussing, trying to apologise, explain.

'. . . and what with the commute to the studio . . . for fuck's sake I'm supposed to be selling this place. Bastards – I mean, it would save so much time in commuting and then I'd see more of Molly and . . .'

He nodded when it felt appropriate and made it past the obstacle course of scattered cuddly toys, books and CDs and found his way to the lounge. The windows were immense; the floor of beautifully Victorian pine, but barely an inch of it visible beneath piles of clothes and more teeming packing boxes. Dot was in the open-plan kitchen area; the units had expensive aluminium splashbacks by some exclusive Italian designer, a full selection of hanging Le Creuset pots and pans, but then in the middle of it all an incongruous bottom-of-the-range white plastic Argos microwave spattered in sauce. Dot's Post-it notes practically covered every surface.

'. . . and Consuela can't travel with me, cos, well . . . I only found out . . . she's not got a real passport . . . Venezuelan

. . . Molly adores her . . . a political refugee . . . but she's so sweet, you'll love her . . .'

He was struggling not to laugh as he tried to find a seat that was not covered in kiddie stuff. There was what seemed an authentic Bauhaus chair, sitting on top of a kitschy seventies vinyl black-and-white-spotted rug. And a cheap Ikea clothes rail teeming with designer dresses right in front of the antique seventies sci-fi-looking TV. A dead yucca was covered in last year's fairy lights and handmade tinfoil angels.

'. . . but I mean I really need to get Molly into a nursery so she can get socialised . . . Montessori would be ideal, there's a good one in Camden, isn't that funny? . . . I mean, really I should be living over there . . .'

She uncorked some wine, took a slug and fussed around looking for glasses in the cupboards. She opened one and it was full of plates, another and it was stacked with DVDs. Above her head, stuck to the glass of what seemed an authentic Warhol of Jackie Onassis, was a kid's crayon drawing of a house with a big smiling yellow sun. It was like she was some magpie student squatting in a stately home. The look could have been called deconstructive if it had been deliberate.

'I have to go east . . . I got gazumped . . . so I'm in a kind of holding pattern right now . . .'

Finally, she handed him the wine in a kid's plastic tumbler, kicked some books from the floor and sat cross-legged in front of him.

'What would you do?' she asked.

So Dot, so Dotty. He couldn't hold it back. The laughter.

Over a dinner of takeaway pizza and a tour of the other rooms, largely stuffed with packing boxes, Owen put together the entire story.

As she spent so much time touring her art abroad, she really needed one big single space that could be artist's studio and crèche, that she and Molly could call 'home'.

105

Really close to a good nursery because she was going to have to let Consuela go. She'd been about to move to a big warehouse in Camden, but the exchange of contracts fell through because of the housing crisis and now nobody was buying so she couldn't sell. So she was stuck, half moved out with no time or energy left to find a new place.

These are the burdens of the international jet-setter, Owen thought as he watched her sitting barefoot by his feet, rubbing her neck. In the silence that followed he sensed it was finally time for what they had been avoiding.

'So how's —'

'I heard you were —'

'You go first . . .'

'No, you . . .'

'Married, yes, not for long and you . . .'

'No.'

The tentativeness, the second-guessing.

'I assumed. Molly's father . . .'

'Oh no, he was really a . . .'

'. . . a bastard? A . . . ?'

'No, a sperm donor . . . Sorry.'

They laughed.

'He sends cheques but he's in New York now. But you . . . married? Owen. Who'd have . . .'

'Well, classic mistake stuff, thought it would . . .'

'. . . make you a better person?'

'Ditto, but you . . .'

'Well, I have Molly . . . How about you . . . do you . . . ?'

'No, no kids. I was a bit of a let-down on that front. You know.'

But of course she didn't know. He tried to change the subject.

'Must be convenient, with Molly, having your folks in town?'

She was silent then.

'We don't talk any more.'

'Oh . . . of course. Sorry.'

Her father and the hospital. He'd been a fool to say such a thing.

'I'm really sorry.'

'It's OK.'

Dot placed a hand on his knee.

'You look so . . .' she said. She smiled. Thank God.

'Different?'

'No, no, well, sort of, but . . .'

There was some discussion of exactly what about Owen was so changed. Dot said he might have filled out, had he been to a gym? He laughed and said it was fat, not muscle. Then she was trying to remember something.

'What was it he used to say about gyms?'

'Sorry, "he" . . . ?'

'Saul. He used to . . .'

The sudden mention of Saul threw him but he thought it his job to try to recall.

'The cult of health is a sickness?'

She shook her head, so he tried again.

'A gym is a gulag one pays to get into.' She laughed, lifted her hand from his knee.

'Never heard that one, it was something about push-ups.'

'Ah! His definition of sex.'

'What?'

'Doing push-ups till you're sick!'

She rolled about with laughter and hugged his knees.

'So have you . . . ?' she asked.

'Had sex?'

'No, silly – heard from him? You were so . . .'

'No, no, nothing.' Silence then. He reached for her hand, her fingers quickly intermeshed through his and relaxation flooded in. He resisted the urge to kiss her. She leaned her head against his knee.

'It was just, well, someone told me about a guy who got thrown out at my opening night, a tramp, they said . . . you don't think . . . ?'

'No, I'm sure he's fine . . . you know him and his cult of the Übermensch, he's probably living in a cave by now.'

'Screaming at the hypocrisies of civilisation.'

'With a hundred disciples.'

'Poor Saul.'

'Yes.'

It had maybe been the wine, or the nostalgia, or the way that one sentence fed the next, or some need to stop talk of the past and end the many questions with the touching of lips.

Molly was having a sleepover with friends, so he could stay, she said, as she pulled away from his kiss and pulled her T-shirt over her head.

'By the way, you don't have to meet her, she's a nightmare, I love her to bits.'

She led him by the hand to the bedroom and finished undressing before him. Her breasts had shrunk and there were stretch lines round her darkened areolae and across her stomach, but she seemed to him more perfect than before. She slid under the covers and he turned his back to her as he undressed, then reached back and pulled the sheets to hide his sex. There was awkwardness as their bodies touched. He tried to kiss her lips but his forehead bashed her cheek and there were apologies. He ran his hand over her pelvis but she said it was too ticklish. She touched his cock and he was nervous about how the nervousness had made it flaccid.

'You can open your eyes,' she said. 'I'm not going to bite.'

They were eye to eye, her fingers round his cock and his circling her clit. He lowered his gaze first. 'Sorry,' meaning sorry for what he couldn't say, sorry for everything.

'Shh,' she whispered. 'I know, me too.'

And so they agreed not to fuck but to sleep, back to back. But over the dark hours in half-waking their breathing rhythms came into sync and their mouths were urgent to dissolve into each other. In his many years since her, it had not been like this with a woman, opening himself as if he was the one penetrated. In between the endless cycles of it, in momentary rest and craving for sleep, he tried to explain it away; told himself it was mercy fucking, just nostalgia, sad really, two people old enough to know better, fucking with their past, mad to open themselves to such naked need. But in the seeping dawn light, her eyes in shadow were over him again, whispering his name as she encircled and pulled him deep inside.

*

The sounds were of objects being thrown, furniture falling over, screams, laughter, what seemed to be dancing, and fluids being spilled – like a murder or a science experiment. It had ceased to be anything that could be recognised as the sounds of coitus and often had me tiptoeing the corridor to Saul's keyhole to see if they were OK. Every night this horror would wake then reawaken me just when I though it was over. For three long weeks I had endured it. I had made plans to leave before Christmas.

To add insult to injury, in the many mornings after, they would pretend that nothing was happening between them. Did they think me deaf or a dummy or did their deception arouse them further? I was not spying, but I could not fail to glimpse their many stolen intimacies: their fingers touching in secrecy beneath the table; the little smiles in the kitchen. The way they fell silent suddenly when I entered his room and sprung apart into grinning silence. Even more galling was the way they made a special effort to keep me included in everything. And so we watched a movie 'together' – another Bergman – but I did not see a single frame, as I was too busy trying to avoid the sight of their fingers finding each other beneath the duvet.

They went to Edna's again and I was not invited. In spite, I went into her empty room and stole a pair of her panties. Back in my room, I sniffed the stained crotch and came violently into the floral fabric. Overcome with shame I told myself I was not becoming sick, it was they that were sick, sick and weak – the Übermensch and his Überwench. As if to prove how weak they had become, she had even invented a love name for him: Sozzle. — C'mon, Sozzle, let's have a drink. — Where are you, Sozzle? — Oh, Soz, you look fabulous. How low the mighty Saul had stooped. The sound of that name made me puke.

I tried to plan an escape but needed money, much more than the scrawny fifteen quid I was getting from the *Hoxton Advertiser* for my weekly book or album reviews. As soon as I had enough money, and paid Dot back the two hundred I owed her, I'd get the hell out and leave them to their squalid secrecies – that was what I thought. Finding work was tough though, there had been more strikes at the main newspapers, and it was Wapping all over again. If I could have filled in an application to be a scab I would have. But I was caught in another catch-22 – I'd have to invest in some new respectable clothes just to get a job, and the contract, being freelance, would probably only last a few weeks, after which time I'd have earned enough to pay back the debt on my new clothes.

It was the recession, I told myself, not my fault, and kept searching: telesales, trainee recruitment consultant, more telesales. Call centres, more call centres. I found a flyer from a car windscreen: 'EARN £50 TO £500 EXTRA PER WEEK WORKING FROM HOME.' It looked hopeful so I called the guy. He kept on about what a unique opportunity it was and asking for my name and details. I could hear him typing, filling in a form. I worked out he was getting paid for getting my details – that was his job. It was even more surreal when I finally found out what the job was he was selling – it was putting round flyers and taking calls like mine. I had to have him clarify – wait, so, the job is getting other people to put round flyers for a job that is getting other people to put flyers round, for a job that doesn't actually exist? He hung up.

'BUDDING ENTREPRENEUR? – CONSIDER RECRUIT-MENT.'

I was stuck, without the finances to move out, and trapped also in a horrible déjà vu. Exactly the same thing had happened to me years before. When, after four months living with Debs, our love turned sour and we were trapped in daily animosity because neither of us could afford to move out. Almost a year of livid hatred. Some sociologist one day had to document this living hell called London.

After another night being awoken by Saul and Dot's orgasmic giggling, I prayed to the dead God to visit a plague upon them both.

I felt almost guilty for how swiftly my wish became real. Within only a month of their initial union their passion started failing. One morning, from along the corridor, I heard her trying to get him to rise.

— C'mon, Sozzle, get up. Let's go shoplifting. You can't just lie there all day and do nothing.

— Oh but I can. Procrastination is an art I practise without hesitation! he groaned in reply, for his nth time.

Her high energy or the force they'd expended sexually had exhausted Saul and led him to a state of regression, sleeping late, becoming sullen and foul-mooded in the morning wakings that soon turned into afternoons. She made the same mistakes I had long before, attempting more inventive and exciting enticements.

— Let's go to Harvey Nicks and spend five hundred. I'll put it on my mum's account.

— I have no enthusiasm for people who are enthusiastic, he replied. — It is all cheerleaders and bombs in Palestine.

— Get up!

— This lady's not for turning! he shouted, quoting Thatcher.

Even though I resented their coupling, I couldn't help but pity her. The closer she got to him, the more she tried to motivate him, the more he froze her out. This was maybe why he vowed never to have a woman again. A certain emotional (and financial) dependence had been exposed in him and he resented it. The big chill had started. I knew because he had gone back to playing his Wagner.

— Penises are everywhere! Dot declared as she sprang through the front door, as was her way in the days that followed. She'd just been to the City Racing opening; it was an old betting shop, near the Oval, turned into an indie gallery. All very trendy, she said, artists exhibiting *objets trouvés* – a basketball and an electric bar fire and 365 used lottery tickets. She met this guy called Pierce and he was doing another show next month and he liked the sound of her video art. She was so excited. I had not the heart to remind her that she hadn't actually made anything resembling art yet.

She was running around the flat, trying to wake Saul. The Revolting Cocks were gigging that week, she announced, and she'd bought us both tickets as a surprise. She'd pay for taxis and everything. Of course, Saul wanted nothing to do with it. I'd been in the kitchen and overheard the whole thing. (I spent rather a lot of time in the kitchen in those weeks. It was between his room and mine. How many hours had I spent staring at the mould on the Artex and the warped Formica and the aluminium pans with burned bases while trying to work out if I should intervene to save them from each other?)

— But you *love* the Revoling Cocks! she protested.

— I never said I loved anything; besides, like certain women I know, they are both repetitive and predictable.

She kept on, thinking her enthusiasm would win. I went to the doorway edge and peered inside.

She was throwing clothes out of his wardrobe, trying to get him to sit up and get dressed, shouting then about Sarah Lucas, she'd met her, she had a kind of art shop with Tracey Emin in Bethnal Green and they were lovely and they wanted her to come and hang out. They were putting on a 'happening' in the next week – everyone had to wear fake beards and do life drawings of a naked man. Wasn't that great? They should go. And there had been this photo Sarah had exhibited, like a bowl of soup but there were things floating in the soup – penis heads, photos of dick heads. And then it was Jake and Dinos Chapman, and their child mannequins with vaginas for mouths and dicks for noses and she'd been reading a story in the paper on the tube about the Operation Spanner trial. It was all very exhilarating. A group of sadomasochists had been arrested for committing violent acts against themselves.

— Penises, you see, they're everywhere! We could make cock art, she said as she tried to pull his foot from beneath the sheets and put on his socks.

— Sex destroys art, Saul said. — There is only so much energy one can ejaculate from oneself. It's the same with love, us real artists have no energy left for it. Please unhand my foot!

— But can't you see, she shouted, — we're so happening? Can I film your cock, Sozzle?

He stared at her impassively, and pulled his bared foot back inside the covers.

— My dear, you are so open-minded that all of your

thoughts simply fall out of your fucking skull. I suggest you analyse the etymology of the word dickhead.

She gave up and marched out. I hid myself in the kitchen as she passed.

Two hours later and her drunken voice screamed from beyond my door.

— Fuck you. I'm getting out of here, going clubbing!

— Fine, fuck off then.

I could hear them out in the corridor. It was well past 2 a.m.

— Just me and Owen, you're not invited.

She had not even asked me to a club. It tormented me that she could use me as a pawn in such a way, as if she could ever make him jealous.

— Good idea, why don't you fuck him too? Saul shouted back. — Then fuck off.

— Fine then, I shall, but we shan't be coming back.

She was at my door then, and I pretended I hadn't been listening.

Just then Saul slammed his door and yelled, — Fuck you, I'm going clubbing – not you! And marched out.

Dot followed him and the argument ensued in the street outside the kebab shop. We never made it to a club or pub; they were both so drunk already and the fresh air must have hit them hard. I carried both their drunken weights back along Old Street. Terrible silences between them and I was the one in the middle, supporting their staggering rages. She tried to punch him and he tried to scratch her.

— Tell your bulimic bitch friend to fuck off and leave us alone, Saul said to me.

— Oh, so he's not speaking to me, she said. — Well, tell your faggot friend that I think he's a loser and drunk.

— Tell her she looks like a pig in shit.

— STOP, BEHAVE! Was I their translator now, their mediator? — Fucking spoiled brats, the pair of you.

They hated me for it, but still leaned on me, for stability. Like some comedy show of two cowards trying to hit each other, knowing that there was someone in the middle to restrain them both. The proof was, when I did nothing they desisted from their violence and both stared at me, as if I was a grown-up denying them sweets. All of this in full public display as we passed the jeering, whistling drunks by the George & Vulture.

If they had made a soap-opera version of Nietzsche's eternal return for TV it would have been our flat; we were trapped in an endless rerun of the same day. She'd gone back to playing her old records, just to piss him off. On one typical morning Saul stormed past me to the bathroom, his eyes burning red through dark foundation, his kimono flapping behind him.

— I have but one goal today, to destroy the cultural hegemony of Joni Mitchell! he proclaimed, then vomited violently into the bath.

— You make me sick, she shouted from her room.

— Puke then, he called back, — it's what you do best! But use the kitchen as the bathroom is occupied, and clean the plates when you're done! And buy some Vim and cheese, would you? I'm a bit peckish.

It would not have gone on like that if they did not enjoy it. I feared I had become some kind of marriage-guidance counsellor or, worse, a pawn in some game designed to heighten their passions.

My position was puerile; as voyeur of their traumas I swear I felt more for both of them than they felt for each other. I sat by my door trying to make out their distant words and silences; I spied on them through the gap. It was like some avant-garde movie, sound and picture out of sync. I spent hours trying to work out the plot as they drifted in and out of shot and I caught snatches of dialogue.

Things were thrown, smashed, doors slammed, feet walking out only to return with screaming. Always her doing the throwing, the walking out, the returning, the screaming again. Always she who accused him of the same damn things. As soon as her foot was out the door he turned his music on full blast. Always the Wagner. There was a pattern to her returns too. Always with a 750ml of Smirnoff and he had never been able to afford Smirnoff and so let her back in.

She was back again with the booze and I was at my keyhole.

— You made me slash my canvases!

— I made you do nothing of the sort. We are each alone and must face the hell of our own making.

— Sozzle, please, just tell me what to do!

— Do you want me to make your art for you? he shouted. Art is dead! Go and kill yourself. I'm sure they'll give you a posthumous first-class degree with honours.

— But you're the artist! Not me, she shouted.

After a long silence she told him about how her chum Sarah Lucas had sold an ashtray to the Lieder Gallery for £65K. An ashtray, that was all it was, full of cigarette butts smoked by the artist.

— But you thought of it first! she was screaming at him. — An ashtray is an artwork. You said it months back, I think I might have even told her. That money should have been yours!

He upturned his ashtray on the floor to prove his point. She screamed: — You thought of it first! But she did it, she had the guts, and what have you done? Nothing, not ever. You break my heart. You're nothing.

— Why thank you, Saul replied. — Like the Buddha I've always aspired to nothingness.

I heard his door slam and her footsteps in the corridor. Suddenly my door was thrown open. I jumped back onto

116

the bed and pretended to be busy. Play-acting the sorting-out of my smalls. She was in tears, wanting a hug, wearing nothing but his Che Guevara T-shirt.

— He's a monster!

— I know, I know. Shh, it's OK.

And as I held her thin body in my arms, I felt myself becoming aroused. Considering it an inappropriate response to her grief, I cleared a space for her on my bed from among the dirty laundry and again found myself in the painful position of playing the role of best friend and confidant while my cock strained against my trousers, screaming at my hypocrisy.

— It's no good, why can't I . . . she said.

I waited for her to finish.

— . . . how does he do it? I spend all day hating him, planning ways to go and then . . . How can I hate him so much but then I see his face and his scrawny legs and that fucking kimono and he's drunk and I come crawling back? Why can't I just . . . ?

— Leave?

— Yes!

But no, I did not want her to leave him because if she did she would leave me too. And so I told her my theory about Saul and black holes and how they are collapsed stars, a negative space where a shining sun used to be and how its gravity was a million times greater than a live star, and how, for me, that was Saul, and how I'd tried to leave so many times too, but his negativity drew me back. How he did this to me too.

— Did he, did he really . . . ? You're so wise . . . so sweet to me.

Her big eyes looked down on me. I tried to put a safe distance between us and so sat on the floor, but it had been a grave mistake as when she crossed her long, long legs, I glimpsed the pink flesh flashing between. I fixed my gaze on the floor. She touched my shoulders.

117

— Oh, Owen. It was so cool last month, when we . . . if only we could go back to being like that again?

How could she sit like that, practically naked, holding my hand and be oblivious to the pain her touch caused me – to the fact that she herself had destroyed that glorious time we had had as three, when the flirtations were infinite and innocent? How could she not know how I longed to take those fingers of her and thread them through mine, to bury my face in those slender thighs just inches from my face, to release my agonised cock within her?

She pecked my forehead.

— You're so wise, you're a chum, a real chum.

That night I placed her panties by my pillow, her sweet musky lust. I could have wept. An impossible idea came to me then: that Saul knew of my longings and had placed her panties in the bathroom for me to find. That they were some secret communication to me – that he wanted me to help him, maybe even take her from him. Like the way he forced me into taking out his rubbish. He had made a mess of it with her and I was always there to clear up after him.

In the days that followed, I made an effort to be practical around the house. I cooked meals of pasta and ketchup and left them outside their doors. But the more I tried to be helpful the more they each seemed to resent me.

Dot's plates of food lay uneaten and stacked by the foot of her door, and so I took the liberty of knocking. She was on the floor, trying to film her face from above with another moustache on, and lipstick, her whole face a mess; there was a half-empty bottle of wine by her side.

— So how's the art coming on?

She pulled the moustache off and threw it down with a sigh.

— Men are fucked! she said. — I told my tutor I was making art in a collective –

— Really? Was that wise?

— Bastard said I could only get one name on my graduation certificate. These stupid old men, I just hate them.

I managed to work out that it was worse than she'd let on. If she didn't attend art school that week and bring a new artwork for the group critique she would be chucked out.

— I can write down ideas, help you brainstorm, like we did before, if you want?

— You're very sweet, but don't waste your breath.

She was even starting to talk like him. Her eyes stared out of her window, to the rubbish bins and that stupid little tree by the fire escape.

— But really, what are you going to do now? I asked. Her hand fell weak on my knee, then suddenly made a fist.

— Fuck it all!

I watched then as she climbed into bed with the bottle and slugged from it. I saw how we could end up. Both of them drinking alone, me caught running from one room to the other, mop in hand, having to feed, clothe and clean up the vomit as they spiralled downward into a void that he would be the only one to climb back from. I needed to get her up and out of the place. My eyes scanned the crap on her floor and, amid a dozen crisp packets, stumbled on her gig tickets.

— C'mon, I said, — it'll be even more revolting than Saul.

I dragged her out of bed and helped her get dressed, with no idea that the night to come would end with the start of an even more powerful spiral, not downward but up.

Saul had already said he would not be joining us, but decided to recant, no doubt because he was without money and she was leaving with the cash and there was, of course, the promise of stealing drinks at the gig, which was an old talent of his. Saul and Dot were on a mutual pact of ignoring each other so the taxi ride there was a hell of silences with me sat between them idiotically trying to get one then the other to say something. We arrived just as the support band was finishing. It was a typical student dive. The kids were grunge cyberpunk and pseudo saddo goth. The DJ started up as the road crew changed the kit onstage. Dot, for all her attitude with him, was wide-eyed like a kid and wanted to dance. (She confessed to me later that it was her first gig.)

Saul took one look at her jiving under the flashing lights, muttered — Philistines, and headed off to pinch some drinks. In less than three minutes he'd abducted three vodkas and Coke and I'm sure had stashed a pint in the lining of his greatcoat because he kept holding it out from himself then swearing as people bumped into him. Dot's excitement was making Saul cringe terribly and as soon as the Revolting Cocks came onstage, Dot yelped and I could almost hear Saul's sphincter tighten. The lead singer was wearing a wrestling mask and nothing else, apart from a foot-long prosthetic penis. — See, Dot shouted, — penises – everywhere! There was a surge to the front as the bass kicked in. An insistent monotonous ominous metallic drumbeat, then the first shriek of guitars. The rest of the band were in leather chaps, bare-chested, bare-arsed, with cowboy hats.

Lyrics were screamed, guitars wailed and the drumbeat pounded like a migraine-fuelled mechanical dildo, the words were all about sex machines and fucking. The hands of the crowd reached out to grab the lead singer's plastic cock. The guy on the synth was crouched behind it, doing something, hidden, a line of coke or a snort of poppers. Then the stage-diving started. Saul's face was unmoved by the spectacle, his arms crossed.

Dot wanted to go forward, pulling both of our hands. Saul refused bluntly. It was too loud to speak but he shouted in her ear. I saw him shake his head, then motion her away with his leather-glove-clad hand.

— Off with you, off with you both!

I was not as choosy as he. No matter what band, as long as it was loud, I threw myself into the mosh pit, well, the safer edges of it. We were standing a good ten feet behind the rest of the crowd and with all the stage-diving it was hard to see. Dot had her video camera out and started filming but was getting more and more frustrated. Shouting (I got the gist of it), — Sick of watching! Come on. She tried to pull me forward. I looked at Saul for permission, his face a picture of stoic negativity. A gig is a mass and he despised the masses. His ideal gig would have been one with him as the only spectator, which he then left after the first song.

To hell with him, I thought. Dot started geekishly jumping up and down so I joined in. Grateful when she pulled me deeper into the crowd, away from Saul's eyes. There were not many girls there — one, totally stoned, was moshing in her bra, her face covered in piercings – green hair. Someone suddenly flew towards us. Doc Marten in face. I put my hands up in time to protect my face, but he must have hit Dot, she was reeling. I held her tight, shouted, — YOU WANNA GO BACK? IT'S SAFER! All the guys were eyeing her up. It must have been about the fifth song. The one I knew – 'Stainless Steel Provider'. Dot shook her head and grinned at me, mad, kid-like; she'd given up on trying to film, the video camera, round her wrist, was annoying her. She shouted something.

— What?

Put her arm round. Sweet smell of her sweat. Repeated it.

— WHA?

Grinned, repeated it and hunched her shoulders when I didn't get it.

— WHA? I DON –

She pulled back my hair and shouted it in my ear, her lips brushing my lobe, sending spasms through me.

— WE NEED . . .

She was jerked from me by the crowd as it surged

121

forward again. I pushed through the seething mass to find her only four rows from the front. I grabbed her hand, but she pulled me in deeper. The lead singer was grinning evil as the bass guitar throbbed and the sampled loop was of a woman coming. He lifted his pink prosthesis and suddenly fake jism sprayed out, as if from a fireman's hose. Guys were jumping open-mouthed to receive it, tongues reaching for the junk spunk. Dot, in hysterics, pulled me closer. I had a sudden desire to kiss her. We were hidden enough from Saul, he wouldn't, couldn't see, ten, twenty rows behind us. But still I sensed his gaze. The lead singer leapt from the stage, mike and cable and plastic cock, all in air. All hands reached to take his weight. He screamed into the microphone, — 'I'M A KILLING MACHINE!' Dot reached to touch his skin as the hands passed his body back to the stage. — I HAVE TO. HAVE TO. That was it . . . Dot had to – she kept shouting. — WHA? WHA? The next track had started. Chainsaw noise cutting through. Explosions. We were right next to the speaker. — PICK ME UP! she shouted, elbowing enough free room to show me with her hands – I had to throw her. I had never staged-dived in my life. Something about her camera, she was shouting. I had to take her camera, for safety. To throw her. I worried she'd get hurt. Kept trying to tell her.

She pulled away, smiling devilishly, gave me a little play-wave, shouted, — BYE! Grabbed my shoulders and hoisted herself up. Other hands took her then, lifted her from me, in the air, threw her, she flew.

I watch. She lands, stands on the stage, at first looks scared. The band are too stoned to care. A security man runs towards her. Hands of fifty men reach for her before she falls back. She looks out and then, mid-fall, closes her eyes, spreads her arms Jesus on cross and falls, forward. I rush to catch her. Many hands have her, feet past me, away from me. Fighting through to get to her. Floating on hands, greedy male fingers fondling her, a hundred, carrying her away to the back. I fought through. She landed feet first, catlike, hugged a man in leather. She threw her arms around me and grabbed my hair, smearing her lips across my face in an urgent embrace. Her tongue was in my mouth and my fingers found the flesh of her waist, our tongues circling dancing around each other, gasping, breathing through each other's mouths in that wet, desperate kiss that went on and on as the lights flashed and my sex pounded and the music rose and our pelvises ground together.

Suddenly I had a dreadful sense that Saul had seen us. I separated from her and we looked into each other's eyes, as if to say, yes, that was real, yes, it happened. She stroked my cheek, then, eyes huge and dark, smiled. I turned back to where Saul had been standing but could not find him. Flashing elbows and heads were blocking my view of our table. I worried he'd maybe left in a fury of jealousy.

– GONE! I shouted to her.

– FUCK'IM. C'MON, and she pulled me back into the throng. — AGAIN, she kept shouting. — AGAIN. She wanted me to film her.

Through the lens the footage was like some form of rebirth, Hindu or Muslim or Aztec or something, some festival of sacrifice, the many hands reaching for her as she flew on fingertips.

Again, she landed, finding her feet in hysterics, just beside me. She shouted it was my turn. Covered me in kisses. Her sweat, wet on my cheek, armpits weeping sex, I shuddered. — YOU, YOU, she shouted, laugh as wide as the fucking sky, and threw me forward, not up. Off balance, hands picked me, arms, arse, then threw. I had a terrible fear of falling and reached to grab – anything. My fingers found metal. I clung, did not fall. Closed my eyes. Still had not fallen. Metal, warm, buzzing flying dream. I opened my eyes and was clinging to the lighting rig. Dot ten feet below, laughing at me, motioning for me to come down. I hung there, for maybe two more songs, too afraid to let go. The hanging man. I had the feeling I'd some day become an anecdote – 'Remember the dork that hung from the lighting rig in '92.' I let go and fell onto the stage. The bouncers threw me back into the sweating mass. Dot was laughing mad as she and others caught me. She held me tight and led me to the back. To safety – to search again for Saul.

We found the empty table with the stolen drinks. A sense of dread seemed to come over us both. We ran a few steps, to the seats further into the dark, and let go of each other's hands. There were only goths, predictably, lurking in the shadows.

She ran down the drink-spilled stairs and out, and there in the changing red–green lights of the taxi rank we found his dark profile.

— What's up? You been out here long? I asked.

He shrugged and sucked on his fag, eyeing me suspiciously.

Dot was raving, trying to explain – the mosh pit – violent communal sexual – constant state of – animal-like – diving – how the music – touch of strangers – won't let you fall – like how jumping is – like how she could weep.

Saul looked us up and down and I trembled waiting for his judgement on the kiss he must have seen. He blew smoke in my face.

— A night in with cocoa and slippers would have been more radical, he said. There's nothing more dull than people trying to be shocking.

So he had seen nothing. I breathed again. As we rode the taxi back home that night I learned something about Saul. He often put down what he envied most in others. Enthusiasm he called naivety, but he was utterly lacking in that spontaneity that emanated from Dot, that infected me, that could energise an entire crowd. The truth was, for all

124

his advocating of 'the leap of faith' he would have been afraid to jump into a puddle.

Back home Dot and I watched the night's recording together in her room. I accidentally hit the slo-mo button and the sound went off. She said, — Wait, don't fix it! The images moved so gently, all the lights pulsing, not flashing. The hands in the air, waiting, reaching up. She turned down the colour, made it black and white. A hundred hands in the air waiting for the body to land, it seemed to take forever, there was some fuzz. I messed around with the cables at the back to try to get a better picture and she was shouting, — YES, YES. By accident the picture had gone into negative. It took ages to get it to stay like that. With some Band-Aids we got the cables in place. Slow and negative. And as we watched it again and again, our kiss resumed, our tongues circling round and round as, on-screen, her body fell endlessly through space.

It would not happen again, I told myself. It had just been drunkenness or adrenalin. But still, her lips haunted me those next long nights. It was as if I could still taste her. I refused to brush my teeth. Hope is for the hopeless, Saul once said.

I'd been shaken by Dot's news. She'd taken the tape to Goldsmiths and played it to peers and tutors. Laughing, she recounted what they'd said, as she presented Saul and me with a celebratory bottle of Croft Original.

— 'Beautiful – reminiscent of religious renaissance art.' 'Of Warhol.'

The tutors had asked to see more works of this nature and stature for Dot's graduation show. All these accolades and enthusiasm were barely believable. It took a while to grasp exactly what had happened; when she got wound up like that she always stopped mid-sentence.

— And Pierce, well, I think that's his second name,

they call him Pierce, he was there too and he loved the tape, anyway he wants it, he's not a gallery owner, more like, I think he's a sculptor, cos it's like a proper group show, kind of anarchist, and it's called *Bug*, I don't know why, in this biscuit factory, warehouse thingy, off Old Street I think, and Hirst and Tracey and . . . you know like City Racing . . .

I could see Saul gritting his teeth through his forced smile.

– . . . And there's no electricity or fire escapes. Isn't that cool? . . . And Saatchi was at the last one . . . the one in the meat factory . . . bought nearly everything, and the Chapmans and Sarah Lucas and . . . and I told them all about the Duchess, all your stories, Sozzle, and Pierce wants you too, he does, he wants you to make a big wall of words . . . and maybe a big essay too . . . and words for the flyers and he's dying to meet you – isn't it awesome? You're such a genius, Sozzle. If it wasn't for you, you grumpy old bugger, making me stop painting and Edna and all the cocks then . . . I mean, all I did was turn on the camera . . . no, it wasn't even me . . . this is all your art really . . . and you too, O. Aren't you both chuffed?

For sure, the show could have been the start of some success for Saul; finally, the gems he'd been polishing for years in the dark could see the light of day. I hoped he would see that. Dot tried to hug him, but he shrugged away, groaning: — Hmmph. It's all just inverted Thatcherism, the artists are in the pay of estate agents. Mark my words, it'll be Greenwich Village all over again. I hope the entire building collapses under the weight of everyone's pretentiousness!

He retreated to his room, grabbing the bottle on the way. I had a sense of portentous doom about it all. Dot was upset and I stayed by her side calming her for half an hour, giving her words of encouragement and praise.

Dot went to the bathroom to wash her face and I was left alone on her bed. Suddenly she screamed. I ran through and Saul was passed out on the floor by his bed. The entire bottle empty on the floor beside him. Dot was in a panic as I dragged him to the toilet.

— I'm calling an ambulance, Dot whimpered. — Ohmigod, the Croft Original!

I shouted at her to be calm and held his hair from his face as he puked in the toilet. He vomited everywhere in mewing spasms in my arms as I tried to remove his soiled clothes. He tried to slap me, yelling out, — Unhand me, you faggot!

As I got him scrubbed down and re-dressed into underpants, I saw the genius of his passivity. In making himself ill he had found a way to make himself the centre of attention again. And what was he puking other than his jealousy? The promise of her imminent success had made him sick and he wanted to bring her down to his level. He would make himself sick and sicker, force her to abandon her career to become his femme de ménage. Such clever devices he had.

She sat by his bed that night, the kitchen bowl by his pillow, stroking his head, gently cooing at him, singing him a lullaby. I told myself that this time he would not win with the power of his weakness. I would be strong and conquer. Her kiss had given me strength.

three

Name Game 3. 2004. Three-screen video loop installation. 20 mins. Variable dimensions. Tobias Lomax Collection

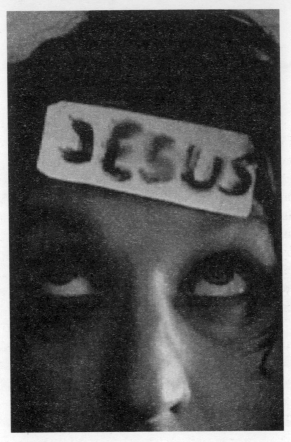

Name Game. 1993. Video still from video loop installation. 18 mins. Variable dimensions. Private collection.

THE WORK COMPRISES three large video-projection screens placed equidistant in a triangular formation. On each is a different person's face (a man and a woman, both early twenties and another man, older). On each head is stuck a piece of paper and on each paper a name has been written. Each name is taken from popular culture and each 'player' does not know the name on their own head, as it has been stuck there by one of the other players without them disclosing the name. The object of the 'game' is for each person to guess what their head-name is through asking questions about who they 'are', which can only be answered with a 'yes' or 'no', such as 'Am I a man?', 'Am I a politician?', 'Am I alive?' The first person to guess who they 'are' is the 'winner'. The game is taken from a popular 'stoner' game.[1] And so again we see the use of the three key elements in Shears's work: play, trust, swapping.

The footage has been shot with three separate tripod-mounted cameras 'in sync' with each other, and in playback gives the impression that the people on-screen are talking to each other.[2] The audio is played back in the gallery in 'synchronised surround sound', which serves to heighten the sense of a real-time event. As such it evokes other technically ambitious works by artists such as Barbara Kruger.[3]

A popular interpretation of this filmed 'game' is that it critiques the influence of media culture on the postmodern subject:

'We are all, almost literally, walking round with names inscribed on our skins. Who I am, maybe a little bit of Bob

*Dylan, plus some Marlon Brando and a little of Germaine
Greer. We consume these cultural identities but in turn they
consume us and constitute the parameters of the roles we
are permitted to play. It is no trivial question to ask – am I
an actor?'*[4]

Appraisal within the post-feminist tradition has
addressed the radicality of the gender reversal within the
'game' – that the female player has a man's name and one
of the male players the name of an iconic female star. Since
devised by a woman, they claim, the 'game' could not be
more serious.

*'Shears deconstructs the notion of fixed gender and
reveals it as a game with power.'*[5]

Further to this, Kate Colliers has claimed that since in
Shears's 'games' we are never shown a 'winner', the focus
is on celebrating the act of shared play and is, as such,
a defiant feminist stance against the male discourse of
conquest.

Reactions from the tabloid newspapers have been
(predictably) extreme due to the high profile of the piece
and go beyond the usual 'this isn't art' controversies.[6]

What many commentators fail to notice, however, is
the subtle humour of the work. Unlike comparable works
(Kruger et al.), which explore the politics of identity, the
effect of Shears's *Name Game 3* is tragicomic – with each
player on-screen growing increasingly exasperated as they
try to find out who they are. Am I a porno star? Did I ever
take drugs? Did I die young? While these may be philosoph-
ical or cultural questions, we must guard against taking the
'game' too seriously. In choosing to show this material in a
gallery, Shears may be poking fun at the pretentious tone of
art discourse, playing a clever double bluff. She has described
the work as 'a joke'.

The reason why the humour is missed may be a result
of the fact that *Name Game 3* is a re-creation, the second

in fact, of an original work from 1993. In comparing the original *Name Game* to *Name Game 3*, the former has the feel of an almost accidental moment between real people, while the latter is staged with actors and scripted dialogue. In *3* the tension between the faces on the screens is less than that in the 'original'. Also, the erratic hand-held movement in the first *Name Game* (with the camera being shared between the three participants) is missing in *3*. Furthermore, Shears herself is missing from *3* (replaced by the actress Glenda Matheson), whereas she was one of the players in the original. All these factors conspire to make *3* a colder, more detached work. It has been said that as Shears's status has increased and her works have become more epic in scale and construction, the 'humour' and the 'heart' have diminished proportionally.

'It has the air of a staged homage to a lost moment. The three screens are like a mausoleum. It lacks the simple spontaneity of that work from her incredible outpouring in the first few years in which her iconic artworks were born.'[7]

Certainly works like *Name Game 3* require expensive multi-screens, hi-tech high-luminance video projectors, synchronised video, feature-film budgets and professional film crews, and as such the intimacy of the earlier 'amateur' work is lost. Other criticisms levelled at Shears's 're-creations' have been extreme, almost as if fans of her earlier works have felt betrayed:

'It strikes me that the artist has attempted to merely repeat the success of those early works by formula. Trust, Walking Blind, Name Game and PlayBoy have all been remade, exposing the fact that no new ideas have been generated in the last ten years . . . It is a great shame to have to witness an artist selling out and rehashing her work just to make sales.'[8]

In Shears's defence, it must be said that, through her

remakes, she has forced us to see how the meaning around an artwork can change over time. The cult of celebrity and global culture has since '93 expanded to such a degree that, by simply repeating the 'same' work, Shears has shown us how our attitudes to celebrity culture have changed.[9] Whereas the original *Name Game* may have seemed a more 'radical' critique of consumerist values, *Name Game 3* exists in a time in which the sociopolitical forms of opposition to consumerism are in crisis. As such, criticisms of *Name Game 3* as 'empty spectacle', 'a sell-out', etc., are really just criticisms of the culture as a whole. The work itself may be a staging of a question that the artist wants to ask herself: in this media-saturated culture, against these images of success which surround me and of which my face has become a part – who am I really?

1. The game is also known as the Rizla Game after the popular brand of British cigarette papers, commonly used for smoking cannabis.
2. A complex technical achievement in collaboration with Sony.
3. Barbara Kruger made a similar work in 2001 with four synchronised screens and 'deliberately wooden acting'.
4. J. Kelly, *'Massage ou Mensonge?'* in *Oeuvres IV*, Gallimard, 2001.
5. K. Colliers, *Gender Fucking!* Semiotext(e), 1996.
6. As part of the 2005 Turner Prize nomination show. The *Sun* ran a headline: 'DOPEY ART – TURNER GIRL GETS HIGH'.
7. T. Schwartz, 'YBA in memoriam', *Sunday Times*, 12 August 2007.
8. M. Cartier, *From Counterculture to Counter Culture*, Chatto & Windus, 2003.
9. A notable difference in attitudes to celebrity in the last decade is what has been called the 'democratisation of success' – the claim being that stars were formerly 'above us' but that through mass television spectacles such as *Big Brother*, celebrities have become 'real people', 'just like you and me.' Counter-criticism to this highlights the fact that these mass cultural forms are sadistic in their viewing pleasure, creating new celebrities only

to shoot them down, that this is in fact turning celebrity status into something 'disposable' not 'democratic', and Warhol's fifteen minutes of fame have turned into fifteen seconds. Ironically, Shears has, through commenting on this, sustained her career for fifteen years.

A SUDDEN MOVEMENT woke him in fright. From the bottom of the bed frame two eyes stared at him, huge, the very image of Dot's. As he tried to focus, the eyes joined a tiny body that ran laughing from the room. He nudged Dot.

'Shit! I think . . . Molly just . . .'

She moaned and pulled the duvet around herself, exposing his every-morning erection. He fought the duvet back and tried to cover himself, searching for his pants and trousers on the floor only to find the used condoms. The voice of the South American nanny from down the hall. *'Bambino, silencio. Mama dormi.'*

This had been the third time he had slept over with her and although he had said he wanted to meet her child, he'd been postponing.

He pulled the duvet from Dot and she was flailing for it, grumpy, trying to hide the light from her face and cover her naked body all at once. He felt a fool, standing wrapped in her duvet, as he hopped about trying to pull his trousers on underneath the thing, then falling on his arse and cracking his head against the wardrobe. As if on cue, the child ran back in with arms full of paper and pens shouting, 'Mummy, Mummy, wake up!'

'Molly,' he should say. 'Hello, Molly.'

He shot Dot a glance. She sleepily extended her arms to the child and brought her to her naked breast. This was wrong, all wrong.

'Mummy, I wanna do a picture, wake up, wake up!'

Owen got his trousers on and turned his back as he pulled on his T-shirt. The child was giggling at him.

'Mmmmm, baby,' Dot muttered, 'you OK . . . ? This is Owen, he's . . . say hello to Molly, Owen.'

Owen raised an embarrassed hand – 'Hi, Molly' – then reached and stuffed the condoms into his pocket. 'Eh, look,' he said to Dot. 'I really should go.'

Dot protested, and even asked him to come onto the bed with her and do some art with Molly. Her nipples brushing the child's cheek, Dot enfolding the child in her naked legs, and covering her four-year-old head in kisses. It was not right. Not right at all. He said they'd speak soon and left them in the midst of the child's screaming for her mother's attention over the sound of his many awkward goodbyes.

He was caught at the door by the nanny who shot him a recriminatory glance.

'See you . . . soon,' he called back through to Dot.

Outside he chastised himself for not having given her a day and time for their next meeting.

In the following week Dot was away in New York taking part in the anthology show on the history of video art. He'd got three emails from her. They all talked of art, of Nam June Paik and Douglas Gordon, and of the stress, and how she was sick of it, dragging Molly round the world and Molly couldn't handle jet lag and it must be the reason why she was such a brat and was unable to focus on anything. And how she needed to change everything or give up art or get married or hire a slave or . . .

None of the messages mentioned their nights together.

So he had called some fuck-buddies.

But with Sue he'd been barely able to maintain the pretence of post-coital conversation. And with Sharon he'd fallen into a funk after the act and asked if it was OK if she left so he could sleep alone. On the second failed attempt with Toni she'd laughed and said: 'So, what's her name?'

Michele had got up halfway through and shouted at him because she just knew he was thinking of someone else. So that was it. Funny as it seemed. What was most offensive to the world of infinite interchangeable bodies was the secret whisperings of love.

Over two weeks since she left and she must have been back in London, but she had not called and he was losing sleep and had to cancel a few pieces of journalism. To be lovesick this late in life.

Maybe this was her revenge. To appear enigmatically then leave again. Like that call from Saul in the night. To make him break the resolution he thought he'd reached, to make him spin out the anxieties for another fifteen years.

Four days of the sickness and then the phone rang. The number was withheld. He knew in his bones that it was Saul. If the number had been there he'd have had it barred. He picked up to tell the man to leave him alone, but it was Dot.

'Owen, thank God, look, I just got in, I'm in a cab, Consuela didn't meet us at the airport, it's a real mess, look, sorry about this but, I've got to be up early tomorrow at the studio to take a call about Zurich, so it would be much easier to crash at yours, me and Moll, would that be too weird? I'm going to have to get another nanny. I've got some duty-frees, would that be OK?

So then Dot was on his doorstep with her grumpy bleary-eyed child in hand. He struggled with the springs and metal of the sofa bed in the living room. He suddenly felt he was being watched. The child was in the doorway in Hello Kitty pyjamas, holding an in-flight toothbrush bag.

'Hello again, Molly,' he said and gave her a little wave.

'Mommy says Kurtie killed himself.' She had an endearing mid-Atlantic posh accent. 'But I think all the other singers murdered him cos they were jealous.'

'Sorry?' He really had no idea what she was talking about.

'Nirvana!' the kid said, stomping her foot.

'Oh, OK. Really, so your mum lets you listen to grunge?' She stared at him.

'You're weird,' she said. 'But that's OK. I'm weird too,' and pootled back down the hall to her mother.

He was bewildered.

Later, he waited alone in his study as Dot read her child a bedtime story.

'"Lady Frogspawn was so tired of being a horse."'

Every word random. Totally bewildered.

That night Dot fell asleep before any explanations were forthcoming. As he held her while she slept, he thought of how it had always been like this with her. Huge life-changing events happened with no discussion or plan. Sentences started up from nowhere and were left unended. Lady Frogspawn and Kurtie. Weird, yes, but I'm weird too, he thought.

It started with contact lens solution, then deodorant, then her toothbrush and woolly slipper-socks; her copy of Plath's unabridged journals that she left by his bedside, that she never seemed to get more than a page or two into before reaching for a kiss or falling asleep, that he sometimes had to prise from her comatose fingers. And her toothbrush lying next to his, his examining of the bristles, the little traces of blood because she brushed too vigorously. That week she'd bought a second toothbrush for Molly and it was there in his sink cabinet. A small investment in their future. It made him laugh. Her hairs in the shower drain; her little Post-it notes to herself, stuck on whatever object was at hand, when-ever a brilliant new idea came to her, that said cryptic things like: TRY VIDEO FEEDBACK and THREE PEOPLE IN A ROOM and MILK THISTLE DETOX.

As he went about his day, finding her hairs everywhere, on his keyboard, on the coffee cup that had been his favourite before she claimed it as her own; the lipstick kiss on the rim of her wine glass; the smell of her perfume in his bed; the subtle scent of her sex on their sheets, it became increasingly absurd to him, this pretence that they were 'just seeing each other'.

There was much talk of the difficulty of selling her flat in the recession and maybe renting it or redecorating it first and of the search, always, for the new perfect place to live, and how sweet he was to be helping her out. And it was crazy that Molly was in nursery in Notting Hill and not somewhere nearer London Bridge because it meant Dot was leaving her home an hour earlier to commute then leaving her studio an hour earlier just to pick Molly up.

'What am I fucking doing?' she said on the phone just yesterday. 'Putting in four hours' work a day and spending the rest of my time running from –'

'Tube to tube.'

'Exactly,' she said. 'I knew you'd . . .'

Yes, he understood, but did she, as to where this was headed? Her impromptu flustered calls brought a sense of expectation to his days. Would she call around four, or earlier? What would her excuse be this time?

'God, I just can't face cooking tonight!'

Or 'Molly's got toothache and we're stuck here in the studio.'

Or 'I've got to do a radio interview at 6.30 a.m. It'd be easier to crash at yours.' Or any of the many excuses that always ended with the same line unspoken. So Owen would find himself saying it for her: 'Fine, just pop over then.'

After their first month had passed, the time of day when she called got earlier and earlier and the pretence that she was just popping round on a whim became increasingly, endearingly, transparent.

He slept at Dot's twice a week and she slept over three or four times at his. Leaving them just a day or two apart, the hours of which were usually spent on the phone to each other. And, absurd, on the days that he slept over at hers, that they'd both have to take the ten stops on the congested Central Line back to Bank, for her to change to go south to her studio which was only, actually, four stops from his flat.

Her aromatherapy night oils, three now, in their bottles by his beside: lavender, thyme and bergamot. And their little spills that had started seeping into the covers of his books. Yes, they were putting on a brave show. Both thriving on the thrilling denial of facing where this was ultimately heading.

And he had committed to writing the essays on the *Nine Works*. There were deadlines now, six weeks till Zurich, and much work to be done, writing about her art with the required objectivity, to be her critic, to make an historical appraisal. The DVDs stacked and ready to watch. A month, it would take.

On their late nights, after a typical dinner of pesto and pasta and Molly put to bed in the spare room, settling down on the sofa with a bottle of Rioja and a movie, he'd find himself stealing glances at her.

They were sitting watching TV in his lounge and her hands sat face down in her lap. Those wrists she always hid from him, the silver scars he knew were there and would have longed to have kissed.

The hands, impassive, looking as if she did not know how perfectly proportioned they were. Just tools for her, two objects she threw in the air when ranting. The way her thighs had filled out so slightly, womanly, that tiny bulge round the top of her jeans, her top, her breasts, braless, as always, beneath, the tiny points of her nipples that made him recall the sucking, the hardening between his fingers. Her long, long neck and the way she rubbed it sometimes as if trying to reconnect her head to her body. The taut tight skin of her cheekbones, ankles, neck, the tiny creases that spoke of survival. And how she tucked her feet under her thighs when on the sofa, the way those long slender feet would brush his leg and she would say 'Sorry', pulling herself into herself. The endearing clumsiness of her every move: she would have laughed at if he ever told her. The way her fingers played with her now long hair, as if remembering how close she'd once shaved it, almost to the skull. The way she would sometimes catch him staring and laugh to herself, and just as he was about to tell her how beautiful she was she would kick him gently with that slender foot and laugh.

'Stop it!'

She had just caught him again. She did not kick, but spoke.

'But you know . . . I don't want to get into a . . .'

The game of second-guesses.

'. . . a long-term thing again?'

'God, yeah, it's so fucking . . .'

'. . . stifling?'

'Yeah, yeah yeah . . . so glad you agree.'

These lines they swapped, taking each other's. Dot sometimes finishing Owen's for him. To remind and caution each other. The words that would stop abruptly as the eyes looked to lips and eyes closed and lips were found. This shared sense that they were doing something dangerous, forbidden. She would break away then and say: 'I'll never do the . . .'

'God, me too. I mean, what does it mean, this . . . ?'

'. . . falling in . . . ?'

'Exactly . . . sounds like . . .'

'. . . like someone's bound to get hurt.'

And in bed she whispered that this was all wrong, that she was not going to be weak again, as she stroked his cock and made it ready, as she climbed onto him and moaned as he entered her, whispering sorry, sorry, yes, yes.

Then it was Molly's Hello Kitty toys and her grizzly bear, and a few extra nightshirts and first one then two then five of Molly's favourite bedtime books, and Owen had found himself online, shopping for Hello Kitty child-sized duvet covers. And all the time, neither of them said anything about the accumulating shared possessions, the little credit-card spendings that were starting to mount up to an investment.

Saul.

On the day that Dot had brought round Molly's inflatable bouncy castle Owen found himself thinking of Saul. There had been maybe three late-night phone calls in that last month. He had turned the ringer off and stared at the flashing light, willing it away. BT informed him that they could only bar a known number, not a withheld one. He'd been developing this paranoia that somehow, impossibly, Saul knew everything and wanted to destroy it. A shadow had been following him on the street. Every time he turned to look there were only strangers with shopping bags. On the nights Dot slept over, he pulled the phone from the wall socket, discreetly.

'Man is one and woman is his negative. History has made her so,' Saul had once said. 'One plus minus-one equals nothing.'

Midway through the ridiculous exertions of pumping up the castle, he found himself saying words to her he'd promised he would never say again.

'Look, this is crazy, why don't you just move in?'

'I . . . I couldn't . . .'

'Seriously, what the fuck am I doing rattling around here by myself . . . C'mon. At least till you find your new place. It'd give you a chance to get Notting Hill cleared up for selling too. You bring enough stuff here for a month, pack the rest and . . . it's not like I'm . . .'

'I know, but it'd be . . .'

A line from Saul flashed through his mind.

'. . . impossible.'

The smile on her face seemed to acknowledge it. Owen finished the line off, to claim it as his own.

'In the era of the predictable, the only thing left to live for is the impossible!'

OK, she said, but it wasn't like she was moving in. Just temporary. They'd see how it went. She'd be off to Zurich in a month and she'd have to have a new artwork come up with, and maybe being so close together would help and she'd finally get a good idea and no more time wasting, cos really he had to make a start on the text for the catalogue. And God, she really had to get with the apartment searching. There were three new potential warehouse places, one in Bethnal Green that looked ideal, he could come and see what he thought, help with the estate whatnots, if he wanted.

The next day he took time off and hired a van and was round at Dot's old place packing things into crates, constantly reaffirming that she'd soon have her new place, just in case. Molly threw tantrums and wanted to take all of her teddies then wanted nothing but to stay. He concerned himself with packing the laptop and DVDs, books and CDs, while Dot threw armfuls of clothes randomly into her travel bags. Six boxes, seven cases and eight hours later Dot and Molly had moved in.

Owen really couldn't believe she had said yes.

Just temporarily of course.

*

TRANSCRIPTION FROM VIDEO FOOTAGE

Harsh top light. 3 people. 3 names.

Saul Metcalf (S) has JESUS written on the Rizla on his head.
Dorothy Shears (D) has SID VICIOUS written on her head.
Owen Morgan (O) has MARILYN MONROE written on his head.

D: OK, am I alive or dead?
O: Yes/No answers please! Like – you say 'Am I dead?'
D: OK, am I?

S: Yes, you are.

Laughter, the camera moves to focus on S.

S: This is dumb.

S touches the paper on his head that reads JESUS.

O: Don't take it off!

S: OK, OK. Fuck . . . am I a film star?

Laughter.

D: No!

O: Nope, sorry.

The camera moves to focus on O.

O: OK, am I a cartoon character?

S: This is so fucking –

D: Shh. No, you're a real person.

The camera moves to D. Exchange of spliff. A drink poured. D drinks.

D: OK, am I a lovely person?

Laughter.

O: Come on, he wasn't so bad! He was just pretending.

D: Aha! So I'm a man!

Off-camera dispute between O and S as to whether O had given away a clue. The camera is passed to focus on S.

S: Am I a writer?

Laughter. S again touches the paper on his head that reads JESUS.

O: No, sorry.

D: Well, there is one book, you kind of inspired it.

O: Stop giving him clues.

Laughter. The camera is passed to focus on O. He stares upwards, comic moment when he flicks his hair back, momentarily obscuring the name MARILYN MONROE.

O: OK, am I a man?

S: I sometimes wonder.

D: Shh, you bitch. No, no, my dear, you are the perfection of all womankind, in a kind of fucked-up way.

Laughter. The spliff is passed; camera is passed to focus on D.

D: OK, so I'm . . . dead, I'm a horrible person and a man.

She raises her eyes upwards. SID VICIOUS on her forehead.

D: OK, did I . . . kill people?

O: No, no, only yourself.

S: Bollocks. Your girlfriend too.

D: No way.

O: Nah, it was an overdose.

S: With a fucking gun!

D: My God, who wrote this on me?

Laughter. The camera passes to focus on S.

S: OK, am I an artist?

O: No.

D: No, no, but . . . you've got your head in the clouds, my dear.

S drinks, smokes. Laughter off-camera. The camera is passed to focus on O.

O: I'm a woman . . . am I . . . sexy?

S: Oh, how trite!

D: Oh yes, very.

S: I never thought so.

O: So am I dead?

D: One question at a time, darling.

O: I just know I'm dead, I always end up dead, why are we all dead?

D: Shhh! Don't tell him.

S: Aha, so I am.

D: Shh, he didn't know he was dead!

O: Well, he's not really, I mean God, sorry, some people still believe in him, millions in fact. Mostly Americans.

D: Shhhh!

Laughter. The camera is passed to focus on S.

S: I couldn't give a shit.

D: Don't spoil it, c'mon. Play the game.

S smokes.

D: OK, you're . . . not a writer, not a film star and there's some debate over whether you're dead.

S: Thanks a bunch.

D: Why do you have to take everything so personally?

O: Comrades, pleeez!

S drinks.

S: OK, did I kill myself?

D: No!

Laughter.

O: You just sort of vanished, and then you came back and
  then you went away again.

*Laughter. S tries to stand. Hand of D restrains him. Off-mike
whispers – encouragements to stay. The camera moves to D.*

D: Is it my turn?

O: We're getting kind of . . . I dunno . . . morbid or –

D: No, it's you.

S: Fuck sake.

D: Your go again, anyway, whatever.

O: OK, I'm sexy, I'm a woman, I'm dead . . . Am I . . . Janis
  Joplin?

S: She's not sexy.

D: She is *soooo* sexy. You don't know what sex is.

Silence. The camera gets passed to focus on D.

D: So I killed my girlfriend and I'm a guy?

S: Yeah.

Silence.

D: Am I Ted Hughes?

S: Oh puh-leez! What is this? The feminist half-hour?

Silence.

S: This is so adolescent.

**THE FOLLOWING FOOTAGE WAS DELETED FROM THE
COMPLETED ARTWORK.**

S gets up, the camera remains on D.

D: Is he OK?

O: He'll be back. Just keep on playing.

A moment, then the camera is dropped. Sounds of D and

O kissing. Camera films the floor: an empty vodka bottle, a Pot Noodle carton full of cigarette butts.

O: Stop, he'll see us.

D: I don't care, you're so serious and sexy-looking.

O: Shhh, we have to keep playing.

The camera is lifted again. D laughing. Putting on a serious face.

D: OK, am I –

O: Isn't it my turn?

D: Sorry. You think he's all right?

The camera is swapped, focusing on O.

O: He'll be off doing some fire and brimstone or taking a shit. He'll be fine.

Laughter.

O: OK, I'm dead and I'm sexy.

D: Dead sexy.

Laughter.

O: Did I kill myself?

D: My God, we've all asked that!

O: Suicide or?

D: I think it was an accident.

Silence. The camera swaps.

O: Your turn.

D looks out of frame, over her shoulder.

D: Am I . . . sorry, I can't really . . . this doesn't really work with just two, it's like . . .

O: Interrogation?

D: Parents, I was thinking parents.

S re-enters frame.

S: OK, my turn.

D: OK, great, you OK?

S: Let's get this done.

The camera shifts hands to focus on S. S lights a cigarette butt.

S: OK, so I'm dead and no one believes in me.

D: I do . . . sometimes.

S: Yeah yeah yeah. OK, am I Jesus?

Laughter.

D: *Yes, yes!*

O: Cheat.

S: What?

O: You went to the bathroom and saw it in the mirror.

S: Fuck you, any stupid fucking kid could have guessed. If you must know it came to me while defecating.

O: Cheat! Can't we just play a simple fucking –

D: Boys! *Pleez.*

S: I just want to know which one of you wrote it.

Silence.

S: You think you're so fucking funny.

O: Oh and what about you writing Sid Vicious on her head, that wasn't exactly –

D: Am I Sid Vicious?

D takes the name from her head, laughs. O takes the name from his head.

O: Marilyn Monroe, what? You trying to tell me I'm queer?

D: No . . . Boys! Please! I wrote it, it was just a –

O: This is so –

D: I'm turning the camera off now. Just a game, Jesus.

*

The new year brought the collapse of Bush's New World Order and Bill Clinton had been elected promising radical change, but I cared little for political ethics. I had gone over to the other side and become an agent of deceit. Not a moment passed without my trying to concoct schemes to have Dot in my arms, behind Saul's back. They had been fighting regularly and I sensed he was onto us so redoubled my guard.

Adultery ideally should happen when one's partner is

away, in a hotel room, in a stranger's apartment, not within the confines of such a tiny flat where all is heard and felt through the thin partitions. Every inch of that stinking flat became a possible trap for me then. I gauged angles of doors and perspectives along the corridor to judge if Saul could see Dot and me together, I estimated how much light seeped into the kitchen and if there was enough darkness in there for us to hide our stolen kisses, which had been many and, although very brief, still intense. The flat was L-shaped and my room was in the middle, their two rooms being at the other extremities, so I was perfectly placed for spying on him to work out when the coast was clear.

I was washing her panties in the bathroom. No, that's not entirely true – let us say, I was in the bath with her panties when suddenly there was a tiny knock at the door.

— Is it you? I whispered.

— Let me in.

I hastily threw the wet panties behind the cistern, stood, then did my best to conceal my erection with the tea towel, it being the only towel we had (and gingham if I recall). I thought, surely the time had come for us to move to the next stage, possibly even consummate our love, but I was overcome with shyness as she squeezed her way inside, in her T-shirt and panties.

— Did you sneak away? Is he sleeping? I asked, anxiously. She giggled and sat on the edge of the bath. I wanted to hold her but was anxious that the tea towel might fall, or worse still, be left free-standing on my erection, as if it were a towel rack.

— He'll be so jealous, she said. — Shh, secret. I had thought the secrecy was about the act I hoped we were about to perform, but she was talking about the art she wanted us to both make.

I sat on the edge of the bath and crossed my legs trying to hide my throbbing affliction while she, surprisingly

150

oblivious to nudity, ranted and raved, her hands drawing pictures in the air. It came to her in a dream she said.

— I'm going to walk backwards with my eyes closed, like the stage-diving, yeah, like this game I used to play in therapy, you walk backwards, like a hundred yards, and they catch you at the end, you know . . . of the room, but this time, I want to do it on the street, and you're going to catch me. And I'm going to film my face walking backwards and you can't let me open my eyes . . . on the street or in the supermarket, like a sleepwalker . . . or . . .

She described it in great detail and it amazed me that she had paid so little attention to the reality of our location, my condition and the fact that Saul could walk in on us at any moment. I pulled the bath plug out and the water started gurgling, rather too loudly. I said the walking blind thing was a brilliant idea but proposed that maybe we should wait till another day because it was 3 a.m. and the clubs would be coming out and the drunks may not have as great a grasp of aesthetics.

— You're so sweet, she said and smiled as she finally came out of her dream state and noticed the tea towel over my crotch. She stroked my cheek and kissed me. I could hear myself moaning as the kiss lingered. She touched my chest, my stomach, my tea towel fell and I gasped. I could not help it. It had no doubt been due to my prepared state of arousal before she'd entered.

– Quick, quick, Saul's come . . . coming . . .

I pushed her swiftly out and tried to hold it in by tightening my muscles. I pinched my foreskin but it was too late. Jism shot all over the Artex wall and gingham as I collapsed with a groan. Thank God, she had not witnessed my weakness, I told myself, and decided that before we could consummate correctly, I'd have to practise solving my duration problem.

*

151

The next morning she ran off in an excited fluster to Goldsmiths, to meet Lucas and Pierce and all her new art chums, to discuss her part in this *Bug* show. No sooner had Dot left than Saul leapt into my room, looking over his shoulder, then out the window checking she wasn't coming back.

— Kitchen! he announced. — I have to speak to you in the strictest confidence. It was absurd, I seemed to be sneaking in and out of rooms with them both, for entirely opposite reasons. As I followed him into the grime and stench, I feared the worst.

— I cannot tolerate this situation a moment longer, he whispered.

I waited for his judgement on my betrayal.

He looked over his shoulder again at the front door.

— OK, if she comes back just pretend we're washing the dishes or something.

At which point he turned on the tap. It blasted back at him, splashing his Victorian cravat and Blonde Ambition T-shirt. He made a play-act of pretending to wash the dishes, even going so far as to pull on the yellow rubber gloves.

— Alone at last, he said finally. – She's incorrigible, like a bitch on heat! You know I can't bear these psychological exertions . . . she's becoming more than a little unhinged . . . *N'est-ce pas*?

I stared at the sight of him repeatedly tapping his temple with the yellow washing glove.

— Well, no, I mean, as you say she's probably just a bit overexcited by your books.

— Dammit, you're right! I should never have told her about the Duchess. God knows, she might be out there tying people up and pissing in their eye sockets.

He stared at the soap bubbles then turned to me.

— I know it's been hard for you to endure, old chum, but I can assure you the game's over, so you needn't be planning on leaving . . . You weren't, were you? I mean, you're not? I couldn't bear to be left alone with her.

I couldn't believe he'd got everything so wrong.

— No, no, I'm going nowhere.

— Nowhere, fantastic! Best place to be, been trying to get there all my life.

And, quite remarkably, he hugged me, splashing bubbles everywhere.

— By the way, I am awfully sorry about all the . . .

I was dumbfounded. He was apologising for the first time and still holding me.

— Sorry, you're sorry about the . . . ?

He quickly withdrew and resumed his pretend washing.

— Look, you have to promise me one thing, OK? You're not to leave me alone with her. OK?

— OK, I suppose.

— Christ Almighty, look lively! he shrieked. — I think she's coming.

As the door creaked open and Dot's smiling face appeared, she must have witnessed a scene of surreal domesticity. Two tramps in the kitchen doing a whistle-while-you work routine.

— Don't worry about us, my dear, Saul said, — just doing a spot of ethnic cleansing.

The coming night, at Saul's behest, I was sat directly between him and Dot on his fungal sofa ('To keep the heated bitch at bay') while we rewatched *The Rizla Game* on telly. After a while he winked at me, as if to say, Shh, don't let her know, we're best off without her. Then within minutes Dot secretly touched my knee and winked, as if to say, Hi, lover boy. I was literally trapped in the middle.

'An excessive tendency towards mediocrity and diplomacy is your failing,' Saul had often said of me, so I decided I had to be decisive and stretched my arm round the back of the sofa to reach for Dot. Our fingers met, her thumb circled mine. Saul jumped up suddenly.

— Ye gads! How now, a rat!

We both jumped, hands separating.

— The bastard, back there!

I pretended to search for the beast behind the sofa. My hands running over dust balls, an old sock, some long-fossilised pasta, many fag ends and what might have been one of Dot's fake moustaches.

— Nothing back here!

— Let me see, Dot said, and soon we were behind the sofa stealing another kiss, tongues circling.

How do you feel towards the one you are betraying? I had started to pity him. If only he knew, every one of his sniping little put-downs over these years was now overruled by the greater truth – 'I have her now and you are a fool, my master.'

But also some small hatred grew. He could not see the anxiety my minute-by-minute performance was causing me. I was lying right to his face and getting away with it, and the world looked none too friendly from that perspective. The cost of getting caught was living in constant fear over the tiniest slip. It was impossible to keep going at that intensity, that degree of attention to detail. That was why people broke down and confessed – not because of guilt or morals – it was simply too exhausting to commit adultery.

That night, Dot waited by my bedroom door. Car headlights outside my window threw her shadow across me. Lit up her eyes.

— Can I come in?

I shook my head. — He's going to find out. We have to pretend like maybe you should give me less attention, spend more time with him, you know, just to throw him off the scent.

She stepped away, her head to the floor and would not turn as I whispered after her.

154

— Dot? No, I didn't mean that. Dot. Dot! Shit!

The very next day I had to endure the hell of my own making as she ignored me almost completely. They were in the kitchen together and she was tickling him as she cooked Heinz Spaghetti. I was livid with jealousy and furious that both he and she could be so fickle in their allegiances. We all sat in his darkened room listening to Nirvana while I had to endure the humiliation of witnessing her pick the spaghetti that dropped from his drunken lips and feed them to his reluctant mouth – like he was a child refusing food, spoiled brat.

He threw spaghetti at her, she threw it back; within seconds the thing had escalated to both of them grabbing handfuls and slinging them.

— Stop it, I screamed, — this will end in tears.

And so it did, with the entire two plates up-ended on the floor and Saul demanding that Dot clean it up and she him. And I was the one who got the pan and brush, while she slammed his door and went back to her room.

— You see, Saul whispered to me, — she's a bloody loony, total liability. Do us a favour and keep her the fuck out of here, would you, there's a chum, I'll roll you a spliff if you do.

When I went to Dot's room she was staring at her floor, streaks of tomato sauce on her hair and cheeks.

— What was that all about? I asked in whisper.

— You . . . ignored . . . me . . . all . . . day.

— Me? You think I . . . Look, we can't do this here, come outside with me.

— Who cares if he hears us? Dot shouted. — Why do we have to sneak about at all?

— Please.

— OK, she said. — Meet me on the stairwell in half an hour.

I paced around anxiously. I did not know if this would be our moment but that day I had bought a packet of condoms

especially, with Sensareeze lubrication – to prolong ejaculation. I heard Dot slip out, put the pack of three in my front
pocket, waited a few minutes, then called out to Saul.

— Just popping out for some fresh air! You coming,
Dorothy? No? OK then, well, I'll see you later, I suppose. I
sounded very am-dram.

I stepped out and the bare walls and piss-smelling
linoleum stared back at me. She was nowhere to be seen.

— Psssst!

I looked up and there she was – up the steps by the
door of the boarded-up first-floor flat. I climbed up and she
kissed me. We were not well enough concealed behind the
metal banister so I tried to work out where we could go to
be alone: the library – no, closed – the subway – no, too
public. The roof of the flat – if there was a ladder – the
disabled public toilets on Old Street, the park, in a bush –
no, not at night, too many gays in there doing their thing
already – our empty warehouse, the back of Dario's Pizzeria,
behind the Portakabin by the jobcentre.

She ran her hand up my inner thigh, felt the bulge in
my jeans, laughed.

— Sorry, I said. It's not what you think, and took the
packet out. She giggled.

— Silly, I'm on the pill.

— Really? But what about . . . well, you know, the
dreaded . . .

There had been that horrific advert at the time with
the iceberg with 'Aids' written on it. The tip of the iceberg
must have been the metaphor.

— You ever had unprotected anal sex or shared a
needle?

I shrugged.

— There's worse things, she said. — My other pill – it
makes babies come out with two heads and no arms and
. . . My dad slammed me on the pill even before I knew

what a cock was, just so I wouldn't make mutants. Bodies are disgusting really. I've always been a bit erratic on the boyfriend front. You know – binge and purge.

— Sorry, binge and . . .?

— Don't worry, I've taken my pill today already. Anyway after my bulimia I think my ovaries gave up. I don't even get proper periods. You can probably spunk gallons into me and nothing'd happen.

Somewhat shocked, I asked if it was OK if we just cuddled.

— Oh, just kiss me, you silly sausage!

She grabbed my face and smothered me in her lips.

At that moment, I heard a noise below. I pulled Dot back from the banister and pushed her down. — Shh! I peered over, trying not to be seen, and watched as below Saul stepped out and looked round furtively. I feared he was searching for us. Dot tried to stand but I held her firmly back. I counted the seconds. In my mind he would climb the stairs and catch us hiding. I glanced over again and Saul was releasing an arc of urine against the steps. Looking around, he tucked himself back in and snuck back into the house.

Dot stood up and started laughing.

— Holy shit, so it's him! I wonder why.

She started walking back down, tiptoeing round the puddle.

— Come on. Why are we hiding anyway? She laughed. — What's the big deal? You think he cares how you feel?

— It's not that simple. Look, if you hadn't started sleeping with him in the first place then –

— You think me and him have been –

I asked her to please, at least, continue this conversation outside. She let me march her through the front door. Round the corner by the jobcentre she was walking ahead of me laughing to herself.

— He hates it when I run off to talk to you or when I

get excited and forget him for just a minute. She squeezed my hand. — He gets horribly jealous.

I really couldn't believe it.

— Him – the king of indifference?

— Oh all that – a bloody sham! He's as insecure as a child, always pawing at me, trying to get his little kisses, God knows why. He has a humungous cock but won't let me touch it. And those noises he makes.

I pretended not to know.

— God, you must hear us, all that screaming and groaning for ages.

— Well, maybe once or twice.

— It's not what you'd think. It's me trying to wrestle him off, and him scratching me, we do this silly play-fighting wrestling stuff, it goes on for half an hour sometimes. He's never really touched me, you know, not in that way. I mean, he just sort of wanks off beneath his kimono as he stares at me and I do the same . . . well, without the kimono of course . . . it's utterly bizarre.

— Really?

— Then he feels guilty and wants his snuggles and then I fight him off, it's this silly game, if I hurt him for real or scratch him too much he goes off in a huff. She pulled up her sleeves, showing scratch marks. Laughing.

— And he's horribly possessive, did you know that? He talks to me all the time in baby language . . . seriously . . . Snooky, he calls me, Snooky-bum, things like that.

— No way, God . . .

— May He rest in peace.

— God, but I thought you two were . . . ?

— God, no, I kind of thought he was like some kind of, I don't know, paternal figure sort of, but no, he's just, we're kind of like twins or something. It's rather sick actually.

— So really . . . I ventured, — do you think he'd mind if we told him we were . . . ?

— That we're . . . ?

I wanted to say 'in love' or 'having sex', but the latter was certainly not true and the former increasingly doubtful.

— You're too, sweet, it's no big deal, and we've done nothing really anyway. Anyway, right now I have to focus on the important thing, she said, — my art.

She walked away, back towards the flat, but then I saw her flash me a smile.

So we tried to focus on art. But beneath that respectable pursuit and behind the back of Saul, stranger perversions grew with art as their alibi. Whether or not Saul suspected our secret couplings at that point, I do not know for sure, but the threat of being caught by him aroused us incredibly.

So it was on a certain day, in Saul's bedroom, that he was reading aloud a chapter from his little book on the Duchess, about an orgy in Manhattan in the twenties, with Duchamp and Man Ray present if I recall, while Dot stood resting her elbows on his desk, so as to support her camera, as she filmed him. I had been sitting on the floor behind her, sorting through records, listening to Saul's voice, amused at how the frigid man loved his naughty book.

— 'She was before me then, whipping the two naked girls beneath her with strings of pearls, while Johnstone smeared her anus in pâté de foie gras. The only thing I could hope to do was to try to exhaust her every urge. Bring her slaves to piss on, money to burn. Anything to save her from herself.'

Perhaps it had been the words, for I had become aroused. From where I was sitting I could look up and see directly up Dot's skirt. I checked round the edge of the desk and Saul could not see me. Just then Dot must have realised that another little game was starting as she readjusted her camera position and put her feet wider apart, thus presenting me with ample opportunity to feast my gaze on her freshly shaven cunt. I lay gazing up at the tight panties pulled between the labia lips, under the tent of her skirt, as she kept on filming. I slowly moved my hand up her inner thigh, feeling her tremble as Saul read on, oblivious to our antics, his voice sounding surreally from the other side of the fabric.

— 'I begged her to vomit on me, to sodomise me with any available object. She inserted the head of the champagne bottle into my torn anus but it gave her no release. Trite bourgeois, she screamed at me, capitalist corpse!'

With my fingers, so slowly, so secretively, I parted the panties from flesh and circled her salivating cunt lips and the mouth of her anus. A shiver ran through her as I teased her tiny clit, and pushed a finger inside her. As the wetness spread over my hand, with my soft movements, I brought it back to my face, feeling the texture of her juice, inhaling its scent, while Saul read on.

— 'I am death, the redeemer, she shouted. Sign a blank cheque for me, open your veins for me.'

I caressed the inside of her thigh, as my thumb fucked her and my forefinger circled her clit. She started shaking and gasping.

Saul paused momentarily in his reading.

— I'm not boring you, am I? I heard him say.

— Nuh, no, no, I'm filming, don't stop! she replied. — Please.

And so Saul went on reading as she went on filming him and although my cock was aching in my trousers and I was close to coming, I denied both her and myself the pleasure of a conclusion, got to my feet and stepped back from her. Dot seemed confused and disappointed, but I stood behind her, looking down at Saul, there, just ten feet away on his bed, raised her skirt and bared her buttocks. Her eyes shot at me to stop, but I did not. There, just feet from him, I stood back to feast on the shocking view: to my right, Saul, sat, as small as a mouse, studious with his spectacles on, reading from his book, while to my left, filling half my vision, was the immense close-up of my fingers sliding in and out of her tight pink lips. His face and her cunt like two obscenely different films running side by side.

We never saw the footage that Dot shot, but I doubt her hand was steady.

My testes were bursting and I knew Dot and I would consummate that very night but we had to wait then till Saul had gone to bed, so as not to arouse his suspicion. To that end, I whispered to her, as I left the room, — Stay here till he's asleep. Come to me before dawn. She did not reply.

In my bed after hours of painful waiting I heard tiptoed footsteps down the hall, past my door, then the bathroom door opening and closing. I tiptoed to the door, put my face to it and whispered, — It's me. Let me in.

A cough from inside. Saul's gruff reply.

— I'm communing with nature, and your request is certainly most unnatural, but if you can't repress your beastly needs, you're more than welcome to join me urinating in the bath, the damned bog's clogged with something again.

I ran back through to my room.

Days went by and each morning she was away before I woke and did not return till late at night. I worried that I had put her off with all my pussyfooting, that she had found me an even greater disappointment than him. All communications from her were about her art and *Bug* – the warehouse – Pierce – Emin – Dinos – videotapes. In her busyness to get everything together for the group show, she seemed to have forgotten of our intrigues. My heart and testicles were aching.

Abandoned, and crazy from frustration, I had taken solace in her panties yet again and had made such a mess of them that they were unwashable, irredeemable. I had some crazy idea that noting the brand and the size (Marks & Spencer, size 10) the colour and shape etc., I could replace them. It should be said that these were not my primary considerations at the time. No, in that week of rejection I had gone back to searching for more work and had even secured an interview with *Riot* magazine in Soho. A place that unfortunately, due to its nature as the sex district, only led me to further ruminations on my problems, my fixation with panties, etc., which then led me to spending an afternoon being interviewed, not by *Riot* magazine but by the Soho police force in a back room of the ladies' lingerie floor of Marks & Spencer. Maybe, subconsciously, I had willed disaster upon myself. The new panties stuffed into my overcoat pocket, I had set the alarm off as I tried to exit. They held me for questioning, asked for my address then sent a cop round to confirm that I was who I said I was, so I had to spend a whole hour alone, locked in, staring at the magnolia walls and packing boxes while I waited for the pigs to return. I made many apologies and promised to reimburse them and had prepared a full confession, which I was thankful for not having let them hear. All of which would have been beyond their limited grasp – of how the situation in the flat and my infatuation with Dot had led me to seek a surrogate.

They let me go with a warning that if any repeat behaviour was reported charges would be brought. My name was noted, they would be watching out for me. I thanked them profusely. When I left I heard them all sniggering.

— Pervert, idiot, betrayer. There were pills everywhere and hash in the ashtray! Police in my home! Double agent! Imbecile. Never darken my door again.

Thus spake Saul as he slammed the door in my face. Dot found it all very amusing and told me not to worry about Saul, he was a drama queen. And a reality check, once in a while, was good, she'd been in jail once for a whole night and she thought me rather cool.

— I had a fascinating chat with the PC. All about Neighbourhood Watch schemes and the understaffing crisis. He was really rather lovely and even let me film him talking.

She took me by the hand and led me to her room and closed the door behind me, a devilish grin on her face.

— So, panties? All you needed to do was ask, she said, chortling.

I could barely face her. She put one hand on my shoulder then balanced on one foot, reached under her leather skirt, then pulled her panties down, bunched them up and handed them to me as a gift.

— Sorry, they might be a bit whiffy. She collapsed in laughter as I sat there humiliated.

— Ah, poor you. I'm sorry. C'mon, let's get out of here.

She led me down Old Street, by the hand, doing her best to cheer me up.

— It's not fair of him to call you a pervert, he's got a pair of silk stockings in his wardrobe, I think he pinched them from Save the Children, and uses them for filtering co-codamol. They're covered in white stains!

She was in hysterics and got hiccups from laughing. We walked past the chippy and she hugged my arm. We headed down Old Street, like an old couple.

— Besides, you're much braver than he is, he's just all talk and books, while you're the one that tries to answer all of his conundrums by doing something. People don't see it in you, but really you're the strong one, so open and brave and he's all boundaries and defence and how could someone so defensive ever be an artist of any kind? He never learns anything, he's so full of himself. But you watch and take things in. I see the way you study me and him, like you're taking notes. Really, you're quite special, even if you do screw it all up now and again.

I told her to stop. We should go home. The street was

becoming dangerous. All these stoned clubbers and her wearing such a short skirt. She kept on and on.

— And he's so jealous of you. My God!

Ridiculous, I told her so.

– No, no. He'd never admit it of course. But really I know he thinks you're the one with the real talent.

— For what? I asked her.

— Well, I dunno, writing maybe . . . no, living . . . or . . . I dunno. He does put you down an awful lot, which can only mean that he really admires you. Everything means its opposite, that's his line. I think he might be in love with you.

— That's crazy.

She kissed my bowed forehead.

— Well, maybe he is. Don't you think he might be? I mean mentally?

— Of course not.

— Or maybe he's a closet gay, or maybe something in his childhood. You know, some trauma . . . maybe manic-depressive. Suddenly she announced: — Now I see why we can never have sex.

— What?

— He's in love with you – and you're in love with him too, aren't you?

That was it, enough. A sudden rage overcame me and I pulled her to me and covered her mouth with mine. It happened so fast, my hand on her breast, her gasps in my ear, us falling back against the wall, her hand up my shirt, her mouth on my neck. The alleyway by the Chinese place. Stink of takeaways, sweet and sour, us sliding by the bin bags.

My finger slid her panties to the side, and found the warm wet. Her fingertips touched my pubes. So soon again I was about to come. Too damn soon. I pulled away and felt the hot wet spasm inside my trousers. Her fingers just millimetres away. I yanked her hand out.

— It's OK, she said. — I'm sorry, I won't tease or come between you both again.

And I could not explain. Every time I pushed her away she thought it because I loved Saul but it was only because I feared revealing my premature ejaculation. What foolish tragedy was this?

She marched away. I called after her, but the clubbers came between us, staggering across the road. For minutes I searched for her, running, calling her name. Finally I found her standing by the bookies. She motioned for me to come closer. Took my arm and snuggled on my shoulder.

— OK, she said, — maybe it's best if we're all like brothers and sisters and you can have my panties when you need them.

It was all going wrong. I could have wept with frustration and rage.

— Look, I said, but could not find the words. The tension was building in me, throbbing in my skull.

— I love you, I blurted out.

She seemed stunned.

I took her hand and placed it over my wet crotch. She felt the stain, confused.

— Oh, did you? Oh. Oh dear, oh, sorry. You are so, so sweet, she said.

She smiled compassionately and kissed my forehead. If I had expressed my love separately from exposing my ejaculation, I might have understood whether it was the declaration of love or the ejaculation that she found sweet. She held my hand as if we were siblings.

— What should we do? I asked, meaning with our lives, with my love . . .

— Well, I suppose we can fib a bit, tell him we fancied some Chinese, or some fags . . . maybe go back home one at a time, not together, like we both ended up on different walks or . . .

At the edge of the street I told her she should go first, but I was still craving more, a kiss to let her know all I could not say, a kiss to hold her there, pin her there, make her tell me she loved me. She pecked me on the cheek.

— And don't worry about old bossy boots, we'll have our little revenge on him soon enough.

Back at the flat, she tiptoed in before me and I waited a few minutes outside before entering, then went swiftly to my room, furious at myself for having failed her. Her door was only ten feet away. I fantasised about taking her by force but knew it too would end in another hilarious failure. I stood there in her doorway, watching her as she slept. Too scared to enter. Her face on the pillow, sweet sleeping face. And words came to me – Oh, Dot, you are my unfinished sentence, we will make up the words to fill the gaps between. My life sentence – my Dot at the end. I came again over her door, then wiped it off with her panties.

Sleepless, I heard footsteps by my door. It was Saul, looking round furtively to see if he was being watched, sneaking in like a spy.

— Shh, I have it!

— What?

— She's to blame for the sorry state you're in. I can see it now. Yes, I have it! I asked him what he had.

— A master plan, you fool. She's always talking about her la-di-da parents – Yes? Well, I propose we pay them a little visit.

His voice heavy with phlegm, grinning Fagin-like.

— When we meet her beloved daddy I want you to be wearing my torn suit and I shall be sporting something profoundly revolting and possibly unclean.

— To what end?

— To what end? Can't you see the genius of it?

All I could see were his bloodshot eyes and all I could smell was sherry-induced halitosis.

— So they'll take her from us, of course! No doubt Daddy will be so glad to save her from us that he'll overlook the nine hundred pounds I owe her! We'll be rid of her craziness and debt-free! You see? Yes? Yes!

I had declared my love and come in my pants and now he wanted her locked in a padded cell. Dot seemed the only sane one among us.

four

Leg Show. 1993. Video still from two-screen installation. Variable dimensions. Private collection.

Leg Show. 1993. Video still from two-screen installation. Variable dimensions. Private collection.

ON TWO SCREENS two figures in women's clothing strike poses. Faces are never seen. It is possible, however, to infer from their appearance, and from the amateur nature of their attempts, that they are, in fact, men 'in drag'. Throughout, a female voice from behind camera makes commands: 'Lift your leg higher', 'Stand on one foot', 'Show me your stockings'. She also compliments the two figures on their performance. 'What a pretty girl', etc.

The audio is out of sync with the actions on both screens, so at times the commands and praise do not coincide with the events on-screen. This creates a sense of estrangement.[1] A gap between sound and image. Command and reaction. Action and repercussion.

The work is largely seen as being comical, as the two male figures stumble around in high heels and strike poses, in competition with each other, for the attention and praise of the unseen female 'director'. Feminists have seen this work as a radical reversal of the 'male gaze,[2] claiming that the process for the artist was one of 'deconditioning' the uncultured femininity she had experienced as a girl, and strategically (and with a sense of vengeance) reversing it back onto the bodies of men. As usual, more mainstream critics have claimed that the work is not in any way serious and has nothing to say at all about any of these issues: 'It's just a couple of TVs on the TV.'[3]

It is worth noting the recurrence of the number 3 in Shears's work. The artworks are always about threes – a third element always enters which breaks down the dualism of object and subject. The third interacts with both – for example, the presence of the director in a film with two actors. Or: image, sound, installation; director, performer, viewer. The three elements are often in conflict with each other. The audio may contradict the picture, creating a third experience for the viewer.

In *Leg Show* there are three people: the two performers (victims, actors) and the woman behind the camera (Shears). There are two screens and one source of audio. The viewer places himself between three pieces of stimulus. Some have found this disorientating. Certainly, those that seek a clear single message from a work by Shears will be confounded. The way to read her work, P. Jennings claims, is to throw oneself into 'the confusion of the triad'.[4] The actors, and indeed the viewers, are complicit in the work, there can be no objective overview. Even in describing this artwork now, this text cannot exist in one form. It is reportage, theory and image. The three overlap but each form is inadequate in itself, while at the same time depending on the two others. Shears's work for certain deconstructionists has a political dimension, not in its manifest content but in the form of its reading and interpretation – 'The works suffer from the same problems that beset democracy', 'We must move beyond the single goal and the opposition with the enemy towards the polyphony of the third voice. In it lies confusion but also a way out of the impasse of the old entrenched dualistic oppositions.'[5]

Certainly, many comments by Shears would seem to imply a fascination with threes. 'Three's company, two's a crowd.' She has said many times in interview that she feels she is not one artist, or even two, but three artists all struggling for dominance. Whereas some have seen this as just another attention-grabbing line, others such as Jennings claim that this 'not one but three' forms the basis for a critique of the role of the artist that runs through Shears's work. From this perspective, we can read a cleverly aimed set of challenges to the male-dominated cultural hegemony of one and (cultural) other.

The bisexual role play and suspension of identity in this work has proven offensive to both straight and gay sensibilities, suspending, as it does, any notions of fixity or resolution over the idea of sexuality. A position that problematises the so-called radical stance of so many brands of 'identity politics'. What has been so problematic to such viewers is that Shears does not 'come out', and declare a fixed identity (hence political position), that the work is really just a game, thus suggesting that gender questioning is a phase to be moved through, as traditional reactionary psychological models suggest.[6]

Shears's refusal to take a position has from some quarters led critics to applaud her courage in 'not succumbing to dated and restrictive models of bracketed behaviour'. As such it is a work well ahead of its time, and as D. Malles has proclaimed: '[Leg Show] is one of the seminal works of the culture of Postmodern Perverse Pluralism.'[7]

1. See *Brecht on Art and Politics*, ed. and trans. T. Kuhn and S. Giles, Methuen, 2003.
2. See L. Marney, 'Visual (un)pleasures', *Stance*, 45–3, 1998.
3. Quote by D. Spencer, 'Transvestites on Television', *Late Show*, BBC, 1995.
4. P. Jennings, *Deconstructing Dualism*, Allegory Press, 2003, p. 141.
5. Ibid., p. 117.
6. Freud's thesis that gender ambiguity and gay experience is an immature phase that prestages the transition into mature sexuality, i.e. monogamous heterosexuality.
7. D. Malles in 'PPP', *Fuck Culture*, Artemis Press, 2004.

HE WAS STARTING to redefine his idea of perfection. He was coming to learn that the huge emotional ups and downs of every single day, in the three weeks since Dot and Molly had moved in, were themselves a kind of reckless excellence.

Each day started with hysterical noise at six thirty as Molly bounced on the bed and dragged her mother from sleep. He would beg for an hour more, which would only last ten minutes as Molly would invariably play hide-and-seek under his bed with Dot laughing.

'Get dressed, scallywag!'

'No-no-no!'

'I'm going to catch you, I'm going to tickle you. I'm going to eat you all up!'

Then there would be the dressing gown and the tiptoeing through the obstacle course of yesterday's scattered play-things: Lego that could jab in the heel; Playdoh already squashed into the carpet; a Hello Kitty toy; a digger: a CD; Doctor Seuss; a sock; a dinosaur, each object backlit by the early-morning light, appearing as if it had always been meant to be there.

Breakfast with the child was always an excruciating exercise in coercion and diplomacy. Molly's worst habit was to refuse to either eat or get dressed. Then she would flip to the opposite – and start spooning cornflakes into her mouth as soon as Dot tried to put her jumper on, thus spilling milk all over her clothes. Her other one was that she wanted to do paintings while eating, leading to predictable but nonetheless regularly repeated disasters with paint and breakfast cereal.

Once some semblance of sanity had been achieved, he and Dot walked Molly the ten vigorous blocks to Upper Street to the new day-care place he'd helped her find. It was expensive and the space was only temporary but Dot considered money no object and was thrilled for Molly to be in day care that was a lot like Montessori.

Then after their goodbyes and Molly's screaming clinging fits, tugging at her mother's legs, when finally the devil-child was prised away by the hippy-looking carer, Owen would take Dot's hand and walk her past the yuppie boutiques to Angel tube station. The walks were filled with Dot's art ideas and plans, and he was always silent, simply staring at her in wonder. The goodbye kiss and then the walk back home, already exhausted.

At his desk, he had to lay out a plan. Having committed to her essay, he now had to clear it with the *Guardian* and *Independent*, *Artforum* and *Frieze*, that he was taking a bit of time out. Each assumed he was angling for a salary because of the recession, and he had to reassure them that that was not the case. In daily emails he had to reaffirm that he would be coming back.

Work on the essay was slow and the flat seemed emptier than ever when he rose from his PC to eat his lunch alone. The pacing would start and he longed again for their many distractions, the games and shouts. It was like a very first love affair, both too hot and cold, all intense.

Come five o'clock, it was the hardest time. As part of the deal, Owen had committed to picking Molly up each day. Invariably, the child refused to acknowledge who he was and screamed. It was only with coaxing and promises of secret sweeties that she left the arms of her carer at all. She always wanted to go to the park. The swings.

'Again' 'Again' 'Higher' 'Higher'. On the roundabout. 'Again' 'Again'. On the slide. 'Again, again'.

After an hour and a half of these exertions, he would, under his breath, be cursing her and all children since time began, counting the minutes, streets walked, and bribery sweets given, till Dot came to save him. Fantasising about her, standing behind him, massaging his shoulders, asking: 'How was your day, O?'

By the end of each day, after dinner and Molly's bath and the grown-ups' rota of sleepy-time story reading, he would find himself in the corridor staring at the child's paintings that covered the living-room walls, from waist height to above the head, above the TV, the doors even. Twenty at least. The one on the kitchen door that had little cartoon versions of themselves, all on skateboards on a big wiggly line, the names Molly had asked Dot to write out for her so she could copy. The Mummy that was Dot and a big smile that went over the edges of her face, the boobs, two big circles; then Molly herself, the M upside down – Wolly – bigger than the grown-ups, with immense flamboyant trousers that were a garden in bloom, thirty carefully drawn flowers. Then himself, little more than a long black line, with Xs all around him, even over his name, making it look like Oxen.

My God, he would tell himself then: is that not the best fucking artwork in the world? Is this not the most fucked-up perfect happiness a man could have? He made a mental note to try to accept this precarious crazy happiness.

Morning again and he could hear Molly running behind him to her mumma, He walked into the kitchen and laid out the bowls for breakfast. Estate agents' brochures were scattered across every surface.

Linton presents: A warehouse apartment, situated within a secure gated development in a former church off fashionable Brick Lane. Property has a large split-level space in living room which has flexible use . . .

There were former school conversions, former hospital conversions, as if the one thing Dot feared was actually living in a typical house.

'Fuck conversions,' Dot said. 'I want to get in before the developers.'

Owen smiled to himself. Dot dreamed of a huge, empty, accidentally discovered space unsullied by the forces of capital that she could convert by herself, but that she had not time to build and refit. In the last few weeks it had become a kind of game with them. He'd encouraged her wildest fantasies of a place in the East End that could unify the three disparate strands in her life and be artist's studio, crèche and home. There was the former sugar factory off Bank, and the warehouse off Tower Hill. In between working on the essay, he, Dot and Molly trailed round the impossible places, with the estate agents in tow.

It had been last Friday and an old church by Aldgate East, advertising a real seventeenth-century stained-glass window as a feature.

'Fuck,' Dot said as they were led in by the estate agent.

The apartment had a section of the rose window. Four apartments probably had a bit of it each. The stained-glass section was brutally cut off by thin partition walls and rave dance music was coming from the neighbouring yuppie. There was a mezzanine to make the place look bigger. Owen stood there as Dot made her assessment.

'It's just so . . . Haven't you got any more churches?' she asked the estate agent guy. Molly ran around the place shouting, trying to get her voice to echo.

'Echo, echo, there's no echo, Mumma!'

'What do you think?' Dot asked him.

'Echo, echo!' he shouted 'No there's no echo, maybe it's the laminate flooring.'

'You said there'd be an echo. Mumma!'

The kid was in a huff.

'It's not very you. You've still got time to find somewhere better.'

The end of another exhausting day had come. Molly was asleep and Dot and he were drinking wine. For some reason he was staring at her feet. Large for a woman, heavily veined. Veins. How many times had he avoided staring at her wrists, the scars cut vertical, upward, not across.

'What?' she asked and his silent smile made her laugh. She was playing with her wine glass, yawning, and suddenly he was struck by the redemptive beauty of it all. Oh, to kiss those wrists. The long elfin fingers, corrupted by the fingernails bitten to stumps. If only she could stop biting her nails, fighting herself. If only they could talk of that night she had slashed her wrists.

She was massaging her feet then, talking about getting some new shoes, maybe with flatter heels. 'Sensible shoes,' she said and laughed.

He had to stop this. His new silence. She was on a big one, trying to work out how to fit in childcare with international travel. Should she take Molly with her to Zurich? It couldn't be good for a child to be always moving from country to country, there had to be one constant, one nanny at least, but they were so unreliable.

She sighed and threw back her head and ran her fingers through her hair, her eyes closed as she massaged that long neck. Look at her hair, the tiny single strands of grey that she pulls out religiously each day from her dyed Warhol white. They were both restless their unresolved tensions finding form in kisses, in clothes shed. They'd just started to make love on the sofa when Dot suddenly broke away.

'It's OK, Molly's fast asleep.'

'No, no, not that it's just . . .'

'You're right, it's not right, we should go to bed.'

'No, not that . . .'

'What then?'

Dot admitted she was distracted, couldn't find the words. His eyes wandered the room, as he tried to find ways to calm her. To finish the sentence that was eluding her. There in the corner by the art books the little light on the phone was flashing. The ringer was off. He hoped she hadn't seen what he'd been staring at. He covered her naked thighs with his shirt, shhing her and whispering. 'Come to bed, what's wrong?'

'It's just . . .' she kept saying, 'just that . . . I dunno.'

'What?'

'I don't know why I'm thinking about him now.'

Saul.

'Shh, come to bed, OK? It's been a stressful day, just come to bed.'

And so he led her from the sofa, past the bookshelves and the flashing light of the phone unanswered and unanswerable that could keep on ringing on mute all night, for days, years, for all he cared.

The way she lay then, after they were spent, on her back, staring into space. He found himself, as long before, wondering if there was a place for him in that vacancy of hers, if she knew how much her beauty caused him pain. That turn away of the head, the tight neck muscles, her eyes searching beyond him to the cornicing that made him jealous of the empty space that was more absorbing for her than he was. Then for her to turn with the smile, almost apologetic for the dreaming drifting time. And that hand of hers reaching, that told him she'd been somewhere very alone and was so glad to be back and see him there, a hand's reach away. She would squeeze his fingers then, but still he worried that the pull of that other place was a sign of the return of her madness or some sad lament for the freedom it had once given her. Her smile on returning was always almost apologetic. It made him cling closer, and stroke her hand, telling her 'I know'. As if he ever could.

She rolled over and placed her hand on his chest. He kissed her fingertips, felt her lungs expand and contract against his chest. In out, in out. As her toes curled round his, he told himself this was real, so real. Oh, to not have to face the tomorrow of work and her tapes and the writing of the essay. To just live in this moment now, and make every day this duplicate image – like the way that Molly knew when she shouted in the park, on the swings, on the roundabout. Again. Again. Again. Again. Again.

'It's not God or the cops that are standing in the way of your happiness,' Saul had once had said. 'It's only you, you've got to kill the cop within, the God, the voices that judge your every action. Happiness requires blood.'

And maybe Saul was right. But to be happy Owen had to learn how to kill the voice of Saul too.

Dot was out at her studio and Molly at day care and he sat himself down to deal with the one thing that could not be postponed – her archive of original master tapes. He had so far looked only at the press tapes.

Something was bothering him. The deadline was in a month and he'd gone back to the start, rewriting everything about her first works. Fretting over telling the world that the person who'd filmed *Negative Leap* had been himself. How the face in *Trust* was his own. If he deleted himself from their history it was tantamount to a lie. The other thought, worse, was that the bigger omission had been Saul. The more he scrutinised the footage the more he saw Saul behind every frame.

'What you need is a leap into the dark, my dear.' And so *Negative Leap* was born. 'You want to be a man? Let me tell you a little secret, it is all a game. All of us men are just play-acting,' and that was *PlayBoy*. And *Trust*. Think of trust.

Dot had been right to remove the ninth work from the show. The one with Molly – it played into the hands of those who were queuing up to shoot her down, who would use that one flawed work to pronounce all of her work as just sentimental personal recordings elevated well above their status. He couldn't tell her this, but really, she had to make a new work, if she was to retain any credibility as a working artist. This worried him.

Tonight was the first big test of their relationship. It was to be the first time they had been seen in public together. An opening of a group show in White Cube, Hoxton. She couldn't face another opening, she said, oblivious to how much it meant to him.

'If we could run off . . . a little cottage, just you and Mozzer, or retire . . . a croft in Scotland, with some cows . . . we could go self-sufficient, or join a commune, or . . .'

While they waited for the agency babysitter, he tried to reassure her. He would be there with her, at a safe distance, watching over her. He made her laugh as she got dressed.

'Just think of all the people who've never been nominated for the Turner Prize, there must be more than a few . . . well, more than a few million. OK?'

On the way in the taxi, her hand in his, Owen reassured her. Of course, it would be wrong for a critic to be seen dating an artist – a little scandal and the media loved its incestuous intrigues.

'Maybe I should just lurk in the shadows and let you schmooze.'

'No, don't leave me alone. Don't you dare! I want to show you off to everyone.'

She kissed his cheek.

The taxi stopped and he saw the hundred outside the gallery door. He let her go first then counted to thirty and followed. Her face was much kissed then whisked away while they kept him at the front door asking if he was on the guest list. He gave his name, quietly, but the girl was too young to have known who he was. He waited as she got someone more superior, and this superior was then so apologetic and of course he was a welcome guest and why didn't he come to openings more often and was he alone? Because he could've brought a friend?

Owen found the drinks table and got a Beck's. Stared round, looking for Dot. He located her, finally, amid a group of young trendies. The way she laughed then suddenly withdrew and they reached to touch her. The way she shook her head and told them, no doubt, that she hadn't had a creative thought in years, and they laughed out loud, thinking it a very witty reply from a Turner Prize-nominee.

Fifty feet away but he did not want to interrupt. He tried to distract himself with the art on show but it was all that new politically correct form of racism, the 'real voice' of ethnic others. Photographs from Afghanistan of families covered in some kind of authentic ethnic mud/blood-like goo. He glanced up but she was gone again. He heard her laughter and glimpsed her hair in the midst of an increasing circle.

He texted her. 'Talk to me. I'm by bar.'

And waited. Some woman in heels had come up to him and told him that she followed his reviews, but didn't he think he was maybe just a bit too cynical?

Dot texted back. 'Bored out of my fucking tits. Am in back.'

The woman told him she'd studied postmodernism and thought him rather reactionary, almost existentialist in his diagnosis of what was fake and real in modern culture. He apologised for having to text.

'Am being accosted by freak. Save me. XXX'

The woman said she found many of the things he said unduly negative, in fact the only reason she read his reviews was cos she found him a truly sad nihilistic individual, and he represented everything she despised. He shrugged his shoulders, apologised. She threw her drink in his face.

People moved away. Embarrassed. Thankfully no one that had a name.

He moved to the back, mopped himself down. No text from Dot. The PR person came and apologised, asked if there was anything she could do. He told her this was not the first time. Another Beck's would be fine.

He waited ten minutes and there was no sign of the beer or of Dot.

He texted her. 'See you back home then.'

It wasn't going to work. Art and Dot and him. The whole thing – nostalgia, nothing more. The daily reality eating away at the memory and the reality was that over the years Dot had become a player; no matter how much she resisted her success, it had branded itself on her. This woman tonight was not the Dot he knew.

'They're so square – and you're so smart and funny, we won't do it again.'

She was sorry – it'd been wrong for them to see all of her old artist friends so quickly after getting together. She'd sensed he found it hard to fit in, she was sorry she hadn't had time to introduce him to anyone. She was drunk and gigglish. 'People,' she laughed, 'I don't hate 'em, I'm just happier when they're not around,' quoting Saul. She was really drunk. Two fucking hours it had taken her to come back.

'C'mere, grumpy,' she said. But when they had made love he had been too overbearing, too needy, and she had been unresponsive to his needs, too drunk to fuck. He had finished selfishly with no care for her. Saying, 'I'm fucking you, I'm fucking you.' Afterwards there had been the silence. He asked what was wrong.

'Nothing, I was just thinking . . . I heard Molly moving round. No, it was nothing. She's so restless here. Forget it.'

'You sure that's all?'

'It's nothing, forget it.'

She rolled away and turned off the bedside light, leaving a space between them.

'HOME HOME HOME!' Molly screamed. It was well past nursery time and she was sitting in a mess of clothes she'd pulled from the boxes; three of her pictures were lying torn on the floor.

'NOW NOW NOW!'

Owen didn't want to tell Dot how to manage her child but she was doing it all wrong.

'Oh baby, I know, but we can't go back now, they're showing people round and you hate it when strangers come marching through your house, don't you?'

'HOME NOW NOW!'

Dot was trying to placate her with her Hello Kitty dolly, which was immediately thrown to the floor.

'Just a few more weeks, baby, and we'll have a lovely new place.'

That was it. The little brat stared at her mother, took a deep breath and held it.

'Now stop that,' Dot said, throwing Owen a worried glance. 'C'mon, don't be bossy-breath, you know Mummy cries when you do that.'

Molly closed her eyes and crossed her arms, puffing her cheeks out.

'Please, baby, stop that, it'll make you sick.'

The kid's face started turning red.

'Ohmigod, this isn't fair, I know you miss the old house, but we can't stay there forever.'

Owen had grown increasingly aware of how Dot's patience was being strained. Truth was he didn't want her to get a new place, and would come up with any number of subtle criticisms of her planned homes just to postpone the possibility of her moving on. It would only be so long till she worked out his little strategies.

Molly knew. Her face started turning purple. Dot was in a panic. Grabbing her arms, shaking her. What the hell can I do? thought Owen.

'Molly, stop that, you're going to faint, stop that!'

Slap her, that's what Owen would have done, or walk away.

The kid's head dropped forward and Dot screamed, catching her.

'My God! Molly! Molly!'

Owen leaned forward to help take the kid's weight.

'Don't touch her, she's done this before, I know what to do. God, how did this start again?'

Dot laid her dead-looking child down on the floor, started whispering and kissing her.

'OK, OK, we'll go and spend the night there, OK? In the old place.'

Miraculously the kid breathed again. The whole thing had been a ruse.

Owen stood there like a fool, useless and resentful that the child had not only got her own way but expressed her irritation with him, his flat and plans. Molly was on to his postponement tactics and suffering because of them.

'Could you just leave us alone for a minute?' Dot said on her knees in the midst of the mess of teddies. He stepped away down the hall and looked back at them both framed in the doorway. They looked like refugees, desperately hugging each other. Don't shut me out, Owen thought. Whatever it takes to stay together, I'll do it.

*

It had been a particularly cold February and Saul spent most of it in a drunken coma, rereading his *Beyond Good and Evil*, dressed in three layers with the bar fire on all day and night beside his bed. I sensed that his drunkenness was due to his suspicion over my affair with Dot. Certainly he'd become more averse to her presence, failing to even attempt to make a start on the text she'd asked him to do for the *Bug* show.

— Don't bug me with your bugs. I've enough in my bed as it is! Go back from whence you came! Back to your parents! First-class airmail, to the bloody turret, to the menstrual hut you must go!

For days he had been seeding references to her parents into his every sentence, leading her to think that the plan for a visit was her own idea.

— Fuck you, she shouted back. — If you ever met my father you'd be shitting yourself.

— Try me, he replied.

I could do nothing to stop it – the gauntlet had been thrown down and the showdown arranged. Dot paid for the taxi to St John's Wood and said there would be lots of free booze because her mother was an alcoholic. She intended to blag or pinch another eight hundred from Dearest Daddy she said (Saul having pissed away all of the last amount Dot loaned him), but she seemed completely oblivious to Saul's plan to dump her there and escape debt-free. Images of what would result if I refused to go flooded me: Saul would be alone with the father, whispering profanities like 'Don't you agree, we could do with another Falklands to keep the number of plebs down?' He'd vomit on their chaise longue as they sat down to tea and cakes and accomplish his plan, with Dot being placed in care that very night. I was caught in the middle again, fearful of exposing his deception to her, but equally anxious of her finding out that Saul had been scheming in my ear behind her back. Why I had not stuck up for her and ceased doing his dirty work, I did not know. I decided to accompany them to defuse the situation.

I'd done my best to dress smartly for the occasion wearing my pinched Oxfam suit and best pair of Docs. There was no polish so I shined my shoes with margarine. Saul had been playing Vivaldi's *Four Seasons* in preparation and emerged wearing his SMOKE CRACK WORSHIP SATAN T-shirt. Dot on seeing this decided to outdo him and put on his COCKS SUCK T-shirt. A petty game of radical one-upmanship ensued, with Saul, quite unexpectedly, taking the opposite tack and selecting his stolen Armani, while Dot went for red torn fishnets and that thing she'd recently shoplifted that she called a skirt that I would have described more as a belt, Saul's army boots and another layer of the mascara added to the accumulated remnants of the last week's. Also in competition seemed to be the amount of alcohol they could consume before even setting foot outside. I sensed that seeing her well-heeled parents might be unsettling for her.

The taxi turned the corner onto a row of huge St John's Wood mansion houses. While Dot paid and tipped the man we decanted and stood in the drive before the vast edifice. There were at least twelve windows with almost medieval-looking frames, and trees and flowers of every imaginable variety as if the place was a botanic gardens; the lawn was a long-abandoned tennis court and there were his and hers BMWs in the drive. An irrational fear of the wealthy overcame me. I registered something similar on Saul's face.

— Home sweet home, Dot said as she staggered to the doorbell. The woman who answered was not at all what I expected her mother to look like. Short and olive-skinned, Portuguese or South American.

— *Hola*, Pilita, Dot chimed. I'm just popping in for a bit. Daddy's not here, is he?

— No, Miss Dorothy. Away till Tuesday.

— And dearest Mamma?

— In Italia to Friday, you not get message?

— Of course, good, good, off you go then, you're excused.

It was a surprise and somewhat scary to witness Dot as an affluent young brat, bossing around the Third World slave. So she had known all along that her parents were away. I started to sense that Dot had another kind of surprise prepared for us. She led us along a corridor lined with images and certificates of her father's glory. Trophies and awards,

187

framed certificates and memberships of this prestigious club and the next, photographs of groups of men in suits.

— As soon as she's gone, we'll steal the booze, Dot whispered.

She gave us the guided tour with an exaggerated posh voice. There was an almost feudal castle-like stairway straight out of *Brideshead Revisited*; teak bookshelves lined with every imaginable psychology text and mini-busts and sculptures of Greek philosophers.

— Of course, Daddy is from a long line of respected psychiatrists, specialising in the neuropathology of women. I was one of his most difficult cases!

She seemed to relish how uncomfortable she was making us feel. She led us along a corridor lined with framed photos. Mostly of herself, always in the centre of the picture, looking like a boy, serious and androgynous, in an all-girls' school, at a sports club, always with awards and certificates. Photos of her with her father's proud hand on her shoulder, the mother nowhere in sight. She seemed top of every class. The hall was like a hall of fame, like they'd built her up to succeed at everything she ever tried.

She caught me staring and pushed me on.

— Over there's the west wing. When I had my episode, I had my deathbed there. They really thought I was going to die.

I hoped to hell none of this was true and that she was just playing a game with us. She winked at me. I could not tell if she was just making this stuff up.

— Charming, Saul muttered. His plan had completely backfired and he seemed almost scared. She led us into Daddy's study and sat in his leather chair at his big desk, flashing her torn fishnet crotch. The entire place looked like a facsimile of Freud's original.

— I think it all started because he'd stopped sleeping with my mum, and then I got boobs and he started freaking out. I tried to make them go away by not eating but it only made it worse. He'd have preferred a son, I think. The three of us drove each perfectly insane. Poor Daddy.

Saul tried to ignore her, his eyes were fixated on what looked to be a stuffed badger. Saul pulled his finger back swiftly from the animal, as if bitten.

Dot laughed at him.

Pilita called goodbye from the front door and within seconds Dot declared that the mayhem should commence. She spun round in her daddy's chair, went into his desk drawer, leafed through his many credit cards, and pocketed one.

— What shall we spend it on, boys, a pizza or a prostitute? Purge or binge?

Many questions were troubling me about her past and her present incarnation. Saul loved stories of the aristocracy and their debauchery, but I could tell he had never come this close before. Dot ran out of the room and we were alone.

— We should go, I said.

— Don't be a chicken, he replied, — this is all quite perversely fascinating.

Dot returned with a bottle of vodka, some glasses and a huge pack of duty-free menthols and threw Saul a packet, then another, teasing him, I could tell, making him reach for them and pick them up from the floor. She poured us both huge shots of vodka.

— But ... what are we actually doing here? I asked. Saul was staring at the huge vodka bottle.

— You're not afraid of a little bit of transgression, are you? she laughed. — Come on, boys, I have a surprise for you.

The scene that was unfolding was a little too like one Saul had told us about the Duchess for my comfort. 1920s New York – an orgy in a rich man's Upper West Side mansion. Artists and aristocrats naked and crawling in blood, semen and broken glass. Saul was too busy lighting a fag to notice my appeals for his intervention. Dot left the room and I caught her at the corner, and whispered, — What's going on?

— Oh come on, I told you I'd have my revenge, let's just see how much he can take. Shh, he's coming.

She led us then, giggling and ranting in her exaggerated voice, to her mother's bedroom. Marimekko curtains and trims, potpourri, festival masks from Venice, a huge bed of seventies-style silky sheets made up like a hotel bed but with fluffy cushions; a Hindu god in ivory by the bedside.

— What if she comes back?

— Oh O, must you always be so practical? She's never here, she can't stand being near the old bugger.

She pulled her mother's clothes out of the seventies mirrored walk-in wardrobe and threw them on the bed. Saul lit a menthol off the end of the last and stared out the window. I asked on his behalf if it was OK to smoke in her mother's bedroom.

— Fuck her, Dot laughed. — She smokes spliffs in here secretly all the time. Tragic really.

Dot held a sixties Chanel dress first to herself, then her eyes shot from Saul to me. Panic surged through me.

— I think . . . this one's for you, she said to me with a wry smile.

— What?

— It's art, she laughed. — I'm going to get my camera in a min. And this – with the utmost seriousness, holding up a floor-length crocheted hippy cheesecloth dress, — is for you, Sozzle.

She must have known that Saul would take offence at that particular garment. If so, it was a cunning move. He seemed oblivious to the greater question of why the hell we would be dressing in her mother's clothes in the first place, as he then searched through the wardrobe trying to find something more 'him'. In his silence he was, perhaps,

190

working out the weight of bottles he could carry home or some other calculation for maximising our exploitation of the capitalist context. I was still counting on him to stop the farce, but he was fully engaged with the textures of silk and chiffon and nylon and I was thrown into confusion as Dot took off her clothes and, naked before us, pulled an eighties business suit from the wardrobe, declaring it 'very her'. She was to dress as her father.

— Come on, girls. You like dressing up, don't you? She winked at me. — I'll get you some panties.

I was terrified then that if I opposed the plan it would only take the smallest slip-up for Saul to know that Dot and I shared a sexual secret. I agreed to put on the Chanel number, in the hope of silencing her, and started to undress.

— You too, Sozzle. He was still fussing over the many styles. A green-and-yellow-striped seventies flared jumpsuit, a ball gown, a Versace in gold lamé. I stood in my underpants, hoping that at any moment he would explode in rage and declare the game over.

— What's wrong, Soz, you scared? She poked his belly.

How clever of her to know that for Saul to seem scared of any transgression was tantamount to an exposure of hypocrisy.

— I'll bet Owen makes a better woman than you do, she added. — I'll award points and a little kiss for the winner.

— I'm a fucking damn sight more of a woman than you'll ever be! Saul snapped back.

There was no way out. Saul insisted on dressing alone in the en suite on the condition that Dot fix him a tall Martini, while he flicked the Versace in her face, picked up a pair of strapless heels and pootled off inside, satisfied that he was once again laying down the rules for us all. I asked her again what the hell we were doing. All of that stuff she'd said earlier about manic depression and her deathbed, was any of it true?

— Shh, my dreary dear, she said, quoting him, — we're making art. Then she ran off to fix more drinks and get her video camera. I was left alone in boxers and socks before the mirror, the little black dress in my hands.

My humiliation grew as my member nodded in approval as I slid the tight dress over my head. I struggled to think of something horrible – the yellow slime in the kitchen sink – the bluebottle infestation in the old bin-bag room – the toilet clogged with Saul's shit-smeared tabloid pages – the breakfast bowl I once found crawling with maggots – anything to make my swelling subside. But the sight of the bulge in the tight material, then that of Dot wiggling naked into the room with the three pint glasses filled with cocktails and her video camera – I sat down rapidly, resting my elbows on my knees, crossing my legs to hide my aching weakness.

The clink of the glasses must have been what roused Saul from the en suite. The image of him then, thick black stubble and the legs of some kind of anorexic gorilla, chest bones from a prisoner-of-war camp highlighted by the sheer lamé dress. Dirty overgrown toenails hanging over the edge of the heels.

— *Et voilà*! he called out, striking a pose. Dot stifled a laugh, and raised the camera – we both knew better than to laugh at Saul for any reason.

She complimented and toasted us both, clinking glasses, as if sensing that a moment of silence would bring it all to an end.

— Oh, but we need to get you stockings, my cherubim! 15 denier, I think, to hide the hair, and foundation to cover the stubble. You both really should have shaved. Oh but you look so glorious! My little peaches – I could eat you all up.

I worried then that we were not making art at all but re-enacting some perverse primal scene that her father had once put her through. But she chattered on, high-pitched and high camp, as her hands rummaged through her mother's lingerie drawers. And part of me did want to wear suspenders and stockings and lacy panties and to beat Saul in this competition of hers.

The cocktails were finished, so then there was gin. Dot poured a huge one for Saul and his humour seemed to come back with every millitre of alcohol more.

— Just a smidge more debauchery for me my dreary dear.

All the lovely expensive frilly thrilling thingies laid out on the bed, and Dot was talking about how her mother had really been a burn-your-bra hippy but her father liked her to dress like a 'real woman', as she put on the old man's double-breasted padded-shouldered suit.

I must have been drunk, because I'd forgotten the why and where of it all. I turned my back to them and tried to pull a stocking on but my foot got stuck. I lost my balance and fell back onto her mother's bed. Dot was laughing, manhandling me.

— No, no, not like socks! She took it from me, rolling it up. — Like this, like putting on a condom. Her fingers through the silk, tight round my foot, winking at me again.

— You should have cut your toenails, silly sausage, we don't want to ladder Mummy's best stockings, do we, she could get suspicious. I made facial expressions to try to express my anxiety. She put her finger to her mouth to shh. I checked Saul's face to see if he'd seen the secret exchange, but he was head down, another menthol lit, rolling on his stockings, mumbling, — Philistine, have you never worn silk before?

Nothing I could say or do. The beauty of it struck me then. Of games, how they eclipse reality and become their own. Life should be a game, Saul once said. I told myself to relax and play it out. We sat so quietly, attentive, in our dresses as Dot put the lipstick on us both, then mascara, Saul play-acting the spoiled girl-child.

— Why him? Me first, me first!

In compensation he demanded a beauty spot, which Dot dutifully gave him.

— Bigger, bigger, he was shouting. — I want to be a slut! Another gin and he was proclaiming that we should, nay everyone should, do this every day.

Dot was up, video camera in hand, filming me, as I forced my feet into her mother's tiny stilettos. A moment of bonding then with Saul in which he laughed at my ill-fitting feet, oblivious to his own, him pouting and blowing smoke rings, Dietrich-style. My knobbly knees. A little game of insults, in the name of competitiveness.

— My darling. You're a dog's breakfast.

— It's a dog eat dog world, I said. Surprised that, for once, I'd come up with a witty riposte.

— Indeed, let the best bitch win!

Dot was silent behind her camera. Her voice instructing. As she led us up another flight of stairs, the walls lined with images of the great English, of the conquests of the empire, I finally saw the joke of it all. Her revenge not against Saul but against the great men in gilded frames. Her camera pointed up our dresses as we stumbled on ahead. She, in her father's suit, made lewd suggestions in a play-man's voice, getting us to pose as she shot us from below, her voice that of a film or porn director.

— That's right, cutie, raise your leg, show me the top of the stockings. Higher, lovely, that's it.

She asked us to stand on one leg, pout for the camera, waggle our bums. At first I was embarrassed, but seeing the gusto with which Saul embraced his part, some ludicrous sense of competitiveness overcame me. So I copied and tried to outdo him, flashing my legs and pouting, as per her instruction. Fighting him for space to show more leg, more stocking tops. Her camera was rolling and it was art.

— That's good. Now kiss each other, a big smoochy kiss. Saul puckered up, all labial lips and stubble, big mwaaa, mwaaas. I closed my eyes and extended my lips. He pulled away immediately, giggling like a man-girl.

She showed us the playback on the big TV in the lounge as Saul opened the fifty-year-old Glenlivet. On-screen was a shot perfectly framed by the banister. It could have been anywhere, another time – a Warhol screen test from the Chelsea Hotel, '72.

— Mmmm, very Andy, Saul proclaimed – the only positive thing he'd said in weeks.

Two drag queens, posing, following commands as a voice made demands from behind the camera.

'Bend over, show me your asses. Shoogle them, let me see those ass cheeks wobbling: Now do the catwalk, and come back to the banister.'

On-screen two drag queens fighting to go first.

'One at a time, girls!'

The queens so studious in their every move, the one that was Saul stumbled in his heels, swore – fuck fuck! Then steadied himself on the banister and sighed deeply like Zsa Zsa Gabor.

'Now pull your dresses up, show me your suspender belts. Show me your pussies. Touch your pussies. Blow the camera a kiss.'

A moment then when both drag queens stared at the camera, falling out of their roles, standing like men waiting at a bar for a pint.

'I'm the winner!' shouted the one that was Saul.

'No, me!'

'Me, me, me, me.'

The voice from behind the camera: 'There's no winner.'

The tape went to fuzz.

195

Dot turned it off and sat back on her haunches.

— So what you think? Is it art?

Saul got up suddenly, spilling his drink, running past us, falling against the wall in the heels he'd forgotten to take off. The sound of the bathroom door slamming, of him retching. I reached for Dot's hand.

— Do you think he knows . . . about us?

— Shh, she said, — listen.

The sounds in the bathroom were not just retching, but something almost inhuman, animal. The puking-up of what sounded like inner organs. Dot got up to go to him but I held her back. Whispered, — Did you tell him?

She shook her head, silent, listening with worry to his every spasm. She ran off to be with him. Her face at the closed door.

— Sozzle, you OK? What's wrong?

I followed and at the door held her hand.

— Saul, you OK?

— EEEE! A scream from inside. — GOD!

— Open this door! Are you OK? she shouted.

— GOD! GOD, I HATE YOU, he shouted back.

We looked at each other then like two children who had upset their father. He shouted – something that sounded like weeping with chunks of food. — IT'S A FUCKING . . . IT'S A FUCKING OBSCENE FUCKING . . . IT'S A . . .

The toilet door fell open, his mascara running down his cheeks, vomit on his dress. He fell forward into our arms, stenching of puke, whispering, — It's a . . . It's a . . . He was exhausted by the exertions — . . . a fucking masterpiece!

I swear his lips brushed my neck and his arms reached to us not only for support.

— 'S fucking masterpiece.

For all of that, though, I found myself in her bedroom, alone as she put him to bed. Sitting there in her mother's dress, the room seemed preserved by her parents as if Dot had died a decade before and everything had to be kept as she'd left it. Like a shrine, like the *Mary Celeste*. The rows of Sindy dolls; arts and crafts; a Swedish rug; a poster of some Scandinavian weaving; Doctor Seuss. The entire twenty-seven volumes of the *Encyclopaedia Britannica*. Inside the drawers in the dresser were trinkets and plastic jewellery, frilly panties, a first training bra, white schoolgirl socks. On the mantel was a hockey trophy from St Paul's, a row of Russian dolls, beside a lovingly crafted horse in clay. Something was missing from the picture, there were no posters of bands or records or magazines, her entire teenage years seemed lost – and nowhere in the house had I seen a picture of the dead brother. I thought of the mad mother and shrink father and shivered. I tried to sleep on the small, single bed. The duvet cover was Laura Ashley, all flowers. It smelled of dust and something sweeter – air freshener or maybe vomit and detergent.

I was awoken by a dark figure looming over me, a man.
— My God!
A hand reaching for me, speaking.
— Shh, silly, it's me.
— Fuck, Dot! What you doing here?
— It's my room.
— Is he sleeping?
She stepped away then, eyes scanning her assembly line of furry animals. She stopped at the window and leaned on the high shelf. Sight of her from behind: the curves of long slender legs, the gap between them running from knee to inner thigh, the shifts in shape as my eyes roamed upwards, following the line that led to her pubis, then the hard black edge of Saul's Armani jacket. I sat up hugging the duvet, trying to hide my mounting arousal. I was deeply troubled by the events of the night, worse still by the things she'd said about her 'episode'. I tried to find the courage.

197

— That thing about the deathbed?

— Yes.

Her back to me, her voice changed, somehow sincere in tone, dark.

— Your episode?

She turned to me then.

— Am I scaring you, should I put something on?

Her eyes, in the half-dark, not her own, seemed drugged. I could not stop her. My eyes fixated on her hands as she pulled something from the drawer, then bent forward, baring her arse to me. I begged her to stop, but she lifted one foot and I saw then – the white schoolgirl panties, then the other foot stepping in, my eye following the fabric as she pulled it up. The feminine flesh bulging over the edges where the elastic bit too tight. She did not turn to face me. I whispered, begging her to stop.

— I'm just getting dressed, she said. — You do like my clothes, don't you?

His jacket slid from her as she stepped towards the bed.

— I'm too big now, they're too tight, why don't you wear my panties instead?

I was close to tears, pleading with her to stop this scary voice, it was no game – this could go no further – Saul was my best friend and if he were to find out. But I had to know about the episode.

She pulled the duvet from me, glanced at the swollen humiliation, then pulled her panties to the side, took my cock in her hand. She fumbled to guide me inside herself, but the angle was wrong and she bashed her nose on my head. So quickly I was about to come. I told her, please, no, NO! I pulled away, shot immediately over my belly.

She had changed again. Not the schoolgirl or the Duchess but Dot, the first Dot, nervous, a little shy, then chuckling, silly. Saying sorry. My cock spasming and her tiptoeing away. She went to leave but I held her hand and pulled her back. I had to know. As if she had guessed what was troubling me she spoke, in whispers.

— My episode?

— Tell me, please.

I pulled her close to me, held her against my semen-wet chest. The room was still and terrible. The first light illuminating her dolls on the window ledge.

— I . . . you don't want to hear this . . . I know you think I'm crazy, I heard Saul talking about it. You both think I'm mad.

— No, not at all, tell me.

She lay back beside me, ran her hand over my stomach.

— Can I trust you?

— Dot, please.

I held her tight to me. Kissed her head.

— It's just this thing I learned, I don't know why, she whispered. — Being crazy, it's . . . I know you think I'm like this person who . . . a lot of it scares me too but . . .

— Tell me.

— They were arguing all the time. This was . . . I was maybe thirteen . . . He was going to leave, both of us, the family, he had a mistress, you know, divorce. It's kind of normal, this was a year or two after my brother died, you know parents break up after something like that. They had been smashing things and screaming, arguing and him shouting, 'I'm leaving, bitch.'

— This is your mum and dad.

— I got into this weird thing with food, because of it. I don't know, I got some kind of, maybe it was psychosomatic . . . I used to stick my fingers down my throat . . . every time they argued, and smashed things, I'd make myself puke.

— Dot.

— So then, you see, he couldn't leave when I was sick so I made myself really sick. I puked so much that blood came and I hadn't had a bowel movement in weeks, my ribs

199

were like fingers. He used to come to my bed and try to feed me, with a spoon, like I was really little again, and I'd wolf it down, to make him happy. And my mum too, she would kneel down and pray by my side. But as soon as they turned their backs, I'd puke it all up again. At first they blamed each other but the sicker I got the more they came to me. When I got really sick they would both just sit there, one either side of my bed. I'd pretend to be asleep or in a coma or something and they'd hold my hands and tell each other sorry and sometimes kiss.

— He didn't leave?

— No, but then the doctors said it was psychological, so they started sedating me and they had to feed me by a tube. It was just too horrible to . . .

I held her hand.

— You don't have to say any more.

— I think that's when I did get really sick, like schizo just to keep them together and . . . it was scary but it was worth it . . . I mean, they're still married right? This was . . . well, it was an institution . . . that really made me fucking crazy, they locked me in, I started hurting myself, eating glass.

— Jesus!

— I was pretty sick. Sorry. I should have told you before.

— My God, no, you're the most sane person I've ever met.

— You're so sweet.

It was me that cried then and her that held me. The tears had been long overdue from somewhere I did not even know. She held me as I wept for her.

Slowly then the holding became kisses, wet mouths, clinging, our mouths finding necks and breasts. — Shh, she kept saying, — let's be slow – and that slowness went on and on for hours it seemed, the gentle rhythms of licking and kissing and sucking, then the pause, and calm, then so gently, she took my sex in her mouth and I took hers, as we lay feeding from each other, lost in circlings of lips and sex.

With many kisses we smeared each other in our mingled sticky scent.

As she slept and my fingers memorised the gentle curve from her pelvis to hip and the muscles of her stomach, I told her many things in whispers: of how I would help her to be all she could possibly be, to serve her even, because she could shine brighter than myself, and to be in awe of her was all I could ever hope for.

It was then that Saul came back to me. Or perhaps some movement of hers on the tiny single bed, but I awoke from these reveries and my eyes roamed the room and there at the doorway I saw the shadow. The shadow moved. Saul? How long had he been standing there? Had he been watching us, maybe for minutes, maybe more, and seen it all? I tried to get up but her naked weight held me down, while from below I heard the creak of stairs.

Saul had left early the next morning and Dot went straight to Goldsmiths and so I spent all of my tube ride home preparing my confession to him, working out emergency strategies. There was no way he would listen. And the truth was I dreaded what the future might be post-confession. He would leave and Dot and I would be left alone together and she would no doubt tire of my neediness in less than a week.

I went to his door. It was only about ten but he was already drinking sherry while dressing in his funereal Spitalfields Market suit, pinched from that stall he said had a scam with undertakers who stole suits from corpses before they were buried. My nerves had upset my stomach.

— Saul, can we talk?

— Cowboy boots or sneakers? he asked. — Do you think the schoolgirl shirt deconstructs the suit or should I stick with the military-disco look?

He put on the Duchamps and relit a fag end from the

electric bar fire, postponing or pretending that nothing was happening, motioning for me to come in.

My fear was compounded by the fact that I was not allowed, ever, to introduce a topic first. He found this very uncool. He had to speak first – as it is with royalty.

— We have to talk, I said again.

— Damn the Duchamps. They're just too solemn for this occasion.

What occasion? Saul tiptoed over to the hundred LPs and rummaged, motioning again for me to be seated. I sat on the edge of his bed. A pair of Dot's panties were lying there next to the Pot Noodle ashtray.

— I'm feeling rather excellent, he said, without looking up. — I've finally realised that it is my fate in life. You know, for the student to surpass the master. She has – has she not?

This startled me – when had he ever said such a thing? It was maybe his next choice of music, Rapeman, that had me feeling ill.

— You OK? he asked. I stammered something out, about things in the house. Things with Dot.

— I'm having a day of revelations, he said. — I'm giving up on art. I'm going to have to get a job.

— You're joking.

— I have never been more grave. Indeed, the grave, it has been on my mind much, so I have resolved to get well. God knows how, but I think food might be something to do with it.

— Really?

— You're looking rather skeletal too. You could do with a good square meal.

How could I say what had to be said?

— But the thing is . . . Dot –

— I shall cook tonight, he said, — to celebrate.

— But the thing is . . . Dot and I –

202

— Shh, he said again, — you're disturbing my internal rhythms.

— Her and me . . . we –

— Shhhh!

— No, you don't understand, I, we have been –

— NO! Must you reduce everything to Oprah? Confessions are for paedophiles and priests.

I felt faint.

— So, he said, — what do you fancy? I've got my dole cheque, I thought some chicken à la Quixote.

I had to lie down, right there on his bed. Rapeman blaring and Steve Albini screaming, that song about Kim Gordon's panties, and Dot's panties were under his pillow, and the stench from the ashtray. I caught the vomit in my hand.

He passed me her panties to clean it up. I muttered thanks. He didn't bat an eye and passed me the sherry. — It's me that should be thanking you, he said. I tried to ask him for what.

— All that seems certain falls away. It's called a paradigm shift, I'm appalled you haven't read more Althusser.

His back was to me as he changed the record again. The Telly Savalas solo album.

— Or cauliflower au gratin, do you think? Of course, we'll have to acquire some fromage but I feel lucky today on the shoplifting front. I'm aspiring to some blue Stilton.

I could not rise to an opinion on choices of cheese. My many questions were drowned out by Kojak's version of 'The Impossible Dream' and with Saul's non-talk that told me asking for explanations would be crass.

— Shh, he said before I could even speak. — Change is the only thing in history that never changes. Do you think they have Stilton in Pricecutter or will I have to forage further afield for fromage?

This surreal meal he made for us. He'd cleared space on his floor and even put a hippy candle in a wine bottle. Whether it was some sick celebration of his acceptance of the adulterous union of Dot and me, he would not say.

The fruits of his shoplifting, he revealed with a flourish – Post haute cuisine! He thought it an innovative combination of the exotic and the banal – a little Thai, a little Jew, and some classic Brit. No cheese, and it was, from what I could gather, Heinz beans on rye-bread toast with salted KP nuts mixed in with the tomato sauce, topped with chilli. Dot found it hilarious. How the peanuts looked just like the beans and how each mouthful was an almost terrifying set of surprises, not knowing whether the next texture was soft or crunchy, all hidden, lurking in the sauce which was excessively chillied to hide the lack of anything else to taste. I sat silent throughout as they laughed together, trying to sort the beans out from the nuts on the side of my plate. I had the feeling, due to their secret smiles and little laughs and hand squeezes, that some deal had been struck to which I was not privy. That I was in some way the object of their mirth, or – worse – compassion.

And Saul fussed around and had Dot in hysterics with his haute cuisine jokes as I yet again crunched my way through what I thought was a spoonful of beans. They were coming up with surrealist food combinations.

— Fish fingers with marmalade.

— Spam tartare.

— Pâté de foie gras with Pot Noodle. And Saul laughed outrageously. So much so that I felt it could only have been somewhat hammed up. He grabbed my face, said to Dot, — Couldn't you just MWAAA? and he made a kissing face. — Really, at times I don't know whether to kiss or slap him.

They were laughing, as if they had agreed this whole night in advance, rehearsed their lines. I could not probe. They were off then on the next culinary rant. Developing theories about how food could be the next art form, that, no doubt, all the yuppie artists would start restaurants.

— Baked Hirst with the formidable formaldehyde sauce!

— Tampon terrine à la Emin!'

— Let's make Charles Saatchi eat his own intestines as a piece of performance art and make him pay for the privilege. Saucisson à la Saatchi. Perhaps he could achieve what every artist dreams of and literally vanish up his own arse!

I could not engage. Suddenly Saul announced that he was tired from all of his culinary exertions and desired the refuge of sleep. Alone, he requested, and apologised for asking, but could Dot sleep in my bed?

Back in my room, Dot undressed. I was profoundly confused by the events. For the first time, she was in my bed with his permission. We could not make love. She clung tight to me, wrapping her feet around mine, her breath slow in my ear, and I could not sleep.

Again, the shadow passed by the doorway. I saw him this time and our eyes met. He was naked and his sex was hard in his hand. He smiled, raised a finger to his lips and mouthed shhh. Then stepped back into the dark.

five

Trust. 1993. Video installation. 32 mins. Variable dimensions. Private collection.

The subject is centrally placed with a strong bright light aimed directly into his eyes. There are traces of lipstick on his lips, and smears on his cheeks. His eyelids have been made up with mascara. Each time he attempts to open his eyes, the bright light forces him to close them again. As he does not shield his eyes we can infer that his hands may be restrained, although this is impossible to determine from the framing of the footage. He seems unable or unwilling to move. Intermittently, the frame is interrupted as others enter; they are seen only briefly and their actions are either kissing, slapping or stroking the subject's face. The number of others is impossible to determine, as is their gender, as is the point of the exercise. A man is being repeatedly slapped and kissed for no apparent reason.

The subject may have been given instructions, such as 'do not move' or 'do not talk' but the viewer is not made aware of these. He appears to be intoxicated, but whether this is due to administered substances or from the experience itself is impossible to determine. The duration of the footage is thirty-two minutes and is one uninterrupted 'take' in real time. The footage repeats when completed. The camera relentlessly films from the same single tripod position as the subject waits for the next touch. Out of the thirty-two minutes, thirty-one of those are simply of the waiting face. While the face waits, noises can be heard from off-screen: footsteps, a glass smashing, a beating of leather on leather, sounds of whispering. The subject demonstrates a surprising range of facial expressions during this waiting, from acute anxiety to an almost ecstatic state. The effect is occasionally comical as the subject goes through what seems a process of excruciating anticipation, counting the seconds, holding his breath, screwing up his eyes, while waiting for a blow that does not come, or for a gentle kiss that turns out to be slap. It has been reported that audience members often experience emotions close to those of the subject, 'a dreadful sense of anticipation', 'a kind of relief'. It has been noted also that viewers often 'jump' when a blow is administered. The work has been described in a wide range of emotive language from 'abusive' and 'sick' to 'beautiful'.

The audio is in sync with the image. But unlike in a cinema where the audio seems to 'come from the screen', the audio is played from speakers at the opposite end of the gallery. This disembodied audio creates an alienation effect between sound and image. Some viewers have described how, hearing footsteps behind them, they had assumed that a real person had joined them in the gallery, only to discover that the sounds were part of the artwork.

Images evoked by the footage have frequently been described as those of interrogation, of consensual sado-masochistic ritual[1] and of 'devotional' religious suffering. The artwork has been banned in several countries with differing laws on portrayals of violence.[2] Islamic groups and women's organisations have, rather surprisingly, joined forces in condemnation of the work, albeit for differing reasons. This kind of reception is typical of the radical ambiguity at the heart of Shears's work.

A man is repeatedly slapped and kissed for no apparent reason, forcing us to ask: to what end? Shears offers no answers and so her work spawns a multitude of interpretations. Most recently, *Trust* has been interpreted as a prophetic critique of the illegal torture of detainees in Guantánamo Bay. But is Shears a political artist or, as others claim, an artist who is demonstrating the political apathy of Generation X – *Trust* being then quite literally a metaphor for the TV viewer who is caressed and bullied into a powerless consensual stupor? Or is her work symptomatic of that apathy and apathetic in and of itself?

Whatever her intent, something terrible and urgent seems to be at stake in *Trust*. It has, for some commentators, indicated the degree to which those who live 'alternative' lifestyles, who 'drop out', ultimately turn on each other in the isolated vacuum they have created. The games they play then, which start out as an escape from the real world, ultimately become psychologically loaded tortuous role plays, in which the repressed returns and the excluded world haunts in the form of an uncontrollable subconscious violence.[3]

1. The work was made at around the same time, February 1993, as the Operation Spanner trial in the UK, a legal first in which a group of homosexual masochists were charged with aiding and abetting violence against themselves. This so-called 'victimless crime' raised an outcry among civil liberties groups until a tape was leaked demonstrating the extent of the acts, at which point such groups found it hard or embarrassing to be legally defending men who nailed each other's penises to planks of wood.
2. Report on the legal battle over the inclusion of *Trust* in the annual art fair, Basel, Germany, *Guardian*, 12 October 2003.
3. The surrealists, situationists and various non-art-based anarchist communes and left-wing revolutionary groups attempted to live beyond the narrow confines of the given culture, trying to decondion on themselves, whether it be through rules on communal sexual sharing of partners, or rotas for eating, washing, childcare, etc. Or, in the case of the surrealists, by rejecting ethics in favour of rules determined by aesthetics, such as committing 'daily acts of absurdity'. The many 'escape attempts' by radical groups have resulted in terrible inversions. Communes in Germany and Holland in the seventies and eighties conducted interrogations of members who questioned the free-sex-sharing rotas, resulting in rape, the victims being largely women and children (many cases of child sex abuse have followed). Men, and usually one dominant male,

asserted the rules that regulated the subservient behaviour of the entire alternative community. Similarly, the surrealists were notorious for bullying, humiliating and banishing their own members for matters as apparently trivial as choice of clothes or music. While the leaders of such anti-groups may have felt powerless in the dominant culture, their isolated world ruled by aesthetic taste became more tyrannical than the conventional bourgeois order it opposed. The idea that 'we cannot change the world so we must transform ourselves' led to many desperate, immoral acts. See Georges Bataille's plans for a surrealist murder, 1912, in which a real victim was picked for ritualistic slaughter in an act intended as a communal rite of passage.

'WILL YOU STAY with me? Not that I mean getting married or anything, but at least share childcare, like between two homes, if that would suit you, because I know I'm not even related to Molly, but it would, for me anyway, not that this is just about Molly, but me and you, in some kind of non-official commitment, cos I don't think we can keep just busking it like this without some kind of plan, some kind of, not that I want to be the big man laying down the rules, given that you are in fact the real breadwinner and . . .'

The more he ran over the words, the more they became some pathetic apology for their own premise. It was the same with Dot's essay. The more he wrote the more he was concealing the passion at the heart of her art.

Dot had wanted to make an offer on a place in Battersea in the next week. And in so little time the deadline for the essay would be up. Their lovemaking had ceased. Conversation had become practical. It seemed to Owen that they'd be stuck in a repeat loop of endless platitudes, until she secured her new home.

He had watched the tapes ten times over while she was away and wept for what they really showed. The growing gap between them. He now knew what it was.

She could not talk of how she healed, of her medication, her many years of therapy and diet, her parents' care, her psychologists, her lovers, Molly's father, of the first person who helped her walk again, or who gave her hope. And he had not asked her if she had ever had a relapse, or what her new drugs were, or if she thought her madness would return. They had perhaps both feared asking, if there was not in her madness a freedom, a blinding flash of total power, that perhaps she secretly longed for.

Old Street.

He turned the corner onto Whitmore Road. 102. It was covered in scaffolding and tarpaulin. The building was gutted, a shell. There would be no gazing in the front window to the dark within to the imagined mess of Saul's front bedroom, the records splayed on the floor, Edna's Hindu rugs hanging from the railing in place of curtains. The big new metal sign said: 'SHOREDITCH TRUST: Changing Shoreditch for Good'.

Fluorescent yellow vests and hard hats passed. He turned and walked away.

The roundabout then, the statue in the middle with slogans cast in iron around it: 'I LOVE HOXTON 2000'. A cast-iron woman painted many colours held a black kid and an Oriental kid in tow, all hand in hand in hand, in frozen running form, the mother's metal finger pointing to Hoxton as if to salvation. She was ten feet high, with a Caucasian- or possibly Asian-looking cartoon face, purple stripy tights, dreadlocks and blue shoes. Like some futuristic manga/communist inspired statue, promoting the left-wing feminist post-colonial dream of a utopia rising from the ashes of the white patriarchal family. A smiling, multicultural, sexy, working single mother, dragging her two ethnically different children into a future of smiling prosperity.

On the walk home, he told himself that nothing short of a miracle could stop Dot from running out of his life.

Music and laughter were coming from inside his front door. It seemed to be many people, a party, Nirvana was playing and the laughter was definitely that of a man.

Molly had not run to greet him as he entered and there was no usual 'Hiya' from Dot. His curiosity pulled him down the corridor past Molly's Lego homes to the sounds in the kitchen. As he opened the door he saw Dot doubled over in laughter, Molly throwing around paper aeroplanes, and someone sitting in the alcove, just another step and he would see who.

'Owen, you wouldn't believe it!' Dot shouted.

A clean-shaven, gaunt, balding, grey-haired man, in an off-the-peg suit and white shirt, turned to face him, lowering his gaze as he tried to shake hands across the kitchen table. Molly's paper aeroplane flew between them as she shrieked with laughter. The old man's eyes at first seemed almost scared, then opened. A smile rising on the aged face as recognition hit.

'No way . . . Saul. My God?'

'May He rest in peace,' the man-who-could-not-be-Saul said so quietly as he negotiated the table edge and stood with hand outstretched. 'Good to see you again.' Dot was on her feet in a frenzy of explanations. The old man opened his arms and pulled Owen awkwardly to his body. He was enfolded in the smell of cheap aftershave, washing powder and cigarettes. Dot said: 'I plugged it in and it rang so I just picked it up and . . . the phone and . . .'

The old man patted his back and Owen awkwardly repeated the gesture. He almost said: 'Good to see you too, old man.'

'Saw her thing on the telly,' the old man said.

'God, fuck the telly,' Dot laughed.

'Lovely place you've got here,' the old man whispered, and Owen felt the warm wetness of a kiss on his cheek. Then Owen was released and the old man stood silent, looking him up and down, smiling to himself.

'Look at you, all grown up.'

Dot was lost for words as she stared at them both, trying to finish her story about the phone call but running to the freezer and shouting back about glasses and celebrating and bubbly.

'Not for me!' the old man said, raising a slender hand, as Dot uncorked the champagne Owen had bought for the hoped-for future occasion when she would announce to the world that they were a couple.

'Twelve Steps,' the old man whispered as he collapsed back into his seat. 'The liver, five years clean now. Not for me.'

'Mummy, Mummy,' Molly was shouting, 'can I have some?'

'OK, sure, I'm sorry,' Dot was saying to the old man and then to Molly: 'No, of course you can't. This is for grown-ups.'

In the silence that ensued Owen took his time to take the old man in: the shoes were brown loafers and worn thin around the edges, the shirt collar had a line of grime; the hair was shorn short and well receded at the hairline, thinning at the crown. He looked some kind of low-grade office menial, a mailroom man, or council bureaucrat.

Dot was unsure what to do with the bubbly, she poured one glass then stopped. Molly thrust a paper aeroplane almost into Owen's eye.

'Uncle Saul made it for me! I did the windows.'

Uncle already, was it? Owen thought. 'That's lovely, Mozzie . . . great,' he said.

The old man was quietly seated and smiling to himself, as Molly climbed onto his knee, doing zoom noises.

'Zoom, zoom,' the old man repeated with a smile to the child.

'Coffee then? Tea?' Dot was asking him.

'Water's just fine by me.'

Say something, Owen was telling himself, but too many questions interrupted and the Nirvana was bothering him and he was becoming increasingly aware that Saul must have known that these last months he had been turning the phone off each night. Molly's zooming paper planes saved him from speech and Dot was back with a bottle of Perrier and slices of lemon and was speaking on Saul's behalf, the old man just nodding in affirmation as she checked she'd got the story right, while Molly got grumpy because the nose of one of her planes had got squished and the man called Saul quietly calmed her and took it in his hands to fix it.

'Saul's a childminder now.'

'Really!' Owen said, hoping that no one had heard that note of incredulity. Dot handed him the poured glass of bubbly as if sensing his nerves. 'For a couple in Knightsbridge, architects. Can you believe it?'

No, he could not. His eyes fixed on the child on the old man's knee, whispering in his ear.

'So, you need to study for that or . . .' Owen asked, 'I mean, child-minding . . . is there a certificate or . . . ?'

Saul turned to speak but Dot jumped in first.

'Saul's doing a degree in child psychology . . . through the Open University.'

'Just a diploma,' the old man smiled.

Molly hugged Saul, and Owen had to take his time to take it in, the quiet non-judgemental intimacy of the old man; the way he placed a hand so gently over the child's soft blonde hair, not touching, then lowered his face to Molly's level, his voice in little whispers, apeing the child's, while on the stereo Cobain sang 'Lithium'.

'Saul's got his own place in Dalston.'

'Well, it's council. Nice place, all new,' Saul said. 'Central heating.'

'Imagine that, he's been there all this time and we never even –'

'Well, seven years.'

It was like they'd rehearsed this, Owen thought. Something was coming. No doubt some sob story had been in great intimate detail in the hours before as they replayed *Nevermind*. She and Saul had come to an agreement before he'd even stepped into his own home. She was reaching for his hand now and Saul was staring at the floor. Wait for it.

'Hell of a schlep to this couple in Knightsbridge, every day. He was saying he was looking for something a bit more local, and then it just hit me.'

She looked at him as if he was the one that was supposed to guess what was coming next.

'You know you've been saying you've not enough time to do the essay, and I'm never going to get the Zurich show ready with all the commuting, well . . .'

And she waited again, for him to speak. But he did not.

'Well, hey presto! I thought Saul could take care of Molly till I get her a new day care. I mean, till I get the new apartment. It'd give us both so much more time in the day. Isn't it brilliant?'

My God, they were cunning, using his ruse of postponing the apartment find against him. Turning his buying more time thing against him. Very smart.

'It would just be for a bit . . . you know, he'd be popping round first thing in the morning, giving her lunch and dinner. What do you think, O?'

She had called him O. For the first time in so long.

'Mumma, who's O?' asked Molly.

Owen's silence spoke louder than it should. If he could just get Dot alone, lay it out, take charge for once.

'. . . or if I moved back to mine. Put Molly back in the old place, none of this would be an issue,' she said.

Now it was Owen staring at the ground and Saul who was speaking.

'Sorry, don't want to cause any trouble.'

My God, had he not learned already that everything Saul said meant the opposite, not only would he be trouble but no doubt had been working out this scam for years. His passive-aggressive strategies. The conniving Machiavellian two-faced dole-scrounging leech.

Just then Molly and Dot turned to him, perfectly in sync, with puppy-dog eyes.

'OK, OK,' Owen said. 'I suppose we could do with an extra pair of hands.'

'I love you,' Dot shouted.

'Thanks, bud,' Saul said. And then Dot was reaching to hug them both but the table was in the way and she bashed her knee. Molly ran around collecting all her paper aeroplanes, asking Saul if he could help her draw windows and little people inside.

'Well, I'll be off then,' said Saul. 'Early start tomorrow.'

'Oh but it's too late. You'll simply have to stay the night.'

Was there no end to this? Owen thought.

'I'll get the tube.'

'But you're nowhere near the bloody tube, Sozzle, I'm not having you walking round bloody Dalston.'

She'd called him Sozzle.

'I can drive him back,' Owen said.

'You've had a glass and a half of wine!'

'OK, OK, I'll fix up the sofa bed.'

It was his study and his sofa bed and there was Saul standing beside him, with a book in his hand and a toothbrush, as if he'd planned this. Owen pulled out the old cranky springed base. It practically filled the entire room and was butted up against his PC desk.

'Cheers, mate,' Saul had said. 'Appreciate this, really.'

'It's fine, no problem.'

But now that they were alone he couldn't meet Saul's eye.

A morbid curiosity had Owen scanning the spine of the book Saul was holding. It was called *Believe in Yourself*. A self-help book. Jesus, how far the guy must have fallen? He was staring at Saul's socks then, they were grey and worn thin at the toes. He was having an almost sadistic pleasure in assessing the man's poverty, asserting his territorial rights.

'Well, you can use my desk light if you want to read. You can put your shoes out in the hall, and feel free to have a shower, it's at the end down there, next to the room Dot and I sleep in . . . So is there anything else?'

'Sorry to put you to this bother.'

Saul's eyes met his and there was something there not seen before, as if about to break through. Saul was the first to lower his gaze.

'Well, goodnight then.'

Owen shut the door and was out and into the hall. It was strewn with dozens of paper aeroplanes. As he bent down to pick one up he heard the faint trace of the voice of the long-dead Cobain floating through his home.

Owen must have sighed again because Dot set down her book on the bedside table and rolled over to face him.

'OK, I know.'

'What?'

'Do I have to play shrink with you? Maybe you could try to be . . .'

No, he wasn't going to finish her sentences tonight.

'To be . . . be honest with me. Why don't you start by saying "the thing is".'

'OK, the thing is . . .'

'Keep going,' she said and so he said: 'Well, you know what he's like, he makes a hell of a mess, he can't hold down a job, he's probably never even had one, he's –'

'He's changed, really, been through a lot.'

'I hope he's not planning on moving in here.'

'He has a place of his own.'

'Does he, have we any evidence?'

She was looking at him now and it was him avoiding

220

her gaze, searching for that bit of cornicing she'd found so fascinating.

'OK, I didn't want to say but he's lived alone for a long, long time and been hospitalised twice for alcoholism.'

'He told you that? Go on, Dot, you're really selling this to me.'

'He's clean now, he just needs some . . .'

'What?'

'Well, a little encouragement. I think doing a bit of work, in a supportive environment, would do him good.'

'Great, so, you've already decided without me. You're giving him a job, now you're planning on him moving in. Thanks, that's just great!

'He's done rehab and counselling. Really, he's totally changed.'

'Really?'

'He seems . . . well . . . gentle now.'

'Mister Machiavelli, Mister Make War not Love? Mister Thus Spoke Zarathustra! You want him taking care of your child?'

'You don't know.'

And she had said that in that way that announced that he would never know the depths that she knew.

'What the hell don't I know?!'

'Shh! He'll hear.'

He'll hear, in my house, he'll hear – Jesus! he almost said, but instead said, 'OK, sorry, I'm not raising my voice.'

Her hand searched for his beneath the covers. Asking him to turn, so he turned and her eyes were so full of understanding and compassion.

'Shh . . . I think . . . He's had a nervous breakdown,' she whispered.

'Well, that was kind of inevitable, don't you think?'

'You don't know, forget it.'

But then there was her silence, wounded girl huffing

221

like her daughter. Minutes it would take. Both of them as bad as each other. Mental age – four.

'Shit, I'm sorry, Dot, please.'

Say her name once again, take her hand.

'Dot, Dot, I'm sure you're right, I can't understand, could you . . . ?'

'Well . . . I can just . . .'

Jesus, so now it was the female high ground, the greater intuition of a woman. Sylvia Plath and women's groups and sharing circles. Fight it, swallow it, stroke her hand, her arm, her neck, say 'tell me' in whispers, say it again, again. She was fighting tears now, hug her, that's it, squeeze it out of her.

'Something in him . . . all the arrogance . . . he's gentle now, so gentle . . .'

Yes, let her cry. 'Shh, shh, tell me.'

'Like he's this old man, like he's taking care of this old man . . . I've seen it before . . . in hospital.'

That word silenced him. This was as close as she'd ever come to talking of her hospitalisation.

'Like he's . . . when you nearly die, willing to, and you choose . . . a razor or tablets or . . . I'm sorry, Owen, you're so good to me.'

'OK, tell me.'

She blew her nose on the duvet, apologised, a little laughter in her eyes, he kissed her forehead, held her tighter.

'Please, we need to talk about this . . .'

'Maybe it's an accident or they find you or . . . but still you made that choice. You puke up the tablets, or the razor – you put it down, but –'

'You're talking about yourself?'

'No, no, but you see, you're split in two, there's always this other you following you around. The one that really did it. You . . . you're haunted . . . his face . . . I just know.'

She was folded up in herself and he held her. He wanted to believe that the tears that threatened him were for Saul, but they were for that second Dot, the Dot that had died, that haunted the living Dot, that was yet another person wandering his home sleepless. He smothered her head in kisses, trying to tell her that he'd almost lost her once, but never again. She was his Dot.

'. . . He's so gentle now . . . his poor face . . . I just feel so guilty . . . poor love.'

Owen stroked her head, whispering. He was glad that in some impossible way the coming of Saul had brought them closer again.

'It's OK, OK, my love, I'm sure it'll be fine having him around. Just for a while anyway, till we sort everything out.'

*

Daffodils appeared unseasonably early and a playwright was elected president of the Czech Republic. Reality had, rather irresponsibly, conceded control to utopian fiction. With Saul and Dot too, an exchange of power had taken place. After he admitted that she had surpassed his mastery he sank into a steady decline.

He had trimmed his hair and weakly made an effort to tidy up the kitchen and hall, not exuberantly or in protest, and without his usual irony. One day, when Dot was away at Goldsmiths, he came to my door.

— What are you writing? he asked. His face without make-up, heavy with days of stubble, his voice gentle and sincere.

— Well, just a review for the . . . I was ashamed to tell him it was a tacky promo – four hundred words on the new Madonna album – and amazed to hear what he said next.

— Can I read it? That is . . . if I'm not intruding.

And so, taking the seat at my busted-up computer, he read, sometimes nodding, sometimes making little noises as I waited for his judgement.

— Not bad at all, he said.

— Really? I mean, she's crap but I can't say that and I'm trying not to use any positive adjectives, but it's –

— A fine use of rhythm, keep it up, he said and went back to the door. — Oh and by the way, if you fancy doing that bit of writing I was supposed to, you know for that damnable *Bug* thing, I really can't face it. The muse seems to have left me. I doubt she will return, ever.

I was dumbfounded. But that was not the end of it. He then thanked me.

— For what?

— Don't feign ignorance. I've been a total bastard, we all know that. I'm amazed you both haven't run off. Anyway, you seem quite happy now, the pair of you.

— You mean, it's OK, me and Dot . . . I mean –

— Shh, he said. Don't be crass. You have my blessing.

And he touched my shoulder. It was unbelievable. Generosity of spirit and then humility. It must have pained him greatly to be experiencing these things for the first time. I couldn't help but wonder if it was perhaps a mask behind which some terrible scheme was being planned. But yet, he was sincere. The reason I knew this to be the case was revealed in the bin bags by the front door. One had burst, and inside I saw six empty boxes of a sherry brand I had not seen before and Dot and I had certainly not drunk. Saul had started drinking secretly, quietly, alone.

I noted also that, for several days on end, by Saul's bed, the jobs page lay open, several boxes circled. It was around then that I had another revelation about his failure. I discovered his oft-quoted original Duchess book, lying in Dot's bedroom covered in her spidery handwritten notes. Therein, I discovered the following. 'Life is a game, she screamed', 'She made me wear her stocking as she spat in my face.' All of Saul's great shocking ideas had been stolen from that book. But furthermore, as I read it I saw it was poorly written and obviously had not one shred of historic validity. It was little more than a tuppenny porno book fraudulently peppered with characters stolen from history to make it seem more scandalous.

'Sporting her moustache she tied the powerless Duchamp to the Louis XIV chair and forced the assembled gentry to tease the prostrate man with tantalising tastes of quim and shaft and with tortures involving whips and knives, while Man Ray, cuckolded, camera in hand, could only record the squalid scene.'

Ridiculously fake and poor Saul had taken it all so seriously. The most troubling thing, however, was how, every day, Dot was becoming more and more the incarnation of Saul's squalid fictional heroine. Increasingly loud, energetic and aggressively fabulous, it was all I could do to calm her, as I was sure her exuberance made Saul feel even smaller, rubbing dirt in his wounds, so to speak. After the torn T-shirts it was ripped tights; she painted flowers on his army boots and wore them without laces, without his permission; she fastened her hair into six short wiry tufts with elastic bands, porcupine-like. She seemed to be spending more time on turning herself into an *objet d'art* than on her art. She returned from Goldsmiths on one such day with an old lady's wig stolen from Save the Children – terrifying to behold. Her blackened eyes peeking out from the matted blonde tufts as she ranted and stripped in my room.

— Some arsehole wants me to do a photo shoot in some magazine. They're all going crazy. He said I look like a junkie. I told him to fuck himself.

She stood before me in her underpants, putting on a play version of Dietrich, the Duchess, or maybe Dracula.

— I vant you to impale me on your stick!

— Shh, we'll have to be quiet? He's pottering around next door.

— He knows anyway, why do you keep pretending he

doesn't? You've even started talking like that silly old book of his.

It bothered me that I had not yet told her that Saul had been spying on our nocturnal couplings those past few weeks.

— You seem to be more concerned with his feelings than mine, she teased. — You fuss over him like an old maid.

As usual such an accusation had me upon her in a frenzy, my fingers groping at her panties as she tore the clothes off me and bit my neck. She freed my cock with one hand, working it hard as she rubbed her clit frantically. We stumbled and fell to the floor. As she mounted me, gasping with that sharp intake of breath, her face suddenly turned to the door. It was part ajar. We both stared at that gap, as if waiting for Saul to find us at any moment. This added great urgency to our fucking, and I pulled out swiftly as I was about to come. Dot held me tight at the stem and pinched the cock head and the cum subsided as she waited, whispering to me.

— I'm sure he heard us.

I got to my feet, shut the door properly and returned to the floor where she was waiting for me on all fours. But after a dozen or so careful thrusts, I was about to come again, and Dot was frustrated, so I withdrew. We were silent for a moment, both staring at my cock, as if it might give us an answer.

— Maybe if we filmed ourselves, she said. And jumped up.

So it was, with the aid of the camera perched on the table by the door and plugged into the back of my B&W portable, that Dot and I watched this young couple fucking in our room as we fucked. Even though in those weeks, with Dot's guidance and pinch technique, I became more proficient and could delay my ejaculations, it seemed that it was only the idea of getting caught and being watched that could accelerate her arousal to the point where we could come violently together. Her camera had become the eye of the absent Saul.

Saul too only aggravated this situation, as every night he found other excuses for Dot and me to sleep together. He claimed to have a migraine, or flatulence, or a job interview early the next morning; he just needed to be alone. On the nights when she slept with him, she would wake me in the early hours, telling me he'd forced her out of bed. It was as if he had pushed us into closer physical intimacy deliberately so he could live through us vicariously. On those nights when she slept in my arms, his face again and again appeared at my door. We did not realise, then, that such games would escalate to perverse proportions.

It started on the night of the games in St Monica's school playground. Swings and roundabouts. The place that in the daytime was bright with the colours of so many coloured children. Their screams and laughter the only thing truly joyful in the slowly gentrifying Hoxton Square. It was dark and the park was empty and moonlit, as if it were a stage. Dot was hyper. She'd been worrying about Saul's increasing isolation.

— Let's cheer him up, she'd kept saying. — Let's party – let's give him a treat. Things like that.

She'd been unable to sleep and had dragged Saul and me out. Saul was looking emaciated in his stained suit, he had not worn make-up in weeks and had almost a full beard. He could not find socks and wore sneakers, he stank of sherry. Dot seemed not to notice any of this, she was on fire with ideas, video camera in hand as she led us through the hole in the school fence.

— Come on, let's do the swings! Sozzle, come on, cheer up.

Saul stood there, silent, smoking, staggering on the spot. He never liked to be told to do anything. So she started manhandling him, getting him on the swing. He struggled, tried to push her away but then it turned playful.

— I'll barf on you, he said. — I can't handle swings.

— OK, so the roundabout. Dot shouted as she ran to it, and spun like a demon round and round. I didn't know what to do. I lifted her camera and filmed. She jumped off.

— Come on, Soz, not scared of a spin, are you? Climb on, trust me, you'll be fine.

— Please, I think I shall go home, Saul said.

— OK, OK, I've got it. Dot said.

She ran to the edge of the playground, then turned by the hopscotch chalk drawings and the concrete dolphin, then walked swiftly robotically towards us, at great speed. As she headed for the climbing frame, I suddenly realised she had her eyes closed. I ran forward, shouting, — Watch out!

— Left Saul shouted. — Turn left!

I was feet from her; she had her hands out in front of her.

— Don't stop me she said, I've got to get to the end by myself. I stepped back as she walked Frankenstein-monster-like towards Saul. He was laughing. Just then a car went past. I ducked down and so did Saul, the headlight illuminated Dot walking, arms outstretched, eyes closed through the kiddie park like a zombie, but the car didn't stop. She kept on and was heading towards the seesaw.

— Watch out! Saul shouted. — Stop and turn 180 degrees! He was becoming quite excited by the game.

— I don't trust you, Dot shouted, — it's a trick.

— Watch out, you're going to bang your knee, I shouted.

She turned swiftly away then broke into a run, eyes tightly closed. She was heading right for the fence. Saul broke into a run and chased after her, shouting, — Stop, Stop. I did the same. We caught her just in time, and we all collapsed in hysterics.

— What the fuck was that? Saul asked.

And so Dot explained it was this game she'd done in

therapy, a trust game, 'walking blind' it's called. You were judged as cured and socially well adapted if you could walk to the end of a hall trusting that people would guide and catch you. People who were paranoid or scared couldn't take more than a few steps.

— I bet you couldn't do it, Sozzle.

— Really? I'm a damn sight more blind than you'll ever be!

So to our great surprise the drunken Sozzle got to his feet, stretched his arms out and started walking away. At first his steps were confident but then he stalled, he turned 180 degrees, then edged forward as if he were in a minefield.

— Watch out for the elephant! Dot called.

— What fucking elephant? he shouted — we're not in fucking Africa!

I sat back and watched a scene of the most absurd beauty, as the moon shone casting long shadows over a blind man who tiptoed with excruciating caution around a tiny enclosure of plastic play animals.

— Take a left, no, no, your right, my left, right? Dot was shouting.

— I can't stand it any longer! Save me from myself! Saul proclaimed as he froze on the spot, eyes closed but to the heavens. We rushed over to him.

— You were brilliant, Dot said, as she took him in her arms and covered his closed eyes in kisses.

— Failure is my fate, my dears, he said, as he rested on a play animal. — Even a pink plastic hippo finds me an object of mirth.

Amid much laughter we drank the remains of the sherry and my last memory of the night was of Saul and Dot on either side of the seesaw, as I stood on the central pivot, rocking them back and forth with my feet, keeping an eye out from my perch for the police as they laughed like naughty children. And I thought that, in a strange way, we had returned to that state of joy we'd first known, before they had paired off, when we shared her affections equally. I have no memory of how we staggered home to bed and it was only morning when I realised which bed. I woke to find an arm round me and it was not Dot's but Saul's. I turned and there she was, one hand between her legs, her naked breasts falling onto the pillow. Her other hand was covering my crotch, which to my alarm I discovered to be naked. While Saul slept on beside me, I unpeeled myself from their bodies and wondered what subconscious desires might have that night have been acted out under the alibi of amnesiac drunkenness.

Most days she was off to Goldsmiths or the warehouse, to talk to Pierce and all the other new artists about who got what space and the electricity problem and what was to be done about flyers. She was all lists and extension cables and power points and video instruction manuals. Her appearance, every day was increasingly devastating to behold. She had shoplifted a fur coat and cut the arms off to make into some kind of armbands or muffler. She tore the collar off and wore it as a necklace of sorts. I sensed that all this manic energy was fuelled by a fear of what Dot was actually getting herself into. It was three weeks till the *Bug* show, a month to her degree show and I still had not seen how she'd turn her tapes into art. I insisted on accompanying her to the warehouse one day to unravel the mystery. I offered to carry her TV there for her and her extension cables.

Bug was in an old biscuit warehouse off Camden Lock above a kebab shop and bookies. The windows on the first floor had been covered in corrugated metal, probably by the council, and the front door had been booted in. As soon as we were climbing up the dusty steps the smell of fungus and what seemed like dead meat was overwhelming, mixed with something sweet, like sugar or vomit. The other thing that overwhelmed the senses were the sounds, many, of radios, footsteps, hammers banging, people shouting. It was hard going carrying the TV and Dot helped me. All along the stairwell walls there were flyers for other exhibitions, *Die Yuppie Scum* and something called *Sale*.

We reached the top stairs and the place expanded exponentially before me. Dozens of young artists marching past with hammers, boards; no one paid us the slightest attention.

A woman with dreadlocks and Doc Martens walked past carrying a mannequin with a dildo for a nose.

— Hi, is Pierce here? Dot asked.

The woman shook her head and looked me up and down. I was obviously not cool enough. Dot showed me the way to her space. The whole place had been partitioned off into large cubicle-type areas. Again, no one seemed to pay her any heed. I'd expected a Pierce or a Hirst to come up to her and greet her excitedly.

We passed some photos of foetuses in formaldehyde, derivative of Hirst but lacking the humour. An older woman had made a sculptural bust of her bust out of something that looked like dog food. There were tins of the stuff next to it on the floor by the plinth and a sign that said 'Sponsored by Kennomeat'. I passed some graffiti sprayed on the wall that read: A PILLAR OF LOTTERY TICKETS THREE THOU-SAND FEET HIGH. And another that read: 365 EMPTY PICTURE FRAMES PLACED RANDOMLY ROUND THE UK.

We followed the hammering and passed a young man who was making pictures entirely out of the red dots that galleries stick on artworks to show they have been sold.

I struggled on as Dot again asked another artist, a terrifying-looking bare-chested bloke with tattoos, where Pierce was. Fuck Pierce, the guy said then sprinted off. There was a weary workaholic sense of commerce, career and competition

231

about them all. The artists seemed to resent contact with each other. Many had draped material over the openings of their enclosure and all they seemed to do was bitch about the others. And this was a 'movement'. How could this disparate bunch of aggressive individualists ever amount to a collective anything? A far cry indeed from the surrealists and the Dadaists and all the other ists that Saul worshipped. I considered trying again to get an article published in the *Guardian*. I had recently got the editor's address.

We turned the corner of a stack of MDF boards and a funky young blond skinheaded guy turned to Dot and smiled. Finally I set down the TV. It was hard to hear what they were saying as someone was experimenting with a stereo, the banging and sawing was so extreme and people were shouting everywhere, but among lots of name-dropping about Tracey and Damien I got the gist. The guy led Dot to her space and so I had to pick up the TV again.

The guy turned to me. — You're a writer then, yeah?

I shrugged.

— You want to see my work? His studio space was right next to Dot's. Dot encouraged me to give the guy a minute.

I smelled it before I saw it. His work appeared to be shit on lollypop sticks.

— Yer s'pose to suck 'em, he said. — Or stick 'em back up yer arse like a cock.

— Really? I said.

— Capitalism's shit, he said, — that's what it's about.

It is never a good idea, as Saul once said, to take a metaphor literally. He handed me his CV and some photos and I smiled to myself as I thought he could rename the work 'poopsickles'. He shook my hand vigorously and again asked me what paper I worked for. I made my excuses and headed back towards Dot, reflecting on how depravity seemed to be 'in'. Extraordinary how many of the poor buggers had abandoned conventional artist's materials to

232

work in shit, piss and blood. I saw tabloids printing pictures of some very average, scared art students trying and failing to be spectacularly offensive, checking the exact consistency of their poo, as if they were da Vinci testing colours of oil paint. It was all perhaps some terribly sincere attempt to prove that their art came from deep within their unique selves, which, since more than five of them were doing pretty much the same thing, seemed not so unique.

I much preferred Dot's videos. They moved in a subtle way, with qualities utterly absent in her peers. With their intimacy.

I pulled the drape back and there she was. There was an old video player and mess of wires on the floor. She had just joined up my extension cable to another that seemed joined to yet another and was about to plug the TV into it.

— Well, here goes, she said.

Thankfully the TV came to life, but with no image, just fuzz. She stared at it.

— I don't really fit in, do I? she said. — They're all so much smarter than me.

— Not at all, I said, — your stuff's going to be great. I plugged in her video player and got one of her tapes from her rucksack and stuck it in, turned it on. The cross-dressing one. — See, I said, great.

But I did worry for her. There was no way she could compete with these wannabe scandalmongers. I tried to encourage her. We sat and stared at the cross-dressing. It wasn't working for her, minutes passed and she was silent, sitting there on the dusty floor, fiddling with the cables. I put on the moustache tape.

— You think I should show just one tape? On different tellys? Or lots?

I shrugged. — Sorry, maybe . . . Uhm . . .

— Or get a big screen and a video projector, they're expensive. Or make a kind of stack of TVs?

I apologised again for my ignorance and her eyes became fixed on the white walls. Behind it and beyond, the sounds of a hundred hammers, drills, feet, purposeful activity. I looked round at the plug sockets, the old TVs. Her breathing quickened, she started hyperventilating.

— Saul would know what to do, she said.

An overwhelming sense of failure came over us both.

— Oh God, oh God, I'm so fucking useless.

I held her, she kissed my neck, bit my ear, whispered in a hiss, — Fuck me!

We were animal, clawing at each other. I fell to my knees and tore her shirt from her. She wrapped her leg around my head as I feasted on her moistening cunt muttering insanities. – My darling, my Duchess! I could feel her looking round, gripping my head, whispering.

— Quick, what if someone sees, we must be quick. I can hear someone coming. There was no one, it was just her little game. I put first one then another finger deep inside her and her pelvis bucked, her spine arched, my teeth tore into her thigh, as my little finger circled her anus. I felt her cunt spasm around my fingers and suddenly a hot gush sprayed my face. Her body writhing, she started screaming.

— Come in my face, come in me!

I covered her mouth with my hand and she struggled as if violated, as we fell to the ground. Around us the banging did not cease and the ground shook with drills. Her legs spasmed and she kicked the wall. I tore her pants off and was soon inside her, thrusting only for seconds before spraying all over her cunt lips, her skirt and face.

We heard footsteps behind us, from the other side of the partition. I made her lie still. Shh. We both looked and saw clearly that Dot's foot and panties were visible from the opening.

Don't move, I whispered.

The footsteps receded and we broke apart.

— Fuck, maybe it was Pierce, she said.

Again it struck me, how the idea of being watched secretly had aroused her.

— Don't worry, I said, — if anyone saw they'd probably just think it was performance art.

She laughed and held me. I apologised for coming too soon but she didn't care, she said, we still had time to work on it.

But what if her art was like my cock, failed and premature. In my mind some absurd equivalence was forming. If I could hold back my ejaculations then her success as an artist would be assured. My fear was that we were just fucking around and wasting time and would be left with nothing.

That night when we got back Saul was already comatose in his bed, with three boxes of sherry denuded. Dot wanted to wake him to ask his advice but I calmed her.

— Shh, he hates being woken. Here, help me take his boots off.

I noticed that a job application lay on the floor, spilled sherry blurring the words he had written. Dot got her video camera; she wanted to film Saul's sleeping face. She plugged it into the back of the telly and his face filled the screen. We sat there silent then on the edge of his bed as he snored, staring not at him, but at his TV face. We managed to get a glass out of the last sherry box and I smoked. Dot lay down next to Saul and I curled up with my head resting on her lap.

— What are we to do? I heard her whisper.

I must have dozed off as I was woken by movement. She was stroking me, kissing me, whispering shh. It took me a while to work out where I was. The ceiling, the posters, the sense of him just beside me, the stench of his alcohol sweat. Then his face still there on the TV screen. Dot's face over me, grinning like a demon.

— Shh, she whispered, her hand covering my mouth as the other reached for my cock. I could not, I would not.

— Shh, stop struggling or he'll hear us.

That was when it happened. At first there were just gentle kisses as we watched the screen, but then things quickly got out of control. Her hand was at my belt again, and her mouth round my stiffening cock.

— My God, no, no, you'll wake him up!

Her mouth full, she could not speak, she motioned to the TV. She was staring at it too, at Saul's face on TV, as if we were to watch it, not him, for emergency signs of his waking. That he was on TV seemed to give us licence to ignore the fact that he was sleeping inches from us on the bed. Playfully the demon pinned down my arms with her knees and thrust her naked sex in my face.

Her mouth already fast at my cock, the smell of her sex, her pubes teasing my lips. I saw Saul's face twitch on the TV and froze.

I prayed for it to be over soon. I could hear him moving in the bed just inches from us. She took me deep into her mouth and was making herself gag on my cock, her teeth riding rugged over my swollen head. From beyond the line of buttocks, where the panties bit tight into her thigh I caught the glimpse of light in her eye from the TV. She was watching the TV. She shuddered suddenly wetting my face with her cum. Her pelvis bucking in spasms and I was thrown into a frenzy sucking the juice from her soaking, twitching cunt.

She got up then, whispered shh, and went back to her bedroom, smiling to herself and I was left to face the sleeping Saul, my face reeking of her. He mumbled something and I froze.

He mumbled again.

— Turn . . . off . . . the light – that was all. I lay there staring at the TV screen. My face and Saul's were together on its surface.

I feared the morning when Saul would work out what had happened.

I must have dozed off because I awoke beside him. He was not abrupt, as I expected. He simply spent the usual reverent time to find a butt end big enough to relight and stared out at his scattered records and clothes as he smoked.

— It's fucking obscene, he said. — Unbelievable.

He stared perplexed at the TV screen with the image of his own feet on it, then, disgruntled, unplugged the camera and stuck on the news.

— Look, I'm really really sorry . . .

He ignored me, kept on.

— These humiliations . . .

I searched for words and he did too as ITN told us that the World Trade Center bomber had just been arrested and another shopping mall the size of a town had just opened and we were bombing in Bosnia, and Damien Hirst had sold his ninth formaldehyde animal for six figures.

— For a man of my years, to have to endure –

— It won't happen again, I said, — We were drunk it was just –

— What are you on about? I'm talking about job interviews. Have you ever been to one? They want me to go to a call centre. I don't even know what a call centre is! I'm going to have to have your help.

That was all he said.

He would not talk of our bedtime behaviours. For many nights similar drunken rituals were performed, but in every episode Saul was the same, eyes closed as if pretending it was a dream. And each day was the denial of the daylight waking reality, as if we were vampires that only lived at night. In the three weeks that followed we three always slept together in many combinations in as many beds and we entered what I came to think of as the 'perverse equilibrium'. Every day I faced the questions and every day it was the denial but come night, when drunken, our bodies found each other.

One morning after another night I decided it was time to confront her.

— Can't you see how sick this is? It's time we sat down with Saul and discussed it all. She laughed in my face.

— My little brother, she said as she kissed me.

I needed to analyse it with him but I knew he would shh me as he did before. Don't be crass. But how could I not talk about it when every night the ritual became more perverse?

There was one night I recall vividly. (Although, perhaps even this memory has been tainted by Saul's squalid texts.) It was in Saul's bedroom again. The curtains were drawn open and moonlight and street light illuminated his rubbish, his clothes in piles, his jackets hanging on nails like a firing squad, an audience.

Dot and I lay on either side of him as he pretended to sleep.

His vast wardrobe doors lay wide open, but nothing was visible inside. It seemed a huge black hole in the room, a portal to another time and place, staring back like an empty eye socket. His books were face down on the ground, food cartons discarded, the interior silver sachet from a sherry box inflated like a party balloon. Every object was illuminated in the same moon-blue light, unified in its mess, somehow an equality between each as if it was carved in stone. And on the TV screen Saul's cock, standing erect, filling the screen. We stared at it, as if it were a pillar or cenotaph. Then she started to suck it.

And the hand that gripped mine as she climbed on top of me, as she sucked him and took my cock and slid me into her wetness, as my hand went to her mouth to stifle her cries – that hand, as I felt her cunt tighten round me as I withdrew and shot over her ass-hole. I am sure of it, the hand that held mine so firmly, gripping so tight, was not hers.

— Morning, he said. Fucking hell, no ibuprofen or Rennies, I'm sick as a dog, couldn't sub me a quid for some cancer sticks, could you? as he passed me on his way to the bath-room for his usual post-booze vomit.

Such banalities. Such necessary lies to keep the un-utterable truth alive for another day. Such beauty that we pretended all was no more than drunken late-night fumblings, forgotten in the hung-over search for food and pills.

The opening night of *Bug* was in two weeks and I was to present my fake attempt to duplicate Saul's Duchess rant, which itself was based on something fake, to Pierce. I had been unable to complete it for these reasons. Dot had returned late and drunk from another day at the warehouse. She was wearing a kid's sweetie necklace and the terrifying wig in two tiny tufty ponytails with a seventies psychedelic miniskirt and sparkly silver disco socks that she'd cut the toes from and so magically transformed into armbands. She wanted to make another artwork right away. If she could just slow down, I told her, decide on one tape, then her exhibition would be done.

— We haven't done the best yet, she kept saying. — We have to keep going.

She had an idea that sounded familiar to me, again from the Duchess book: Duchamp tied to the chair. Something about sacrifice, paying the price for being bad. I didn't want to burst her bubble or to let Saul know that I'd worked out that his heroes were phoney, so I agreed to go ahead with the new artwork. The vodka she brought helped.

I drank and watched as she arranged the camera and tripod, marvelling at her manic energy. It was OK, I told myself, just one more game, but I worried for Saul. His hand was shaking as he poured the vodka and his fore-head was sweating. It was late in the day but still he was still only half dressed. Pinstripe flares, barefoot, bare chest with kimono.

She set a chair in the middle of his room, throwing clothes and ashtrays to the side to make space and pointed her camera at the seat. I helped arrange the anglepoise lamp before the chair as she collected Saul's ties and belts to use as restraints, along with a glass and a high-heel shoe which would be 'props'.

She had not decided which one would be tied to the chair and did not meet my eyes as she went through the procedure. My heart was aching for a little glance to tell me it was all a joke, but there was nothing. We were to draw straws but had none, so it was cigarette butts. Her fingers did not hide the fags well enough, we could all see which was the shortest, but I sensed it was a secret message from her – a sacrifice had to be made to validate our sacrilegious union. I waited till last and took the shortest.

More vodka was required and Saul volunteered to go to the off-licence with her money. I tried to ask him if he was OK with all this, but he left with no more than a shrug of shoulders. We were alone together.

— He seems to be a bit weirded out by . . . you know . . . our um . . . sleeping arrangements. He seems . . .

— I know, she said, — don't worry.

She told me I should be brave, this was going to be the answer to everything. She kissed my cheek. — Trust me, she said and I tried. I gave her my hands which she tied behind my back round the chair. — A lovely little game, she said.

She stood back and stared at me as if admiring an artwork, her eyes critical, but a tiny smile on her face, and I could not help but recall Saul doing exactly the same thing to her, that night she cut off her hair.

— Vodka, I said, but there was none and my arms were

restrained. She whispered, — I know, O. Shh. She went next door and came back through with her wigs and make-up.

— Who would you like to be tonight? she whispered.

I knew it was only minutes till Saul returned and did not want him to find us kissing but was so desperate with need. I told her I would like to be a girl, make-up would be required, that way she would touch me more.

She painted my face. Her eyes focused on the act, as if I was a canvas. Eyeliner, mascara, lipstick. I surrendered and it started to make some sense. For us three to be together, I had to re-enact her own transformation in negative, to take the leap, become her.

— My beautiful girl, she whispered.

Saul came in the front door and she pulled away. Vodka with no mixes and two new packs of Marlboro and the Velvet Underground to get us in the mood. I wondered what his motivation was. To punish us or accept our union. Some ritual had to be gone through. An end to the pretended secrecies. Dot danced, arms spinning, waving round the bottle to 'Venus in Furs'.

She adjusted the lamp and the camera on the tripod and turned off the top light and plugged the camera cable into the telly to show me my pretty face, as if all the world was watching. She ran back and forward from the TV, checking the framing. I closed my eyes as she painted a beauty spot on my cheek.

— So beautiful she whispered. — Just stare at the light, like you're being interrogated. My eyes burned and I could see nothing. Whispers in the dark.

— No way, Saul said. The album had ended.

— Shh, it's secret, she said to him, then to me so close in my ear, so gentle.

— We're going to do little things to you ... and you can't move or talk OK, that's all you have to do, try not to respond, OK?

It started with many giggles. The camera had been turned on, she said, we were recording. I had to keep a straight face. I couldn't, was laughing at how this whole thing was absurd and sorry for spoiling it all. My hands were not tied at all well and soon were free and I was holding them up to the camera and saying, — See! He was behind me then, trying to retie in the dark and the top light had to be put back on so he could do it properly and, laughing, I called him the Marquis and it still wasn't tight enough so I called him a wimp. — Tie it tighter, you wimp! Finally I was tied and the lights were off but nothing was happening. They were whispering beyond and I was laughing. — C'mon, this is a joke, but they did not respond.

Minutes passed and I was bored, but then sounds behind me of heels, stilettos. I was laughing at how contrived it all was, was that really all they could come up with? I really couldn't see a thing though, was sure the lamp was too near my retina, all burned shapes. A whisper close to my face, his. — Shut the fuck up and face the light!

A sharp noise then to my left. I turned to see but was light-blinded. The sound again. Of leather or wood, a strike. Dot's command again to face the light. Fear then of punishment.

A hand so gentle stroking my cheek, or the brush of a kiss? Who?

I waited, my face muscles contorting in a smile, I fought it, was thinking about the image of my face on the TV, this was for her, her art. The more I fought it the more hilarious it became, this pathetic DIY grunge attempt at sado-masochism.

A slap shot through my face and I reeled from it. Then nothing, nothing. I waited for a second blow. Noises behind me, like steel on glass. Then no, the front door, opening then closing. My God, had they left me? Was this the plan? They'd be out all night and I'd be tied like this till the joke wore thin and they'd been out clubbing and if they were sober enough then they might untie me, what, four hours later? Or one of them had left for good and the other was running after.

I felt wet on my face. My God. I turned to see who, but was blind. Hands held my face firm from behind, aching to know that soft wet again.

A slap. Cheek hot from it. Sound of breath, quick in my ears. Rush of blood. Craning to hear, trying to anticipate the next blow. Sound of what? Plastic being crushed. Nothing. Then nothing more. Starting to panic, hands struggling to get free. Whisper in my ear. His voice I think.

— I love you.

Sharp sting on my nipple — teeth? I looked down but my hair was pulled back by the roots. The urge to beg. — Please, please, stop!

Nothing for minutes more, something in me weeping, please, please, don't make me wait, hurt me even, just please, not the waiting. Cold sweat alive down my arm. The lamp moved closer to my face, the burn of it on my cheek. Do something, please. Struggling so hard not to cry out.

A mouth on mine, lips hot wet, full, no stubble, hers then, a tongue on my teeth, smell of patchouli, of sweat.

Laughter behind me, both of them, it seemed, or another. How was that possible? Someone else in the room there with them? I turned to look, in a panic, but hands held my head and others tied a blindfold over my eyes. My feet then all that was free, kicking, but hands then, many it seemed, holding, tying them firm, a gasp from some voice not Dot or Saul.

The waiting, the weeping, I became animal, gasping, could I talk? Would I be struck? Would they gag me? Had Saul, in the off-licence, told some strangers about this freak tied up and invited them round? I tried to cry out but lips were on mine, then firm hands holding my mouth. I tried to speak but my lips trembled so much I could not. A voice in my ear: — Shhh, shhh. A glass smashed behind me. A face came close, sniffing my skin, then nails, a nail or glass, scraping my chest. A hand over my mouth.

The waiting. No sound behind.

The front door? They had left me alone, tied and bound.

Please God.

And how many times did I cover my eyes and hide myself in the darkest place while I heard the plates smash and the screaming and the door being slammed, and the fear of my mother's lover coming home drunk, then beating her. Her begging him to stop, to leave, then begging him to stay. And all that silence, waiting, and my mother's hand would find me in the ironing cupboard, hidden beneath the sheets, telling me she loved me more than anyone and we would get away soon, just the two of us. But the two I did not trust, not him and her, or her and me. Not two, ever.

Something broke in me then. I could not stop it. It came from some force stored in muscle, hot flush through my skin. I closed my eyes and surrendered to it. Every muscle taut. A rush of tears and insane laughter.

The light was turned off but I was blinded and speechless.

— It's OK, the camera's turned off now, Dot said and the hands came to free me. — You can open your eyes. But I did not want to. I wept as their hands and voices reassured. — You OK? Was just a game. Hope we didn't freak you out. You freaked out? Sorry, baby. Let's put the top light on. Shh.

A hand was on my shoulder, then a kiss on my cheek.

— It's OK, we stopped filming ages ago, you can come back now.

A kiss on my other cheek.

— Poor baby, he's lost the plot.

— Beautiful, she said.

— Yes.

Lips then on my eyes, my nose, hers I assumed. Then a hand through my hair. A mouth met mine, then moved from me and I heard them kiss inches from my face. My every sense was heightened in that state. The burn had faded from my eyes but I kept them tight shut, savouring. I heard the saliva in their mouths, the breath through teeth, the meeting of lips sticking and parting. Her lips returned to mine and our tongues circled. Her head fell back and from the movement beside me I imagined that he had started biting her neck. With closed eyes I leaned for her other side and found that soft skin and started to bite too. She fell onto me and as her teeth grazed my ear a shot ran through my spine, stiffening my cock. A shudder ran through her and a hand fought with my pants, freeing me. Two or three hands were over my chest then and a mouth. It had to be hers, but I would not open my eyes to see, each sensation had to be prolonged. As a hand pulled my hair, a mouth ran down my chest to my belly as two hands lifted me up and out of my pants and held my thighs tight. The mouth took an age to hover its warm breath over my aching cock, then plunged wet around me, sending gasps from my lungs. I did not know if Saul was holding my hair or hips, or watching us both or if he too was doing things unseen to her body. She sucked and circled and I heard the fall of clothes by my ear, felt the brush of hair and limb against my shoulder. I would not open my eyes. Her hand travelled up my chest, over my shoulder to that place beside me where I sensed he stood erect. I felt then the beating of her wrist against my chest as, inches from my cheek, her fingers pumped. I heard her fabric fall and her lips found mine and I could taste the sour sweat of my own sex. Her lips left mine and I heard the gasp of breath and the gag and saliva of her taking his length deep to her throat. I found her neck and felt her head move forward and back again. I could no longer bear my blindness, but forced myself not to look. In my mind I saw a perfect silhouette of her lips stretching round the veined length of his shaft, strings of saliva dangling from her lips. Her hand gripped my cock, as she paused, then suddenly, her weight on my lap, she guided me into her soaking cunt, gasping and gagging on his cock as she did. He was groaning and I was close to coming. I placed my hand on hers to ask her to stop, but I did not speak. I knew it would all be over if I came, all eyes opened in embarrassment.

She slid off me slowly and let me go and I slid from the chair, my eyes tight closed again, pinching my cock head, so as to delay. My pants, still round one foot, had thrown me a little and I soon kicked them off and found my way round her solid thighs to her buttocks. Eyes closed, I followed her sounds and smells. Above my head in the dark I could hear sounds of her frantic movements and smelled her musky sex. Suddenly a finger touched my chin. In my mind I saw her hands between her legs, vigorously fingering her cunt. She pulled my chin closer. I raised my tongue into her taste and followed the salt mucous trail of her engorged clit. I smothered my face in her, soaking from eyes to chin as her juices flowed. Her pelvis bucked and she whimpered. She ground her pelvis into my cheekbones, her cunt quivering. Then all sounds were lost as her thighs gripped my cheeks and the first orgasm spasmed through her.

I tried to form an image of our positions in the room. But all sense of space had gone, and as a hand touched my cheek and shoulder I could not sense if it was his or hers. There was a movement, something fell and the fingers had left me. I had to see.

Through half-shut eyes, I glimpsed a sight unbearable in its perfection. The light had fallen to the side and cast a thin sliver down one side of her perfectly shadowed form. She was on her knees, her buttocks in the air, her sex hidden in darkness. As she arched her back the light caught the rise of her spine, causing a perfect white line to rise from her anus up through her waist along the widening of the ribs, between the dark arcs of her shoulder blades to the curve of her neck, to disappear, finally, into the darkness of her head. This white line then seemed to continue, disembodied as the hard shaft of Saul's cock. I looked down and there too was my cock, a line of light.

She moved, groaning, onto me then, and I vanished into her wetness. I looked up and Saul's cock was once again revealed. In that state of delirium it seemed as if our sexes were the continuation of her spine. As she pulled back from him, she sucked me in deeper; as she moved away from me, so she took him in. I looked to Saul but his eyes were on her. Her pelvis was bucking, her juices wet on my leg. I was close to coming so made my body still and tried to control my muscles. But her cunt gripped me tight and Saul's slow thrusts rippled through her spine and I could hear them both gasping and could no longer bear it. With a scream she threw herself onto her back, reaching for our cocks, as her body bucked and howled. His eyes shot to mine, eye to eye, cocks in her hands, his jism sprayed high over her neck and breasts and I poured over her stomach and we fell into her open arms.

As we slowly found our breath we stared into each other. Eyes wide open.

six

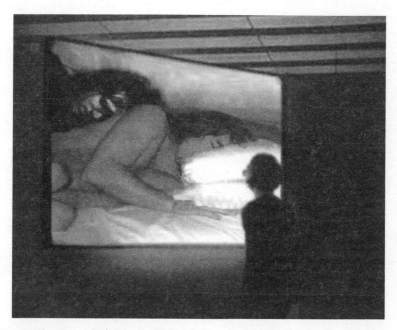

Watch Over Me. 1997. Video loop. 3.42 hrs. Installation view.
3.2 x 2.4 m. Max Lever Institute Collection.

THE WORK COMPRISES video footage three hours and forty-two minutes in duration. The image is of two almost naked young men asleep on the same bed. It starts in near darkness, and then grows lighter as ambient early-morning light starts to fill the room. The men go through a series of different sleeping positions: at first with an empty space between them, then facing each other but apart, then with backs to each other, then gradually moving closer till ultimately they are holding each other. The sequence abruptly ends when in full daylight, one of the men wakes and tries to cover the lens, violently.

The footage seems almost anthropological in its unyielding gaze. As such it evokes the earlier structuralist works of Warhol, such as *Sleep* (1963) and *Eat* (1961), which documented 'real' events in real time. The significant difference, though, is that whereas the Warhol footage was filmed with the use of a tripod (and in many instances the camera was left unattended, without an operator) Shears's work is hand-held, betraying the constant and subtly shifting presence of the camera operator.

The audio is in real time, the sounds of the men, moving in their sleep, snoring, one of them mumbles to himself. Also, the sound of the camera/operator/artist breathing is audible throughout and on two brief occasions whispers can be heard, although no words are discernible.

Viewers are often touched by the 'vulnerability' of the sleeping men. Others have been moved by the subtle humour in the negotiation for space on the bed, and possession of the quilt. Others still talk about the beauty of watching man, 'the sleeping animal'.

The irony is that the one thing that is not represented in the image, i.e. the artist, is the presence that is often felt the greatest. Some viewers have been disturbed by the presence behind the camera. The viewer is never far from being reminded that there is an unseen person (a woman) in the room recording the sleepers. For some, this presence has been described as 'gentle', 'a compassionate gaze', an act 'of devotion or love', the title 'Watch Over Me' implying romantic associations, or care and perhaps even maternal responsibility – to watch one's children/friends as they sleep. The fact that the camera had been held in the artist's hand throughout the three hours and forty-two minutes implies an act of endurance and hence commitment, if not to the people within the frame, then at least to the act of watching. Others find it disturbing to be placed in the position of silent watcher.

The duration, too, is unsettling, forcing many to ask the question: what could possibly be the mental state of someone who watches two men sleeping for nearly four hours? The lack of 'anything happening' on-screen has led some viewers to run out, not from boredom, but with a 'dreadful sense of foreboding', of 'something terrible about to happen'. The constant sound of the artist's breath has been described as 'terrifying'.[1]

The title also raises serious questions. As the filmed subjects are plural, the 'me' of the title cannot have originated from the 'them' (or if only from one of them then this would imply that consent had been given only by the one). The 'watch over me' seems, by inversion, to be a request from the watcher/artist. But why would she ask two sleeping men to watch over her? This provokes many further issues. One such is that, perhaps, in cultural terms, it is a question the artist could not ask of the men when they were awake. A woman asking two men to care for her could be seen as weak, as conventionally stereotyped feminine behaviour, so she utters it quietly to herself, almost in shame. The work triggers many such conflicting interpretations, questions and, indeed, emotions.

Gertrude Wellbeck[2] claims that Shears has deliberately turned the tables on gender, rendering the men portrayed as 'castrated', passive objects, and that the filming is a violent act of 'reclamation', 'a secret, subversive act of control'. Thus raising serious questions about consent and trust.

One incident on the footage that some have found contentious is as follows. When the first man wakes he tries to stop the filming, covering the lens with his hand. The sudden abrupt movement and violence of the action is in stark contrast to the preceding three hours and forty-one minutes of restful peace. This aggression seems to imply that a violation of consent has taken place. Other feminist readings of the work have found Shears's blurring of boundaries around gender and interpersonal consent highly problematic – as 'violation', 'an inverted rape fantasy'.[3]

It has been noted that numbers of viewers watch the footage for in excess of fifteen minutes.[4] As with other duration-based artworks there is considerable debate as to whether the piece must be viewed in its entirety for complete appreciation of the work to be possible.[5]

A point of interest is that this footage was shot in 1993 but not exhibited till 1997. Over the issue of consent, this could only be addressed if the men in the footage had been identified. To date, the sleeping men have not come forward or raised objection to their portrayal.

1. Ed Weaver has commented on how the work deconstructs the conventions of the slasher movie, with the hand-held point of view of those asleep always being that of the killer before the act of murder. See *The Darkest Light*, Interim Press, 2001.
2. G. Wellbeck, 'Stealing the Camera – Appropriating the Male Gaze', in *Face-Off*, Angel Press, Mass., 2004. Also 'Portrayal is Betrayal', D. Smeaton, ibid.

3. T. Balzarro. *Boundaries*, FPP, 2001.
4. A considerably greater length of time than the conventional duration for art appreciation, which is fifty-six seconds. See A.K. Ridge, *The Psychology of Perception*, UNQP, 1996. See also T. Thomas, 'The First Nine Yards', *Guardian*, 12 August 1994, in which he raises troubling statistics on the amount of time consumers spend in a bookshop and the limited mass-market discounted produce they have to access in that time/space.
5. An issue brought up in the 1992 work, *24 hour Psycho*, D. Gordon.

IT WAS THEIR first attempt at shopping together. Molly was sitting in the trolley baby chair, even though all had acknowledged that she was too 'grown up' for that now. Owen was pushing the trolley as Dot marched on ahead and Saul followed behind. Owen stared down at the almost empty trolley – so far, after many squabbles over brand names and whether they should be shopping organic or free range and exactly what it was they should be buying for dinner for four, all they had managed to buy was a bunch of bananas. The idea, which Owen was growing tired of, was that collectively they could decide on a meal together. Dot was fed up with the bickering and left them to it.

'Something big, to feed us all,' she said. 'I'm off to find some nuts.'

Owen pushed Molly to the poultry aisle with Saul in tow. An elderly woman with a basket of leeks had stared at them passing, perhaps, Owen thought, assuming they were a gay couple. Stupid bitch, he thought. Yes, he was a bit tetchy, since Saul was round every day now, and sleeping over twice a week.

A large chicken was thrust in his face. 'You think this'll do?' asked Saul.

Molly giggled. 'Tofu!' she said.

Owen turned to her. 'Sorry, Mummy wants a big thing.'

'Tofu.'

'You know you need more meat, don't you,' Saul said, 'if you're going to grow up big and strong? Chicken tastes just like tofu anyway.'

This week Saul had convinced Dot that her largely

255

vegetarian diet was not suitable for a growing child. In subtle ways Saul, Owen thought, was starting to be his old controlling self.

'Oops. This one's not organic,' said Saul. And rummaged around getting another. Owen saw the price.

'No way, fourteen pounds for a bloody chicken.'

'Bloody chicken. Bloody chicken,' Molly repeated.

'Shh,' Owen hissed.

'Don't talk to her like that,' Saul said.

Enough, thought Owen as he grabbed another chicken. Already Saul was shaking his head.

'Uh-uh, full of chemicals, hormones, all kinds of shit. Dot'll never agree to it.'

Really, how would you know what she'd agree to, you dole-scrounging scum? Owen thought.

Owen put his chosen chicken in the trolley. Saul picked it back out again and got the first one back.

'I'm not paying for that!' Owen said. 'You can buy it for yourself if you want.' A low blow, he knew, since Saul was after all in the pay of Dot.

'Tofu!' shouted Molly.

Saul walked off. 'Where you going?' Owen called after him.

'To get some bloody tofu.'

'Bloody tofu, bloody tofu,' Molly sang.

'Don't be ridiculous, we can't cook chicken and tofu.'

'Why not, since we can't agree? Molly can have tofu, you can have cheapo chicken and me and Dot'll have the organic one.'

That was it. That made him mad.

'That would require three ovens!'

Owen pushed Molly at speed towards Saul in the tofu aisle.

'That's just typical of you, why don't we all eat in separate rooms too, for that matter, in different houses?!'

Molly had reached into the trolley and yanked a banana off the bunch. She pointed it at Saul's face, making peeooow peeooow gun noises, then at Owen's. He grabbed it from her.

'OK, OK,' Saul said. 'Tofurkey!'

'What?'

'Tofurkey, tofurkey.' Molly repeated.

'What are you talking about?'

Saul held the package up to his face.

Tofurkey. Turkey-flavoured tofu in breast-like strips.

'Jesus Christ!' Owen shouted. A teenager with her mother scuttled past, embarrassed.

'Look, it's my money, we're eating in my house so I'm choosing, OK?!'

'Tofurkey, tofurkey,' yelled Molly.

'Fine, abandon democracy then, it's always easier to have a dictator.'

'Tofurkey! Tofurkey!'

'Are you attacking my fucking politics now?'

'I'm going to hold my breath!' Molly shouted.

Oh, Jesus. She took a deep breath and held it. Saul stared at her, perplexed.

'We have to get her to stop, she faints. Dot'll kill us!'

'Ridiculous,' Saul said.

The kid was turning bright red, eyes tight shut.

'Fine,' Saul declared. 'I'm going to hold my breath too, till she starts behaving!'

Saul took a very audible deep breath and crossed his arms. All around in the aisles, shoppers were staring. This was madness. Molly was turning purple and Saul competing in a bloated crimson.

'Please, both of you, stop it. Everyone's looking. Mummy will be here soon.'

Just then he saw Molly open one eye and peer at Saul. Saul was turning light blue, his cheeks like balloons. Molly took a deep breath and reached to shake Saul.

'MUMMA! MUMMA, HELP!'

Owen turned and there was Dot standing before them with armfuls of food. 'My God, what's wrong?'

Saul finally gasped for breath and started wheezing. Molly hugged him.

Sheepishly, Owen tried to explain, but Molly interrupted.

'He went all like a balloon and zombie, Mumma, scary.' She promised she would never ever hold her breath again. 'Ever ever ever.'

'Good, well, I'm glad we've achieved something here,' Dot said. 'But I see you still haven't decided what we're eating tonight.'

'Chicken,' Owen said.

'Turkey,' Saul.

'Tofurkey,' Molly.

That was it. Owen started laughing and Saul did the same. They had to hold each other to stop themselves from falling back into the substitute meats section as Dot pushed Molly away, shaking her head.

'Boys.'

Owen had to admit that there were basic material improvements, what with Saul taking Molly to nursery each morning, then picking her up at three and taking her to the park and then feeding her. Which all gave Dot an extra three hours in her studio each day to prepare for Zurich and extra time to resume her apartment search.

And yes, Saul could cook. To Owen's great surprise Mister Pot Noodle had become the new Jamie Oliver. In the last week they'd eaten ratatouille, fricasseed chicken with plum sauce, Thai green curry, and Moroccan bean stew with a 'harissa sauce' that Saul and Molly had ground from the unused spices in the rack that had for years been little more than decoration.

And Saul had a way with the child. He talked to Molly

in a quiet voice, slow and clear, sometimes so quiet that she had to come closer to hear. In only two weeks the holding of breath and the tantrums had vanished completely.

It had been lunchtime and Owen could hear them next door in the kitchen.

'If you have ice cream and want to bounce on your trampoline at the same time then what would happen if you bounce too high?'

'I'll drop my ice cream.'

'And it would be all over the trampoline, wouldn't it?'

'Yes.'

'And would you want to bounce on a trampoline covered in ice cream?'

'Yuck!'

'So we do one thing at a time,' Saul told her. 'We sit down and eat the ice cream and it tastes so much better because we're concentrating on every mouthful, and when we go on the trampoline it's better, isn't it, not with the ice cream?'

'Of course!'

'Do we see a man riding a bike and eating pizza at the same time?'

'No.'

'Do we see an elephant making paintings and jumping at the same time?'

'No, that's silly.'

'And why's that?

'Cos if you do two things at the same time it always gets into a mess.'

'So clever, did you work that all out for yourself?'

And the old man was quiet, non-intrusive. He had not drunk a drop of alcohol since he'd arrived. Owen had even started to feel guilty about checking the bottle every day after Saul had been there.

And Saul's gentleness was not that of a scheming inter-locutor. He seemed to really be a man who walked about as if any passing accidental thing might shatter his whole self. He was gentle with Molly because he needed to be gentle with himself. Saul now found cars and music too loud, and light too bright and avoided the television and seemed almost threatened when Dot talked about the daily news. So strange, Dot had even started trying to make up questions for him just to get him to speak. And the man's silent smile. How he seemed to listen, to take his time to process what had been said, then smile as if it would take longer still. They had almost joked about it – how they almost missed the old Saul.

On the nights when the adults stayed up late talking, it was agreed that it would be easier if Saul just slept over. Owen did not object and so prepared the sofa bed in his study.

Owen came in with the bedding. Saul stood there, looking sheepish, holding his child psychology book.

'You sure this is OK? I could get a taxi back.'

'No, it's fine, really.'

'Sorry to be any . . .'

It was a thing that Owen did not want to admit, but since Saul's arrival, the intimacy between him and Dot had grown. They made love now with a careful attention to nuance in mood and sense and touch. Dot said it was because she was getting another two hours of sleep each night, as Saul put Molly to bed, but he sensed it was also something to do with Saul's proximity.

In their bed, as she reached for his cock beneath the duvet and laughed and whispered, 'Shh, we'll be quiet,' Owen found himself replying to a question she had not even asked.

'It's OK, he can stay as many nights as you like . . . well, I mean, till things are sorted out.'

On the video he and Saul lay fast asleep. Saul wrapped his toes round Owen's and Owen reached back and held him. Dawn light was seeping in. Dot's breath could be heard from behind the camera.

It was midday and Owen was sitting alone before the PC and the VCR. The entire tape lasted nearly four hours and he had watched nearly all of it, transfixed.

The text he had written read: '*the sleeping men have not come forward or raised objection to their portrayal.*' It was a lie and it had him stumped. How could he write the names 'Saul' and 'myself' in the essay? If he did then he'd have to rewrite the whole damn thing, reveal that the 'faces' had names from the very first artwork to the last. The whole thing would have to be a memoir and the tabloids would get it and it would damage Dot's career irreparably. But how could he erase himself and Saul from Dot's history?

He had to get out and walk.

The walk led him three times round the block, past a screaming car alarm and nowhere but round his mind in circles.

He was guilty of a thing or two. He had been doing all he could to postpone Dot's finding of a new apartment, and he'd been postponing the end of the essay. So what was it that he feared in reaching conclusions? Maybe this weird life with Saul and her and her child could not face itself, could not face a conclusion; maybe this happiness was just a postponement of reality.

'*The sleeping men have not come forward.*'

Maybe an awakening was coming as violent as the one on the video.

He walked for hours, postponing home.

On opening the door there was laughter. And a chain of paper people that hung from the ceiling, festooned all the way to the kitchen. Saul, Dot and Molly were at the table all with scissors, absorbed in their work. It took a second then more for them to register his presence at all.

'Hiya, we're making people,' Dot called out.

'A community,' Saul added, face not turning from the cutting of paper.

'It's so great. Saul and Molly found a whole bunch of

261

posters at the Sainsbury's paper-recycling thingie and we're making people.'

He pulled off his jacket.

'We're going to cover the world!' Molly said earnestly, folding paper and aiming her scissors with the precision of a scientist. Saul, interrupting, telling her not that way, not too far or they'd all come out separate, just up a bit.

Dot passed him the scissors. 'My hands are tired, must be RSI from typing – you take over.'

So then Molly was in charge. She traced the human outline on the folded pages and was so bossy when she taught him how to fold the paper and cut the outlines, don't cut there cos that's the hands. He did as she said. And when done, opened it, to screams of laughter from all. Chains of paper people holding hands.

'All the faces are different!' Molly protested.

'So they should be,' Saul said. 'It'd be boring if they were all the same.'

Molly had for some reason reached to hug Owen then, and her sudden movement had made him cut through the hands. He knew it had gone wrong but she asked to see.

He held up the paper chain and it hung together, as long as an arm's breadth, but then fell apart, all the paper people falling into twos.

'It's OK,' Molly announced. 'We have Sellotape.'

As she went off to find it and Saul went to help her, Dot's hand was on his.

'You OK? How was your day?'

He wanted to tell her that today he'd almost been afraid to come home again, but the failure of the paper chain made him reach for her open hands. Molly came back though with the Sellotape, and it was an unwritten rule not to let Molly see too much adult emotion so Dot's arms peeled back from his neck, as Molly, enthusiastically, held up the tape, but then couldn't find the end, and was so quickly screaming in frustration. Saul quietly took it from her and said that many things in life were like that, all it took was patience. Saul found the end and pulled out a length.

'LET ME, LET ME!' screeched Molly and Saul was laughing. Saul let Molly bite the Sellotape all by herself to make the tear. Beaming with pride, she passed it to Owen. Slowly he applied it to the broken hands and then the two were four. He held up the four, Dot squeezed his hand, but Molly was pointing at the pile of paper people on the table.

'MORE SELLOTAPE!'

He wanted to tell Dot then of how unbearable such happy moments were for him. She smiled as if to say 'I know' and squeezed his hand. Molly offered him the Sellotape, face beaming.

'Why you sad?' Molly asked. Her face so close to his.

'Am I? I'm not really – see, I'm smiling.'

Saul's hand was on his shoulder as if he knew too. Squeezing hard.

'Owen's had a hard day at work,' Saul said.

Molly, content with the simple answer, fastened the last hands together and ran with her garland of paper people to the corridor to fasten it to the end of the last. Dot followed her. Saul ruffled up Owen's hair and sat facing him.

'Old man,' he said, 'you're such a sentimental old fuck.'

Owen stared at the floor.

'I . . . just don't know why . . . She is so . . .'

'Isn't she?' Saul said, rubbing his shoulders.

'I just don't know how . . .'

'I know, no one ever taught us how to be happy.'

Owen put his hand back then and held Saul's at they both stared out at the festooned hallway and the mother and child.

There were poles in the middle of the playground where there once must have been swings. Molly was running round and round chasing a little black kid in fluorescent bodysuit.

'Sorry I couldn't make it yesterday,' Saul said, 'I had something I had to do. I've been meaning to tell you. I mean, I've noticed, well, I thought it would be good for us to talk about what happened.'

Owen sat on the roundabout next to Dot as Saul stood. They were still turning slightly, from when Molly had been on the roundabout minutes before. Owen was a little concerned by Saul's tone of voice, almost confessional.

'The desert,' Saul said. 'You have to see it. I mean breathe it,' Saul started, then stopped. Then smiled. 'Maybe it's not the right time . . .'

'Tell us,' Dot said. 'The desert? You were . . .'

Owen stopped the roundabout from turning so they could face him.

'Messiah syndrome,' Saul said. 'You ever hear of that?'

Owen hadn't, neither had Dot.

'The security forces stop them at Ben Gurion Airport, Tel Aviv. A thousand of them a year, still to this day, all these poor bastards from all over the world thinking they're the next messiah, turning up in loincloths and all that. It's like Monty Python or something.'

Dot laughed. Owen was curious as to where this was heading.

'I was there, seven years ago, my mum had just died. You sure you want to hear this?'

Owen did not, as if if they all went into confession then it would be trauma and tears and blame. He stared up and located Molly. She was being chased by the little black girl; they were both hiccuping with laughter as the kid's mother watched over them.

'Go on,' said Dot.

'I'd been, well, in a hell of a state with drink. I woke up one morning, some party some junkie had had, I was staggering round Soho, Oxford Street, a real mess, I ended up down Marble Arch, all those big embassy buildings, really fucked up. I heard some music. It was the synagogue, you know the big one down there, it's got a beautiful dome, I'll take you there some day, if you like.'

This whole thing seemed impossible to Owen, Saul the hater of religion, the Antichrist. Saul in the desert – had that not been one of Owen's fantasies?

Dot nodded for Saul to go on.

'Anyway, this song, my mother used to sing it. I must have staggered into this place. I don't know what happened but they took me in, this Lubavitcher got me a place to stay. I was fucked up, I don't know, maybe it was just the guy's face, like he'd seen people like me before, like he cared. I don't know. Relinquish, that was the word he used, accept, surrender, words like that. I had to see the desert, he said.'

Owen could hear the quiver in Saul's voice. Dot gripped his hand. Owen looked out to Molly and the black kid as they headed towards the slide. The mother of the kid looked around for Molly's mother. Owen made hand signs to her that it was OK for the kids to play there, he was watching. Saul went on.

'They paid for my ticket, flight, food, everything, got me dried out.' Saul laughed to himself. 'I was the oldest student there, in the kibbutz, by far. And it's hard work, every day the same stupid jobs, like the fucking Stone Age in a tent. And I had to fight it, the naive faith they had. It drove me nuts, you know, made me want to drink and trash it all. But the Lubavitcher, it was like he knew. He'd look at me with these eyes and it'd tear me up. He'd hold my hand and say "I know."'

Owen heard Dot sniff beside him. He wrapped his arm round her. Saul went on.

'So one night, it was just, you know, a hundred yards away. I went to the desert. I mean, it's not what you'd think. Like a beach with no water, but really cold at night. Anyway, I was waiting for this big religious conversion or something. I actually went kind of nuts, you know, screaming at the sky. FUCK YOU, GOD! and all that jazz and of course there's nothing, it's just a stupid desert. And I thought, I'm a Jew – what's wrong with that? A Jew in a desert! I don't know why, I went crazy, howling and giggling, and the desert, I suppose I expected it to laugh back at me or something. You know, you look into the void and it looks into you. But it was just silly. I mean, hysterical, I was. When the Lubavitcher found me he said I had the divine laughter. So I go to synagogue every Saturday. That's why I couldn't help out yesterday. I don't know why I'm telling you this.'

'C'mere you.' Dot burst into laughing tears, reached out for Saul's hand and brought him closer. Owen sat back and let them hold each other, as Dot hugged and kissed the head of Saul. Saul reached to take Owen's hand. Something in the movement must have set off the roundabout because they started spinning.

'Jesus Christ!' Dot muttered and that set Owen off. All three were spinning on the roundabout holding each other. Owen looked out and the mother by the slide was staring at them as if they were mad, while Molly waved.

Owen could not bring himself to look at the last two tapes. The violence within them. Slaps, blood, screaming. He was at his desk and unable to face the impossible essay. Dot was putting pressure on him about Zurich. She needed the text finished and since the touring childminder situation was, as always impossible, she wanted either him or Saul to come to Switzerland with her.

Down the corridor, they were making houses. Saul had constructed a little tent with sheets thrown over Molly's bed and had brought her dollies inside. Words only half heard and guessed at but he was sure Saul was asking her all their names, his bare feet peeking out onto her alphabet rug.

Owen couldn't focus. A tiny gap through the door, down the hall through the sheets, and he was sure he saw Saul being served make-believe cups of tea. And Saul holding his plastic kiddie-cup like an old lady, like Oscar Wilde, his little finger pointed outwards. 'It's delicious.'

The child's laughter and he himself had never found time to play under Molly's drape. Perhaps Dot was right, the old Saul was dead and we had to get to know the new one. But the inner peace of the new Saul scared him. He was ever-conscious of the lurking messiah.

Owen was on his feet, walking towards that small tent of whisperings. But then, stopping before the sheets, he heard words from inside.

'Tea is a funny thing,' Saul said, 'just some crushed leaves from India.'

'What's India?' Molly asked.

'Well, I'll tell you in a minute. But milk comes from England and sugar from Jamaica. It's all very strange and wonderful this thing called a cup of tea.'

Owen had to step away, there were things going on in there the like of which a normal four-year-old would never have heard. The deconstruction of colonialism, and Saul, his voice in whispers, his fingers maybe drawing maps in the air, telling Molly about the world. As Owen made it back to his room there was an understanding of Saul's new place in the order of things. On one level it was tragic that he'd had to find a four-year-old as his new student, but on another, just imagine, to be that child and for that adult to take that cup with its imagined tea and for him to tell you of holy Hindu cows and how to milk a teat and how sugar boiled down from cut vines in the West Indies. And to see this man's eyes, wide open, as he again teaches himself the wonder of words he had once found predictable. For the most cynical

267

man in the world to find joy in the eyes of a child who waits on his next word. A word that might redeem him. If only he could live with them under that little makeshift tent. If only there was no essay and no Zurich, no career to build and no homes to find. No tomorrow to fear.

*

To be three is the one for me.
To be two, would you?
It makes me sick and it makes me spew.
To be one is no fun, unless you like sticking
    things –
– up your bum. Up your bum (or sitting alone with
    a bottle of rum)

We were all drunk and Dot had made up a song with Saul playing along on his beaten-up guitar, as we brainstormed threes: three strands in DNA, green, red and blue make white light. Three for two in the off-licence with Sauvignon Blanc. The third term of Tory rule. Three hours to Goldsmiths and back. Jesus predicted that Peter would deny him three times. Hear no evil, see no evil, speak no evil. We live in 3D. Bad luck comes in threes.

Three wise men, let's say it again.
Three is company, two is a crowd. Gonna shout it
    loud.

As Saul struck the final chord he collapsed, drunken into the depths of his wardrobe.

We were high on our threeness, floating on vast quantities of alcohol. Our lovemaking in that month had drifted into a somnambulist semi-waking sensuality, in which we never knew or admitted we knew who was touching who.

Our limbs and mouths dissolved into each other, but still not a word had any of us said about what we were really doing. Dot thought we had finally become a work of art, that art and love could be bedfellows. But neither art nor love can thrive without the silent third element and that is social reality, and it was rushing at us, fast.

It was the second week of May and only a week till Dot's premiere in *Bug*. The problems with electricity and lighting and her choice of tape had been solved: she was going to exhibit our slapping kissing tape on a TV on a plinth somewhere. Everyone told her she was headed for success but there was an electric air of restlessness around her. She could not sit still for a second. She'd shoplifted a bodice and bowler hat to wear to her opening. Her lipstick was black or was maybe eyeliner, or possibly permanent marker. I hoped not. She wanted to film everything, all the time.

Saul had already drunk two boxes of sherry on the day when it happened, and his snoring was filling the flat. Dot asked me to come with her to his room and for us all to sleep together, for once, deliberately, eyes wide open.

— You're right, she said, it's silly to keep on pretending like this.

I suggested it may not be such a good idea to wake Saul and expect him to be happy about it.

— Perhaps we should bring him a coffee and some ibuprofen before our discussion?

— A discussion? She laughed, quoting an old Saulism back at me. — Must you always explain away the fabulous?

She had her video camera with her. — Come on, she kept saying, as she pulled me through Saul's doorway, over his piles of unwashed clothes.

— I can see it in my head, she said, — a thing of beauty, to make all humanity weep.

— Pardon?

— Get in beside him, I want to film us sleeping.

It made sense, we had filmed everything else we'd done, what would be the harm in it? I decided to keep my pants on, and when Saul woke, to sit and quietly discuss our situation.

I was woken by screaming. I tried to keep the peace but they were both in hysterics. Dot was picking up her camera, the lens seemed broken. Saul yelled: — How dare you? Get the fuck out!

He was trying to cover his nakedness, kicking Dot out. He screamed so loud they couldn't hear me.

— Psycho bitch, you've no fucking right!

She was in tears, didn't understand, saying sorry, sorry, telling him that we looked so beautiful together, her eyes shooting to me for help.

— Tell him, when he sleeps, he's so –

Saul pushed her back. She fell and banged her head on the stereo, writhing in pain as she clutched her skull. Saul ran from the room, dragging his clothes, screaming back: — CUNT! Never darken my door again!

I was left alone with her. I found that I was more naked than I had thought and searched for my underpants. She wanted to show me what she had filmed, by way of explanation. Saul must have dressed quickly out in the hall and found some boots because I heard the front door slam. I tried to be practical, plugged her camera into the VCR, rewound and hit 'play'. It was just some footage of Saul and me sleeping, harmless.

— Don't you see how sweet you are?

I sat and watched. She had woken between us and got her camera. She'd filmed the space between us where she had been. Slowly Saul and I, in our sleeping sense of her lack, rolled over and held each other. Saul was naked, and I wearing only my shirt. Saul muttered, I snuggled up against him. Then he rolled over and I went into spoons, holding him from behind as he curled his hand under his chin like a little kitten.

— So beautiful, she said over and over, as I reached for her hand, my eyes stuck to the screen. She started staring at her upturned hands, chanting sorrys and beautifuls, as if in mantra.

On-screen, the smile on Saul's face as he nestled his chin into my neck. As his hand reached back and held me closer. The voice from the recorded footage then, the same as the voice beside me, whispering, — So beautiful. Then the face of Saul waking. Then in shock. He lunged for the camera. His eyes flashing furious from between the dark fingers that obliterated the lens.

I realised then what had happened in the mind of Saul.

— What did I do wrong? Dot kept asking, but I could not tell her.

She had broken his one unspoken rule: to keep the repressed repressed. It was not a portrayal but a betrayal. Or maybe something more simple, more base and selfish: he was the only one allowed to make an artwork of his life. She had reduced him to an object in her art. The one thing Saul could never bear was to have his powerlessness exposed.

She wept on my shoulder but I could not hold her, my hand floated by her side. She had plans to buy him presents, to give him sherry, flowers, money, five hundred pounds. She sat on the edge of the bed, inconsolable.

— Will he ever speak to me again?

I lied, said, — Maybe . . . We'll see, sure. Let me try and smooth things out with him, OK?

— Would you?

— Sure, trust me, it'll be fine.

But I knew that she had destroyed what we had, because it had been a secret we could not reveal even to each other, and she had filmed it with a video camera, for all the world to see.

Pills. I didn't think she had any left, thought she had got rid of them all, but she had to take some to calm herself. There were two new large bottles in the bathroom, Valium and something else.

Saul returned with two boxes of sherry, and would not speak to me. I went to his door – it was locked – and whispered through the wood.

— Open up, we have to talk. Please, Saul.

After ten minutes I heard him hiss from the other side.

— We need to need to ditch the bitch! I told you she was sick. Months back and you wouldn't listen.

— Please, try to be reasonable, and lower your voice.

I waited and waited, then his voice, dark and phlegm-filled: — If you can't get rid of her, then you'll be forcing me to take care of the situation myself.

I sat in silence on his doorstep. Then his hissing words came.

— So be it!

I couldn't wait around worrying or let her worry for a second, so I made myself indispensable and kept us both furiously busy over the next few days, drawing up lists of to-dos, shopping for her, for extension cables and scarts and other video things, reassuring Dot that her TV on a plinth in the midst of the vast warehouse was a great artwork, that the thing with Saul would blow over. The frenzy of exhibition preparation, generated by the many artists fighting over exhibition space, distracted me from the fear of Saul's smouldering scheming.

On the night of the opening as Dot and I prepared to leave without him (his door had been close to us for three days), Saul, to our surprise, asked if he could join us. He seemed perfectly benign. He'd even given her some hope, talking politely, about how important *Bug* must be for her and almost apologising for his mood of late, then excusing himself to get dressed. I tried to encourage her.

— See, he's over it, it's just his way. He hates being emotional and never likes picking up his own messes, he'd rather pretend nothing happened at all. Trust me.

His appearance when revealed was resplendent, head to toe in all of his leathers: trousers, waistcoat, gloves, with his overcoat with antique Nazi regalia. I told her it was his way of being funny, his sign of forgiveness, he was, after all, Jewish.

— Let's just let him shock everyone and steal some posh wine and within the week he'll have forgotten every-thing and we'll be back to day one again.

She was still afraid to talk to him. She did not wear one of her new radical outfits but only jeans and a T-shirt, and it took her three hours to decide on even that. I heard her talking to herself from behind her door.

— It's OK, it's going to be OK. I'm sorry, I'm sorry.

On the way, in the tube, Saul was silent, sitting across from us. I took Dot's trembling hand and every time she jabbered her nervous sorry and thanks to him, I gripped her tighter.

— Thanks, Saul ... You've no idea how much this means to ... You'll get to meet Sarah Lucas and take the piss out of Hirst if you fancy or ... It's not really my art but yours. I mean, you should be taking all the credit.

He simply nodded, staring out at the passing stations.

Inside, he marched ahead of us, up the many dusty stairs. There was a DJ playing a Happy Mondays/James Brown hybrid, and maybe two hundred people. She clung to my hand and so I led her on with encouraging whispers. Apart from her single TV screen showing our cross-dressing tape, the rest of the art was of little consequence: some things that looked like archery targets painted onto the walls; the usual exhibiting of banal consumer objects as if they were some damning indictment of our time, à la Jeff Koons – in this case, a cappuccino maker on a wooden plinth and some slogans on hand-painted cardboard on sticks as if made for a demonstration that said, ironically: 'DON'T ASK ME' and 'I'M WITH STUPID'. There were some packing boxes that I'd seen before, assuming they contained art ready to be unpacked, which turned out to be the art themselves. There was some *tableau-vivant* diorama of a working-class domestic living room as an installation in the middle of the space, right next to Dot's TV, which no one had seemed to notice.

— It's great, I said, — maybe the TV's a bit too small, but I'm sure folk will look at it later.

But her eyes were scouting around for Saul. Finally she found him and pointed him out to me – in the midst of a crowd at the free bar. Dot wanted to wait for him but I considered it better to mingle and let him find us and that would also be a sign of his forgiveness.

So Dot introduced me to so many artists and gallery owners. Adrian Searle, from the *Guardian*, was there, looking fashionably knackered but marvellously aloof. Dot got chatting with Tracey Emin about men's underpants as if discussing Kant's aesthetics. I wanted to butt in but there were so many people around them and my underpants were not a fit topic of conversation. I glanced over and some girls in seventies retro wedges were touching Saul's leathers, giggling and whispering in his ear. I told Dot everything was going to be fine and tried to make her laugh. Pointing out the female performance artist walking round wearing nothing but a black plastic bin bag, asking people to give her their empties. Clinking around with empty beer bottles and plastic cups inside. Nipples exposed as the weight of crap increased around her. She was from Northern Ireland, she told everyone, it was an artwork all about the Troubles. Dot got the guts then to leave my hand and within minutes was in the midst of the throng, ranting about Saul's ideas, how life itself should be an art form. The tall man with the retro glasses, Pierce I assumed, was flirting with her, telling her how wonderful she was and how rumour had it that one of Saatchi's buyers was here tonight, undercover.

I looked around for Saul but he had abandoned the girlies. I presumed he was downing swift ones at the bar. It was the explosion that located him.

The space cleared rapidly around the commotion. He was standing in Dot's space, bottle of wine in hand. The TV lay smashed on the ground. The man who must have been Pierce marched over to him.

— Please step away from the art!

Two hundred people fell silent.

— I don't see any signs around saying don't touch, Saul shouted back, flicking back his hair. — Really, if you're going to put *objets d'art* on display you should at least make sure they're securely fastened.

Pierce grew increasingly irate. Dot headed towards him through the crowds. Saul was smirking, waving the bottle. — So we're in the Victoria and Albert, are we now?

Dot tried to quieten them both, taking Saul's arm, all apologies to him and the strangers around.

— Get the fuck out of the art, Pierce shouted, as Saul wandered over to the next artwork, the realist diorama, and started picking at the fake authentic fifties wallpaper, pulling off a strip, smiling to himself.

— So this is art, is it? he pronounced sarcastically, loud enough for everyone to hear. Dot tried to pull him away but he shook her off violently. There were mutterings beside me of 'drunk' and 'loser.' Women in designer grunge turned away. Searle headed for the door. I was frozen to the spot.

— I must apologise to you all, Saul declared. — I was bored and simply wanted to watch TV, but then it fell over. I'm sure this is a wonderful radical work of art, and that we're all having a lovely time being truly 'out there', I was just decon-structing, it all seems to come to pieces quite easily. You're more than welcome to join me. Take a piece of art home.

And he tore off yet another strip of wallpaper. That was it. Pierce stepped inside the diorama and tried to remove Saul by force. Saul dropped the bottle. As he bent to pick it up, Pierce grabbed his arm and he staggered back against the fake wall. It fell to the ground with a bang, blowing dust into faces. Dot started shouting sorry, sorry, in the ruins, as Pierce struggled to try to lift the wall back in place, but he started sliding in the broken glass of Dot's smashed screen, cutting his hands. The warehouse was rapidly emptying. The almost naked woman in the bin bag marched over to Saul, Dot and Pierce.

— No, he's right, she shouted — this is all decadence, think of the starving in Bosnia!

Saul broke into hysterical laughter and the woman by his side was paralysed with confusion.

— Fuck Bosnia, he yelled. — Fuck Ethiopia! Bomb the lot of them! She clinked away from him, joining the throngs of the leaving. Pierce grabbed Dot's arm, shouting, pointing a bloody finger at Saul.

— Is this cunt a friend of yours?

Dot stood there silent and Pierce headed for the door. She ran after him, and slid in the glass, tearing her jeans and skin, apologising, trying to explain. Someone had started taking flash photographs. My final glimpse was of Saul, throwing beer bottles to the floor, one after another as if listening to notes they made, singing along to some song in his head. Probably Wagner – Dah dahdey dah dah, dah dahdey dah dah.

I could not sleep through her screams at his locked door. Through the gap in my door frame I glimpsed her, on her knees, weeping: — Please, please, open up, I'm sorry for whatever I did . . . I don't know what I did wrong . . . just please, open your door.

All she had left now was her degree show and it was such a cop-out and made her sick, sick, please, please, she repeated. I couldn't bear it any more, got up and tried to take her from that place but she shrugged me away, her face weeping mascara, her fingers bloody, a smudge of it too on her cheek.

— Take your fucking hands off me! . . . You did nothing, you stood there and watched like a fucking . . . you did nothing . . .

I walked away. The whimpering resumed as again and again she pleaded I'm sorry, I'm sorry, I'm sorry, I'm sorry, please, please, please. I glimpsed her curled on his doorstep like an obedient dog. Back in my room, I heard the William Shatner album start up. His excruciating rendition of 'My Way.' Shatner was a failure. Saul was a failure, now she was. We all were as shit as Shatner. Saul once again had it all, his way.

I wanted to run but could not for fear of seeing her face in the hall. She ran past my door, slammed hers, then the noises were of things being thrown, crashing and smashing. I covered my head in my stinking pillow, knowing that she was right in her judgement of me. Once again, I did nothing.

All that long night her howling kept me awake as I tossed and turned and tried to find a way to save her. I would borrow money from her and we would leave together, that was the compromised plan. When I finally found sleep light was coming up.

Awake, I found the flat silent. I waited outside her door, listening for a noise inside. Then knocked. No reply. I opened the door and witnessed the aftermath. Her stereo was smashed and thirty or so records lay in pieces on the floor, littered among the thousand torn pages of his books.

In the toilet I found another, lying face down. The *Oxford Dictionary of Quotations*, as if one of them had left it there for me to find. Many pages were earmarked. Quotations underlined in pen. As I leafed through I learned that the many aphorisms and epigrams Saul had spouted over the years were not his own. Valéry, Barthes Niezsche, Wilde, La Rochefoucauld, Cocteau, Chesterton.

'The future is a thing of the past.'

'Stop all this talk of equality. We only want to be equal with our superiors!'

The charlatan had sat there for hours each day memorising aphorisms to make himself sound intelligent. From a cheap book of quotations. It was even worse than his Duchess book – it constituted almost every word he had ever said. The plagiarist. I decided to write up my proof and present it to him, as a gift, on our departure. As he was out and she too, and I could do nothing, I sat and read all the underlined quotes and took apart the basic arithmetic of his so-called intelligence.

How to create a Saulism:

You take a simple proposition, widely accepted as a commonplace truth, say 'work ennobles man', then you swap the words around and invert the proposition, thus: 'Work is noble but I have never seen a noble who ever worked.'

Or just take a word, say 'desire' and turn it against itself. 'My only great desire is to cease desiring.'

Or: 'Indifference seems to be the only thing I'm indifferent to.'

I had wasted years marvelling at his witty ripostes, and all of them were an equation, a formula, for ignorance, in fact.

'There is nothing more ugly than the manufacturing of beauty.'

How piteous a character to always be just playing with words throwing them back in people's faces, to make them laugh at the undoing of what they'd just said. But never to progress beyond reaction, as those you have played with are given pause and say, 'How true, how true.' And what a hollow victory.

'I can think of nothing less natural than people communing with nature.'

Oh yes, I saw him clearly then, after years wasted worshipping his words. He would weep, I thought, when he read my analysis.

'Staring into the void is greatly overrated.'

And people found him a wit.

'Wilful stupidity seems to me to be the only intelligent course of action.'

'Blind faith is the last refuge for those who have seen too much.'

And his other variations:

'Never forget that we live in the era of forgetting.'

'Ignorance is bliss is a thing I've only ever heard intelligent people say.'

'I feel rather lured by the allure of failure.'

We had believed in him and he had trashed us, like so much rubbish. He could no longer pretend to a life without repercussions. Finally, he must have seen there was a cost. Finally I had the courage to spit in his face and leave.

I heard the door open and his boots down the hall. I made my preparations.

— Can you come through? he called out.

I took a breath and headed to his room, brandishing the book of quotations.

His appearance, when I opened the door, seemed completely haggard. He was still wearing the clothes from the night before. He had the Duchamps on very quietly. 'Disparu'. His face smeared with wept mascara. I fought against the impulse to pity, raised the book in my hand.

— Shh, listen, he said as the singer reached that horrible crescendo with that screaming so out of tune and the audio samples of people wailing as if dying against the plinky-plonky eighties synths and the vocals with north of England accents singing *Nous avons disparu*.

— Look, I've had more than enough of . . .

The sight of him kept me from finishing. He burst open a sherry box and pushed the plastic lever and started guzzling it. His eyes were bloodshot and I noticed a fleck of vomit on his chin. As if remembering I was there he offered the box to me. I refused. All over the floor his records and tapes were scattered as if he'd been trying to finally find the sleeves for each.

— 'bout time you saw this.

He was holding up some newspaper clipping. Of a band from the early eighties, posing. I glanced to his wardrobe; in the back there was a pile of maybe twenty or thirty empty sherry boxes. His brow was sweating vinegar piss.

— Read it, he said.

I sat and gave him another minute, looked at the stupid clipping.

LOCAL BAND IN TOP 100. It was from the *Hull Courier*. 1984. 'In at number 89 in the charts, Ashton Bar favourites the Dooshamps . . .' Even the spelling was wrong. In the photo five guys in their early twenties were dressed with scarves round their waists à la Spandau Ballet. Each was androgynous with tons of face paint, like Cleopatra. One was obese, another anorexic-looking; by way of unity they had 'pirate' boots sprayed silver and ribbons in their hair, all pulling very serious expressions. One had a fist in the air, another had a keyboard strapped round his neck and a growling expression with black lipstick. What this was about I had no idea.

Saul tried to relight a fag end and broke into a hideous cough. I was about to hand the clipping back when he raised a finger and pointed to a body half cut off, no face visible, just an elbow at the edge of the frame.

— I did tambourine, he said, — on track four.

I was in shock. I was close to laughing even.

— No way, you?

He nodded, fell silent, smoking and pointed to one of the other faces. The one on the edge.

— Edna, he said.

The fat boy with feathers in his hair.

— No way!

Saul had blown smoke into his own eyes and they were watering. I felt about to burst into hysterical laughter. The song ended.

— I want you to be honest, he said.

I nodded. Waited.

— It's really not very good, is it?

For the first time ever he had reached to hold me and it was me that withdrew. Even at risk of offending, I could not stay a second longer and had to hide my laughter. I got up and along the hall came the sound of the cough, then the retching. Alone in my room I allowed myself a little giggle then chastised myself for being so weak again – I had gone there to assassinate him, but had emerged with only pity. How could I not? The source of everything he thought was true and unique and good, the basis of his aesthetic tyranny, and all he had ever achieved in his life had been this. An elbow in a photo of the band that wrote 'Disparu'. From my room, I suffered the sounds of his vomiting, his guts tearing themselves inside out trying to find something solid to puke up, but finding nothing.

All the rest of that day and through the night I waited for her to return. A 10 a.m. the next morning I heard the door open. Her face was sleepless, maybe stoned. She said she'd spent the night at Edna's. She let me hug her. Her clothes were dirty and she stank of booze. I took her into my room and helped her off with her jacket. She was talking deliriously.

— We could just get on a plane ... go to Tuscany ... my dad's got a villa there, or Rome ... we could get high ... or take Edna ... or run away or ...

I tried to calm her, get her to lie down. No point running away.

— Just tell me what to do, she said.

— Well.

— Tell me and I'll do it. Please.

Her eyes waiting on me, her hand gripping mine.

— Well, I'll help you with your degree show, we can do it together, then once you graduate we can maybe go away, I said. — Let's stay a few more days, wait and see, we'll work it all out, together.

I reached to kiss her but she raised her hand to say no.

— Just wait and see, she repeated, just do nothing?

No, no, I said, and tried to explain. But she stood and walked away. I tried to grab her back but her fingers slipped from mine and she was gone. I knew it even then. She'd needed me to take the lead but I'd been practical, passionless, pathetic. I sat on my bed as next door, back in her solitary room, I heard her picking up her many broken things.

In the days that followed violent fluctuations left her ever more drained.

— I have to apologise to Pierce, she whimpered over and over. — Poor Pierce, I have to find him and say sorry.

— Forget him, let's just think about your degree show, OK?

And she'd flash with rage.

— Fuck art school! Did fucking Duchamp kiss ass to get a degree, did the Duchess? That cunt Pierce. I'll slash his fucking face.

She truly did not seem to care if she graduated at all. I kept her busy and away from Saul, whom we hardly saw in those days as we were up at dawn. I practically dragged her out of bed every morning, dressed and fed her, although she pushed every meal away. She also cared little about her appearance. On the tube to Goldsmiths, her T-shirt was torn and many eyes stared at her bra, some laughing, whispering. I wanted to ask her to cover herself up but any mention or touch of her body made her shrug away from me.

I tried to get her enthusiastic as we entered, pointing out the students who were turning the studios into gallery space with their boards of MDF, hammers, nails and gallons of white paint, but I could tell the repetition of the same scene we had seen at *Bug* drained her.

A tutor accosted her. She still hadn't told anyone what she was going to be exhibiting. It would be unwise to spring a surprise on everyone, he said. I saw him eye her from head to foot, intimidated or perhaps aroused. She should come to his office and discuss it, he said. She walked away from him, with utter uninterest. I followed her, past large cibachromes of breasts and weeping faces, a sculpture made entirely out of Coke cans in the shape of Michelangelo's *David*.

A young male student stopped her and asked what dimensions she needed her space to be. Did it need to be blacked out?

— No idea, she said. — I don't even know where the fucking thing is.

She pushed past him. He gave directions and I took note and followed. Her blankness I knew from before, from the night of Valium, but she was more down and distant, so much more than before. She would not meet my eye.

— He said to the right and past the cardboard car, I said.

— What?

— Your space.

A female student was hanging dozens of medical blood bags and catheters from the ceiling. Two men in overalls were painting the walls white. Dot stopped and stared.

— Institutions, they're all the fucking same!

— Sorry? It sounded like something Saul had said.

She paced away again. I located the cardboard car and found her space beyond. White, empty, a Post-it note with her name on it on the wall. I got her to stop, took out my list of things to do. The video projectors we needed and some screens delivered from the company I'd found for her. I asked – where would they go? Should we hire a technician? Could she afford it?

— This place is sick, she kept saying. Her mouth was slow, wet, as from pills.

The empty white space seemed to scare her.

— If you could just tell me what to do. Please. I took her hand in mine.

— Take your fucking hands off me.

— I just want to help.

— Oh, so very you, always helpful, always trying to fix everything, mother's little helper. Don't you have any desires of your own?

I couldn't leave her like that no matter how much she seemed nauseated by me. She was belching, almost gagging on her words.

— We have to try to calm down.

— We? You're like a fucking mirror. Empty when no one's there.

— Dot, this is –

— No, no, I see your game. That's what you do, you just tell me what I want to hear, give me what I want. I thought it was his fault, him. But it's you. The weak always bring the strong down to their level. You've dragged him down. He wouldn't be such a failure if it wasn't for you. If you didn't clean up his shit all the time, he'd face his fate. You're nothing compared to him. You do things deliberately to upset him . . . I know your game. Soap and toilet roll and God knows what suicidal crap . . . Why don't you just admit it – you're begging for his big cock to fill you up cos you're empty! Weak . . . so fucking . . . !

I waited for her to run out of steam.

— Dot? Are you OK?

— Stop it, just stop it!

— What?

— If I'm sick let me be sick! Stop taking care of me, it makes me sick, really fucking sick!

— Sorry.

— Stop saying sorry . . . Leave me alone. Go! Go home to your lover boy, before I stab him in his fucking sleep! GO!

I froze. She pushed me and I stumbled back. I reached to hold her, but she pulled her hand away, put it to her mouth.

— You break my heart, she muttered as she turned and ran out, leaving me in her big empty space. You break my heart.

Other footsteps sounded beyond from her partition. A young trendy-haired student came in, all big smiles, and asked if I knew where to find Dorothy Shears. He'd been appointed to help with technical things. Within seconds of having my attention he started talking about his own work. He made sculptures out of microwaves and was inspired by the ecology movement and Joseph Beuys, he said. Was I here to buy art? I excused myself and left to look for her.

Corridors and then the refectory and no sign. I ran to the station, and she was not there.

I waited for the train, then headed home to make sure Saul was OK.

seven

Walking Blind. 1993–2004. Video loop. Variable durations. Installation view. Variable dimensions. Various collections.

IT IS NIGHT. A woman walks backwards with her eyes closed. Her face is held in exactly the same position while the background moves behind her. It becomes clear, through time, that she is holding the camera to her face.[1] She walks, eyes closed, through a series of locations, a shopping centre, a city street, a park. At times she bumps into things, or narrowly avoids obstacles, some of which could potentially cause her injury. At other times she comes to a stop entirely, seemingly gripped by fear of hitting something unseen, even though there is no visible threat. She does not open her eyes throughout, even though, at times, the viewer can sense her powerful desire to do so.

Like earlier works by Shears, the face dominates the image and the work is a document of the human emotions expressed on a face during an arduous 'game of trust'. The activity of 'walking blind', although first developed as a group psychology experiment[2] is now widely used, from Stanislavsky's acting 'method' to New Age 'rebirthing' and corporate human resources exercises. The difference, which some see as a radical critique of such exercises, is that, in Shears's version, there is no one at the end of the walk to catch her.

Where this work departs from these games formats, and from Shears's earlier work, is that the game is no longer played out in a 'safe', familiar environment, 'among friends'. If it is a game of trust then how can it be played alone? Who is Shears trusting, who will save her from hurting herself? Is the work not in fact documenting a lack of trust; its loss? Can we even trust the artist?

This sense of jeopardy and the question of the purpose of the game is deeply traumatic for many viewers. Dramatic reactions have been noted, with viewers shouting at the screen. In interview, they have commented: 'I couldn't bear it, she was going to hit this window behind her, I started shouting, "Go to the left", "Watch out!", things like that. You want to help her but you can do nothing. It's horrible.' 'It's like she wants to hurt herself.' 'She wants to shut her eyes and make it all go away.' 'It's like she's screaming inside and no one can hear her.' 'It's a cry for help.'[3]

More so than any other work, *Walking Blind* has created heated controversy, with different groups taking polarised positions on single issues within the work. Around the issue of 'passivity', some feminists regard the work as 'irresponsible': the image of a woman walking blind at night, in public, plays into stereotypes that women are powerless; that they want to be taken care of as much as they want their sexuality to be taken care of for them. Although there are no images of a sexualised nature, the word 'rape' comes up again and again in criticism of the work. The NO MEANS NO movement[4] see in the image an 'every woman's worst nightmare scenario' – 'of walking blind and alone through deserted streets'. The voluntary 'eyes closed' is seen as being doubly metaphoric: on the one hand women are seen as being conditioned to this role of passivity, on the other it concerns our culture's blindness to the issue of rape. From this perspective Shears is criticised as being ethically irresponsible.

On the other hand, many post-feminists passionately argue that the image means exactly the opposite – that *Walking Blind* is a test of strength, the first step towards self-emancipation. They highlight the courage Shears exhibits in walking eyes closed for fifteen minutes without giving up, or asking for help, giving in to fear, etc.

It is no doubt because the work can contain such a

multitude of differing interpretations that this has become Shears's iconic work. No other image from the YBA period, save perhaps Hirst's formaldehyde shark[5] has been so pastiched and recycled as this.[6] That so many interpretations have been spawned may be a result of the dreamlike quality and the lack of any guiding text by the artist, thus leaving the image open to 'projection' of meaning by others. Any comments that Shears has made about the work have only served to increase the enigma.[7] One of the main reasons perhaps why Shears never discusses the meaning of her work is that she may not want it to be reduced to the biographical, no doubt because there has been such a great deal of fetishisation in the press around her mental health.[8] Ironically, very few of her peers seem burdened by the same concerns. Quite the opposite, in fact, with several becoming infamous for their 'wild' behaviour (Emin) and for, in fact, documenting their own transgressions as artwork.[9]

It should be noted that this one work is not one but at least three, in a series over an extended period of years.[10] The three versions (1993, 1999 and 2004) have only recently started being shown together. In each, the central figure is the same – Shears herself. It is as if, over the years, Shears has tested herself by enacting the same ritual.

In the third, most recent work, there is a sense of the event being staged. Shears walks blind with a confidence bordering on indifference, as if whatever she did, whichever way she moved, she would be safe. In fact, records show that there was an entire production team in the wings waiting to catch her, do her hair and make-up, photographers to record her, TV teams to interview her, after the fact. It is perhaps precisely that control that she wanted to escape from but she is caught in a double bind. There is no escaping her career, even if she were to trip and fall that too would become art. This newest work is chilling. It seems, ironically, to represent a desire perhaps to fall away from the lights and the cameras into a darker place, where vulnerability and danger might coexist once again. To return to the power of that first work, where she walked blind and alone into the darkness.

1. As Carol Jenning noted, '[Shears] holds the camera to the face as a suicide would a gun.' From *DEADARTLIVES*, Riot Press, 2002.
2. Charcot, 1866, experiments with female in-patients in Salpêtrière. See Foucault.
3. Documentary, *WYMEN*. FBC, 2004.
4. NMN-UK, women's helpline and resource centre.
5. The work is entitled *The Physical Impossibility of Death in the Mind of Someone Living*. Hirst's most recent work *For the Love of God* (a real diamond-encrusted human skull) was recently sold for a record-breaking £50 million.
6. The image from the award-winning 'Eco-Diesel' advertisements for BP. A number of other 'artists' have latched onto the image, such as the neo-punk band Xeon, who pastiched the work in the music video for 'Deliver Me – (From What I Want)', ref. J. Holzer. It is almost inconceivable how this one image can be seen as containing a radical feminist message, while at the same time is seen as being a symbol for the anti-globalisation movement. The common interpretation seems to come from the idea of 'walking blind into the future' and the image is sometimes renamed 'The Angel of the Future' – see W. Benjamin – the eyes closed being seen as a double-edged symbol, as manifesting 'a desire to turn our eyes from the horrors of consumerism', but also as an image of our moral blindness.
7. Shears has claimed that the idea came from a friend saying, 'You're always walking round with your eyes closed.'
8. Controversy over whether latter acts of violence, reportedly committed by Shears, were actually artworks or 'happenings' or acts committed while 'ill' and thus not breaches of the law.
9. Emin has succeeded in surpassing Damien Hirst in terms of notoriety in the eyes of the general public. See her drunken outburst on a Channel 4 TV discussion, 2003. See also the many autobiographical works charting her adolescence in Margate and the artwork entitled: *Everyone I Have Ever Slept With 1963–1995*.

10. Shears has produced twenty-one artworks from 1993 to the present. Eight of these are 'remakes'. While this in total may seem a small amount, many artists who have produced more have found that collectors have shelved, stored or in some cases destroyed some of their works in order to elevate the prices of the remaining ones and young artists are now being encouraged to 'produce less'. Author's note: it is possible that the idea of being an 'artist for life' is more to do with the needs of the market and of branding than it is to do with the actual processes of art-making. Many artists find that they have 'a good five years', others that they have only one or two in which creativity flows. Having to reproduce mechanically the semblance of that original outpouring, long after it has been spent, has been the condition many biographers claim is to be blamed for the suicides of many painters and musicians. See D. Weaver, *Hate Me Again – From Pollock to Cobain*, Chatto & Windus, 2002.

A LETTER FROM Lloyds TSB: 'We confirm that we would like to you offer mortgage facilities to the amount of £895,000.'

Terence Conran's *Super Home* book cover. Before and after images of a factory by a sewage-strewn canal, converted into a glass-walled open-plan waterfront apartment. A similar space converted into a trendy open-plan studio with bean bags, hi-tech entertainment consoles, sunken bath, sheet-metal kitchen and vast glass table.

An image of a Victorian hospital. The text read: 'Development Opportunity.' Further images of the space from five different angles. Of the view from the window.

A message from the arts editor at the *Guardian*, asking why he'd said no to the last two articles they'd offered him.

A printout on gazumping.

A letter from Lloyds TSB, extending the bridging loan on the sale of the property in Notting Hill.

Flyers Dot picked up on her trips to Bethnal Green, from community groups, Bangladeshi. Images of coloured faces in bright coloured clothes.

A computer-generated image of the projected new Bethnal Green architectural redevelopment plan for the area between Cambridge Heath and Mile End.

A call from the Lieder Gallery asking if Owen could deliver the text for the *Nine Works* asap – the Zurich show is in four days' time.

FedEx boxes arriving every few hours.

That one image of her on the tape – walking backwards eyes closed, at night through unknown streets, in danger. Walking blind.

A week of fragments and passing images. No continuity. Everything disparate moving fast. At his desk, Owen was caught in the midst of it.

The phone rang.

'Hello, can I speak to Dorothy Shears please?'

'She's not here. Who's calling?'

'It's Jenny from Lambert and Higgs here, I'd like to confirm the property viewing.'

Owen took the details, then turned off the phone and walked through the flat. Dot had started packing Molly's toys into boxes. Premature, he thought. All month he'd made himself change and adapt to their ways, forced himself to give in to the happy chaos.

He looked into the room that had become Molly's. The stack of paintings that were almost as high as his knee. He picked one up. A picture of a house. Another beneath it was the same in a different colour, and the one beneath with two big trees and four big windows. He pulled the blue moon-and-stars covers back on her bed, tucked them in.

Musical beds. Most nights he had been woken by Molly and had to take the cold, dark walk to her tiny bed while she snuggled up to Dot. Other nights Molly had woken and gone through to Saul, and after he had talked her to sleep Saul had carried Molly into their room and placed her beside them. Owen couldn't help but feel that Molly was doing this deliberately, that she sensed the subtle tension within the three and their imminent fragmentation when homes and jobs were worked out.

Dot had been losing sleep over Zurich, a week, tossing and turning and more than half of them with Molly invading the bed. Last night had been a night of hell. Molly complaining of a sore tummy at three in the morning. Dot rubbing her tummy, putting her between her and Owen till she fell asleep. Owen taking the sofa, then being woken around five by the sounds of Saul's feet carrying Molly back to Dot's bed. In the morning, when he got up to pee, he saw Saul's door open and his bed empty. He tiptoed to his own bedroom then and saw.

Dot and Molly and Saul asleep together.

Dot was all high energy. Talking about four things at once on the tube to Bethnal Green with Molly on her knee, getting her all exited about their future.

'It's big with lots of space for, well, anything!'

Saul was away at another job interview, she said. She wished he was here to see it, then swiftly jumped topic.

'But God, if I don't make that ninth work. I mean, you must have an idea, if you could just give me an idea, I could film it, we could turn it round in a day, unveil it in Zurich.'

'I don't know.'

'And the text, you going to get it finished in time? If we don't have the text I don't know what'll happen. There's so much riding on this, even the mortgage. You have any idea how much this bridging loan is costing me? Is the text OK, you get to the end yet? Can I read it?'

'Not yet, I'll get it done on time, trust me.'

They were out of the tube, Molly bored and yelling for sweeties.

'Shoosh, darling, don't you want to see the nice new house?'

Dot led him past a mosque, the many shoes that lined the doorway and the voices from inside. They passed what must once have been the silk mills – one was now a discount clothing warehouse, a gang of Asian-looking kids brushed by them, listening to music on their mobile phones. In the not too far distance were the concrete schemes of Globe Town. They passed an arrowed street sign for the Museum of Childhood, but there was no sight of the museum.

Finally they arrived.

A new conversion, she'd said. The back court of the old Bethnal Green Hospital. Beyond the Victorian edifice were more modern ward buildings, post-war, vast, fairly featureless. Two or three of them had already been converted and had gardens outside. There were new trendy VW Beetles in fashionable yellow and a BMW parked outside.

The estate agent guy was ingratiating and Dot asked if she could view the property by herself, just give her ten minutes.

'It looks great, aren't you just so excited?' she said to Molly.

Molly reached back for Owen's hand.

'Don't worry,' he said, 'this could be our new house.'

Dot pushed the door open – 'Tan-tara' – and led them inside. She fished around for a switch. Neon strip lights came on. The place had been gutted and new power points had grown from the walls; the old lino must have been ripped up to reveal the concrete beneath. But the vast emptiness of it, the line of thirty windows on each side, the traces on the floor from what might once have been a nurse's office, marked it all clearly as what it was – a hospital ward.

'Wow, it's perfect. Over here, I'm thinking, we'll put up a fake wall, maybe out of glass bricks, you know, so as to let the light in.'

The space she wandered around was empty, but in her mind she had images of a place he could not see. Molly ran about picking plaster chips and nails off the floor and throwing them at the walls.

'This would be the kitchen, I'd separate the work space from the living space with another glass wall and I'd have one of those walk-in bathrooms, no walls, just tiles everywhere, a wet room, showers and a sunken jacuzzi. Molly, where would you like to have your bedroom?'

The child looked perplexed.

The incongruity of it all struck Owen. Dot's episode and her attempt and her hospitalisations.

'What do you think, O?' she shouted out. 'Isn't it perfect?'

He looked at her, so far away, at the other end of the big empty space. He could not picture the walls, the furniture, the fireplace and kitchen, the bedroom and glass walls. All he saw was the woman he loved standing shouting to him from the opposite end of a hospital ward. Molly came up to him.

'And when Saul's got his new place he'll be just a bus ride away and so easy for Molly and you're . . .'

If flashed before him then that she might say, '. . . going to have your study right here and this will be our bedroom.'

She smiled. '. . . I suppose you'll have to change at Bank and then onto the Central Line, but it's so close, don't you think? Half an hour tops. Great, eh? I mean, can't you just see it?' as she spun round, her hands in the air.

Molly gripped his hand. The kid couldn't see the pictures either.

'Where's your room, Uncle O?'

He squeezed her hand.

'I don't think I'm going to have one,' he said. 'I'll just come and visit when Mummy's finished making it all lovely for you both.'

He looked up at Dot.

'It's brilliant,' he called out. 'I can really see it.'

On the way back to his on the tube, he noted that the child cuddled up to him more than usual, as if she sensed that her mother's plan for the future did not contain this man she'd grown used to. And he felt pity for that child, because maybe she knew even more about abandonment than he did. In two days' time her mother would be off to Zurich, and it had still not been decided whether the child would travel with her mother, stay with the grandparents, or with Saul or himself, or if he or Saul would make the trip too.

On the tube images flashed by like the faces of many races.

The child looking up at him.

The hospital.

Dot's mouth moving fast, but her words inaudible over the train noise.

He closed his eyes and saw again the child's drawings. Many different colours but they were all ultimately the same. Of the same house and in that house there were not two or four but three people.

It was footage of three different films edited together in three adjoining vertical strips. On the left-hand screen Saul walked through a park in 1992 with his right hand extended. On the right-hand screen Owen walked through a supermarket with his left hand extended. The footage was from a month ago. On the middle screen Dot walked through a street with both hands extended. The footage seemed from five or so years ago.

'So what do you think?' she asked.

They were all sitting round her laptop and she was nervous. This was the great unveiling of the art she'd been making all month in her studio. She'd been through all the old tapes and found these three pieces of footage all from different times and places. It was to be the ninth work. She liked the arithmetic: three people times three films equals nine. The footage froze on the screen. And Dot's face was expectant, staring first at Owen then at Saul, asking what they thought.

'Can we see it again?' Owen said, playing for time.

'God, you hate it, don't you?'

'No, no, not at all.'

He hadn't hated it, and could see what she thought she'd been doing. She'd been trying to create the illusion of three different people in different films walking holding hands together. But she'd failed. The placing of the hands did not match up between the screens. Sometimes the hands were cut off halfway up a body or too low and ghost fingers and knuckles would appear on the edges of the frames, betraying the rough amateur assemblage. And the idea was hopelessly romantic, like some kitschy image from the sixties. Sentimental.

'Shit. It's crap, isn't it? Fuck, what the hell am I going to do?'

'Calm down,' Saul said. 'If you don't like it don't exhibit it.'

'What? And just have eight works in a show called *Nine*!'

'Well . . .'

'You were supposed to help me, Owen. It's fucked, if Zurich's fucked then we're fucked!'

She stormed out and Saul ran after her.

Owen stared at the screen as the three people in their three different times walked alone into their three different futures.

*

On the run home I had prepared a plan. If she could loan me five hundred we could get a place together, I'd get regular work, pay her back. I'd find a place in New Cross, close to the art school.

I burst through the front door.

— Dot?

No reply.

— Saul, are you OK? Has she been back? No reply.

His room was in almost total darkness. The stench of urine, sweat and sherry was overwhelming. The TV flickered blue light to the sounds of a crowd cheering. I reached for the light switch, and nearly tripped over him. He was naked, but for his kimono and one plimsoll, and lying on the floor. I tore open the curtains and acid-bright light burst in revealing many silver bags from the sherry boxes. He must have pulled them out and inflated them as if having a party by himself. Twenty or more, like space-age pillows, like Warhol's silver balloons. I propped him up on the edge of the bed and he reached immediately for a sherry box. I took it from him and he struggled for it, like a child fighting for sweets.

— Give, give me!

It burst between us.

— Idiot! Look what you've done.

— Please, Saul, stop!

He fell backwards, his words slurring.

— I'm not gay, though I wish I was just to piss off the homophobes, that's what he said, you know, on TV.

— Saul, concentrate. Have you seen her, has she been back here? When was the last time you saw her?

— He's going to die.

— What? Who?

He stared at me blankly, pointed drunkenly at the screen. — Fucking cunting Kurt!

He pointed at the TV. On it Cobain was wearing a wedding dress with fake saggy tits and was being brought onstage in a wheelchair. The drummer was in nothing but a bra and jeans.

— Listen to me, she's run off. We have to find her. I turned off the TV. Saul was flailing then, hands at the buttons, turning it back on.

— Fucking hell, leave it alone!

Cobain started playing 'Smells Like Teen Spirit' then stopped after the first three notes. — We don't do that song any more, he said world-wearily to the audience.

— See, Saul said. — He hates them, he used to love 'em ... throw himself off the stage ... they're killing him. Won't last a year. Mark my words!

I could make no sense of what he was saying. I tried

to get him dressed. All of his clothes were dirty or Dot had stolen them. I got him into his pink BABY T-shirt and a pair of my own jeans. I took the rest of the booze away from him and went to make him a coffee.

From the kitchen I heard the next song start up. 'Lithium'. It got me thinking about Dot's tablets. I thought about her father and her episode and tried to focus away the dread with the coffee-making. When he hit the chorus Cobain started detuning his guitar and screaming, not singing, relentlessly flat, out of tune.

I came back through with the coffee. Saul was fishing through the ashtray for a butt to relight.

— A gun, he said. And started singing that Nirvana song with the chorus about a gun. About not having a gun.
— He's a pacifist, BANG! Won't last the year. Bye-bye, Kurty boy, we love you, man.

— Drink your coffee, I said.

— Only make him famouser. Funny ha ha, eh? Five years, mark my words, everyone'll have one . . . like fucking Che Guevara. Poor fucker. Brains to the wall, fucking T-shirts everywhere, face all over the place . . . collector's items, wait and see.

Enough. I turned off the TV again. Put myself between it and him.

— Don't be silly, I said. — Cobain'll be fine. Drink your coffee and sober up. We need to try and find Dot. OK?

He stared at me hard as if trying to focus. He reached to hold me.

— D'you think I'm a bad person?
— No, not at all.
— Could you sub us a fiver for some . . . juice?

I called Goldsmiths. I called Sarah Lucas's shop and ran down Old Street to Dazed to see if anyone had seen or heard from her. I even ran into Sadhi's corner shop and asked there.

I took the liberty of going into her room and trying to find her address book, to find her parents' home number. Books and things on her floor; soiled panties and half-eaten food; make-up, empty pill boxes and vodka bottles; crisp packets in their dozens; Mars Bar wrappers; empty food packets hidden in corners and under the bed: Pot Noodles; a multitude of Post-it notes, covering the walls in layers: JOIN A COMMUNE; A BIG PROJECTION ON THE HOUSES OF PARLIAMENT; IMAGES ON WATER; ON CLOUDS; FILM A SUICIDE – WACO. A piece of paper on her desk, scored in marker pen, underlined: THE TRUST GAME – IN SUPER-MARKET – ON STREET – WALK BLIND.

Her camera charger was there, but not the camera. The wrapping for a pack of twelve tapes lay on the floor. I pictured her, walking around alone filming herself, walking aimlessly, falling into things, people, eyes closed, stumbling into danger.

There were three Shears in the phone book in her part of town. One on Harley Street. Her father. I dialled and I got through. — Hello the Stratford Clinic. I hung up.

I took the train all the long way to Goldsmiths. No sign of her in the corridors, in the hall, or refectory. I tried the studio. Video equipment had arrived, the screens and video projectors I'd ordered for her lay in huge boxes, unopened, while all around the other students were hanging their pictures, assembling their structures.

A hand on my shoulder. I turned and it was the shit-is-art student from before. Before I could speak he asked me, — You seen her? She's leavin' it a bit late, mate.

He asked me if I knew what instructions she'd given for her show. Everyone else was done, the tutors were going nuts.

I didn't know. Had no idea, but since I could think of nowhere else to search for her I thought it best to venture some suggestions. Something had to be saved. Given that

303

she wanted to show video clips on screens it had to be dark. I took the liberty of telling him to construct a space a bit like a cinema. He seemed content with that.

— So where do you want the projectors, mate?

— Sorry. Uh, no idea, I guess, facing the screen? Eh, look, sorry, I'll get her to call you as soon as I find her. OK?

— It's gotta be finished tomorrow, man.

I made my apologies and was running out again.

I opened the door to home, calling out for Saul, but his room was empty. The hall floor was streaked with vomit in trails all the way from his room to the bathroom. It was getting late and the rain was pissing down. I cleaned up his mess with a cloth and some Vim and paced the hall, waiting for just an idea of what I could do. She was out only God knew where wearing fuck knows what.

Looking for clues I went back to Saul's stupid Duchess book.

The epilogue said there were no surviving artworks by the Duchess. She committed suicide the day before her first group show, the 1923 surrealist retrospective in NYC – in which she was to have exhibited herself dressed as a chesspiece. She had been missing for a week. Her naked corpse was found in a dumpster on Twenty-Third and Fifth. Deep holes had been cut into her flesh, around the genitals, the breasts and mouth. Some claimed she was murdered by jealous male artists. Others that she had had a history of self-mutilation and satanic ritual. After her death Duchamp became a millionaire and declared surrealism dead. He vowed never to make art again and took to playing chess. It was a patchwork of total lies and half-truths, but Dot had believed it real and inspirational. She could have been at that very moment living out the tragedy of the Duchess. I was thrown into total panic.

I paced my room then charted its contents as the

minutes became hours. The lowered ceiling and walls of dust-filled swirly Artex. Posters of Gerhard Richter's Baader–Meinhof portraits covering the holes in the walls. The old broken typewriter found in the street. The sign 'Danger of Death', drunkenly pinched from the electricity generator on the corner, the plastic Amstrad stereo with the two mismatched speakers, found in the street, linked by many sections of electricity cable stripped from kettles, computers and TVs all found in the street. My old BBC personal computer, with its green text on the black screen that gave me migraines. The two single mattresses piled on top of each other, one with kiddie hot-air balloon patterns on it, that together were so soft that it was impossible to get up from them. The broken Xpelair fan on the window. The many books of Saul's I had borrowed and only ever half read. The three years' worth of stolen charity-shop clothes in a pile as big as a corpse. The fungus spores on the wall that connected to the bathroom. The many bits of paper with Dot's ideas scrawled on them. Covers of videotapes, stickers for video spines. A pair of her panties under my bed resting among dust balls. The iron bars on the windows. The broken fire escape, missing its first five steps. The lights of cars on the overpass. Vertical shadows against my wall, like bar codes. I looked out and pictured myself out in the rain on that road, walking under the pissing sky, camera to eye, screaming at the cars that screamed past. I thought I saw a figure out there. I pushed my face to the cold glass, but couldn't see. The dirt on the outside softened every detail into grey. A shadow passed between the headlights. It stopped, by the railing, seemed to hold something to its face, a bottle, a gun, a camera.

I ran outside, trying to locate that space, up towards the pedestrian walkway. A few figures ran past with umbrellas, one in a shellsuit. I turned the concrete corner onto the bridge, and there ahead was the figure again, hunched over the rail, in the middle, an inhuman form, that somehow seemed familiar to me. The six lanes of cars speeding white and red light below its feet.

— DOT! DOT!

The figure turned as I ran forward. It was a man, seemed an old man. The old tramp, I thought. As I got closer there was a flash of skin beneath his trench coat. Rain obscuring bare chest, cock in his hand, dribble of piss in air, falling to the cars below. I stared in disgust but then the face flashed in the headlights.

— Jesus, Saul! What the fuck . . .

He tucked his cock back inside, rubbed his eyes.

— Come on. You're going to catch your death.

I put my arm round him and took his weight, leading him away.

— Sorry, sorry, he said. — It's all my fault.

— It's OK.

— You find her?

I shook my head. He was trembling all over.

— Got to call her dad . . . or pigs . . . sick girl . . . got to call her dad.

But what would her father do but take her from us?

— Let's get you home, I said. — Maybe she'll be back there waiting for us.

Car lights threw dark dreams across my pillow all that night as my ears strained to make every creak of wood, every passing footstep or slowing car cohere into her form. No sleep before the sun rose and no word and I could not endure the waiting with her words circling in my head: 'Wait and see, that's all you ever do, you do nothing, nothing! Empty man, mirror man, gutless!'

The number of her father's medical practice was in my trouser pocket. The repercussions of calling it were horrific to imagine. I had to do one thing first.

I went to the public library to check the medical dictionary. I already knew the names from the empty pill boxes she left in the bathroom. Diazepam was easy enough. Lithium – a mood stabiliser – taking the edge off both the highs and the lows – it built up slowly in the system like salt or nicotine or smack. Three months it took after withdrawal for the levels to reduce to zero and the withdrawal had to be phased so as not to risk triggering mania. Hers had been total and abrupt. Cerebrex – used in the control of extreme manic episodes. Manic depression can have seasonal triggers: up in spring and summer, down in autumn, winter. She was up and it was spring coming into summer. Can be triggered by exposure to cannabis.

I sat there in the empty library, an old woman on a Zimmer frame passed me by. A clock ticked. Seventies lino and fake wood. A display showed the latest Jeffrey Archer. An institution. If I called her father, Dot could be placed in an institution again.

I read on, looking for excuses. But the evidence mounted against her. Her sudden eruptions of hatred then quiet whispering, then touch, then withdrawal. Further signs of mania: the subject talks in quotations – they may have been studying, reading obsessively. It is not uncommon for manic patients to expound totalising world views, end-of-the-world theories, to have sudden conversions to obscure religions, to have an answer for everything, to laugh at your questions, to show signs of extraordinary conviction – that only they have the key to understanding it all, that these visionary insights are too complex to explain to a normal person – to identify with extreme historic figures, to suddenly give up on projects that have been worked on with commitment for months on end. Bulimia is common, as is an increased testosterone level and erratic, heightened libido.

I felt dizzy and nauseous.

Goldsmiths was the only place to look for her and I

dragged myself onto the tube but then, halfway there, all the bodies tight round me, I thought I was going to faint, vomit. I needed air.

I walked the streets of Soho, trying to get my head together. Past the fruit-market stalls and the stink of last night's pubs, the crushed fruit underfoot. A pair of stilettos clicked past me and cockneys whistled. Was I to blame? Had I not encouraged Dot to give up her pills? Only to expose her to hashish?

I passed adverts for sex shows, cards for prostitutes in phone boxes; the Ann Summers shop and XXX video stores with handwritten signs tacked up on their blacked-out windows. FIST FUCK IV, TEENTOTTIE.

But she had not really been sick that time, in her teens. I tried to remember the words she'd told me. She'd pretended, with her parents, and then the pretending made her sick – that was what she'd said.

A skinny-looking woman in a corset and fishnets was sitting on a stool in a doorway before me.

— Fancy a show, sir? Only two pounds.

The sign behind her said 'LIVE COUPLE FUCKING'.

And I had watched Dot and Saul writhing naked. 'VIDEOS VIDEOS VIDEOS' a neon flashed. Dot and her videos. If she was mad now, it was not the drugs, not that at all. It was the video-making, the inability just to live – 'The unrecorded life is not worth living.' It was the tyranny of Saul's aesthetics that had made her mad.

'XXX. YOU MUST BE OVER 18 TO ENTER.' I entered, maybe to drown out judgement, to kill the growing guilt. The sounds of video orgasm flooded the shelves. Three hundred varieties of sexual perversion available from *Anal Intruder* to *ZooGirls* to take home on VHS for £15. The guy behind the counter turned his TV screen round to show a waiting client, Saul's voice was over my shoulder. 'There is nothing less sexy than sex.'

308

No, the fault was mine. Me and my weakness for sex. I had pushed both her and Saul into it, from some sickness inside me. Fuck it. There were at least three arguments in my mind from every perspective. Three sides to every story:

Two scroungers had exploited a rich girl, taken her money, ruined her career and driven her insane. A failed artist had manipulated two youngsters into acting out his debased fantasies as a revenge against the world that had rejected him. A bored rich girl with a history of madness dragged two innocents down into her cyclic condition without giving them forewarning.

I was inventing alibis. I was to blame. The fault was all mine. Mine, fuck me. I needed to do the stupidest most extreme thing possible. Dot had made us wear her mother's clothes. I had wanted to wear her mother's clothes. Fuck me. Fuck me dead.

Madame Jay's, the back-street transvestite bar, I had passed it many times. The dark purple smoked glass mirrored my daylight grey self back to me as I hesitated at the door. It was still early, and there were very few customers there on the purple velvet seats. The place smelled of bleach. A tall TV girl came over to me in a spangly dress, fishnets and heels, fake eyelashes and rouge that on her black skin looked like a bruise. Could I buy her a drink? Her voice not just a man trying to sound like a woman but a cockney trying to sound like an American queen. Her many flirtatious questions and her hand on my shoulder kept me there as I tried to leave. She talked about her implants and stroked my thigh. She wanted to show me. We could go to the toilet. Thirty and she'd give me a suck, fifty and I could fuck her. She took her hand and put it on her thigh. I could feel her cock through the fabric.

— I got quantity and I got quality.

I tried to excuse myself, didn't want to offend, she had been very charming, I said, I couldn't afford it, was on the dole, but she brought down her prices.

— Ten for a suck. You get finance, I give you romance.

The briefest flash, then all hell broke loose within me, why not, why not fuck a trannie, get fucked, get addicted, get sick, get pills, live to fuck to forget to fuck again till you die of it. Fuck me and Dot and Saul and all our petty little problems we thought so important.

She crossed her muscly legs. Then it came to me. Edna.

I didn't have Edna's number but something visceral told me Dot was there. I excused myself, and ran to the door, down the street, past the stench and sex to the tube. This madness had started with Edna. Yes, Dot would be there, where else in the world could she be?

eight

Trust 3. 2001. Circular video loop. Double screen installation.
2 x 3.4 x 2.8 m. Frederick and Gerhard Scholl Collection.

THE FOOTAGE IS in slow motion and is of people being slapped. The number of faces is around thirty. The act of slapping echoes that which took place in the earlier, similarly titled *Trust*,[1] but whereas the slapping in *Trust* was within an intimate setting and focused on one person, in *Trust 2* and *3*, there are many subjects who receive a blow and the context is public. Faces of onlookers can be seen in the background and it is clear that the location for each 'slap event' is, in fact, an art gallery.

As *Trust 3* is one of Shears's remade works it is interesting, the transformation and change in the nature of footage between *Trust 1*, *2* and *3*. (1993, 1993, 2001 respectively).

Trust 2 appears to be amateur footage of Shears slapping people at a gallery opening. Her voice can be heard off-mike, asking people to take part in a 'social experiment'. There is a playful party atmosphere and much laughter as Shears convinces people, individually. After slapping five or six, very hard, a commotion starts up, and judging by the footage (erratic, thrown around) it would seem that Shears was forced to stop filming.

The slapping that had been so gentle and understated in *Trust* has, by the time of making *Trust 2* become violence enacted on strangers, with only the most tenuous consent. The work began as an exploration of the power of the camera: what could someone get away with, what rules of conduct could they break, simply by virtue of the fact that they were recording an event that was being called art? In *Trust 2*, Shears's 'game' becomes dangerous, antisocial.

Trust 3 was made in 2001. This time again within a gallery setting, but the footage shows a slightly older group of people, of mixed ethnic backgrounds, fashionably dressed. Whereas the original footage was hand-held and raw, the footage in *3* is filmed on Steadicam, the room is 'lit' and the 'slapping' seems pre-organised. There is none of the process of coercion/talking people into taking part that was on the first footage. Each person simply stands facing the camera, waiting for their turn to receive the blow. It cannot be ignored that several of these 'people' are film and music celebrities, others respected names in the art business.[2] As such the change from the first work to the last is a material indicator of the rise of Shears's career.

Some have seen it as an impassioned critique of the art market, quite literally Shears striking out against it all, or even against 'the image of her own celebrity'. Exponents of this view cite the 'subversive role of play in the social context'.

Others claim, to the contrary, that the work is an example of the impotence of such rebellious gestures – the act of rebellion itself being recuperated back into the canon of art. As with Dada and surrealism, the anti-art statement ultimately becomes just another commodified gesture/ object. A more balanced interpretation is that the work comments, on a meta-level, on the processes of recuperation and is in fact an ironic critique of the idea of 'rebellion' through art. The attempt is futile from the start and that is the point. Critics of Shears's work have pointed to this work as the end of the period of 'playing games'. As J. Thompson wrote, 'We all knew this would end in tears.'[3]

There is a sadness about this work. As the many faces of the rich and famous line up to be slapped in turn, there is a sense of the artist's desperation. She strikes out with raw violence, unimpeded by concern over the degree to which she might hurt each person. But no matter how hard the slap is, no matter how much a cry for help, or expression of anger, there is always a next face waiting for her to 'do her worst'. Thus the role of the artist is parodied and inverted. The artist is asked again and again to express rebellion to an indifferent world, only to be applauded for how 'expressive' and 'angry' she is. These attacks occur in a vacuum. They are without repercussion or, worse still, only fuel the mechanisms of publicity. The faces seem pleased to have been slapped by the artist, as if they have just received an autographed print, 'a real Shears'. Shears's voice from behind camera, her grunts and gasps as she strikes, are deeply disturbing, and after witnessing so many faces being slapped, focus tends towards the sounds of Shears's own voice behind the camera.

As a critic and friend of Shears has said: 'This is really an act of desperation.'

It is ultimately not the faces who are slapped that we feel for, but the person off-screen and unseen. The work is really about Shears striking out against herself and what she has become. She must perform the role of rebel, day in, day out, and the act is increasingly as empty as the waiting faces. We sense that behind this violence all she wants perhaps is to reach out and touch with the gentleness she once knew, before success placed a screen between her and the world. As in her first work called *Trust*, which was truly about trust, and not its attempted, and failed, betrayal.

1. *Trust*, 1993.
2. It has been noted that two of the 'names' were former 'partners' of Shears, gallery owners and media celebrities. A well-known indie photographer, acclaimed for capturing the movements in grunge and heroin chic, was among them.
3. J. Thompson claimed that Shears had made a career out of filming

drunken party games; that her art was a product of a generation so politically disenfranchised and disengaged that their only possible reaction to the serious adult world of responsibilities was to poke fun with 'ironic and childish games'. 'The Party Is Over', *Independent*, May 2002.

THEY WERE BOOKED on the 09.30 KLM 472 for Zurich. She said she'd pay for his ticket, at the last minute even. He calmed her, telling her his flight had been booked for two days' time and he would join them both, just in time for the opening night, with the text. He'd have to rewatch all the DVDs, check his references and endnotes, work round the clock to get it done on time and apologised again that it had thrown their plans to travel together. Such a pity, he'd been looking forward to the two adjoining rooms in the Hilton. I know, I know, he said, but this is for you. He'd join them as soon as he could. But secretly, he wanted Dot and Saul to share that bed, to give him the excuse he needed to end it all.

They were all packed and excited on that morning and hugs and kisses at the door with their bags and Dot lingering to ask him if he would be OK, and Molly gave him a little hand-drawn card with big love hearts and kisses.

'Good luck with the show. Don't worry, I'll email the text over as soon as it's done, you'll be fine. We'll find a way round the problem of the ninth work,' he said. 'Be good, and don't worry.'

Then they were away to the waiting taxi and he was alone.

Drink was what it needed.

The essay would never be finished. Their whole plan of making sense of the past was a pathetic fallacy. She had already left him and taken Saul too. This must have been the revenge she'd been planning all these years.

He'd got five texts from her that day. The second last

read: 'Horrible city but show looks good. Sozzle and Mozzer send love. XXX'.

The last said: 'Wish you were here my O. X'.

He could just see them walking round Zurich together. Their hands in Molly's hands, swinging her along the streets. He saw the city. The old buildings and the concrete motorway that cut through its centre, ripping the heart from the place. The boulevards that lacked the grace of Paris. The centre that had been a sex district last time he'd been there. He saw himself in a video cabin ten years back watching some hardcore fantasy tape, the naked woman held down by two men, screaming *nein, nein, nein*. A couple of marks it had cost.

He had willed them gone but now that they were it was too much.

Saul would be there at her gallery opening, all wit and clever one-liners, at his best and walking hand in hand to the hotel with her. They would sleep together tonight. Making love in the hotel room, taking great care not to wake Molly.

He paced the flat. The many things scattered; the paper people on the walls; her clothes; the toys; the three adult toothbrushes in the sink, the small child's one; Saul's child psychology manual, the page folded over on Bowlby's maternal deprivation theory; the wine glass with her lipstick kiss; their plates from their last meal together, stacked above the dishwasher; Dot's Post-it notes. One that read: WE ARE FILMS – THREE FILMS.

In her mind he was going to get the KLM flight the day after tomorrow. Fuck her and Saul. Fuck them forever. Owen couldn't sleep. It was back to the mobile again and the list of fuck-buddies, texting them all the same message.

'Hiya, how you been, you free for sum fun 2nite?'

Only one reply from Liz, she was in Ibiza.

He placed the mobile by his pillow. If one texted or

called back he would fuck her. Get her in a taxi, pay for it. Right here in this bed that was his and Dot's. No sleep for fear of what he would do if a reply came and he was given the choice.

He knew what he had to do.

First, put on her panties. The empty rooms told him so. No choice but to see it to the end, no more questions. It was their fault for leaving him alone. Ideally it would have required a hotel room; a vodka hip flask, an ounce of hashish maybe, or a gram of coke, a bottle of poppers; sex with strangers, perverts, transsexuals. In homage to Edna, may she rest in peace.

But look at yourself now, Owen, thirty-nine, and still you don't know anything much. As if sex had an answer and you are scared of going outdoors to Soho where sex is sold.

Owen got the bottle and went through to her room and opened her drawers. Shirts and bras and panties. Holding them to his face. Washing powder – no trace of her. A pile of used clothes. Another drink and her panties on his face, mask-like and then it had to be the music.

The CDs. Versions of the old albums. All were there – Dinosaur Junior, Parliament, Foetus off the Wheel, Wagner, the Revolting Cocks, Rapeman – Nirvana – these songs Dot played to her child as if there was something to be learned from them.

Fuck it, play them all, have another fucking drink, coward yellow-belly.

Rapeman. The band name that had Albini banned from Europe, and more voddie and it was pathetic really how much he had invested in that year. Hear the music now, really listen to it. So many attempts to shock, to over-throw the dominant order – through doing what? Buying some videos and some CDs? Pathetic. A refill from the voddie. Pills, it needed pills. Dot always had her stash, the hundreds of things she took and then didn't take, the bag in the bathroom.

Ibuprofen, diazepam, Valium, Sertraline, Propranolol, lithium. Lithium then in homage to the song by Cobain and Saul had been right, the fucker didn't last the year and maybe that had been the better way to go, better that than this. And Saul must have been deeply disappointed when the millennium bug hadn't destroyed civilisation at 00.00 hours on 1 January 2000.

All her tablets, one from each packet, ten packets.

Tonight we're gonna party like it's 1999.

A line like a song lyric running through him: you've made me like this, you made me do this and now you'll pay.

Throwing back the pills like they did on that first night. When Saul came in, when she said she was going to give them all up because she had something better now, before she flushed the rest away. Pink and blue and white and semi-transparent in gel capsules. Diazepam, Valium, lithium, Sertraline.

That great artwork, that one with him and Saul in her mother's clothes. So be it. *Leg Show*, and no one to see it but the mirror.

He is in the bedroom, stripping naked, going through her boxes and bags, trying to make himself hard. He finds her tights. Five pairs packed. He must have the old ones, used ones, that smell of her. Bathroom for another diazepam, the ones she said made her happy, sleepy, sleepy happy.

Feel the denier on your hairs. Laugh at it, laugh at yourself.

So naughty, telling himself shh. He pulls them on so slowly because he doesn't want to rip them with his toenails, but then remembers that when she comes back he is going to have to. Yes, finish that sentence for once, for both of them. Yes, tell her she has to leave, her and Saul. She will be gone in a week anyway, he can start tonight, packing her boxes, and Saul will only be a matter of days. He will carry Saul's boxes to his car, and wish him well as he drops him at his new council flat.

Shh — as he throws back the rest, as he, the stockings now on and tight-fitting fabric round his cock, looks at her rack of dresses. And it was a mistake all along to let her move half of her stuff here. Because women need security and a man they can trust and he is dangerous still, more than ever he was before, and it makes him laugh how they both came to him for security and maybe this is his revenge, finally. He could kill them both now in sweet Valium indifference, make them pay. He is in hysterics as he pulls her sparkly minidress over his head, as he bursts the seam, as he takes a minute there, to pose in the mirror like she did in that artwork called *PlayBoy*. As he pulls the dress up in the mirror and looks at the legs and tells himself higher higher as she did in that artwork called *Leg Show*.

Am I a film star? Am I a man? The mirror tells him he is a man, nearly forty, overweight and laughable, wearing his girlfriend's clothes. Oh, but she is not his girlfriend, she is neither girl nor friend and his attempts to bring her back have failed. All he wants is to just for a minute to take stock, as in a photo, to say I am happy or sad. Just one thing finally resolved.

Saul's old songs. And wine uncorked because vodka done.

Rapeman was screaming thoughout the flat. He tried to sing along. Another CD. To hell with it. Go the worst. The Revolting Cocks. 'I'm a killing MACHINE!'

He found the heels, the ones she'd worn on the TV broadcast of the Turner Prize. His toes bursting the seams, he took one off and sniffed it, dizzy. Considered wanking into it, his cock between the straps. Soft, old softie walkover Owen, wimp and sucker. No more booze. Fuck, how many tabs had he taken?

And she had swallowed every pill she had, they said, then slashed her wrists.

'Killing machine', 'Killing machine'.

The album was all wrong. He staggered through in the heels, catching himself in the hallway mirror. Maybe the lighting was wrong. The hairy legs, the big shoulders. Not like Dot at all. He bent over to change the CD and felt the rip at his arse. His fingers reaching back to find the tear. Dot would kill him. I'm a killing machine.

Tomorrow he'd pack all of her things. She had to go, he'd write her a cheque for the torn Dolce and Gabbana. Another for childcare. So, stoned fingers through the CDs – Slint, Psychic TV, Nirvana, Einstürzende Neubauten.

He stumbled back as the Nirvana started, tried to turn it into a dance. He was moshing, James Brown-ing, Prince-ing and funkadelic-ing in the living room, struggling to stand, reaching for the wine bottle, thinking of them in Zurich, walking round like fucking Lord and Lady Muck of fucken' Muckenddoo. They had left him again and they would pay.

The Duchamps. It had to be there somewhere. He'd found it on eBay just a tape with a photocopied cover. To walk the street blind tonight in Dot's clothes and be Duchamp's Duchess. To write a name on his head and ask everyone who he was. Am I Elvis, am I Cobain? The faces passing scared in the street. Fucking tell me – am I dead or alive?

Owen fell head first, bashing his face on the wall, as he tried to put the tape in. It was the heels, he told himself. Hello, he said to the face in the mirror, but it did not reply. Hello, baby, who's a cute girl? Love you, I love you, I . . . To just have a slap in the face, or a kiss, to wake up. His head falling. Wasn't it beautiful, though, the way – the face in that artwork. The way it waited for the touch. And he was there at the start of the filming. Dot stage-diving and him waiting anxious to see if they would catch her. He needed to sleep, the room spinning.

And 'Disparu'. That fucking song, maybe it was even Edna singing, and it was crap, so crap, but beautiful because it showed how weak and pathetic and vain people were and how crap the eighties actually were, and the irony of that would be lost on everyone now cos irony meant nothing any more and it wasn't here anyway, gone and lost and smashed and no one would ever hear that fucking song again. Up in smoke. Poof. DIS – PAR – OOO! French lyrics and Yorkshire accent. Hilarious. *Nous avons* need to puke. Going to. Can't move. My God.

Up somehow, he chokes the puke through his nose, pulls off a heel and falls to the floor, Molly's Lego castle breaking under his cheekbone, winded and gagging. He reaches for the phone line, pulls the phone to himself, along the floor. Its voice saying PLEASE REPLACE THE HANDSET AND TRY AGAIN PLEASE REPLACE THE. His fingers can't find the number. Temazepamwithalcohol, the other one, pink, somegovthealthwarning. 'Disparoo'. This is her big show and she has to be there to meet her fans and he has maybe done this just to fuck it up for her. He hits all the phone buttons. Her mobile – speed dial 2.

Ringing, ringing. Poor Saul's voice, in his head, singing along to the stupid song. 'Noose avons disparooo.'

Ring ring ring.

'Disparoo.'

A click, a hello. Dot.

'Hi, Owen. How you doing?'

He couldn't speak, old Saul was singing loud in his head.

'Owen? You OK?'

His head spinning, vomit rising again, he tries to speak, but his lips, numb.

He's asking her about 'Disparu' but his mouth is all wrong, he has to focus. 'Pills' is all he can manage.

She's screaming. Sound of her, dropping phone, footsteps running, many things. Off-mike, off-camera. And Action.

Saul is there then.

'Owen, talk to me. YOU FUCK! YOU DUMB FUCK.'

It's a movie and artwork. Dot screaming in the background – she knew something like this would happen. Listen, they are both there in Zurich.

'Wake up! I knew we shouldn't have,' shouts Saul. 'Talk to me. Tell me something. Keep talking. You selfish fuck! . . . Fuck. Look, OK, you have to talk to me. She's calling an ambulance. Wait, she's . . . she's . . .' He is shouting at her. 'SHUT THE FUCK UP.' He is back. 'We're going to get the next flight back,' he says. 'We're going straight to the airport. OK, talk to me, you fuck, please fucking talk to me.' She's saying keep him talking. Then it's Dot's voice on the phone.

'Owen, talk please. QUIET! I can't hear. Sorry, I was talking to Saul, tell me something. Talk to me, keep on talking, the ambulance will be there soon. Owen, say my name.

'Dot.'

'OK, I want you to tell me something, anything, the first time you met me. OK?'

'OK.' And so Owen focused on each word and each word was slow but it took him away from the nausea.

'Gallery. Old Street.'

'Yes, yes. Can you remember which one? And the show?'

'Dazed . . . was called *Arseholes* . . . pictures of arseholes.'

'Was it? How can you remember that? Got to keep you talking, the ambulance'll be there soon. Wait, and you had a rucksack and you were wearing a . . . can you remember? I can't . . . what were you wearing?'

'Army trousers, Doc Martens . . .'

'Can you really remember all that? OK, OK, what was I wearing?'

'Woolly jumper, grey . . . blue jeans . . . Hush Puppies . . . mousy hair . . . no make-up.'

She was sobbing.

'Was I really like that? My God, what'd we do without you? We should write this all down so we never . . .'

Her voice in his ear, he's trying to tell her of the way she stood so still while everyone else was in a panic of activity, of how she stared down at her own hands, of how he'd never seen anyone so out of tune with her time, of how her face had seemed timeless, like a very old painting, like a queen, like a duchess . . .

'Owen? Don't go quiet on me. Owen, my love! Jesus Christ, wake up, please, you fuck. Talk to me. Little brother, wake up. Wake up, Owen! OWEN!'

Her voice so far away, so sleepy. Then Saul is in his ear whispering in a new language. *Baruch atah Adonai.* Take my hand, he says, take her hand, we're going to walk together now. *Hamotzi lechem mien haaretz.* Like four notes in a song. *Hamotzi lechem mien haaretz.* Lovely old song, so sleepy, like a prayer. Hand in hand in hand.

*

The concrete maze of estate houses. Five youths in hooded shellsuits loitered by the metal fence, kicking at cans. I stopped running so as not to draw attention to myself and got to the security door. Tried to remember the button. Most of the names had been erased so I pushed many.

— Hi, that Edna?

— The intercom buzzed and whistled and one then another voice came on.

— What? Fak off! Izzat de council?

— I'm looking for Edna.

I heard glass smash behind me and kids' laughter. The street gang were watching, getting closer. I pushed more buttons and stared up at the many concrete windows, boarded up with metal. The intercom whistled again.

— Is that Edna? I'm looking for Dot. Is she there?

There was silence. Then a voice, maybe Dan's, cockney.

— Fack off, ya puffy cant! Make me cam dawn there I'll fackin' rip yer face!

— Look, I need to know if Dorothy is there.

Just then another voice came on, speaking some language unknown to me. The buzzer buzzed. I pushed my way through the door. Up the steps of broken glass and piss and graffitied walls, I turned the corner and there was Edna's ridiculous doorway, the plants and shoes outside. Sandals, plimsolls and definitely Saul's hobnail boots. The ones Dot wore. She was here.

I hesitated. There was no point ringing the bell. There would be a scene and Dan's huge bulk would promise violence. So I retraced my steps, and there at the bottom of the stairwell, under the steps, in the dark, amid the broken glass and syringes, I waited. No one came or went in what must have been an hour. I didn't want to give up my hiding place, but needed to pee. I peed in my own space and had not choice but to crouch in it.

His boots, her feet, were the first thing I saw. Her fish-nets were torn to shreds. She was dressed in Saul's cut-off wedding dress and her bra over the top, with the wig she stole, half painted pink with dayglow highlighter pens. In her hand she clutched her video camera. I did not call out. I waited for her to get to the front door and out, before getting up to follow her.

At a safe distance I followed her as she walked back through Hackney into Hoxton. Block after block as the faces turned from black to white. McGregor Court. The Enfield cloisters. The off-licence advertising cheap booze. The George & Vulture, Pittfield Street. St John the Baptist Church. To the corner of Whitmore. She stopped and I hid myself in a doorway.

Minutes I waited and then peeked out. She had not walked home, but straight on. To the orbital streets of Hoxton

Square. Camera in her hand. Her pace was picking up as she approached a gallery. There was a crowd of people outside, sipping wine. An opening was taking place. I recalled her words from days before – 'Pierce, rip his face.'

— Dot! I called out.

She turned and her face scared me. Her expression beneath the streaked mascara, the moustachioed mouth, of almost total vacuity.

I ran to her. Stopped, could not touch her.

— You still here, you're like a dog, she said. — Can't you just leave me alone?

— You OK? What you doing here?

Behind us, the talk was loud, the many dressed up for their trendy opening, glasses clinking, cigarette smoke and flirtation in the air.

— Saying sorry to Pierce, she said, but the words seemed as empty as her eyes.

And the smile that followed was almost terrifying. And why Pierce? What had he to do with anything?

— You should go home, little brother, you might get hurt.

And she turned to walk inside, through the masses. I had no choice but to follow her.

She went round the entire party, three hundred people, whispering in their ears. They laughed as she took their video portraits. It seemed like a game. I stayed a good distance away so as not to intrude, and crept slowly closer. A woman beside me was talking to some guy, posh voices.

— Is it some kind of video diary?

— Artwork, I think, some kind of slapping game, sounds a bit daft.

— It's been done before, Douglas Gordon, what was it called . . . ?

— I think that was kissing.

From between the shoulders and glasses of the many

I saw that Dot had lifted her camera to her eye, and a young man stood before her. He smiled then nodded. Suddenly she slapped his face. He reeled then broke out laughing. The laughter spread and then another guy came forward to Dot, offering his face. Again Dot slapped and the sound was audible. People turned to stare.

— It's OK, someone called out, — it's only art.

— Any volunteers? another called out. — We need to do a hundred faces!

There was much laughter and Dot had become the focus of the entire show. The couple beside me then started on performance art and Vito Acconci slapping himself. No one seemed to notice that Dot was striking each person harder and harder. It was absurd, they had started lining up to be slapped and each time, as she hit them as hard as she could, they reeled with laughter after and thanked her and gave her their cards.

I sensed a great danger and got closer. Just then, I glimpsed Pierce. He was with some foreign-looking types. Dot broke away from the circle around her and marched up to him, interrupted him mid-schmooze.

She explained the process again and told them it was an artwork, a hundred people slapped in the face. He was embarrassed, reticent, but his friends egged him on.

— OK, just the one, he said, as he went to set down his wine glass. Before he could, she lashed out at him, he tried to defend himself. His glass was in the air, smashed against his cheek, blood on his face, she screamed at him, punched his chest. — BASTARD! BASTARD! The place fell silent. People started to run, chaos broke loose.

I pushed through the bodies and hauled her away. Her camera hit the ground. I grabbed it as I pulled her outside into a run.

— Come on!

Out through the hysterical crowd, out through the

square. She was falling everywhere, tripping, dead weight. I managed to get her onto Old Street and into an alleyway. There was a phone box, fifty yards beyond.

— Stay here, I'm going to get help, right here, I love you, OK, I love you, I'm going to get help. Trust me, OK.

She stared catatonic at the place where my face had been. I didn't know if it was safe to leave her but there was only one thing I could think to do. The number in my pocket – her father. I ran to the phone box and tried to find change, the fucking phone wouldn't take my money, I dialled again and again, then finally got through.

— Hello, Dr Shears please, this is an emergency.

— This is his secretary. I'm sorry, sir, but Dr Shears only sees patients by appointment. Would you like to make an appointment?

— No, it's about his daughter. Dorothy.

It was then that I heard the touch on the door beside my head. I looked up and there through the graffitied glass was Dot. She looked at my hand and the number within it, then at my eyes. Her mouth fell open, all blood seemed to drain from her face.

— Hello, can I help you?

I swear I heard her gasp for air. She fell back as if winded, the breath forced out of her. Eyes wounded, confused, a child betrayed, looking into me, asking why, why.

— Dorothy!

I turned and slammed into the glass. She fell away from sight towards the road. A scream of cars skidding, a crash, and thud. I couldn't get out of the box. I put my weight against the door and fell out. Beyond, two cars were crushed into each other, a flash of her legs, voices screaming. Past the wreckage she ran, between skidding cars, away, for her life.

For hours in the night I was cross-examined. The same questions over and over from the two policemen in my room.

329

Saul was interrogated for three hours. I puked with nerves. One of them was in her room taking flash photos.

Night willing day, willing her return. 7 a.m. and no word and so the aching train ride to Goldsmiths. I paced outside for an hour, then, when the doors were opened, ran inside. Her tutor accosted me, asking me where she was – her degree assessment was to be that afternoon. I lied, said she was sick, said she had given me instructions for the layout of the show. All day I fought the fear with the many technical questions, the placement of screens, the plugging in and testing of video projectors, the choice of tapes. I was no artist but it had to be done, something had to be saved. I spent hours going through the video cassettes in boxes with no labels, trying to work out what her intentions had been. Back and forward to the phone to call Saul, her father, but 'no word' were the only words.

The screens and video projectors, when erected and plugged in, flooded the room in light, but I had no time for reverie. Three screens had been hired, so three tapes had to be chosen. I did not know which and how. There was the Rizla game and the slapping game and the dressing in her mother's clothes, and her filming herself with her moustache – earlier conversations she'd filmed with me and Saul, laughing faces. Hundreds of hours of other things I watched in fast-forward while I fought the mounting hysteria around me from students and, it seemed, the press, the many whispers of 'police', 'missing', 'newspapers'. I put a board over the opening to her space.

At midday the tutors arrived. I begged for more time. An hour and they said time was up. One, German, asking me if the show was ready. I had no choice, I picked three tapes. The slapping game and the Rizla and the mother's clothes. The video technician was on hand; I told him where things started and ended and how they had to be repeated. I ran to the phone and called Saul again, but no word, her father the same. I came back through and after half an hour with the adjusting of projectors and distances and focal lengths, I saw it all on three screens. Flickering faces on huge screens. It did not seem like art at all, more like home videos, nothing else. I stayed only for five minutes, as the tutors took notes. A journalist tried to corner me and I ran from him.

Helpless stupid tears on the train then street then home and she was still not there. Saul seemed blood-drained. He was chain-smoking. I offered him a drink, he refused. He would never touch a drop again, he said, and would not let me put on music to kill time. He was to blame for it all, he said, he understood now. There had to be an end to it, he said, as he broke into tears. His arms reaching out for me. He had to start again he said, crying, clinging, asking me to forgive him. The phone rang and we both dived for it.

Hospital corridors endless. Saul could not face her and so I went alone. I got to the counter, gave my name, asked if it was OK, visiting hours were over. It was fine just for five minutes, they said. Her parents had been in. As the nurse led the way I asked my questions. All too abstract for the woman to answer. 'Pills,' she said. 'Stomach pump.' 'Wrists,' she said. I asked where this had happened, how. She had vital signs, the nurse said, hadn't woken yet but they were confident it wasn't a coma. 'Here you are' – she motioned to a door.

My Dot, not that body hooked up to intravenous drips with monitors and cables and face so grey. Her poor face as I sat beside her. I was scared to take her hand in case it would hurt, worrying over the bandages round her wrists and her IV drip. Her fingers tight like spiders. Big bandages, brown stains through the fabric.

I squeezed her fingertips. No response, but her heart-beat monitor pulsed, she was breathing, eyes closed.

Her hair – like she did that first time with scissors in the bathroom, her hair in the sink, but this time cropped almost to the skull, tufts and bloodied scabs, my poor boy-girl. And her mouth, the tube in her mouth.

A nurse came and said best if I came back tomorrow. Dot needed rest. They'd call me when she woke. They would tell her that I'd been here. Was I her boyfriend? What was my name again?

Saul was packing. He would not talk and had been on the phone for hours. Every time he put it down it had rung again he said. He'd leave enough to cover one month's rent when he went. He was sorry, he said again and again, but he had to leave tomorrow. Something had to change and it was him, he said again, again. And again the phone kept ringing. Saul pulled it out from the wall.

Later, dark, I plugged the phone back in to wait for the hospital's call. The line beeped. You have twenty-nine messages. I listened to the first and it was a gallery, then another – the Lieder Gallery, they wanted to talk to Dot. I tuned the ringer back on and it rang almost immediately. A woman calling from some other gallery.

On-screen was my face. Our Rizla game. I was asking, — Am I a man? To my left, the other screen – the dressing-up game – Saul and me.

Her voice. — Show me the tops of your stockings.

A laugh from a woman in the crowd around me in the dark.

Behind me was the waiting game. I couldn't face it. My face in light, waiting for that kiss, that slap.

The voice from the first video. Saul asking, — Am I a celebrity?

I could not sleep the night before. I called the hospital and could visit at three, Dot still had not regained consciousness, they were doing more tests. There were hours to kill. I came to her show as soon as I could because I sensed Saul needed to be alone in his packing.

The crowds. Some laughed, some talked in whispers, others, silent like me, sat between the three screens. Waited on the next question, the next words. The videos, different in length, repeated when finished. It was impossible to look at just one. When I tried, voices came from another, or a slap.

You turn and start to watch but then there are voices from another. After hours, you learn this, to treat the three as one, to let the voices that interrupt lead your eye astray. To not try to focus on the one. I was staring at my face on the screen waiting to be slapped and I heard Dot's voice from behind me.

— So, I'm dead and I killed my girlfriend and I'm famous.

And on another screen I saw my face flinching as Dot's mouth entered to kiss me.

I turned to watch the Rizla game and Saul was on screen, Jesus written on his forehead.

— Did I ever write a book? he asked and Dot's voice laughed, told him that he didn't but he inspired one, a big one. And I turned and watched Saul and me in her mother's clothes, shaking our legs cabaret-style and hear her voice from behind me.

— Do people hate me? she asked, from behind.

Three hours and never the same image and sound, endlessly out of sync, as the eye roamed from one screen to the next. And in that time these three videos that distract from each other did not detract but add. The space between, the floor, the ten feet of floor, in which you stand, and some sit, the images and sounds. The spaces between things. Between people, these were alive.

A middle-aged woman was weeping beside me, she had

been there for a whole half-hour, transfixed. Her partner asked — What's wrong? She was telling him she was fine. — Just leave me, please, give me another ten minutes, love. There was laughter too, from the young people, a crowd of eight, in hysterics over the cross-dressing, over the Rizla game.

My voice from the screen.

— Am I Marlene Dietrich?

The man behind me took notes.

As I left I heard some man at the door announce his credentials to a woman and ask where he could find Dorothy Shears. Handing his card. The woman said she'd been trying to contact Dot for days, she'd put him on the list. There were whispers about the police. There were others too, waiting to get inside. Dot's name on many lips. As I left, I passed endless studio spaces, young artists sitting alone, staring at their white walls, waiting for just one person to enter and look at the work they had spent four years making.

He had fallen silent, in that last day as we waited for word of her waking. He'd cleaned up the entire flat all by himself, silently. And his appearance: the stubble gone, no trace of eyeliner, his hair, washed clean, his clothes – his first attempt at looking respectable. My jeans and a white shirt, shoes polished, in every way the image of every man he once despised.

The vodka was my going-away present. I put the Duchamps on repeat and we sat in my room drinking it from coffee cups, silently staring at the little wheels on the tape player going round and round. *Vous avez disparu.* Then it stopped.

— It's scary, he said.

— She's going to be OK.

— No, the silence, he said.

— I like it, I said. — Always have done.

— You scare me too, he said. — Always have done.

I told him, shh. In the silence the question came to me, one that had been unasked for too long. I think he sensed it too. I had to know if the hell we'd put Dot through had been some product of something repressed between us. I could only ask it with touch.

I got undressed and climbed under his covers. I asked him just to come in and not worry. He sat there for another ten minutes, finishing the bottle; he held it upside down and let the last drip fall to the carpet.

— Scared, he said.

— Shh, let's just sleep.

So slowly he removed his clothes. I recall just fragments. I kissed his neck and he resisted. He pinned me down, wrestling, using his weight against me, his dick soft against my leg. I reached to kiss his mouth and for a second our lips touched, our tongues met and circled, I felt him grow weak in my arms. Then he threw me off.

I tried to hold him, he hid his face, pushed me away, turning his back to me, curling up into himself. I tried to sleep, but was unsure where to put my hands. At least the question was answered. I had not been aroused. There was nothing in that way between us, not without her. But the greater question loomed, was this not a foretaste of what would come with others, years later? When alone with just one, I would be haunted by the trace of the other.

He fell asleep in my arms, snoring. Hours later, I pulled back the covers to look at him naked. I kissed his shoulders, his back. He did not wake. I watched over him as he slept. The rhythm of his lungs against my chest. I held him all night, his foetal form in my arms. My friend, my father, my once role model.

Cars and daylight woke me. I turned in the bed and his bags had gone. I stood in his room. So many things he'd left behind. So many of his special things. The snakeskin cowboy boots that he never let me wear; the Nirvana T-shirt, his Palestinian scarf and pinstriped flared seventies suit, his leather chaps, his SALE T-shirt. Eyeliner sticks, his hundreds of records no longer scattered but in two stacks as high as my chest, his books, my God. Books are heavy and his bags must have been small, Nietzsche and Wilde were still there by his bed. And his sheets. The dark mark on his pillow where his dyed black hair had rubbed off. His many improvised ashtrays, a coffee cup teeming with butts.

He said, that night before, that he wanted to go to France but would not give me details of where. France was dead, a museum culture, he'd said it himself. He would not find Sartre or Henry Miller there. It was a little lie and his tone was not one of hope but of resignation, as if heading back, not forward. I sensed he had gone back to his mother, wherever, whoever, she was.

He didn't say goodbye. I was too hung-over, too in need of sleep to hear the door, a pillow over my head. Maybe it was better that way. He was never good in the mornings.

I called the hospital to ask after her. I wanted to tell her about Saatchi and the Lieder and her sell-out success and how she'd graduated with first-class honours and won the Schwartz Prize. All these things from the messages.

— She's sleeping, the nurse said.

— Is she . . . ?

— She's out of danger. She's stable.

— Stable.

— Yes. She woke in the night, she was wide awake. You can call around midday.

— OK, I said. I'll call back, thanks.

But I could not face hearing her voice so distant, on a phone.

The more I thought about it, the more hours I sat in silence, the more I realised that neither could I truly face her face.

She would wake and I would not be there. I would not

plead for forgiveness, or seek reconciliation or try to explain. It would be better that way. Better for her. I would do my penance. Never again would I let anyone get close enough for me to hurt them. Best if I stood on the sidelines, remained at a safe distance, cautious, critical. Best to kill my need for touch, to save others from it.

That was what I told myself as I carved the date into memory.

That last day.

He had gone and she would live.

The 3rd of June 1993.

nine

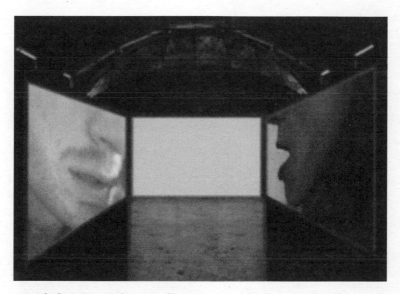

Untitled. 2009. Video installation. Variable dimensions.

TWO VOICES IN the dark. Him and her.

 She: Wake up!

 He: Let him sleep, he needs to rest, that's what they said.

 She: Wake up please.

 He: You're tired, go home and sleep, I'll stay with him.

 She: I'm going nowhere. You go!

 He: It could be hours yet, you look tired. You go and I'll stay.

 The voices seemed half dream, each sound, so close to his ear; the sticky smacks of saliva, the sighs and small movements, slowly forming into an image around him. He did not want to wake, did not know if he even could, felt comforted by the voices, like some half-memory of being half awake as his parents fussed over him as sick child, if that was even his own memory, or was it something Dot had said, maybe something from her memory once told to him – borders were not clear. Keep your eyes closed, feel them holding your hands, pretend to sleep and suck in all that affection, because it will disappear as soon as you open your eyes and re-enter the world of the questions asked and answers expected in the light of day.

 As he came to fuller consciousness, there was pain, in lower gut and arm; he fought the impulse to take stock, wake and talk.

 She: He just moved. I saw his eyes flicker.

 He: He's probably just dreaming.

 She: How do they know it's not a coma?

 He: They've done tests.

 She: What the fuck do they know?

He: Why don't you go check on Molly?

She: Why don't you stop telling me what to do?

A beep of a heart monitor in rhythm. Funny. It must have been his own. The other sensations then were of tightness, in arm and hand, both hands.

They were on either side of him, his bed, so he must be at home, but He had said, Go home, so it must have been . . . yes, the smells confirmed it: a hospital. And the pressure in his hands was theirs holding his, one on either side, and maybe a drip in his wrist. This was the image unseen, but imagined as if from above. He could hold them here as long as he kept his eyes shut.

She: God, I'll never forgive myself.

He: Shh. It wasn't your fault.

She: Whose then? Yours?

He: Both of us, maybe not. I don't know.

She: OWEN!

What was it Dot had said? – I made myself sick and they held my hands. I pretended to be asleep and they stayed by my bed.

He: Stop shouting. He can't hear you.

She: How do you know? Just shut up.

She was weeping for him now, and He was reaching over to hold her.

She: Don't touch me!

He: I was just –

She: This is all your fault.

It was a struggle to keep his eyes closed. He did not want the fighting to start, for one to leave. He moved slightly and they did as he wanted, separated and the silence could only have meant that each was staring at him.

She: Owen, my love, are you OK? Can you hear me?

He: Hey, buddy, you all right?

Time stretched in the pretending. It seemed like hours passed, and gradually each fell silent and the hands left his and they each went back to their own ways in the waiting. It pained him then to hear her fussing.

She: You know, to hell with the show, if he doesn't wake up I . . . I'm giving up art forever anyway . . .

He: I know, I know.

She: If I hadn't been so selfish this would never have happened.

He: No, it's my fault, if I hadn't turned up, you two would have been . . . anyway, he's going to be fine.

She: What if he's not?

Something came to him then. Not a thought or feeling. But an image through the dark. He was walking into a vast darkened space and to his left and right were two separate screens facing each other, huge, the size of a cinema each. On each were moving images of mouths talking. One female and one male. But not talking to each other. They talked to the third screen, on which there was no image, no sound, nothing. Blank, bright white. They talked to it as if begging it to come to life.

It took all the energy he had to suppress the urge to sit upright and tell them.

She: If he doesn't wake, we're not going to make it.

He: Me and you. I know that. Come home with me now. They'll call us when he wakes.

She: Don't touch me, please.

It seemed then that each gripped his hands tighter. And although he felt for their distress the grip of the image was tighter on him. In his mind he stood in the gallery watching the screens. He turned and saw the third screen reflected back in the eyes of the audience. He saw tears as they stared into the empty white that represented fear, total fear of loss, inexpressible. This artwork was the ninth and the one that would save her career. And the image was not of her making at all, but maybe it was – as it had always been – his own.

She: Why did you come back anyway?

He: Just wanted to see my buddy.

She: Bullshit, you were afraid no one'd remember you. You must have heard about the essay and wanted to be in it. You make me sick.

He: You've always been fucking dumb, you know that. You'd forget where your fucking head was if I wasn't there to tell you.

She: Oh, really.

He: Yeah – in fact, if I hadn't come along you'd still be doing fucking watercolours and listening to Joni Mitchell.

She: Well, actually, I think you'll find, Owen was a bigger inspiration – in fact, we did most of my work together.

He: That a fact?

She: Oh, fuck off and leave us alone.

He: After you, madam.

Don't fight, little children, he thought. Daddy's here. How they were in terror of being left alone, together, with his absence. They would each beg him to tell their story. And he could change everything, all the details, put words into the mouths of each other, finish Dot's unfinished sentences and make Saul speak with his own voice, even have the man erased entirely. He could rewrite everything, make himself the victim or the hero and still they would thank him for it. Maybe they were all he could hope to shape or mould in the world, but maybe that was enough.

A hand was holding his again. The other hand clasped then, as if the second was jealous of the first.

She: Owen, I'm sorry, can you hear me?

He: Whatever I've done, mate, whenever, all of it.

He was bursting with it. He knew, finally, that in the hands that clutched his he held not only the story of their pasts but their hopes for the future. He must have been gripping hard because both started talking, excitedly.

He: He squeezed my hand.

She: His lids are moving – look.

He felt the energy flow from skin to skin and fought the desire to open his eyes and confess.

She: Owen, please wake up.

He: Please, mate, please.

Yes, he would keep them waiting like this in their warm need, a few minutes longer, maybe more. He wanted only to make this moment go on. He was both their sickly child and their caring father. Their judge and creator. Joy welled inside him, he was at their very centre holding them both together and apart. Caught between weeping and laughter. Compassion and control. My God. He had to keep a straight face. Be quiet, make it last, he told himself, just another moment. They squeezed him tight. He kept his eyes shut and felt the power they had given him. Felt what it was like to hold a life in each of his hands.

He: Look, he's smiling.

She: Owen, it's me. Can you hear me?

He: We're both here.

She: I love you, Owen.

He: We're right here.

acknowledgements

The author would like to thank the following people: Emily Ballou, Lucy Luck, Roger Palmer, Brian Brown, Irvine Welsh, David Mackenzie, Pilitia Garcia, Ron Butlin, Malcolm Dickson, Michael Storm, Dan Franklin, Hannah Ross, Beth Coates and all who have supported and/or provoked me over the years.

'Art is dead. Long live art.'

www.vintage-books.co.uk